CLAY
310
A F⃗ ☑ P9-CLO-337
Dekker, Ted, 1962-
Obsessed /

03/05

CLAYTON COUNTY LIBRARY
RIVERDALE BRANCH
420 VALLEY HILL ROAD
RIVERDALE, GA 30274

DISCARDED

Praise for
Ted Dekker's novels

"With the release of *White,* and the culmination of the Circle Trilogy, Dekker has placed himself at the fore of Christian fiction. His tale is absolutely riveting, and the redemptive value at the heart of the series only makes it all the more remarkable."

—MICHAEL JANKE
CM Central

"One of the highlights of the year in religious fiction has been Ted Dekker's striking color-coded spiritual trilogy. Exciting, well written, and resonant with meaning, *Black, Red,* and now *White* have won over both critics and genre readers . . . An epic journey completed with grace."

—Editors, BARNES AND NOBLE

"Dekker is a master of suspense and even makes room for romance."

—*Library Journal*

"My advice is to sit back, curl up, and savor *White* for the triumph it is. It's so rare that we get stories as well plotted, perfectly paced, and told with real heart like this."

—*FuseMagazine.net*

"Full of heroic action, deep meaning, and suspense so palpable your fingers will dig grooves into the book's outer cover, *Red* magnifies the story of *Black* times ten, raising the stakes to epic proportions. But Ted Dekker's biggest ace in the hole is that he understands what so many others never realize: substance and meaning *can* go hand-in-hand with exciting, cinematic storytelling. *Red* is a thrilling, daring work of fiction that not only entertains—it inspires. Why aren't there more stories like this?"

—ROBIN PARRISH, editor,
Fuse Magazine, www.FuseMagazine.net

"*Black* has to be the read of the year! A powerful, thought-provoking, edge-of-your-seat thriller of epic proportions that offers great depth and insight into the forces around us."

—JOE GOODMAN, film producer,
Namesake Entertainment

"As a producer of movies filled with incredible worlds and heroic characters, I have high standards for the fiction I read. Ted Dekker's novels deliver big with mind-blowing, plot-twisting page turners. Fair warning—this trilogy will draw you in at a breakneck pace and never let up. Cancel all plans before you start because you won't be able to stop once you enter *Black*."

—RALPH WINTER
Producer—*X-Men, X2: X-Men United, Planet of the Apes,*
Executive Producer—*Star Trek V: Final Frontier*

"Put simply: it's a brilliant, dangerous idea. And we need more dangerous ideas . . . Dekker's trilogy is a mythical epic, with a vast, predetermined plot and a scope of staggering proportions . . . *Black* is one of those books that will make you thankful that you know how to read. If you love a good story, and don't mind suspending a little healthy disbelief, *Black* will keep you utterly enthralled from beginning to . . . well, cliffhanger. *Red* can't get here fast enough."

—*FuseMagazine.net*

"Just when I think I have Ted Dekker figured out, he hits me with the unexpected. With teasing wit, ever-lurking surprises, and adventurous new concepts, this guy could become a real vanguard in fiction."

—FRANK PERETTI

"[With THR3E] Dekker delivers another page-turner . . . masterfully takes readers on a ride full of plot twists and turns . . . a compelling tale of cat and mouse . . . an almost perfect blend of suspense, mystery, and horror."

—*Publishers Weekly*

"Ted Dekker is clearly one of the most gripping storytellers alive today. He creates plots that keep your heart pounding and palms sweating even after you've finished his books."

—JEREMY REYNALDS,
Syndicated Columnist

"Ted Dekker is the most exciting writer I've read in a very long time. *Blink* will expand his fan base tremendously. Wonderful reading . . . powerful insights. Bravo!"

—TED BAEHR, President,
MOVIEGUIDE Magazine

obsessed

Other novels by Ted Dekker:

Black
Red
White
Three
Blink
Heaven's Wager
When Heaven Weeps
Thunder of Heaven

With Bill Bright:

Blessed Child
A Man Called Blessed

obsessed

TED DEKKER

CLAYTON COUNTY LIBRARY
RIVERDALE BRANCH
420 VALLEY HILL ROAD
RIVERDALE, GA 30274

WESTBOW
PRESS
A Division of Thomas Nelson Publishers
Since 1798

visit us at www.westbowpress.com

Copyright © 2005 Ted Dekker

All rights reserved. No portion of this book may be reproduced, stored in a retrieval system, or transmitted in any form or by any means—electronic, mechanical, photocopy, recording, scanning, or other—except for brief quotations in critical reviews or articles, without the prior permission of the publisher.

Published by WestBow Press, a Division of Thomas Nelson, Inc., P.O. Box 141000, Nashville, Tennessee, 37214.

WestBow Press books may be purchased in bulk for educational, business, fundraising, or sales promotional use. For information, please email SpecialMarkets@ThomasNelson.com.

PUBLISHER'S NOTE: This novel is a work of fiction. Names, characters, places, and incidents are either products of the author's imagination or are used fictitiously. All characters are fictional, and any similarity to people living or dead is purely coincidental.

Library of Congress Cataloging-in-Publication Data

Dekker, Ted, 1962–
    Obsessed / Ted Dekker.
    ISBN 0-8499-4373-6 (hard cover)
    ISBN 1-5955-4031-8 (international)
    I. Title.
    PS3554.E43O27 2005
    813'.6—dc22

                                                        2004015647

Printed in the United States of America

05 06 07 08 09 QW 7 6 5 4 3 2 1

This one's for The Circle

1

Hamburg, Germany
July 17, 1973
Tuesday Morning

ROTH BRAUN SLOWLY TWISTED THE DOORKNOB AND GAVE THE door a slight shove. A familiar medicinal odor stung his nostrils. Outside, the sun warmed a midsummer day, but here in the dungeon below the house, the old man lived in perpetual twilight.

Roth imagined a Jew stepping into a delicing shower and let himself relish the horror he might feel in that moment of realizing that more than lice were meant to die in this chamber.

Roth was in a very good mood.

The smothering quiet was broken by the sound of the old prune's tarred, seventy-eight-year-old lungs rasping for relief. Gerhard's wheezing annoyed Roth, ruining his otherwise perfect mood.

The only living soul he despised more than the Jew who'd stolen his power was Gerhard, who had allowed the Jew to steal his power.

He glanced at Klaus, the gangly male nurse who had tended his father for three years. The white-smocked man hovered over Gerhard in the corner of the room, refusing to meet Roth's eyes. Gerhard Braun sat in a dark-red leather recliner, blue eyes glaring over the nasal cannula protruding from each nostril.

"Good morning, Father," Roth said. He closed the door quietly and stepped into the room, pushing aside a curtain of tinkling glass beads that separated it from the entryway. "You wanted to see me?"

His father looked at a servant, who busied himself over the table in the adjacent dining room.

"Leave us."

By the trembling in his voice, either Gerhard really was dying, or something was upsetting him, which invariably sowed its own sort of death. How many men alive today had been responsible for as many deaths as his father? They could be counted on two hands.

Even so, Roth hated him.

The servant dipped his head and exited through a side door. The steel door closed and the nurse flinched. Glass in a cabinet behind the table rattled despite the room's solid-concrete walls. The nineteenth-century Russian crystal—one of dozens of similar collections pilfered during the war—had once belonged to the czar. The Nazis' defeat should have sent Gerhard to the gallows; instead, the war had left his father with obscene wealth. The paintings alone had netted him a significant fortune, and these he owned legally. He'd shipped them to Zurich, where a hotly contested law made them his after remaining unclaimed for five years. Compliments of the Swiss Federation of Art Dealers.

Until the day I suck the energy from your bones, I will love you for showing me the way.

Until the day I suck the energy from your bones, I will despise you for what you did.

Gerhard held up a newspaper. "Have you read this?"

Roth walked across the circular rope rug that covered the black cement slab and stopped five feet from Gerhard. A hawk nose curved over his father's thin, trembling lips. Wispy strands of gray hair backlit by a yellow lamp hovered over his scalp. Skeletal, blue-veined fingers clutched what appeared to be a *Los Angeles Times*. A stack of newspapers—the *New York Times*, *Chicago Tribune*, London's *Daily Telegraph*, and a dozen others—sat a half-meter thick on the small end table to his left. Gerhard routinely spent six hours each day reading.

Gerhard flung the paper with a flick of his wrist, never removing his eyes from Roth. It landed on the floor with a *smack*.

"Read it."

The male nurse pretended to fiddle with the oxygen tank. Roth stood still. This attitude of Gerhard's was no longer simply ruining his mood, but destroying it altogether.

"I said, 'Read it'!"

Roth calmly bent and picked up the paper. The *Los Angeles Times* was folded around an article in the Life section, "Fortune Goes to Museum." Roth scanned the text. A wealthy woman, a Jew named Rachel Spritzer, sixty-two years of age, had died three days ago in Los Angeles. She'd been survived by no one and had donated her entire estate to the Los Angeles Museum of the Holocaust.

"So another Jew's dead." Roth lowered the paper. "Your legacy lives on."

His father clutched the arms of his chair. "Read the rest." His chest sounded like a whistle.

If Roth wasn't a master of his own impulses, he might have done something stupid, such as kill the man. Instead, he set the paper on the windowsill and turned away. "You've read it, Father. Tell me what it says. I have a ten o'clock engagement."

"Cancel it."

Roth walked to the bar. Control. "Just tell me what has you so concerned."

"The Stones of David have me concerned."

Roth blinked. He poured a splash of cognac into a snifter.

"I'm finished chasing your ghosts." He swirled the brandy slowly before sipping it. "If the Stones still exist, we would have found them long ago."

Gerhard managed to stand, trembling from head to foot, red as a rooster around the neck.

"They *have* been found. And you know what that means." He launched into a coughing fit.

Roth's pulse quickened a hair and then eased. If the man wasn't dying, he was losing his mind. Surely the Stones hadn't been found after all this time.

Gerhard staggered three steps to the windowsill, pushing his startled nurse out of the way, and grabbed the newspaper. He leaned on the wall with one hand and held the paper up in the other. He threw the paper toward Roth. It fluttered noisily and landed on the black slab.

"Read it!" Gerhard's eyes drilled him. So then maybe there was something to this.

Roth picked up the paper, found the article, and slowly read down the column. What if Gerhard was right? What if the relics did exist after all? They would be priceless. But the Stones' monetary value didn't interest Gerhard—he already had enough wealth to waste in his final years.

Gerhard's obsession was for the journal that had gone missing with the Stones.

And Roth's obsession was for the power that had gone missing with the Jew who'd taken the journal.

He had spent nearly thirty years tracking down innumerable leads, searching in vain. There was no telling how much wealth had been stripped from the Jews when Hitler had gathered them up and sent them to the camps. Much of the fortune had been confiscated by the gestapo and recovered after the war, but a number of particularly valuable items—priceless relics that belonged in museums or in vaults—had disappeared. Some of those treasures could be found in this very house. But any well-heeled collector knew that the most valuable collection had vanished for good in 1945.

The Stones of David.

One stunning item in Spritzer's collection is an extremely old golden medallion, better known as one of the five Stones of David. According to legend, the medallions are the actual stones selected by David to kill the giant Goliath. The smooth stones were subsequently gilded and stamped with the Star of David. The collection was last verified in 1307, when they were held by the Knights Templars. The collection was rumored to be held by a wealthy Jewish collector before World War II but went missing before the claim could be verified.

Alone, each medallion may be worth over $10,000,000. But the collection in its entirety is valued at roughly $100,000,000. The relic will be displayed in a museum yet to be disclosed with the following cryptic caption at Rachel Spritzer's request: "The Stones are like the lost orphans. They will eventually find each other."

Sweat cooled Roth's palms. He set the paper on the bar, set an unsteady finger in its margin, and scanned to the end.

> *Rachel Spritzer lived alone in an apartment complex she owned on La Brea Avenue and died a widow. The complex will be sold by the estate, along with much of Spritzer's noncollectible property.*
>
> *Rudy and Rachel Spritzer immigrated to the United States sixteen years ago, five years before Rudy was killed in an automobile accident. (See B4.)*

For a moment Roth's vision clouded. His mouth went dry.

"Now I have your attention?" Gerhard demanded.

Roth read the article again, searching for any phrase that might undermine the possibility that this Jew could be anyone other than whom Gerhard was suggesting.

"She was sixty-two," Gerhard said. "The right age."

Roth's mind flashed back to those war years when he was only twelve. Even if the connections were only circumstantial, he could hardly ignore them.

"I *knew* the Jew survived," Gerhard said.

"She donated only one Stone. There were five."

"If one Stone exists, then the journal exists. Someone has that journal!"

"She's dead."

"You will make her speak from the grave." Gerhard swayed on his feet, right fist trembling. His eyes looked black in the basement's shadows. "She knew. She knew about the journal."

"She's dead!" Roth snapped. He took a deep breath, irritated with himself for losing control. The fact was, Gerhard's history with the Stones gave him knowledge that no one else could possibly have.

"You know well enough that the journal implicates the entire line of elders. It lists each of our names and the names of the women we killed. It must be found!"

Mention of the women triggered a coppery taste in the back of Roth's

mouth. The last time he'd seen the journal, it contained 243 names. Roth
would one day surpass that number, he had vowed it.

But even a thousand or ten thousand would not compensate for the
one that had escaped Gerhard.

"That woman would toy with me even in her death," the old man
said. "In her house, in her belongings—somewhere, the old bat left a trail.
You will go to Los Angeles." The nurse, Klaus, moved to assist Gerhard
back to his seat, but the old man shook him off. Klaus retreated.

Gerhard was right. The Stones could lead to the journal. The journal
could lead to the Jew. The Jew would lead to power, a supernatural power
that his father had never attained. But Roth would.

The prospect of finding the Jew after so many years felt delightfully
obscene.

Roth realized that his fingers were trembling.

"The United States," Roth said absently. "We don't have the same
liberties there."

"That's never stopped you before."

The notion swarmed Roth like bees from a disturbed hive. Hope.
More than hope—a desperate urgency to possess. Pounding heart, dry
mouth. He was no fool. He would neither fight the emotion nor show it.
After lingering so long on the edges of his mind, the desire to possess this
one lost hope swallowed him. This is what Roth lived for, the purest form
of power found in the very emotion that at this very moment raged
through his body.

In his mind's eye he was already flying to America. He would have to
move quickly, set the trap immediately. There was no telling how long
they would keep the old Jew's collectibles in Los Angeles.

Roth stared into his father's blue eyes for a few long seconds, torn
between the man's mad obsession with the past and his own with the
future. What Roth did for tomorrow, Gerhard did because of yesterday.
Who was the better man?

He remembered the first dead Jew he'd seen in the camps twenty-eight
years ago. He'd been eating fresh eggs and sausage prepared by one of the
Polish servants from the village for breakfast. It was the most delicious

breakfast he'd ever tasted. Perhaps leaving his mother in Germany to spend the summer with his father up in Poland would be a good thing after all. He was twelve at the time.

"Papa?"

"What?" his father asked, walking toward the window overlooking the concentration camp.

"Why do Polish eggs taste better than German eggs?"

His father pulled back the curtain, and Roth saw a woman hanging from the main gate. Gerhard answered him, but Roth didn't hear the response. The year was 1942, and hers was the first of many dead bodies Roth would see in Poland. But there was something about the first.

Roth let the memory linger, then returned his mind to the Stones. His father's eyes glistened with tears; his face wrinkled.

"The Jew took my soul. *She* took my soul! I beg you, my son." Roth felt a terrible pity for him. A single tear broke free and ran down Gerhard's right cheek.

"If the Jew is alive, she will be drawn by the Stone," Roth said.

"Forget the Jew. I must have the journal. You see that, don't you? More than anything, I must have it." He held out a spindly arm laced with bulging veins. "Swear it to me. Swear you'll bring me what is mine."

Roth looked at the large swastika on the gray wall, sickened by Gerhard's weakness. He would make it right, because the Stones meant far more to him than they could possibly mean to his father.

"Come here," Roth said to the nurse.

Klaus glanced at Gerhard then stepped out from the shadows.

Roth backed up and stepped off the rug. There was the right way and the wrong way to do this, and the purest in mind knew the difference.

"Farther, to the middle of the rug," he said.

Klaus took another step so that he stood near the center of the rug.

"I would like to repay you for your care of my father," Roth said. "Few men could put up with a whining old man the way you do. Is there anything you would like?"

No response. Of course not.

"Anything at all?"

The nurse lowered his head. "No sir."

Roth pulled out his gun and shot Klaus through the top of his head while he was still bent over. The slug likely ended up in his throat.

The man dropped in a pile.

Roth looked at his father. "You should have sent him out."

"You're working against your own kind," Gerhard said. "He was pure."

"Then I did him a favor by sending him to his grave pure."

2

Los Angeles
July 18, 1973
Wednesday Morning

STEPHEN FRIEDMAN MARCHED ALONG THE SOUTH EDGE OF THE vacant Santa Monica parking lot, mind whirling. This was a primo deal, baby. Definitely, absolutely, one of the most primo deals he had come across in the seven years he'd played the real-estate market.

His partner on occasion, Dan Stiller, followed closely at Stephen's heels, black portfolio under his arm.

Stephen leaped over a chain and kept an energetic pace along the uneven asphalt. Tufts of stubborn brown grass grew among the cracks. The crumbling brick wall across the lot had been decorated by hundreds of white droppings. Seagulls. Someone had scrawled some word art on the wall: BIG DADDY ROCKS. To any ordinary pedestrian, the parking lot would have looked desolate, and perhaps worthless.

To Stephen, this piece of ground looked like a slice of potential paradise.

He smiled at Dan, who'd walked around the chain. Prevailing Santa Ana winds slapped at the wide lapels of Dan's plaid polyester blazer and whipped his hair back. The effect accentuated his sloping forehead and turned his bulbous nose into something that might have fit a Boeing 747. But behind that nose, Dan's brain was proportionally as large. They made a good team for the odd investment—two young Jews, both immigrants, carving out a new life in this magnificent land of opportunity. Where Dan's conservatism held them in check, Stephen's enthusiasm drove them on.

"It's a natural," Stephen said.

"Like the condo in Pasadena was a natural?" Dan referred to the complex Stephen had insisted they convert to a neighborhood amusement park. But the notes came due before construction could begin.

"I got us out of that, didn't I?" Stephen said.

"Involving a crook like Joel Sparks isn't exactly my idea of getting us out."

"The mob rap is totally hearsay. He's a businessman; he has money. He bailed us out."

"We lost a hundred thousand dollars."

"You've never lost a hundred thousand before? You win some, you lose some." Stephen turned to the vacant lot. "Besides, this one's a winner, guar-an-teed." He took a long whiff of the air. "I can practically smell it. You smell that, Dan? That's money you smell."

"Actually, that's exhaust I smell. And it's the carbon monoxide in the exhaust, the stuff you *can't* smell, that worries me."

"It may just be me, but I get the distinct impression you have some doubts. You don't trust my nose?"

Dan wiped his brow. "I don't doubt your ability to choose them, Stephen. But, yes, I'm struggling with this particular idea."

Stephen had made and lost a million dollars a dozen times already— and they both knew as much. The very same impulsive passion that pushed him to seize opportunity also landed him in trouble from time to time. He made a million dollars easier than most. He also lost it easier than most.

Never mind. The fact that he now understood this about himself tipped the scales in his favor. He was up at the moment—eight hundred thousand up. Not bad for a thirty-one-year-old immigrant from Russia. Dan, for all his cautiousness, was only liquid to the tune of half that much. Which was why he needed Stephen. The only real issue separating them was what to do with the property.

Stephen tapped his temple. "You have to imagine it, Daniel. Open your mind!" He scanned the property and spoke with animated gestures. "Americans love entertainment. Cotton candy, ice cream, a roller coaster." He pointed to the deteriorated brick wall. "Right over there you see gull droppings; I see balloons. This lot is most definitely a coastal amusement park begging to be built."

Three teenagers passing by on the sidewalk turned to look at Stephen as his voice grew louder.

"I'm not saying that it couldn't happen, but a museum is more reasonable, if not to you, then to the city planners. Stephen, think. We have to submit our intentions with the down payment by next Wednesday. There are two other parties bidding. If the city rejects our plan, we lose the deal. All I'm suggesting is that we go with a more conservative plan."

"And I say the people here are secretly crying out for a roller coaster. They're praying every night for us to put thoughts of museums and office buildings out of our minds, because they want clowns and the sound of laughing children to invade their neighborhood."

Dan stared at him.

Stephen saw an opportunity and seized it. He stepped toward the teenagers and motioned to a boy with long blond hair and a pooka-shell necklace. "Excuse me, Sir Hamlet, there. Could I get your opinion on something?"

The blond boy glanced at a younger rail-thin girl with large freckles and an embroidered blouse, and a skinny boy who towered over both of them.

Stephen fished out a ten-dollar bill. "I'll give you ten bucks for five minutes of your time."

"Ten bucks?"

"Ten bucks."

"For what?"

"Just to act something out for me and my business partner here."

Dan objected. "Come on, Stephen."

"Act what out?" the blond kid asked.

"We're investors, and we're trying to decide if this parking lot should be an amusement park or a museum." Stephen pointed to the freckled girl. "I want you to stand over there"—he pointed, then gestured toward the other two—"and you two over there and there."

"Ten bucks for each of us?" the boy asked in a small voice.

Stephen saw that they were sloppily dressed. Not *cool* sloppily, but poor sloppily. The girl's sandals were tied together with string, and the tall skinny kid's bell-bottoms were ankle-high. For a moment he just stared at them, struck by an odd sense of empathy that he couldn't place. The city was full of kids like this—why these three suddenly pulled at his heart, he didn't know.

No, he did know. At this moment they were him. They were decent, wide-eyed kids mesmerized by the possibility of making a quick ten dollars.

"What's your name?" Stephen asked the blond boy.

"Mike." If the boy were a smart aleck, Stephen might have changed his mind. But no snot-nosed kid would have answered the question so innocently. Several others on the sidewalk had stopped and were watching.

"I'll tell you what, Mike. I'll give you each *twenty* dollars if you help me out here. That's a lot of money for five minutes, but my friend and I are going to make a bundle on this piece of property, so I think it's fair. What do you say?"

"You mean it? Twenty dollars?" the small girl asked, eyes wide.

"I mean it."

One last glance at each other, and they scrambled over the chain to their posts.

"What do we do?"

"I want you to pretend you're an amusement park." He pointed to each in succession. "You're a Ferris wheel, you're a merry-go-round, and you're a roller coaster. Just stick your arms up like this"—he threw his hands up over his head—"or like this"—he waved them out at his sides—"and when I tell you to, pretend you're machines."

"You better not be pulling our legs about the twenty dollars," the blond boy said.

"Scout's honor," Stephen said.

The kids adjusted their arms.

"Perfect!" Stephen faced Dan. "Okay, Dan, now you stand over here—"

"I'm not doing this, Stephen."

"You have to! I need you to do this. You need to stand over there like a statue. How else are we going to compare?"

"No way."

Stephen took his arm, turned him from the kids, and whispered. "Be a good sport, Dan. For their sakes. Look, you need my five hundred grand, right? Just go along with me here."

Dan looked at the three kids and then walked to one side.

"Act like a statue, Dan," Stephen said.

"I am like a statue."

"Stick an arm up or something, so you look more like a statue."

Dan hesitated and then raised an arm and went stiff, like a German soldier saluting.

The gawking crowd on the sidewalk now included a dozen kids and several adults. Stephen faced them.

"Ladies and gentlemen, we're conducting a quick survey here. We have to decide whether we want to build an amusement park or a museum here. You guys are the judges."

He spun and faced the three kids like a conductor cuing up his orchestra. "Ready?"

The freckled girl chuckled. "You're pretty crazy, mister."

"You'd better believe I am. Ready?"

"Ready."

"Okay, make like an amusement park." He waved his arms.

The tall skinny kid was the roller coaster. He stuck his arms out like a cross, which wasn't Stephen's idea of how to show a coaster, but at least the boy was playing along. The girl turned in a slow circle like a merry-go-round, and the blond boy made a circle with his arms. Ferris wheel. They grinned wide.

"Sound! Sound!" Stephen called.

"Sound is an extra five bucks," the blond boy said.

"Make it ten," Stephen said. Shoot, he'd probably give them forty if they wanted it. "Give me some sound!"

"*Vroom, vroom. Whir.*" Wasn't much, but it earned some laughs from the gathering crowd. "*Honk honk,*" snorted the girl.

"Excuse me," Stephen said. "What's *honk honk*? If I'm paying ten bucks for a noise, I need to know what it is."

"It's the line of cars waiting to get in," the girl said.

Stephen smiled wide, delighted. "There you go, then. Cars waiting to get in to the amusement park!" He faced the crowd. "All in favor of the amusement park, raise your hands."

Two dozen hands went up amid chuckles.

"All those in favor of a museum"—Stephen pointed to Dan—"raise your hands."

A middle-aged couple walking by raised their hands and grinned.

"There you go. Case settled. Thank you for your cooperation. You're dismissed." Some loitered, some moved on.

The kids ran up to him and Stephen handed each thirty dollars.

"That's it?" Mike asked. "We're done?"

"You're done. Don't blow it all at once."

They hurried off, looking back over their shoulders.

Dan shook his head. "Okay, Mr. Hot Shot. So you have a bit of charm with the locals. I can assure you that the bank, which holds the papers on this lot, doesn't care about your antics. And I guarantee the city will look more favorably on a museum than on a playground. Especially a museum that already has its backers. You know the Jewish Public Affairs Committee has talked about bringing the Holocaust museum under its umbrella and then relocating it. Why not here? If they follow through, we'll do well. That was the whole idea."

"Just because we're Jewish doesn't mean everything we do has to promote the Jewish cause," Stephen said. "This is nothing but business."

"Of course. But you *are* a Jew. A secular Jew without much sentimentality for our history, maybe, but still a Jew. You can't ignore that. You're irrevocably tied to the war."

Stephen's morning paled. Dan's problem was that he knew too much.

"No, Dan, nothing is irrevocable. Especially not memories of the war. This is the United States of America, not Poland. Just because my great-great-great-great-grandmother dug potatoes in Poland or wherever doesn't mean I have to build a monument to her here."

Stephen had left both Russia and his past at age twenty to find a new life, and for the most part he'd succeeded. Anything that threatened to take him back, even if only in his mind, offended him.

"You're being unfair," Daniel said quietly. "You owe your life to your mother. And you know very well that she probably gave her life in one of the camps. How can you turn your back on that?"

"Because I don't *know* that she died in a camp," Stephen snapped. "I don't even know who she was. Why do you bring this up? I'll give you money for your museum. Just don't pretend we're crusaders here. I spent twenty years trying to find my mother and finally came here to give up that search. I don't have the stamina for that kind of thing."

"Seek and you will find—"

Stephen flung an arm into the air, his irritation flaring to anger. "Don't patronize me. For all I know, my mother and father *were* killed in some gas chamber. Whoever brought me into this world obviously suffered enough—is it incumbent on me to suffer too? As far as I'm concerned, it never happened. I don't have a mother. I'm not even Jewish anymore."

He paused, surprised by the emotion shortening his breath.

"And if there's a God in heaven who cares that I should seek, then I challenge him to create something . . ." He pinched his thumb and forefinger together. "Even a small morsel of some goodness worth seeking. Anything but the death that turns up everywhere I look."

Dan blinked at his outburst. "I'm sorry—"

"Then leave it. Give me some breathing room. Build your museum, but don't exploit my conscience."

Dan held up both hands.

For a few seconds that stretched into twenty, they stood in the vacant lot, making a good show of studying it. How they had managed to go from amusement parks to prison camps was beyond Stephen. Why, he wasn't entirely sure, but the subject never failed to resurrect ugly feelings he couldn't deal with.

Actually, he could deal with them. By burying them. Burying them deep and letting them lie dead in an unmarked grave. Certainly not by building a monument to them.

"You know, you may be right," Dan said. "An amusement park could transform this neighborhood."

"Forget it," Stephen said. "You already have backing for the museum. It's the safer plan. Though not as much fun, you have to admit."

"No, not as much fun. Your call."

"Couldn't we build a museum as part of an amusement park?"

Dan chuckled. "Now, there's an idea. I have three hundred thousand. We need eight by Tuesday. Can I count on you for the five?"

"Yes. And forget the amusement park for the time being. I'll run some comps and get the money to you by Tuesday."

"Okay." They shook hands.

"Sorry, huh?" Stephen said. "I can get carried away sometimes."

"Don't be ridiculous. I shouldn't have brought it up." He nodded at Stephen's blue Chevy Vega. "Go buy yourself a new car; it'll help you feel better."

"What, you don't like my car?"

"It's a bucket of bolts."

"It's my friend. Maybe the only one I have. Other than you and Chaim, of course. And I just installed an eight-track." He snapped his fingers to a few bars from James Taylor's "You've Got a Friend."

They stared at each other. For some strange reason a great sadness crept into Stephen's chest. He suddenly felt very lonely. He was standing in the middle of a parking lot in Santa Monica, surrounded by pedestrians and cars, contemplating a deal that could make him hundreds of thousands of dollars, and he felt oddly abandoned.

Like an outcast. Or like a child who couldn't find his mother. Both.

Stephen swallowed. *Bury it.* He grinned and slapped Dan on the back. "Man, you have got to stop being so serious. I'll see you later."

Dan smiled back. "Okay."

3

ROTH BRAUN STOOD ATOP THE GUTTED BUILDING ACROSS THE street from Rachel Spritzer's apartment. The warm California breeze swept over his face, through his hair, around his arms. He hated America, but he loved the purity of nature, and despite the smell of exhaust, the wind held some of the power that came with that purity. Even those who thought they understood the psychic energy in nature rarely really understood its true unspoiled power.

It was the energy of a million nuclear detonations.

It was the force of a billion dying babies crying out at once.

It was the substance of creation—raw, staggering. A plea to reverse the chaos suffered at the hands of ruined humanity.

Purity. This was the true meaning behind the Nazi swastika.

Roth unbuttoned the top three buttons on his black silk shirt and let the breeze reach inside. The others were waiting in the car with the agent who would show them Rachel Spritzer's building. Roth had insisted they wait while he scouted out the neighborhood. The Realtor had objected, and Roth wanted to crush his windpipe, but his practiced and generous self-control had allowed him simply to repeat the demand and thereby receive a nod.

The Realtor undoubtedly assumed that Roth was walking around the buildings to get a feel for the value of the adjacent land. Instead, he had climbed the stairs of this abandoned building opposite the Spritzer place and now stood unseen above them all.

Like a god.

Still, they were waiting; otherwise he might have performed a ritual to the spirit of the air, right here on the black tarred roof.

He'd slept less than four hours since shooting the male nurse in Gerhard's flat, but he felt as though he could go another week without closing his eyes. This time, the success of his mission was within reach.

Roth put his hands on his hips and walked to his right, keeping his eyes on Rachel Spritzer's apartment.

"Who are you, Rachel Spritzer?" He spoke low. "What secrets do you hold? Hmm? Who will come to find you? Who, who, who? I know who."

He did not doubt that this rather plain-looking four-story apartment complex held the secret to more power than most of the neighbors who'd lived like rats around it for the last thirty years could imagine. He knew this because he had disciplined his mind to connect with the psychic energy that said it was so.

The Stones had surfaced through the death of yet another Jew. Fitting. There was Gerhard's fortune to be found, yes. But more. Much more.

Roth lifted his eyes and scanned the city stretching into the haze. He breathed deeply and closed his eyes. In his younger days, before he'd perfected his exquisite self-control, he might have succumbed at a time like this to the compulsion to kill. The discovery of Rachel's Stone called for a celebration, no doubt about that. But he would wait until the sun was down. What he had in mind here could not be compromised by weak-minded indulgences.

What he had in mind here would make an indiscriminate killing laughable. He would discriminate with utmost care.

Roth exhaled completely, allowed a shiver of eagerness to work its way through his body, and turned to the roof access.

Let the game begin.

4

TWO OR THREE TIMES A WEEK, STEPHEN CAME HOME FOR LUNCH. Today was one of those days, and Chaim Leveler was glad. The boy was clearly troubled by an altercation he'd had with Dan Stiller.

Evidently, Stephen had said a few things he now regretted. For all his ambition, the lad was actually quite sensitive. He tried to cover up the deep wounds of a hapless past, but no spin could change what had happened. Stephen would always be a war child: subject of all worlds, master of none. Lost in the folds of history without a true mother, a true father, or a true home.

Stephen sat at the chrome-rimmed dining-room table, spreading mayonnaise on his bread. "You should spend less time figuring out how to make money and more time thinking about love," Chaim said, laying a hand on Stephen's shoulder as he walked to his green vinyl chair. "Look at you. You are smart, good-looking. Although you could use a haircut, never mind what is culturally accepted. Either way, what woman can resist a dimpled smile? You're thirty-one. You should have three children already."

"Yes, of course. Sylvia."

"Now that you mention it . . ." Chaim had always thought Stephen and his bright young niece, as he insisted on calling her, would make a handsome pair.

"Please, Rabbi, I don't need a matchmaker."

Chaim wasn't technically a rabbi, at least not in the eyes of the synagogue. No Messianic Jew could truly be a rabbi. But the retired fire marshal had never been able to suppress his spiritual fervor. Not that he ever tried. He smiled at Stephen's term of endearment and rounded the table, stroking a full beard. The smell of fresh mint tea and salmon sandwiches whetted his appetite more than he cared to admit. Age had snuck up on him like a wolf on a rabbit; he had to stay fit enough to flee the snapping fangs. He touched his belly.

Chaim had left Russia immediately after the Second World War. Two years in the Sobibor prison camp had exhausted his interest in Europe. His brother, Benadine Leveler, had survived the war fighting with a Polish resistance group. Afterward, Benadine had stayed in Russia and opened the orphanage where Stephen was deposited as a child. At times, Chaim felt guilty for coming to this land of plenty, but how could he feel bad with Stephen at his table? The lad may never have come to America if Chaim hadn't blazed the trail.

The call from his brother, informing him that Stephen was coming to America, had been one of Chaim's brightest moments. It had been a pleasure to help Stephen, no longer a child, find his feet. As it turned out, Stephen hardly needed help. He'd completed his studies with honors and entered the lucrative world of real estate at the age of twenty-four. Still, Chaim felt he could take some credit for that.

The boy had elected to live in Chaim's two-bedroom home all these years despite the alternatives his considerable earnings provided. Even in the best years, Stephen never ran out and bought a new Mercedes or otherwise advertised his wealth. America had a difficult time understanding Stephen. He didn't run through women, didn't drive fast cars, didn't spend half his earnings on parties and clothing. But not because he was too frugal or conservative.

Stephen could walk into a Las Vegas casino and drop a thousand dollars in a game of craps inside of ten minutes. He was as impetuous and bold as they came.

Stephen didn't flaunt his success for the simple reason that the trappings of American life didn't appeal to him. At least not the kind of trappings a few million dollars could buy. When Stephen dreamed, he dreamed of owning jets and buying islands. Of obscuring the past and buying himself a new future. He was a tie-dye dreamer; he dreamed big, audacious, colorful dreams that held certain appeal, even if they were absurd fantasies to most.

"What you need, dear Stephen, is some love in your life," Chaim said again.

"You don't give up, do you?"

"Why should I? Pass me the mayonnaise, will you?"

Stephen passed the jar.

"It wasn't so long ago that I was in love, you know," Chaim said. "Sofia. A beautiful Jewish girl in St. Rothsburg. When she entered my life, the rocks began to smell like chocolates. Nothing became everything overnight."

Stephen shook his head. "Enough."

Chaim acquiesced. They made small talk and ate their fish sandwiches. Delicious.

Stephen finally wiped his mouth and stood. "Speaking of love, didn't you invite Slyvia to supper tonight?"

"Dear me, I had forgotten!" Chaim stood and hurried to the sink. "And I'm cooking, yes?"

"We could order—"

"Nonsense! She loves my cooking. Did I promise her anything in particular?"

"Veal parmesan, wasn't it? Or was it fondue?"

"You're not sure?"

"I had more on my mind at the time than the menu." Stephen lifted his chin, stepped onto the kitchen floor, and began dancing with an imaginary partner. His lips twisted into that whimsical, dimpled smile. "Love, dear Rabbi. Remember? Love is in the air, and I am caught in its draft."

"Nonsense. I don't think you would know love if it smacked you upside the ear. Seriously, Stephen. Was it veal?"

Stephen spun around once. "Love, Rabbi. The food of life itself. Cook us love for dinner."

"Be serious, boy! I've forgotten what I told her!"

"It won't matter what we eat. Feed us stones, and we'll think they're chocolates, Rabbi. You do remember love, don't you?"

"Ha! I was born for love." Chaim impulsively stepped around the counter, grabbed the taller man's upheld hand, and swung into his dance. "Although I doubt I make a suitable partner."

Stephen didn't miss a beat. He spun Chaim around and feigned a swoon. "Abandon yourself, Rabbi. Tonight, I will feed on love."

Chaim dropped Stephen's hand, suddenly embarrassed. "Oy, what has become of us? What am I going to do about dinner?"

Stephen spun into the living room and abruptly dropped his arms. He walked to the stereo and punched the power button. "Veal sounds wonderful. I'm certain it was veal. In fact, I was sure all along. I just wanted to see your moves."

"My moves! Please!"

The telephone rang shrilly and Chaim picked it up.

—⁓—

THE RABBI was right, Stephen thought. He really could use a little romance in his life. He spun the radio dial. Stopped on the alto voice of Carly Simon. Stephen returned the mayonnaise to the refrigerator while Chaim spoke into the phone. Of course, it meant finding the right woman to romance or, more to the point, finding a woman who wanted to be romanced by him. He'd had one major love fresh off the boat as a freshman in college. *"You gave away the things you loved, and one of them was me,"* Carly drawled. A girl named Betsy who had been utterly infatuated with him for two weeks before moving on to some other prey. The experience had left him less than confident. *"You're so vain, you're so vain."*

"Are you sure?" Chaim's tone caught Stephen's attention. "How is it possible?"

"What?" Stephen asked, closing the fridge.

Chaim responded by turning his back.

Something had happened. Stephen walked to the table to clear off the remaining dishes. Perhaps it was Marjorie Stillwater, the old lady from Chaim's church. She'd died? Or was this Joel Sparks, insisting that Stephen owed him money? What if something had happened to Sylvia?

The suggestions trotted through his mind, but none paused. It was probably nothing.

"Thank you, Gerik." The rabbi set down the phone.

"Well? What was that about?"

Chaim still didn't turn.

Alarm spread through Stephen. This wasn't like Chaim. Not at all.

"What's going on? For heaven's sake, tell me."

When the rabbi turned, the blood had faded from his already pale face—he looked like a ghost. He reached for the newspaper, flipped through the sections, stared at a page for a moment, then showed it to Stephen. "Did you hear about this?"

The page was open to the story about Rachel Spritzer's death. They had all heard of the reclusive woman, of course, at least of her reputation. Stephen glanced at the paper and shifted his eyes back to Chaim.

"I heard of it, yes. She lived alone in an old, vacant apartment complex off La Brea. The property is worth roughly five hundred thousand dollars, demolition costs factored. Why? You know something I don't?"

"She had in her possession one of the Stones of David, which she donated to the museum."

Stephen looked up. "No, I hadn't heard that." Surprising. Even stunning. But this information wouldn't have turned Chaim white. "You're serious? The Stones of David?" He reached for the paper. It came out of Chaim's limp hand.

Stephen glanced down the article, settled on the part about the relic, and read. His interest in the Stones of David had been started by his foster father. He glanced up, saw that Chaim was staring at him, and returned his eyes to the paper.

"I knew about the listing," he said. "But I didn't know about the Stone. This is proof, then. They do exist." Stephen quoted from the article: "The Stones are like the lost orphans. They will eventually find each other."

The rabbi was still quiet. Stephen closed the paper and dropped it on the table. "What gives?"

"She was an emigrant from Hungary," Chaim finally said. "A very wealthy emigrant who had in her possession one of the Stones of David. Not too many wealthy Jews survived the war."

"I can read that much for myself."

"She used to visit Gerik down at his antique shop. She left a note with him to be opened in the event of her death." Chaim stopped. "Evidently, she'd been sick for some time."

"And?"

"Do you mind . . . would you mind showing me your scar, Stephen?"

Odd request. He had a scar below his collarbone—a crude half circle with three points inside it, like a half-moon some creature had taken a bite out of. He'd searched for the meaning of the mark. Chaim had asked Gerik about it once, and the old man drew a blank. It was a mark from the war; they guessed that much, but no more.

Stephen pulled down his collar, revealing the scar.

Chaim stared and seemed to shrivel.

Stephen released the shirt. "What? Tell me—what!"

"Stephen, Rachel Spritzer's note says that she branded her son—who was born in a Nazi labor camp—with the image of half a Stone of David."

The words made no sense to Stephen. Rachel Spritzer marked her infant son. Half a Stone of David. Surely this wasn't connected to him.

Tears filled the rabbi's eyes. "She had been searching for her son since the war, but she had to be very secretive."

"You're not saying . . ."

Stephen felt the air slowly vacate his lungs. Heat washed down his neck and back.

"I'm saying that I think you've found your mother, Stephen. I think that Rachel Spritzer was your mother."

The room shifted out of focus. Stephen reached out to steady himself on a chair.

He couldn't breathe.

5

Poland
April 24, 1944
Early Morning

MARTHA PRESSED HER EYE AGAINST THE THIN CRACK BETWEEN the two boxcar planks for the thousandth time in four days. Outside, dawn colored Poland's horizon gray. Where in Poland, she didn't know. Why to Poland, she didn't know. But she was certain if they didn't stop soon, some of the women in this car never would know.

How long could a human live in a cramped box without food or water?

There was this gray sky above them, and there was this constant *clank, clank, clank* of railroad tracks below them, and there were vacant stares inside, and there was enough heartache to have wrung the tears from every one of them days ago, and that was the sum of the matter. Nothing to say, nothing to do, not much even to feel anymore.

Except for the baby. She had to feel for the sake of the baby inside her.

Martha clenched her jaw, turned back to the dark car, and slid to her seat. She hadn't urinated for two days, but the dull pain was manageable for the time being. There were three waste buckets on the far side, all full after the first day. Having nothing to eat or drink did have its advantages, however small.

The freight car held roughly seventy women, made up of two groups: a motley crew of fifty who'd accompanied her from the prison in Budapest, and another twenty who'd joined them much later, well inside Poland. Late on her second night in the car, the train had pulled into a large plant with huge smoking stacks. Martha had stared through the cracks at hundreds, maybe thousands of men, women, and children. They wore gaunt

26

faces and walked slowly in long lines to the big brick buildings near the train's caboose. Music floated over the compound—Bach. Something felt horribly wrong with the scene, but she couldn't put her finger on it.

Soldiers swapped out the buckets, hustled the new prisoners on board, slammed the gate shut, and locked it tight. The boxcar began rolling again about an hour later.

Ruth had been in the second group, which was mostly comprised of Jews from Slovakia. The petite young woman had eyed Martha for a full day before edging past the others to her side. She'd taken Martha's arm at the elbow and stood in silence.

Martha smiled as best she could and placed her hand on Ruth's. They remained like that for several hours. No need for talk. Human touch was all the young woman seemed to want, and Martha found it indescribably comforting. *Everything will be all right because I can feel you, and you are all right. See, it's not so bad—your arm is warm.*

Ruth had finally stretched up on her toes and whispered into Martha's ear. "Are you from Hungary?"

Martha nodded. "Yes."

"I am Ruth Kryszka," she said in decent Hungarian. "They took my husband a week ago from a farm where we were hiding in Slovakia. I think they may have killed him." Her voice trembled slightly, but she seemed brave.

Martha drew her closer and felt compelled to kiss her on top of her head.

"Who are you?" Ruth asked.

The question was Martha's first normal exchange in four weeks, and it made her want to cry.

"I am Martha," she whispered. "Martha Spieller." She wasn't entirely sure why they were whispering. Perhaps because they clung to their own histories as the last bastion of meaning in a world gone mad. Sharing it was like sharing the deepest secret.

"I am from Budapest," Martha said.

"I studied in Budapest once," Ruth said. "It's a beautiful city. They are killing Jews in Hungary?"

Killing Jews? She said it as if she spoke of eating bread.

"Some. Not so much in Budapest, but my father was well-off. The gestapo came with the gendarmes three or four weeks ago. They confiscated our house and my father's collections. I was taken to the prison outside of Budapest, and now I'm here."

"Are you married?"

Martha had cried herself to sleep for two straight weeks in prison, remembering the brutality of that day. They'd been eating lunch— imported Swiss cheese and strawberries with a wonderful white wine— listening to Father talk confidently about the return of better days, when the pounding came on the door. Not just a knock, but smashing fists and shouts. For a moment they'd all frozen, even Father. Then he'd dabbed his lips, pushed back his chair, and assured them it would be all right. Yes, of course, he'd set things up with Kallay's high-ranking officials. No harm would come to his family.

But they all knew that one day harm would come. Most able-bodied Jewish men already had been sent to labor camps. All Jewish property had been legally confiscated.

Martha closed her eyes, doubting whether she could share this particular secret of hers. "My husband and father were killed in our home," she said with an ease that surprised her. "They took my mother and younger sister, but I haven't seen them."

It was enough for a few hours. After a period of rocking quietly with the clanking train, Martha rested her cheek on the shorter woman's head and quietly cried for the first time since boarding.

They whispered above the sound of the tracks several times over the next day, exchanging precious secrets that were really not secrets at all. They were both Jews. They had both lost their husbands and their homes. They were both young—Ruth twenty-five and Martha thirty-two—and above all, they were both on the same train, rolling and grunting and whistling its way steadily closer to some unknown destination.

Now, the dawn outside marked Martha's fourth morning aboard the cattle car, and still the train rumbled north, always north. Ruth sat next to Martha, knees bunched up to her chin, brown eyes bright, a fighter who'd accepted whatever comfort Martha could offer.

Ruth faced her and whispered. "Do you think we will both be in the same place?"

"I don't know where we're going."

"To a labor camp."

"A labor camp? You know this?"

"I think so." Ruth hesitated. "Do you know what they are doing? The Germans?"

"In the war?"

"No, to us. To the Jews."

Martha had heard rumors, hundreds. "They are killing some and forcing the rest to work."

"They are exterminating us," Ruth said. "It's why Paul and I went into hiding. The station where I was put on the train—I think that was a camp called Auschwitz, where they kill us like cattle. There are other death camps, but not this far north, I don't think."

Martha stared into the darkness. Surely Ruth was exaggerating. "They can't just kill like that."

"But they do. I heard it from someone who escaped from a camp called Sobibor. They kill with gas and then burn the bodies."

A chill swept over Martha. Gas?

She felt Ruth's eyes on her. "You're pregnant?"

"What?"

"You're pregnant, aren't you?"

Martha sat up, terrified that her secret was known. Was it so obvious? A cotton shirt and a loose wool sweater hid her belly well. This was her first child, and even without the loose shirt she wasn't showing much.

"I am also," Ruth whispered.

"You . . . you're pregnant?"

"I don't think we should let them know."

Martha was at a loss for words. If Ruth could see that she was pregnant in this dim light, surely others would see it as well. She'd refused to consider what the Germans might do to her when they learned of it, but she couldn't escape the certainty that they would eventually discover her child.

"How did you know?" she finally asked.

"Don't worry, it's not so obvious. I see these things."

"And they won't?"

"If they do, they'll know that I'm pregnant too," Ruth said. There was a comforting sweetness in her voice. She had a heart of gold, this one.

"How many months are you?" Martha asked.

"Six."

"Six? I am almost six!"

"Five then? You hardly show! It's your first? It must be your first."

Martha wondered if any of the others could hear their excited whispers. She lowered her voice.

"Yes, my first. And yours?"

"Yes."

For a minute, the secret lives they carried within them overshadowed any sense of pending doom. Martha could feel Ruth glowing beside her.

"What will you name it?" Ruth asked.

"I . . ." Now the desperation of their plight surfaced again. Martha looked away. "I don't know."

Ruth placed her palm on Martha's belly. "He feels like a David to me," she said.

"And if it's a girl?"

Ruth hesitated. "Esther. David or Esther."

———

THE TRAIN'S whistle pierced the silence. The cadence of the wheels immediately slowed. Martha tensed, then stood and peered through the thin crack.

"What is it?" Ruth asked over her shoulder. "We're stopping?"

"I don't know."

"Do you see buildings?"

"Yes. Yes, there are buildings!"

Murmurs swept through the boxcar. A woman to their left demanded that someone tell them what was going on. It occurred to Martha that the question was directed at her. She had the best eye-level view out of this box.

"I think we're stopping," she said. "There are buildings and a fence."

"A fence?"

Voices bubbled up in the car. A loud hissing confirmed her suspicions. The train was stopping.

Martha's palms were wet already. Good news might greet them here. A drink of water. Some soup and bread—stale, soggy, moldy; it wouldn't matter. There would be a toilet. Even a hole in the ground would be a welcome sight.

Ruth laced her fingers with Martha's and squeezed tight. "This is it! This has to be it."

"I think so."

The air felt electric.

Only Martha and another woman, who poked her head past Martha's knees, could see clearly. The train passed guards who held back dogs straining against their leashes. Soldiers lined a road beside the tracks, rifles slung, some staring casually, others smoking. A tall fence topped with rolls of barbed wire ran along the perimeter of a compound, which housed dozens of long rectangular buildings.

Martha glanced over her shoulder. The women who could stand had done so. They'd grown quiet again, eyes wide in the dim light, staring at her or at the cattle gate. Their door to freedom.

Ruth leaned into Martha's ear and whispered. "The strong are allowed to work. Stand tall and suck your belly in."

Martha put her arm around the woman and drew her tight. "Thank you, Ruth." She kissed her head again.

She wasn't sure why she was thanking young Ruth.

"Promise you won't leave me," Ruth said.

"I won't."

The car jerked to a standstill.

They heard the dogs then, a chorus of barks that seemed to have started on command. The lock rattled. Martha's heart hammered at twice its normal rate.

The gate swung open, and light flooded the car. Martha strained for a view.

The first thing to catch her attention was a German officer standing thirty feet away beside a line of trucks. He wore a freshly pressed SS uniform with a bright red-and-black armband, arms folded behind his back, legs spread in bulging slacks, shiny black holster at his side. But more riveting than these were his eyes. Even at this distance, she saw them clearly. They were blue. And they were dead.

The next thing Martha saw was the sign above the gate.

TORUŃ

"Out. Step off the train and line up by the trucks." A guard pointed at a caravan of seven or eight flatbed transport trucks behind him.

For a moment, none of the women moved.

"No need to be afraid. Hurry!"

They surged out of the train as quickly as aching joints would allow. Ruth released Martha's arm, and they walked down the ramp into the crisp morning air side by side. All the way down the train, women emerged from the freight cars, which were fewer now than Martha remembered from when she had boarded in Hungary. Maybe ten cars remained.

"Make a line. Make a line!" The guards hustled the women into a long line, several deep. They weren't beating or shooting, simply bringing order to a situation that required it. This was not the way soldiers intent on extermination behaved.

Martha hurried for the line, Ruth by her side. The morning air felt fresh; she could smell something, maybe baking bread. They might even have hot showers. It had been a month since her last hot shower.

Or perhaps they would be gassed.

"Follow the guards into the camp. We have food and blankets. Follow the guards into the camp."

They hurried as best they could past the gate and into the camp called Toruń. Martha gazed at the sprawling compound and tried to remain calm. The other women weren't hysterical. Ruth wasn't crying or showing fear. She had to be strong. Martha straightened her back against the terror.

The yard was a slab of brown mud beaten into submission by thousands of feet. Not a blade of green grew between the buildings. Four guard towers rose above the fence, each manned with three guards. Overlooking the entire yard, a red house stood on a rise to the right. A large German flag rolled lazily on a pole from the highest gable.

"Form a line, form a line!"

"I think we might be in for some trouble," Ruth said, staring at the large brick buildings to the left.

"Silence! Single file!"

The women extended their line until they stood shoulder to shoulder at the center of the yard. A dozen women dressed in frayed shirts and slacks, women who apparently lived here, walked past the new group in single file, watching. Several others dressed in gray uniforms worked with the new arrivals, jostling them into order, issuing commands even though they looked to be prisoners too.

Martha saw an SS officer from the corner of her eye; she turned. Ruth glanced over, saw the man, and stood still. It was the officer Martha had first seen, the one with dead eyes.

The officer strode toward the group from the left, a long overcoat now draped over his shoulders, a stick gripped in both hands. He walked to the middle of the yard and faced them.

"You have arrived at Toruń, subcamp of Stutthof, in Poland. My name is Gerhard Braun, and I am god." He spoke in Hungarian, and his eyes remained flat. They settled on Ruth and lingered there as he spoke.

"I have selected each one of you. For that you should feel fortunate. Your train came through Auschwitz, yes? In Auschwitz, you would never receive such personal service.

"Now, I imagine that most of you would love a bowl of hot soup and the opportunity to relieve your bladder. Am I right?"

None of them responded.

"Answer me when I speak!" The officer's face flushed.

"Yes," Ruth said loudly. Martha hesitated, unnerved by her friend's bold response, then mumbled the same with the others.

He paced, calming himself. "I was sent to this stink hole only because I speak Hungarian fluently, and I will tell you that this place easily can put me in a bad mood. In fact, most of the time I am in a bad mood. There's no need to exasperate me. At this very moment, my thirteen-year-old son is watching us from the window of my house. He's visiting from Germany. His name is Roth. I would like all of you to wave at him."

Martha glanced at Ruth and then up at the red house a hundred meters away. First a few, then all of the women waved at the window, though they could see no one behind the glass.

"Good. Now, I have a decision to make," Braun said. "I can send you to the barracks where you'll be assigned duties and then fed. Or I can send you to the building to your left." Without turning, he let his stick flop in the direction of a large brick building. "This building is where we give you a shower. Has anyone heard of the showers?"

Martha felt her muscles stiffen, but she dared not speak.

"No? The showers at Auschwitz are ten times as large as ours. They say you should never hold your breath while taking a shower." He paced, lifted his face to the sky, and then faced them.

Martha's stomach twisted. Surely he didn't mean to kill them. Birds were chirping in a huge poplar by the gate; the morning sun was bright on the horizon; they'd done nothing wrong. Besides, he surely wouldn't toy with them in this manner if he intended to kill them. She let out a slow breath.

None of the women had spoken.

"Take your clothes off and leave them on the ground with your belongings. Now!"

"Suck your belly in!" Ruth whispered.

Martha quickly pulled off her shirt and then her slacks, holding her belly as tight as possible. In less than thirty seconds, they were naked.

Braun stretched his arm toward the showers. "Move!"

They turned and filed through the mud like a flock of white geese. Two female guards hurried them on each side. The dead-eyed commandant watched them go.

Martha refused to let her mind assess the situation. Thoughts of warm showers and hot soup had fled. Perhaps being treated as cattle on a cattle car had been better.

They marched into the brick building, past a line of square wooden toilets, and into a large cement room with a dozen shower heads protruding from one wall. Martha felt a wedge of panic rise in her chest. She had to be strong!

She bumped into Ruth, who had stopped in front of her.

"Keep moving!" one of the guards yelled. "Move!"

Ruth spun, eyes wide. "It's a shower!" She ran to one of the shower heads that dribbled a steady stream of clear liquid, cupped her hand to catch some, sniffed it, and whirled about.

"Water! It's water, Martha!"

The showers suddenly began to spit and spray. Ruth grabbed handfuls of water and splashed her face and mouth. Martha stood rooted to the concrete as the women rushed to the flowing water, crying out with delight. How many of them had suspected something other than water, she didn't know, but she felt their rapture.

To her right, two expressionless female guards watched.

"Martha!" Ruth called.

Martha ran into the cool streams. Life flooded her skin and reached into her soul. She lifted her hands and shrieked with exuberance. She couldn't remember feeling so alive.

There was a God in heaven, and he was kissing them with this water. Or was he?

6

Los Angeles
July 18, 1973
Wednesday Afternoon

STEPHEN AND CHAIM APPROACHED RACHEL SPRITZER'S ABANDONED apartment building from the north. Ordinarily, Stephen drove with the ease of someone who'd found a thousand addresses in Los Angeles— one hand on the wheel, the other on the listing; one eye on the map, the other on street signs. Today, the nervous twitches of a new driver ran through his bones. Both hands on the wheel, both eyes glued to the windshield.

They'd stopped by Gerik's antique shop to retrieve the note, an unexpectedly innocuous note written on white paper with thin blue lines. The words still bounced around Stephen's head.

> *I have searched all of Europe for my son. An orphan after the war, perhaps.*
> *His name is David, and his father died during the war. I placed half of*
> *David's Stone on his right shoulder, under his collarbone.*

That was what the note had said just above a sketch identical to Stephen's scar.

And, *They must not know that he is my son. I would fear for his life if they were ever to find out.*

And, *I had hoped he would come because of the Stones, but I could not*

make it widely known. This note is my only remaining hope. Tell no one
unless it is he. May God forgive me.

That was it.

So who was Rachel Spritzer?

How had she come into possession of a Stone of David?

For that matter, who was *he*? Stephen's foster father had named him, upon collecting him from an orphanage in Poland. But his name was really David. It simply had to be.

Gerik had been little help. He had been as surprised as anyone that Rachel had harbored such a treasure all these years. Rachel had given Gerik the note six months earlier when her health began to fail. But he hadn't opened it until after her death, as instructed. If Chaim hadn't made a comment about the scar on Stephen's chest, Gerik never would have connected the note to Stephen.

Whatever had prevented Rachel Spritzer from revealing her connection to a lost child had held power over her until the day she died.

Stephen had received the note with a trembling hand and paced for fifteen minutes, asking unrelenting questions. But there were no answers. Not from Gerik, who knew Rachel better than most, he said. Rachel was a private woman.

Three blocks off La Brea, the traffic thinned considerably. Amazing how neighborhoods changed from one street to the next. Here stands a million-dollar home with elegant palms and a mermaid fountain in its front lawn. There, a mere slingshot's distance off, stands a home surrounded by lumps of clay.

"It could be coincidence," Stephen said.

"Yes, it could," Chaim responded. "I can't see it though. Can you? The mark on your chest matches the sketch in her note."

"Still. Could there be any proof?"

"They've already buried her. I don't know."

"What about the will? Maybe she mentioned something in the will?"

"Gerik said no."

Stephen nibbled on a fingernail and tried to think clearly. All these years his mother lived not twenty miles away? He wasn't sure whether it was preposterous or tragic. Why hadn't she found him? Why hadn't he found *her*?

This couldn't be his mother. Not this rich woman who'd died and made the local news. The woman may have abandoned him in Poland, then gone on to live a life of luxury while he scraped to build a life from scratch. The woman quite possibly had given birth to him, but she could not be his mother.

"It should be up ahead on the left," Chaim said.

Stephen fought a sudden urge to turn back, afraid of what he might find. Or what he might not find.

You are my Stone of David, his foster father, Benadine, used to say, kissing him on the forehead. He asked Benadine what it meant. His foster father had smiled. "You are a survivor, Stephen. No Goliath can touch you." That was enough to make any boy of six walk around with a puffed chest for the day.

You are my Stone of David.

But he'd never been Rachel Spritzer's Stone of David.

A tall, gray structure loomed ahead. He glanced at the listing and scanned the building again. Four stories high. Cracked and discolored stucco siding. Chipped red-tile roof. Mexican tiles displaying the building numbers embedded in the stucco under an exposed light bulb. A Caldwell Realty sign in the lawn.

"This is it," Chaim said. "I have the distinct feeling that your denial has been compromised. Perhaps this is all for the best."

"I'm not in denial," Stephen said. "I'm living beyond the past."

Chaim didn't respond.

Stephen pulled to the curb and peered up at the structure. Dying vines spilled from flower boxes below dirty windows. A lone palm tree listed slightly, its dead, bushy fronds in desperate need of a trim. Concrete steps led to a single brown entrance door. A patchy brown lawn surrounded the corner lot, separating it from the nearest structure—a dilapidated apartment building with boarded windows across the street.

The buildings looked to have been built at the same time, although Rachel's building was in far better condition than its twin.

They climbed out of the car, Stephen clutching the newspaper with its old black-and-white photograph of Rachel Spritzer and her husband, Rudy, shortly before his death. Three yards to his right sat a dog, stubby tail madly twitching, tongue hanging limply out of its jaw. It was a cocker spaniel, not fully grown, perhaps a year old or so.

"Are you okay?" Chaim asked.

Stephen gazed up at the four-story building. "Yes."

"Arrff!"

"Easy, boy."

The dog offered a brief whine, bounded toward him, stretched up on its hind legs, and tried to lick his hand with a large wet tongue.

Stephen glanced around, saw no sign of the dog's owner, and tentatively petted the spaniel behind its ears, welcoming the distraction.

Stephen straightened and flipped his hand "Go home. *Shoo.*"

The dog sat on its haunches, tilted its head, and stared at him with big brown eyes.

"Go on now. *Shoo!*"

The dog turned away and bounded a few feet before turning back and sitting again. Good enough.

"Maybe it would be best to come back later, after you've had more time to digest this news," Chaim said.

"No." Stephen let out a long breath. "I don't know why I'm so nervous. It's just a house."

Chaim said nothing, but Stephen was sure he was thinking *denial.*

They walked to the entry. Chips in the stucco and small cracks in the door's brown paint showed the building's age. A lock box hung on the door handle. According to the article, Rachel Spritzer had spent the last month of her life in a hospice facility, where she'd made preparations to settle her estate. The complex had been on the market for a week. Stephen entered his code, removed a corroded brass key, and opened the front door.

Chaim poked his head in, then studied Stephen. "I think I'll wait in the car."

"There's no need for that."

"Yes, I think there is. You should be alone."

Stephen nodded. "Okay. I won't be long."

"Take your time." He descended the steps. "Please, take your time."

The dog suddenly barked and bounded up the steps and into the building.

The dog had no business inside, but the moment Stephen stepped in, a sense of wonder swept away any thought of issuing the canine out. The entire entry level had been converted into a parking garage similar to those found under office buildings. Three rows of bare steel posts stood in the place of load-bearing walls. Judging by two large cobwebs, the garage door hadn't been opened in at least a month. He noticed a single elevator to his right, next to a door that read, "Stairs."

This was his mother's house?

The dog had stopped ten feet in and once again stared at Stephen, head tilted.

Stephen shut the door behind him. "You can't be in here," he said. But again, he welcomed the dog's presence. Despite Chaim's insistence, Stephen wasn't sure he wanted to be alone.

The dog bounded for the elevator, sat by the door, and stared eagerly at the call buttons. Seemed to know the building. What was the chance that this was Rachel's dog? Surely she would have made arrangements for it, as she had for the rest of her estate.

Stephen walked toward the elevator, breaking the silence with the *clack* of his shoes on hard concrete. With a whole lot of remodeling, the apartment building could be restored. Then again, if the rusted pipes overhead were any indication, the entire infrastructure would need an overhaul. Cheaper to start over.

See, it didn't feel like his mother's house to him. He was a Realtor examining a building, not a son coming home. Maybe because he wasn't really her son.

A twinge of guilt pricked his mind. He should feel more like a son.

"You stay here," he told the dog. But the moment he cracked the door to the stairwell, the cocker spaniel bolted for it, squeezed between Stephen's legs, and disappeared down a flight of steps.

"Hey!" His voiced echoed through the stairwell. He considered following the dog into the darkness below. "I'm going up." He was talking to this dog as if it could understand. "You hear me? I'm going up. Don't you dare poop down there."

Stephen headed up the concrete steps. He would deal with the dog before leaving. Letting it wander around the basement for a few minutes wouldn't hurt anyone.

The second floor still housed three apartments, but they looked as if they'd been abandoned for a decade, maybe two. Green carpet, fifties all the way.

Third floor, same as the second. Musty, dark, and vacant. She had lived in the building only a month ago, but where? Caldwell may have removed her belongings, but the first three floors had been vacant for a long time.

Stephen walked up the last few steps, saw the heavy oak door that led into the fourth floor, and stopped. This was it. His hammering heart was driven as much by nerves as by the climb.

The dog sat by the door. Must have run up while he was on the third floor. Maybe this really was Rachel's dog. Did that make it his dog? It really was a beautiful dog, and by the look in its eyes, quite intelligent. No, this wasn't his dog. Rachel had left everything to someone else. To a museum.

"You poop down there?"

The dog barked and Stephen jumped. "Hush."

This was ridiculous. He should just go in there, see what this Rachel Spritzer had left, and then be on his way.

He gathered himself, transferred the newspaper to his left hand, pushed the door open, and stepped into the fourth floor. A smell that reminded him of cherry blossoms tinged with licorice filled his nostrils. The odor of . . . Russia. His foster grandmother's apartment in Moscow. If he was right, he would find some mothballs hanging around somewhere as well.

The dog ran around him and headed straight for the back of the apartment. Stephen peered through the dim light. He was breathing through his nostrils. Loudly. He opened his mouth. Better.

The entire level had been converted into a single apartment. Plush carpet, textured gold wallpaper, lavender drapes—Turkish, if he was right.

A light switch to his right brought a large crystal chandelier to life in the entryway. He walked farther in, taken by the contrast between the floors below and this one. Judging by a scattering of empty picture hangers leaning against the walls, someone had selectively removed some of the paintings. Undoubtedly, the museum had picked through her belongings and taken what they considered truly valuable. There certainly weren't any Stones of David lying around.

You are my Stone of David.

Stephen stood in place for a full minute, gazing about the room, trying to decide what it meant to him. Was there some deep, mysterious connection between the apartment and his life? He tried to imagine Rachel Spritzer living here. He lifted the paper and stared at the picture of Rachel and Rudy Spritzer. The black-and-white photograph was slightly out of focus. Dark hair pulled up in a bun. A kind face. Thin. Before coming to the United States, and during his first year here, he had searched for any record of his true parents. Nothing. Not a scrap of information in the hundreds of war records he'd pored over.

He folded the paper, took a deep breath, and walked into the room. He would look around, sure. It would be good to know who had given him birth. But to pretend there was any meaningful relationship between this woman and him was nothing more than misguided sentimentality. He'd shut this door once and had found a certain amount of peace in doing so. He couldn't afford to open that door now. This was about closure, not a new beginning.

Stephen walked slowly through the sprawling five-bedroom apartment, feeling distant from it all.

Some of her clothes still hung in the master-bedroom closet, clearly the source of the mothballs he'd smelled. A king-size canopy bed sat draped in lace. The kitchen boasted the latest appliances. A cookie jar with a rose inlaid in gold leaf still held sugar biscuits. Although the museum evidently had no interest in the furniture, most of the pieces in the living room were antiques, probably from Europe, and would fetch some money with the right dealer. The dinner table was hand carved from cherry.

History seemed to leak from every knickknack and every doily. But Stephen didn't want to engage that history right now. The trappings of unmistakable taste were everywhere. No photographs though. She hadn't even left him a photograph.

Stephen stopped in the middle of the room, struggling against a terrible urge to cry. He couldn't, of course. He was a grown man. He didn't even know if she really was his mother. And even if she was his mother . . .

A wellspring of sorrow rose through his chest. He struggled to hold back tears and failed.

He stood straight, sniffed hard. It was enough. He'd come, he'd seen, and he'd cried. He couldn't afford any more.

Stephen walked to the dining room table, slapped down the paper, and cracked his knuckles. All right, then. There you have it. Finished. Chaim was waiting. He headed for the door.

The dog.

"Hey, do—" His voice cracked and he cleared it. "Hey, puppy?" He headed back to the master bedroom. "Hello? Puppy?"

A brown nose poked out from under the bed skirt. No eyes, just the nose. "Come on, Spud, time to go."

In response, the spaniel eased its head out, still flat to the carpet, eyes rolled back for a view of Stephen. The dog was certainly no stranger to this apartment. If it wasn't Rachel's, it had to be one she'd befriended.

"Come on." Stephen turned and walked into the living room, hoping the dog would follow. It bounded past him, pulled up by the elevator, and barked.

"You want to ride the elevator? Is that the way you normally go?" He punched the call button. "Sure, why not?" He was feeling better already.

He punched the call button, stepped in behind a happy cocker spaniel, and pressed the lowest button before realizing it had a B on it. Basement. The number on the button above was worn off, and when he pushed it, no light illuminated. The car rumbled slowly for the basement. Stairs would have taken half the time.

Stephen rested his head against the wood paneling. What would he tell Chaim? He would be reasonable. He had found some closure. Maybe they could come back later and walk through the apartment together. Maybe they should take a closer look at her will—she may have left something for him in the fine print. Something that had meaning.

He tried again to imagine the Jewish woman who had carefully packed her precious treasures and crossed the seas in search of a new life. Rachel Spritzer. She'd survived Hitler's reign of terror. He'd spent the last ten years pushing it from his mind.

The car reached the bottom, and its door slid open. He hit the close button, but the dog leaped through the gaping doors.

"No, Spud, not here! Hey!" Stephen stepped from the elevator, hit the switch to his right, and let his eyes adjust.

The dog stood by a door across the empty room, swapping expectant looks between the door and Stephen.

"You know this place, don't you? Is this where you slept?"

Curious, Stephen quickly poked his head into three other doorways. Two led to empty storage rooms, the other to an old coal room. He cracked the door Spud had fixated on—utilities. The dog hurried toward a plump, black cast-iron boiler that sat against the far wall, then found an old blanket in the corner. Spud had obviously slept here on more than one occasion.

Stephen scanned the room. The building had been constructed in the forties or fifties, before electricity dominated the water-heating industry. Black water pipes ran out of the boiler and disappeared into the ceiling. A newer electric water heater stood in the corner. Several fifty-five-gallon drums lined the wall next to the black boiler. The room smelled a bit like kerosene. Or was that charcoal he smelled?

He walked to the drums and tapped them. Two gonged loudly, empty. The third thudded, and the liquid caught in its rim vibrated. It smelled stagnant. A drop splashed on the drum, and Stephen glanced up. The culprit appeared to be a slowly leaking pipe.

He grunted and was about to turn when the dog caught his eyes. Spud was sniffing at a round plate set in the concrete floor behind the boiler. Something like a manhole cover, only smaller, maybe eighteen inches in diameter.

"You find something?" He crossed the room and leaned over the dog for a better view. Spud was pawing the edges of the cover now. Careful not to rub against the boiler, Stephen squeezed behind, bent down beside the dog, and examined the dirt-encrusted surface. A pattern had been stamped into the steel, but he couldn't make sense of it. The cover probably gave entry to a sewer system or a large drain. Of course, you never knew with these old buildings.

He straightened, dug for his keys, and scraped at the dirt. No luck. A screwdriver or crowbar would probably do the trick, but he didn't make a habit of lugging around either in his back pocket. Interesting though. The dog was certainly taken by it.

It occurred to him that he was squatting over a sewer grate behind a potbellied boiler with a dog. The day's revelations had messed with this mind. He grunted and stood. Black dust covered his right hand, and he wiped it as best he could against the cement wall.

He found a certain quality about the utility room appealing. The fact that it had survived all these years, maybe. Its utter silence, perhaps. Peace and bliss at the bottom of a hole. Or was it isolation and death? Abandonment. Misery loves company.

"That's it, Spud."

The dog looked up wistfully; returned a longing gaze to the circle.

"If only my life were as simple as yours. Let's go."

Amazingly, Spud obeyed.

They opted for the stairs this time. The ancient elevator deserved a wrecking ball through its gut. It was amazing that the thing still worked. Stephen pushed his way into the garage and stopped.

The rolltop door was open. A black Cadillac with tinted glass gleamed under the lights—a rental from California Limousine Service, according to the insignia on its doors.

"Stephen Friedman, what on earth are you doing in a dump like this?"

Stephen turned to face Mike Ryder, a Realtor he'd bid against on a piece of property in Hollywood last year. The dog ran past Mike and through the garage door.

"Hey, Mike. Never know where you'll find the deals. You showing the place?"

"Second time today. To the same party. That mutt follow you in?"

"It slipped in before I could stop it," Stephen said. No sign of Chaim. "Know who he belongs to?"

"I think he's a she," Mike said. "Used to belong to the owner, but I guess she found another home. Been meaning to call the pound."

"Who's the lucky prospector?" Stephen asked, glancing around.

"German investor. Working on an offer."

Stephen arched an eyebrow. "Just like that? How much?"

"Asking price. He's on the top floor now with two business associates. Forget this place, Stephen—no short-term money in this one."

The thought of someone buying the building struck Stephen as profane. He may not have a legal right to the place, but if Chaim was right and he was Rachel's son, his own history was tied to this building.

Stephen nodded and looked at the limousine again. Odd for a foreign investor to snap up a property like this so quickly.

"Your listing, right? Can you give me a day on this?"

"You really interested?" Mike wore a crooked grin. He shrugged and headed for the elevator. "Nothing's going to happen in a day anyway. You got it. But don't tell me I didn't warn you. You may have a nose for a deal here or there, but trust me, this ain't one of them."

"Appreciate it."

Stephen left the building feeling dazed and confused, and clueless as to why. It was just a building from the past. Like the Holocaust, he should just leave it for history.

The thought made him sick.

7

Los Angeles
July 18, 1973
Wednesday Evening

THE RICH AROMA OF VEAL GREETED STEPHEN WHEN HE STEPPED into the house at five thirty. He'd dropped Chaim off after their visit to the apartment and gone for a long drive before making some inquiries at the courthouse and the museum that had acquired Rachel's estate. In the end, he'd learned nothing new. The afternoon had been a complete waste of his time. He had to get beyond this crazy assault on his emotions.

But Chaim and Sylvia would want to talk about it. Maybe it would be for the best.

He stood by the door and gathered his resolve; the last thing he wanted to do was spoil the evening with his problems. The fact was, he really didn't have any problems. Nothing had changed, really. Only history. So he'd been born to a woman named Rachel Spritzer. Maybe. So what?

He walked toward the sound of voices in the kitchen.

"The carrots and onions do the trick, I'm telling you," Chaim was saying.

"Smells delicious." Sylvia's soft voice. "You really didn't have to go to so much trouble for—"

"Nonsense. Besides, Stephen insisted."

She chuckled. "I hate to break it to you, dear Rabbi, but Stephen is only a friend. And I think the feeling is mutual."

Stephen pulled up short.

"Are you accusing me of meddling?" Chaim objected. "How does an old man like me propose to meddle in the lives of two young pups?"

A pot boiled gently on the stove.

"Two lovely, beautiful young pups, I might add." Chaim said. "A lonely man and a lonely woman, searching for love, practically ordained for each other."

"Please! I don't know where you get the idea that I might be interested in Stephen. As a friend, sure. But trust me, he's not my type."

"Oh? And what is your type? You're both Jewish."

"There's more to a relationship than religion."

"You don't find him physically attractive? And he's ambitious, smart, strong willed—you could never go wrong with a man like him."

"Don't get me wrong, I like him, I really do. I just can't imagine him as any more than a brother."

There was a pause. Long enough for Stephen to realize that he'd started to sweat.

"I think you're wrong about him," Chaim said.

"Please, what's wrong with a brother?"

Stephen backed up a few paces then walked forward, hoping they could hear him. He rounded the corner, saw Sylvia kiss Chaim on the forehead. Brown hair fell to her shoulders. She had a small nose, dwarfed next to the rabbi's. Chaim was no beast, but Stephen couldn't help but think that Sylvia was indeed the beauty kissing the beast.

"And you're like a father to me," Sylvia said.

"What is that incredible smell?" Stephen asked, stepping into their view.

Chaim and Sylvia both started.

He winked at them. "Is this the talk of love that I smell? Or is it veal parmesan?"

"Hello, Stephen." Sylvia exchanged a quick glance with Chaim. "It seems that God has informed the rabbi that you and I should fall madly in love and raise a dozen children in marital bliss."

"Oy, I said no such thing!"

Stephen stepped to Sylvia and kissed her on the cheek. "Thank you for coming."

"My pleasure."

Stephen withdrew a box from under his arm and handed it to Sylvia. "In case the rocks still taste like dirt."

"Chocolates." Chaim arched an eyebrow.

"Rocks?" Sylvia asked.

"Chaim was telling me this morning how even the rocks taste like chocolates when you fall madly in love. From his own vast experience, of course."

Sylvia took the box. "Thank you. These look wonderful."

Chaim eyed him. "Are you okay?"

"Fine? Why wouldn't I be? Today I found my mother. Her name was Rachel Spritzer. She was a very wealthy woman. A few days ago she died and left me nothing." He shrugged. "So what has changed? Nothing."

"She was your mother," Sylvia said.

"Was she? And what is a mother?"

They both looked at him.

"How is the district attorney today?" Stephen said. "Keeping our streets safe from thugs?" He made no secret of his skepticism when it came to her boss, Ralph Ferguson, the bald, potbellied DA who'd come to Los Angeles from the East Coast seven months earlier. Sylvia still hadn't committed to liking or not liking the man, even after going on four months as one of his attorneys fresh out of law school.

"That would be the police chief's department," she said. "We only lock them up."

"Lock 'em up . . . take 'em off the street . . . same thing. People don't give you enough credit. That whole department would fall apart without you."

She laughed. "Last I checked, I was still chained to the research desk, but thanks for the vote of confidence."

They avoided the subject of Rachel Spritzer for the next twenty minutes. They were all thinking about it, Stephen knew. It was in their eyes and on the tips of their tongues. But they were giving him the space he demanded.

The veal smelled wonderful, but Stephen hardly tasted a bite. They made small talk about the church Chaim attended, about Sylvia's research, about the deal Stephen was working with Dan Stiller.

"I visited the Holocaust museum," Stephen finally said after a stretch of silence.

Chaim set down his fork. "You did?"

"Yes. And the will makes no provision for any other party."

"You told them who you were?" Sylvia asked.

"I told them I was Stephen Friedman."

"But they knew you're related?"

"Of course not. How am I supposed to prove that? 'Hi, my name is David Spritzer, son of Rachel Spritzer; hand over the goods'?"

"There has to be a way."

"I don't even know if I *am* her son."

"You must be," Chaim said. "How could she ever know about the scar? No, there is no doubt."

"Legally there could be," Stephen said.

"Hire an attorney," Sylvia said.

"I don't *want* to hire an attorney. I want closure. And I think I have it now. She was my mother; I can probably accept that. End of story."

"It can't be the end of the story," Chaim said. "She alluded to some danger. Sylvia, can't you talk to the police about this?"

"Please, no," Stephen objected. "Really, whatever was in her past is in the past. Finished. I just want to get on with my life."

Stephen pushed a piece of meat into his mouth. "I'm not the only one she abandoned. Her dog's on the street as well." He immediately regretted the remark.

Chaim raised his eyebrows. "That was her dog?"

"I think it might live in the basement."

"The building has a basement?"

"Not so uncommon for a building that size. Nothing but an old boiler and utilities down there."

"How old is the place?"

"Built in 1947. The boiler isn't in use, of course. Maybe she stashed all her gold in the sewer." He couldn't seem to stop this flood of spiteful comments.

Sylvia looked up from the meat she was cutting. "What sewer?"

"There was a manhole in the boiler room. I assume it leads to an old drainage sewer of some kind."

Chaim glanced at Sylvia and then back. "A manhole? How big?"

Stephen set down his empty fork and indicated with his hands. "About so." It was absurd to think that Rachel Spritzer would put anything in a sewer. Besides, the cover hadn't been touched in years.

"Since when do they put entrances to public sewers in private buildings?" Chaim asked. "In Russia maybe, but not here."

"They don't," Stephen said. "But if the sewer predated the building, it's possible. I've seen it. These days, they would simply collapse the sewer and reroute it, but not in the forties."

"Could be submerged utility valves," Sylvia said.

The rabbi began to eat again. "Could be a bomb shelter."

"It could be a secret entrance to Fort Knox," Stephen said. "Please. It was in the utility room."

"How big did you say?" Chaim asked.

"Eighteen inches?"

"I would think that was a floor safe," Chaim said.

"No, it was a manhole cover of some kind," Stephen insisted.

"How do you know this?"

"Well, I don't."

"There you go, then. A floor safe."

"Makes sense to me." Sylvia winked. "You walked away from a fortune without knowing it."

"The cover was caked with an inch of grime," Stephen said. "No keyhole either."

"Still, I like the idea of a safe. A woman who owned one of the Stones of David would like the idea too."

Stephen rolled his eyes. "Don't be ridiculous. Nobody has touched it for years—does that sound like a safe to you? I can't believe we're even talking this way."

Chaim nodded. "You're right. It was a drain." He sliced into a potato. "I'm very sorry about all of this, Stephen. Maybe Sylvia is right. You should hire an attorney."

"I don't need an attorney. I have Sylvia. Honestly, I don't have a case, do I?"

"No telling without digging deeper," Sylvia said.

"But from what you know."

"No, probably not. But you never know until you dig deeper."

The image of that manhole cover, or whatever hid behind the pot-bellied boiler, fixed itself in Stephen's mind.

"I don't think I could handle digging deeper. I'll just . . . things will be fine. I'm working on a very good deal with Dan; I have a wonderful home. Wonderful friends." He attempted his best smile. "This will all pass, and things will be fine. You'll see."

———

SYLVIA LEFT at nine, and Stephen retired to his room at ten.

He climbed under the sheets and turned off the lamp, but he could not sleep. What if Chaim was right about the safe? Absurd. Eighteen inches—about right for a safe. A big safe, anyway. Too small for a manhole, really. Floor safes weren't that uncommon, although a safe behind a boiler was odd. Maybe he should return with a few tools and clean off the lid. Settle the matter. A safe would have a lock of some kind.

He tossed and turned. The hour hand on the white-faced alarm clock by his bed crept past midnight.

Say, for the sake of argument, that there was a safe behind the boiler. And say that there was more to Rachel's estate than what her will revealed. Wasn't it possible she would have left it in a safe? Maybe for her real son to find? He considered the note.

I had hoped he would come . . .

Even if the circle behind the boiler did belong to a safe, there might be no way to open it. Short of owning the building, breaking into the compartment was out of the question. Had she hidden a key in the base-ment? Or in her apartment?

Stephen crawled out of bed at one, went to the bathroom and returned, careful not to slough off what little grogginess had set in after three hours in the dark. *Sleep. Please, let me sleep.* He plopped into bed and shut his eyes.

What would she hide in a safe anyway?

The Stones of David.

No, she'd donated the one Stone in her possession to the museum. If she would have had two or three or all five, she would have donated the entire collection.

She'd had a month to settle her estate before dying—surely she would have itemized her estate. Rachel hardly seemed the kind who would lock up a treasure in a floor safe and then forget to list it among her assets. Especially something so valuable as the Stones of David.

Unless she wanted her son to find them without tipping off whomever she was afraid of. There was a thought. A silly, stupid thought. But a thought that kept him awake.

———

ROTH BRAUN sat in the black sedan and peered into the night. It was now well past midnight, and the long journey from Germany had worn him thin. If not for his anticipation of the satisfaction that lay ahead, he would have collapsed long ago.

But Roth wasn't fueled by regular flesh and blood and muscle and sinew. He drew his power from the blackest part of night.

He picked up the penlight with his gloved hand and snapped it on. A round circle of light lit the book that lay on his lap.

A telephone directory of greater Los Angeles. A monstrous thing that he would have preferred to leave back at the hotel. But he needed options in the event that the Jew he'd selected was unavailable or hard to reach.

There was always the possibility that he might select the wrong woman. Name alone couldn't confirm heritage. For all he knew an American Indian married a Jewish man and now bore the name Goldberg. But that didn't really matter. The selection of a Jew as opposed to an Indian or a German wasn't critical, though certainly more rewarding.

It did have to be a woman. His father had selected women. A woman had been his father's undoing. Yes, it had to be a woman.

His penlight illuminated the first name he'd chosen. Hannah Goldberg. Sounded like a Jew. Certainly a woman. Hopefully living alone.

According to the phone book, she lived across the street from where he was parked now. The number on her mailbox read 123423. Such a big number for an address. The Americans were far too many.

By night's end they would be at least one fewer.

Roth snapped the light off and set the book on the passenger seat. His fingers were trembling, but he knew he could subdue this visible anticipation with a single squeeze. He had this power. For the moment he would indulge the slight physical response.

Roth picked up a red scarf, ran the silk under his nostrils, inhaled slowly, then tucked the long scarf into his pocket.

He opened the car door, stood in the night, glanced up and down the vacant street, pushed the door closed. He rounded the hood and headed across the street. A single porch light lit the entryway. Otherwise the house was dark.

It was going to be a good night.

8

Los Angeles
July 19, 1973
Thursday Morning

BLINDING RAYS STREAMED THROUGH THE WINDOWS WHEN Stephen pulled himself from sleep the next morning. He swung his legs to the floor. Nine o'clock. When had he fallen asleep?

He hurried to the shower. First stop, Rachel Spritzer's apartment. He considered running the comps he'd promised Daniel first but decided that could wait. He had to get this other business out of his blood.

He'd go, find nothing, and be done with his mother's apartment. End of story.

He couldn't remember ever feeling so knotted up. The obscure hope that had kept him awake last night now demanded that he get into the apartment complex and down to the safe.

What if?

No, Stephen, not what if. Impossible, crazy, stupid.

But what if?

From his clock radio, Diana Ross was belting out "Ain't No Mountain High Enough."

THE REALTOR'S sign was missing from Rachel Spritzer's yard when Stephen pulled up an hour later. Huh. Even if the Germans had made an acceptable offer, the sign usually remained until closing.

A single brown car Stephen recognized as Mike Ryder's waited along the curb. No pedestrians. And no cocker spaniel. Probably off licking someone else's hand.

Stephen got out of the Vega, grabbed a hefty screwdriver and a hammer from the floor behind the driver's seat, shoved the first in his slacks' front pocket, and slid the hammer into the inside pocket of his blazer. The folds of his pants easily concealed the screwdriver; the hammer wanted to lean out. He tried to flip the hammer around so the head would sit in his pocket. No luck. He would have to hold it in place with his left forearm.

He patted his left breast pocket and headed toward the front door. If he was lucky, he would miss Mike. A quick trip down to the basement, and he would be gone. He was a Realtor with legal access—he wasn't exactly breaking and entering. Still, sweat glistened on his brow. Hot day.

Stephen stopped at the door. No lock box. No sign; no lock box. For a brief moment, he actually panicked. How could . . .

The door swung open and Mike stood in the frame. "Stephen!" He clearly hadn't expected anyone. "Whoa, too strange. I was just going to call you." He stepped out and shut the door behind him, then donned a pair of mirrored aviator shades. "Sorry, man. It's off the market."

"What do you mean, 'off'? Pulled?"

"Sold."

"Sold?"

"Closes tomorrow morning. Impossible, I know, but true. What can I say? Sometimes they go your way; sometimes they don't." A slight smile curved his mouth.

"How can it close tomorrow?" Stephen asked, seeking a new angle. He still wanted in, to satisfy his curiosity if nothing else. "Paperwork takes longer than that."

"Not necessarily. Clean title, cash deal."

"The German?"

"Roth Braun. Asking price. Paid for the furnishings too. Signed the papers yesterday."

"He's here?"

"Not at the moment, but I'm sure he will be. Sounds like he intends to live out of the top floor for a few days while he finishes his business here in the States." Mike locked the door and walked down the steps.

"Any chance you could let me in?" Stephen asked.

"In? Why? It's sold."

"Not technically. It'll be sold tomorrow morning. If they make closing. Either way, I think I left my wallet somewhere inside."

"As far as I'm concerned, it is closed," Mike said. "They put half down in earnest money. Two hundred fifty thousand smackaroos, my friend. That sound anything but done to you? I'm not sure I'd want to be caught inside the property when Braun shows up. Considering the size of the deposit, we're giving him access. I'm surprised he's not here already."

Stephen almost walked away then—he really had nothing to gain at this point.

Except maybe an inheritance that was rightfully his. Except maybe four more Stones of David.

"I'll be sure to hurry. Just let me in. I'll lock up. I'm a Realtor, for heaven's sake. This is what I do. Five minutes max. For my wallet." The hammer felt heavy in his jacket, and he turned slightly away.

"If he shows up—"

"My *wallet*, Mike! He won't."

Mike looked around and shrugged his shoulders. He pulled out a key, jogged up the stairs, and unlocked the door. "Locks from the inside. Make it quick. Trust me, you don't want to run into Braun. The dude gives me the creeps."

"If it becomes an issue, I'll tell him I entered the building while you were still inside. You left without knowing I'd come in, and I left shortly after."

"Yeah. Okay. You have a hammer in your pocket?"

Stephen froze briefly. Recovered. "Oh, yeah. I forgot it was still there." He pulled it out, thinking it was impossible to forget such a bulky object. "Pounded in a sign just a bit ago."

Mike stared at him for a moment. "You always keep hammers in your jacket pockets?"

"Gosh, no. I don't know what I was thinking. I was in a hurry." He pushed his way past the door. "You sticking around?"

"Not a chance. You're on your own. Don't forget the door."

Mike left wearing a puzzled expression. Stephen closed the door and let out a sigh. Not exactly the smoothest of cover-ups. A few white lies. He *was* going to pound a stake, if he could call the screwdriver a stake. Hadn't exactly done it yet, but he wouldn't call it a bold-faced lie. Never mind, this was his mother's house. Or had been.

He took the stairs to the basement, flipped the light switch, and gazed around. A single caged incandescent bulb cast a yellow hue over the four doors, all closed. Had the German been down here yet? He crossed to the boiler room, stepped in, and lit the room with another switch.

Three fifty-five-gallon drums, large water heater, potbellied boiler. Nothing had changed. The smudge marks where he'd wiped his hand yesterday stood out on the wall behind the boiler. A small hiss from the water heater broke the stillness.

Stephen pulled out the screwdriver and walked to the boiler. The circle in the concrete hadn't been disturbed. He moved one of the empty drums to gain working space. Settling to one knee, he chipped at the dirt that encrusted the lid. It broke off in small, crusty chunks. At this rate, cleaning the lid would take ten minutes at least.

He paused to listen. Silence. What was he doing? This was nuts. An image ran through his mind—him spilling out of the building, smeared with dirt and sweat. *Hello, Mr. Braun. The boiler works just fine, just fine. No need for a plumber. Yeah, that's what I am, a plumber.*

He attacked the lid with determination, needing to be done with this madness. The screwdriver kept catching on the pattern's small edges. Could be anything. He cleared the edges and saw that the lid was indeed just that, a steel lid set into the concrete.

Questions racked his mind as he worked. Why would anyone put a safe here? Assuming it was a safe, which it probably wasn't. But then why would anyone put a sewer entrance here? Unless it wasn't a sewer entrance or a drain or anything of the sort. Unless it was really a safe . . .

He shook his head and used his fingertips to brush the surface clear. The relief appeared to be a single insignia stamped into the metal. Still no keyhole, which meant it probably wasn't a safe. Not a chance this thing was a—

And then, suddenly, there was a keyhole.

A dime-sized slab of dirt flipped off the lid, revealing a round cylinder and the telltale zigzag of a key slot.

Stephen knelt over the lid and blinked. He ran his eyes around the edges and then refocused on the keyhole. His heart pounded. It had to be a safe!

He stuck the screwdriver into the slot and tried to turn it but gave up immediately. There had to be a key.

So, it was an old floor safe, hidden here behind an ancient boiler. Didn't mean it held anything but air. On the other hand, what if? What if there really was something hidden in there? For him. Rachel's son.

Stephen stood and hurriedly looked around for a key. The wall, the boiler, the furnace. Nothing. He paused to listen. Nothing. How long had he been here? Ten minutes at least.

He took a deep breath and sighed. Now what? He stepped up to the safe. The overhead light bulb glared on it. He'd actually managed to clear most of the grit from the surface. Small dirt chunks now ringed the safe. Anyone setting foot in the room would see it immediately. *Here I am; open me and find hidden riches.*

The least he could do before leaving was sweep away the dirt and make some attempt at hiding his hack job. He was about to look for a broom when the steel edges of the lid's pattern suddenly tripped a wire of recognition in his brain. Something familiar. Letters?

Stephen fell to his knees, snatched up the screwdriver, and attacked the dirt with renewed vigor.

The dirt came up in stubborn flakes but slowly revealed letters and then words. He tossed the screwdriver in favor of his fingernails. He clawed at the surface, brushed the dirt off again, and jumped up.

The Stones are like the lost orphans. They will eventually find each other.

Stephen's heart rose into his throat. A high-pitched ring sounded on the edge of his consciousness. *The Stones.* At his feet was a hidden safe that made specific reference to the Stones of David. He was a Stone of David. He was David. This meant what?

His breathing sounded loud in the chamber. *You're jumping to conclusions, Stephen. This is where she once kept the single Stone she owned. You're letting your imagination run wild down here.*

A faint *hum* ran through the walls. Stephen spun. The garage door! It had to be the German. And unless he was blind, he would have noticed the blue Vega parked out front.

Sweat covered Stephen's face. He instinctively wiped it away and then swore when his hand came away smeared black. He dived for the safe. Landed on his knees hard enough to send pain up his spine.

Using his arms as two brooms, he swept all the loose dirt back over the lid. Never mind the huge smudges that dirtied his blazer; he had to hide what he'd done here. The building might belong to some German named Braun, but as far as he was concerned, this safe belonged to him.

Footsteps sounded faintly above. He jumped to his feet, grabbed one of the empty drums, and drag-rolled it along the wall as quietly as possible, which was far too noisily.

If they barged in on him, what would he say? The plumber thing wouldn't have a prayer. Maybe he was from the city inspector's office, checking on compliance issues. A requirement for closing on the property. Cross the t's and dot the i's and all that rot. Unfortunately, he'd gotten a tad involved, thus the painted face and smudged arms.

Stephen grunted and maneuvered the drum directly over the floor safe. He stepped back. Looked natural enough, except that now a ring showed on the concrete from where he'd taken the drum. He brushed at it with his feet and managed to at least confuse the issue.

He ran from the room. Doubled back, grabbed his hammer and screwdriver, checked the room one last time, and headed back out. He hung out at the bottom of the stairwell for several minutes, begging a God he didn't really believe in to make the people upstairs disappear.

They ascended in the elevator. *Thank God, thank God.* Good enough, then.

Stephen crept up the stairs on his toes, poked his head into the garage, saw no one, took a deep breath, and headed for the front door.

He made it all the way without taking a breath. Unfortunately, he was forced to breathe before he got out. His gasp echoed through the garage. Perfect stealth.

Stephen ran for his car. If the German was to look out the window at the moment, he would see a dirtied man making a break for the blue Vega. Let him draw his own conclusions. At least Stephen was in disguise of sorts.

"Arf!"

He pulled up ten yards from his car. The dog sat by his door, stubby tail wagging furiously.

"Shoo! Shoo!"

Spud did not shoo.

Stephen leaned over him and unlocked the door. He expected the dog to bolt then. Instead, Spud licked his hand.

The dog had bad timing. At any minute someone would begin yelling out the door for Stephen to get back in there and explain what in tarnation he'd been doing in the basement.

"Okay, okay, go easy on me. I'm not a salt lick or whatever it is you guys—I mean gals . . ."

The dog jumped into the car, hopped into the passenger's seat, and looked away.

"Out." He didn't want to yell or make a scene. "Get out, dog!" he whispered harshly.

Spud refused to acknowledge him.

"Get out!" he whispered again.

No luck.

Stephen slid in, closed his door, and leaned across to open the passenger door so he could shove the mutt out the other way. Now Spud turned huge, eager eyes on him. The dog licked his hand as Stephen reached for the lock.

Maybe he should take the dog. Stephen straightened and gripped the steering wheel. Mike planned to call the pound, which meant the cocker spaniel might find a new home. Or an early grave.

Now was not the time to weigh his options.

Spud barked.

"Okay, but just for a day. That's it." He fired up the car and pulled into the street.

The dog looked forward, apparently pleased.

"And if you poop in the car, you're out for good. You got that?"

She whined and lay down on the seat. If Stephen didn't know better, he would think Spud here could actually read his intentions.

Which were what?

To find out what was in that safe. Rachel's safe. Mother's safe.

A tremble in his fingers refused to settle. He studied them. He didn't think he was prone to shaking.

He fought a sudden desire to wheel the car around, slip back into the apartment, and have at the safe. But he rejected the idea immediately. His eagerness might have landed him a case of the shakes, but he hadn't lost his mind to this thing. Right?

9

B E THANKFUL," GOLDA SAID IN A SOFT, HUSKY VOICE. SHE MUST have heard Martha's hushed cry. Only one day had passed, and Martha doubted she could survive another.

Moonlight cast gray shadows on the wall opposite the small window. A hundred women crowded Block D, the barracks reserved for Jews. Most of them slept, exhausted from a long day's work at the soap plant. Martha couldn't remember ever feeling quite so hopeless, lying here on the planks they called beds. At least in Budapest, she was in a familiar city. Here, she was abandoned and so far from home. Golda was right, she should be thankful, but she couldn't bring her emotions in line with her reason.

"You're alive," the barracks leader said. "Full trains leave Stutthof for Auschwitz all the time. And you came on a train *from* Auschwitz. There will be no crying in my barracks."

Martha could not answer. An apology seemed unwarranted, and any defense would be insensitive to the hardship they all faced.

On the bunk opposite Martha's, Ruth rolled over, rose to her elbows, and faced Golda. "Your body's alive, but maybe they've killed your heart. Who ever heard of such a rule, no crying?"

"In another week, you'll be begging for a dead heart," Golda snapped under her breath. "When the war is over, you may cry all you like. In here, you will keep your driveling to yourself. You aren't the only one trying to survive this madness."

Ruth didn't retreat, but she didn't respond either. Martha could see the whites of her eyes glancing from Golda's bunk to hers. Maybe she was tempted, as was Martha, to tell the hard woman that pregnant women couldn't afford to shut down their hearts, for fear it would shut down the child's heart within them.

Toruń was a labor camp for about five thousand women, mostly Polish dissidents and political prisoners from the Baltic region, but quite a few Jews lately as well. The food, a daily helping of a liquid they had the nerve to call soup and one slice of a white cardboard substance they called bread, was not enough to keep both mother and child alive. Martha had spent her first day at the plant, thinking the problem through until her head throbbed. As long as a woman could work, she was spared death, but between disease and malnutrition, life expectancy was only a few months at best. Between disease, malnutrition, and a growing baby, she couldn't expect to live more than half as long.

Unless she and Ruth found a way to eat more, neither would likely bear their babies.

Ruth's eyes returned to Golda. "Don't think that because we're new here, we don't know the meaning of suffering in silence," she said. "But if you can't protect your passions in this life, then stepping into the next might be better, don't you think?" Ruth, the brave one. "What good is surviving if you survive with a dead heart?"

Golda hefted herself to one elbow and studied Ruth. "What, you're a rabbi? There *is* no passion in this place! It was the first thing the Nazis stole from us."

"Not from me. The desire to live and thrive is a drive granted by God. Fine, we will learn not to cry, but you waste your time trying to kill our passions."

The leader squared off with Ruth in silence.

"She's right," a voice said quietly from above Martha. Rachel, another Jew from Hungary who'd been here for a month already, leaned over the bunk. "It's the most sensible thing I've heard since coming here. If we can't have hope, then why live at all?"

"Animals don't feel hope," Golda said.

When no immediate response came, Golda lay back down, satisfied she'd made her point. "We should be thankful for one thing only, and that is that we are alive," she said. "Braun might be the devil in white skin, but if you play by his rules, you may actually live awhile. Talking of hope and passion will only get you killed."

"Some things are worth dying for," Ruth said.

"Not your passions. Trust me, you can't afford to be passionate."

"I can't afford not to be passionate," Ruth said, soft and sweet, like an angel. "I'm pregnant."

Martha felt her pulse surge in the sudden vacuum created by Ruth's statement.

Golda sat up, swung her feet from the bunk, and stared at Ruth.

Rachel slid to the floor. She sat on Ruth's bed. "You're with child?" she whispered.

"Yes."

"I have a child. A three-year-old boy. They took him away in another holding camp."

Martha could hold her tongue no longer. "I'm pregnant too," she said.

They turned to her as one.

"Six months," Martha said. Her voice held a slight tremor.

"*Both* pregnant?" Rachel asked.

"Yes," Ruth and Martha said together.

"Do you know what this means?" Golda demanded.

"It means that we both carry joy and passion in our bellies," Ruth said.

"Don't be a fool! You'll likely be dead by tomorrow evening!"

"Don't be so harsh, Golda!" Rachel said. "You can't know that."

"I'm required to report this immediately. You have no idea what this means to the barracks."

"You have no right—"

"If they are discovered without my reporting it, five of us will be shot for hiding it!"

Martha felt a welcome resolve sweep through her. She could only hide so much without sacrificing her sanity. "Then tell him," she said. "I can't hide forever. Report me—"

"Report both of us," Ruth said. "We're not afraid, are we, Martha?"

Martha considered the question. "I'm scared to death."

Ruth stared back, white. "So am I."

Rachel and Golda did not move and offered no words of comfort. Were they so insensitive? Martha could understand Golda's dilemma, but the woman's silence sent a chill through her bones.

"What has the commandant done to others who are with child?" she finally asked.

"He sends some away." Golda's voice sounded tempered, perhaps by Ruth and Martha's display of strength. "He's allowed only one to have her child. This one finds some twisted pleasure in exercising power over life. Letting one live extends hope. He uses your hope as a weapon, to make the suffering worse for everyone."

Martha took a deep breath, fighting to hold on to courage. "Even if he does allow us to live, we don't have enough food to keep the babies alive."

"We will depend on God's will," Ruth said.

"God's will?" Golda said. "God's lost his will. I'm not sure God hasn't lost *himself* in this war."

"No, Golda," Ruth said. "Don't mistake man's weakness for God's."

She humphed. "Braun will want to see you." She sighed impatiently. "Whatever you do, don't slouch or look stupid. Don't anger him. And don't try to seduce him. If he tries to seduce you, resist, but not too much. It's a dangerous game. He's not permitted to touch a Jew, but that doesn't mean he won't."

The thought nauseated Martha. "I . . . I couldn't."

"Think of the little bundle of passion in your belly, and you can do anything." Golda faced Ruth. "There's your sentiment for you." She swung her legs back onto the bunk and lay still.

"I would pay any price to keep my child," Rachel said. She paused and looked at her hands. "I marked my son before they took him away." Her lips began to quiver with emotion, and she lifted her fingers to cover them. She stifled a cry and whispered. "I burned him. What else could I do? He's too young to remember his name. How will he know I am his mother? I had to mark him so maybe one day I could tell him that mark means he's my son. I could write letters and search for him that way. I wanted to tattoo him, like they do with all of us, but I didn't have the ink, and they were going to send me away the next day."

Martha wondered what could drive a woman to burn a mark on her baby. There must have been a better way. She could never imagine doing anything so painful to her own child. But to question this tormented woman who'd lost her boy felt scurrilous.

Rachel glanced up, anxious, as if realizing how shocking her confession must seem. "It's not so different from giving a baby a shot, is it? You poke a needle into the child so that he won't become ill. He screams today, but you've saved his life. It's all I did."

"Yes," Ruth said, rubbing Rachel's back. "It's exactly what you did, Rachel. And it's what I would do too. These are not normal times. We must cling to each other—to our children, our families—no matter what the cost. It's all we have left. This is our hope."

Martha lay back, empty of the courage she'd felt less than a minute earlier. If only she weren't pregnant. What had she and Paul thought, even considering bringing a child into this cruel war? It had been her idea. She'd practically begged him, and now look at her! What a fool she had been, thinking that a baby would make her feel alive again.

Martha stared at the pitted bunk boards above her, blinded by bitterness. She hated herself; she hated the war; she hated Golda; she hated the baby.

The baby? Tears sprang to her eyes. Dear God, what was she thinking? No! She could never hate the life that grew within her body. *Never!*

10

T HE NEXT DAY CREPT BY, TORMENTED BY THE BURDEN OF THE unknown. Golda had made the report to one of the guards before the eight o'clock work bell. Ruth and Martha were assigned to the fat vats, a hot, grueling place that would have sweated the women dead in a single day if not for the extra rations of water.

The bell signaling the end of the workday customarily rang at six. At five, when one of the guards signaled for her and Ruth to follow him, Martha rose from her stool with terrible anxiousness.

The guard marched them to the red house on the hill.

The air felt cool, promised rain. Birds chirped, full of life, a far cry from the deathlike hissing of the fat vats. Martha glanced over her shoulder at the camp below. From this vantage point, it looked crisp and clean, except for the huge mud hole in the center yard. It could easily be a Hungarian factory or a large college for boys.

A prisoner tended a flower bed that lined the walkway to the porch. Her eyes caught Martha's for the briefest of moments and then turned away. Did she know something? No, how could she? Except perhaps that few prisoners who entered the house fared well.

Martha swallowed and climbed the steps, legs weak and shaking.

Be strong. Don't slouch. He likes pretty women.

Both she and Ruth were pretty. Maybe that would give them favor. A petite doll from Slovakia and a tall brunette from Hungary. The thought sickened her.

Ruth took her hand and squeezed. She could feel a slight tremble in the fingers of the younger woman, who was brave not because she didn't feel fear, but because she faced it with surprising strength. Little Ruth needed her, didn't she? It was why she'd found Martha on the train. It was why she had taken Martha's hand now.

Martha squeezed back. "Be brave," she whispered. "He will never send away two such beautiful women. We are in God's hands, remember?" She didn't know which hope would prove true, that they'd find themselves in God's hands or that the commandant would find something in them to favor. Maybe both, maybe neither.

The guard opened the door and pushed them in. A young boy standing behind a chair, perhaps Braun's twelve-year-old son, stared at them for a moment and then ran down the hall.

The door shut behind them. They faced a spacious living room, handsomely decorated with crystal and paintings and golden velvet drapes, not unlike her father's country home outside Budapest. Leather couches surrounded a large, turquoise Oriental rug, well-worn but tightly woven. A long dining table was set with silver goblets and tall red candles.

Without warning, Braun stepped into the room from the kitchen. He'd been waiting there, staring at them with his dead, blue eyes.

It occurred to Martha that her hand was still in Ruth's. She tried to pull it free, but Ruth clung too tightly. The commandant wore his uniform slacks and knee-high black leather boots, but above his waist, only a white undershirt. His eyebrows arched.

His eyes drifted over them. "The two pretty ones." He walked to a cabinet and withdrew a bottle of red wine. "Would you like to join me in a drink?"

Martha heard the question, but she felt as though she were trying to breathe through syrup. Her heart sounded too loud in her ears. Her hand was still in Ruth's tight grip. They should decline, right?

"That would be nice," Ruth said evenly, finally releasing Martha's hand. "Thank you."

"Wonderful. It's not exactly German wine, but it is quite fine." Braun pulled out the cork and sniffed the bottle. "When in Poland, do as the Polish." He grinned, poured three shallow glasses, and stepped forward with two.

Ruth and Martha each took a glass.

"Thank you."

"Thank you." Martha thought her voice sounded like a mouse, and she determined to be stronger.

Braun retrieved his own glass. "So I understand that these two feisty Jews are pregnant. Honestly, I never would have guessed. You're both so"— he turned—"*fresh* looking."

Ruth lowered her eyes. "Thank you, sir."

Thank you? Was Ruth going too far?

Braun regarded Ruth with a pleasantly surprised look. Maybe her friend was onto something. What if the commandant chose to let her live, but sent Martha away?

"You're too flattering," Martha said, lowering her eyes as Ruth had done.

"Hmm. Yes, I suppose I can be. But you should know that I detest the fat guts of pregnant women. Especially bloated Jewess guts. If I know that the pure Aryan race is to be extended by a birth, I can stomach the sight. Otherwise I find myself wanting to vomit."

Martha stared into her glass. For a moment, he had seemed almost human. Now, she resisted a sudden urge to throw his wine at him and scratch out his eyes. Not even Ruth had a quick answer.

Braun was watching them carefully. "Which is why, whenever I over-saw the execution of Jews before being sent here, I personally shot the pregnant women. Himmler insists that no more than two bullets be used for each Jew. When I shoot a pregnant whore, I can take out two Jews with one bullet. How does that strike you?"

"It strikes me as inhuman," Martha said evenly.

Ruth glanced at her, then back at the SS officer. "It strikes me as dia-bolical. Only a coward would even find such a thing admirable."

Braun's grin seemed to stick in one place. They'd surely committed themselves to death.

He suddenly grinned wide and set down the glass. "Fortunately for you, neither of you has a pig gut. Lift your shirts, please."

Martha hesitated only a fraction of a second before lifting her shirt to reveal her belly. Ruth did the same.

"Amazing. You can hardly see it. They tell me six months."

"Yes."

"I like children, of course. I love children, actually. Even, dare I say it, the odd Jewish child. Young, impressionable minds waiting to be formed. Innocence. Innocence can be intoxicating. That's why we sometimes kill a hundred Jews at once, you know. So that when we kill only twenty, we are practicing a kind of innocence."

"I can see the logic," Ruth said. "But wouldn't killing *no* Jews lend itself to an even purer innocence?"

Braun stared at her, as if considering the argument for the first time. "But then we are confronted with another evil," he said.

"Allowing Jews to live?"

"Precisely." He held her gaze. "Sometimes the death of one satisfies the wrath of a just God. Isn't that why God demanded blood sacrifice from the Jews?"

"The death of a lamb," Ruth said. "Not a human. A long time ago."

"The last sacrifice of the Jews wasn't a lamb. It was a man. Jesus Christ. You don't remember?"

"You use the indiscretion of a few men to justify a slaughter?"

He stared at her and then abruptly diverted his gaze. "You will both live. You will be given double rations and allowed to give birth, should you survive so long. In exchange for this, I ask only that you visit me on occasion. You don't need to be afraid; I won't touch you, although I do find you both very beautiful. I would just like your company from time to time."

Ruth dipped her head without removing her eyes from his. "Thank you, sir. You can be very kind."

"Well, I suppose we all have it in us." He walked to the wall and plucked a red scarf from a hook and handed it to Ruth. "I would like you to do me a favor. Take this scarf into your barracks and place it on the bed five down from your own. The woman will know what it means."

Ruth took the scarf. "Just place it on the bed?"

"Yes. Just drape it over the bed. Will you?"

"Of course."

Braun smiled. "Good. Good, then. You may leave."

Ruth folded the scarf and tucked it under her waistband.

Martha wasn't sure how to feel about their good fortune.

The barracks were still empty when they arrived. Together they ran to the window and watched the guard walk away. Ruth was clearly more elated than Martha. She lit up like a Christmas bulb and threw her arms around her friend.

"See what Golda says to that!" Ruth said. "You see what passion can do?"

"It's not over, Ruth. It's a beginning, but—oh, you're right! Thank you!" She kissed Ruth on the cheek. "Thank you, thank you, thank you."

Ruth pulled out the scarf and walked to the bunk five down from hers—Rebecca's, if Martha remembered right—and unfolded it over the corner of the bed.

"Come, let me show you something," Martha said. She led Ruth to her bunk and slid onto the bed, where she'd scratched ninety small marks into the wall. "This is how we will know when the baby is due. Each day, I will cross one off."

"I can hardly believe he's agreed."

A morsel of doubt tempted Martha. Golda had insisted that the commandant only lifted hope to crush it. She pushed the thought aside.

"The end of July."

The door suddenly creaked open. Women began filing in, worn to the bone. Ruth and Martha exchanged a glance and then bounded out of the bed.

"Where's Golda?"

Golda was the eighth person to step through the door. The first seven had stopped and were staring. They knew? Golda had frozen in the doorway. They knew already? They *all* knew?

But Golda wasn't staring at her, was she? Not at all. Her eyes were fixed past Martha's shoulder, down the aisle. They were all staring down the aisle.

She turned with Ruth, but there was nothing to see. Only the red scarf.

Martha faced Golda. "What?" The woman's face had drained of blood. "What is it?"

"The scarf," Golda said matter-of-factly. "It's on Rebecca's bed."

"The commandant told me to put it there," Ruth said. "Is—what does it mean?"

Golda walked past them, picked up the scarf, stared at it for a second, and then set it back on the bed. Two dozen women now crowded the aisle by the door, all eyes fixed on the red scarf. A few lowered their heads and walked off.

"What is it?" Ruth cried.

"It's Braun's game," Golda said softly. "Every few days, he orders a guard to place the scarf on a bed. The selected woman is required to visit the commandant at six thirty for dinner."

"For dinner? Oh, my dear, poor Rebecca. I had no idea! I didn't—"

"The woman does not return. The next morning she is found dead, hanging by her neck from the front gate." Martha felt the blood drain from her face.

Ruth lunged for the scarf, but Golda stopped her short. "You can't do anything! Stop it!"

A loud gasp silenced the group. There in the doorway stood Rebecca, eyes fixed wide on the red scarf. She slowly lifted a trembling hand to her mouth. Her face went white like paste. Nobody moved.

Then three women converged on her. They placed their arms around her neck and began stroking her hair in a kind of silent ritual that struck terror in Martha's heart. No one made a sound.

Except Rebecca. Rebecca suddenly sagged and began to whimper.

—⁓—

"YOU'RE THIRTEEN—grow up! This isn't a world made from fairy tales. It's a world where lions eat sheep and powerful men eat inferior animals like Jews."

Roth watched his father, terrified and in awe at the same time. He lowered his eyes to his knees, bared between his shorts and knee socks. No matter what Father said, thinking of other boys his age as animals was still a little strange, although he wouldn't dare admit such a thing.

This was his third visit to the camp, and each time the sights became easier to accept, but he doubted very much that young boys were meant to see the things he saw. His friends back in Berlin walked around all proud in their uniforms, but they hadn't seen what he'd seen.

"Come here," his father said in a softer tone, stepping toward the window. He stretched out his arm and beckoned with his fingers. "Come on, I want to show you something."

Roth approached and looked out at the work camp below them. It was brown everywhere. Mud and dirty buildings and women plodding around in brown clothes. Some of them wore white scarves on their heads.

Father placed a calloused hand on Roth's shoulder. "What do you see?"

Roth thought about it. "Jews?"

"Yes, that's what most would say. Jews. But when I look I see more than Jews. What I see separates me from most men."

Roth looked up. There was something almost magical about the way his father looked at him with those mesmerizing blue eyes.

"What do you see?" Roth asked.

Father lifted his eyes. "What I see isn't for children."

Roth felt a stab of disappointment. The feeling quickly changed to humiliation.

"But I'm not a child," he said. "How can I grow up if you don't let me see things that other children don't see?"

His father considered this.

"Once you cross the threshold, there's no turning back. Are you sure you're ready for that?"

He wasn't sure. Not at all. But he nodded anyway. "Yes."

Father stepped back and arched one eyebrow. His eyes dropped to Roth's feet then up his body. Roth stood tall, uncomfortably aware that he was quite short for such a bold statement.

But judging by the look on his father's face, Gerhard was proud of his answer. He'd stood there like a man and said yes.

The commandant stepped forward and smoothed Roth's blond hair. "You come from good stock, boy." He paced in front of the window, one hand stroking his chin. "Do you remember what I told you about the swastika?" he asked.

"Yes."

"Tell me."

"That it is an old symbol that has been changed."

"The Sanskrit word, *svastika*, means good fortune. It's a spiral spinning with the sun. Only those who have a clear understanding of the occult know that a chaotic force can be evoked by reversing the symbol. This is behind the design of our swastika."

His father stopped and turned to him. "This war—all that the Third Reich is doing," he stretched his hand out to the camp below, "in camps like these—is about power. It's about reversing the effect of a terrible degeneration that has ruined civilization over thousands of years. This is the führer's primary objective. Do you understand?"

His father had tensed and his hand shook a little. It made Roth nervous.

"Do you understand?"

"Yes, Father."

Father stared at the camp. "When I look at that mud hole down there, I don't see Jews. I see degenerated humanity. I see a wrong that needs to be righted. And I see the perfect solution. In ridding the world of them, yes, but not in the same way I did at Auschwitz. They are killing enough Jews each day to satisfy our objective. Marching them into the chambers like zombies, ignorant of their fate." The man's lips twisted in disgust. "Here . . . here our task is far nobler. Here we are finding a way to power the new world."

Roth followed his stare. How Father saw a way to power the world with the sad-looking Jews below was beyond him, so he said nothing.

"They are like batteries," his father said.

"Batteries?"

"Psychic fuel cells. If you know how to take that power, it becomes yours and makes you strong. Like taking the power out of one battery and putting it in your own."

His father had closed his eyes. His lips trembled. Roth quickly lowered his eyes, afraid to be caught looking.

"Do you know what hope and fear have in common?"

Was he meant to answer? Roth wondered briefly if his father was speaking to him, or to himself.

"They both hold great power. But that power is dependent on both fear and hope together. Think about it. Without the fear of something terrible, you cannot have the hope that it won't happen, you see? Without having hope for something wonderful, you can't have any fear of losing it. They work together, the two most powerful forces we possess."

Father turned from the window, walked to the bar, and poured a drink into a glass. "I play a game of high stakes here, Roth. I play for the kind of power that few men will ever have. Not the power of deciding who will live and who will die—that's child's play. But the power of taking another human being's power. The power to harvest their souls."

He paused, eyes glimmering, as if this was a great revelation that should impress Roth. And indeed it did. His heart was beating very fast.

"I lift their hopes to the heavens"—he lifted his hand high in the air, then swung it down hard—"then dash them. *Why?* you may want to know. I'll tell you why. The anguish they feel in that moment weakens their will. Their resolve turns to putty. Their anguish becomes my power."

Then his father said one more thing that would never leave Roth.

"This is how the Prince of Darkness has always gained his power—through the suffering of his victims. That's how he took the life of the Christian God, Jesus Christ. Raised him up and dashed him to the ground. And he was a Jew too."

Father chuckled, took a drink, then set the glass down with a satisfied sigh.

"There are many of us, Roth, not just me. Our work is meticulously recorded, and one day I will show you what we have done. The deaths of our enemies—these Jews—is a happy bonus. But it is the power that feeds us. Does this excite you?"

Only then did Roth realize that he was squeezing his hand into a fist. He relaxed, but he found that he couldn't speak.

Father smiled reassuringly. "Not to worry. It was all quite strange to me as well. I still remember the first ritual I witnessed. It scared me to death. But the power, Roth . . . the power was intoxicating!"

He laughed and Roth joined, glad for the relief.

"Would you like to join me tonight?" his father suddenly asked.

"Join you?"

"Well, not join me. You can watch me through the slit in the door. I've picked a woman. At this moment she's down there in the camp, plumbing the deepest wells of her soul, dredging up horror. Tonight I will ravage her soul. Don't worry, it won't be gory or brutal. I have no need for theatrics. A little blood is all."

Roth said the only thing that came to mind. "Okay."

Father beamed his pride, a look irreversibly seared into Roth's mind. "That's my boy!"

11

S TEPHEN RETURNED HOME TO FIND THE RABBI GONE. YES, OF course; Chaim always spent Thursday afternoons down at the mission, serving soup and spreading good cheer. But this was good. Stephen couldn't tell anyone about the safe, not even Chaim.

Two things had changed during his last visit to Rachel's apartment. The first had to do with secrecy. Some things in life had to remain private. Matters of love. Matters that were deeply sacred. If Rachel was his mother, and if she had gone to the grave with some deep, dark secret, then he should pursue that secret with reverence.

The second change had to do with objective. The scales of his desire had tipped from a simple need to discover to a surprising need to possess. If Rachel, being his mother, had searched for him as the note to Gerik claimed; and if taking out a full-page advertisement in search of her son placed him—David—in terrible danger; and if, failing to find him, she'd secretly hidden something for him, then it was his right to possess this last remaining link to his mother.

The Stones are like the lost orphans. He was an orphan. The other orphans would be the other four Stones of David. Either way, he had the mark; the safe had the mark, or at least the words. The safe should be his.

Stephen left Spud on the front porch. He brought the dog a bowl of water and some lunch meat, which Spud gulped down without chewing. "Stay here." Stephen pointed a finger. "Don't move."

He hurried into the bathroom and stopped in front of the mirror.

78

He'd forgotten about the black dust. He looked like a native warrior trapped in a business suit. It was a wonder Spud hadn't barked at him all the way home. Now that he thought about it, several drivers had peered at him quizzically on the trip home. *What's wrong, never seen a treasure hunter before? Just returning from a coal mine where I've found a stash of diamonds.*

He stripped off his shirt and paused to trace the small scar near his left breastbone. Whatever he'd speculated about it before, he now knew the truth.

Stephen showered, dressed, and drove straight to the library with Spud in the passenger seat. "You have to stay in the car, you know. No way I can take a dog into the library."

He parked in the shade of a jacaranda and cracked the window. "I'll be back."

His first challenge was to research without tipping his hand. He couldn't very well run around conducting interviews about his mother without bringing attention to the possibility that she had hidden the other four Stones in her apartment.

A series of searches through the periodicals turned up nothing on Rachel Spritzer. As Gerik had said, she'd lived privately. She had been hiding her secret.

Who were you, Mother?

Stephen turned to the Stones of David. He flipped through library cards, found dozens of titles that contained information on the Stones, and pulled five of them. Settling in a quiet corner, he began to read.

None of them told him any more than he already knew. He'd done a research project on the Stones for a history class nearly a decade ago. But now he read the coverage in each book with renewed interest.

Although the biblical record made no mention of what happened to the five stones David chose to slay Goliath, historians' first note of their existence cropped up in 700 BC, when they were taken to Babylon along with other treasures from the kingdom of Judah.

They next appeared in AD 400 in Alexandria. Christian folklore claimed the Stones represented the seed of David, the purest surviving symbol of Israel, which was Christ. According to Genesis, God put enmity between the serpent's seed and the woman's seed, and the woman's seed would crush the head of the serpent. David had crushed the head of Goliath with a stone, and the Messiah had come to deliver the final deathblow.

Nevertheless, most Christians weren't even aware of the relics. They'd been lost again in AD 700, and for a thousand years their very existence was in dispute. Here the record became somewhat fragmented. Various rumors surfaced and then faded, until the Knights Templars claimed to hold them for almost two hundred years before the order's sudden demise in 1307, when the French king Philip IV drove them into obscurity. *You are my little Stone of David.* Why would his foster father use that particular phrase of endearment for Stephen?

Most experts valued the collection at between $75 and $150 million. The idea caused the slight tremble to return to Stephen's fingers.

Rachel had donated a Stone of David to the Los Angeles Museum of the Holocaust. He returned to the library's newspaper section. Virtually every major newspaper in the country had picked up the story, and several already debated the existence of such a relic. Others doubted the authenticity of Rachel's Stone. But to think that a World War II survivor such as Rachel would lie about the Stone seemed somehow profane. It *had* to be genuine.

As for the Spritzers, they had immigrated to the United States sixteen years ago from Hungary. They spent their time working with orphanages around the world. Low-profile. Wealthy. That was all he could determine.

Stephen checked out three of the volumes and headed home, nerves taut. He'd learned nothing new.

The rabbi still wasn't back. Stephen led the dog into his room and ordered her to stay in the corner. Spud jumped onto his bed, eyed him as if asking permission, and, when Stephen made no objection, curled up by the pillow.

Stephen looked at the books. Who was he trying to fool? There was only one way to do this. He had to get back into the building, find a key, and open the safe. He was just delaying the inevitable, subconsciously try-ing to work up the courage.

But he couldn't just waltz up to the front door and demand they let him look for a key. The moment the owner sniffed anything remotely like a safe, he'd slap the crazy Realtor with a restraining order and take the treasure for himself.

"Stephen?"

Stephen whirled. Chaim stood in the doorway.

"Sorry, didn't mean to startle you." The rabbi looked at him question-ingly. "You okay today?"

"Why wouldn't I be? Sure. Why, what's up?"

"That's what I was just asking you. Isn't that the dog from the apartment?"

"I'm just watching over her for a day or so."

"So you went back?"

Stephen shrugged. "Just to collect the dog. I'm okay, Rabbi. Really."

The rabbi shifted his gaze to his left and Stephen followed it. The books lay on his desk, one cracked open to a chapter titled "Stones of David: Fact or Fiction?"

"Maybe you should take a few days off," Chaim said. "Your mother has died. You missed the funeral, but you should grieve in your own way."

"Grieve what? I didn't know my mother."

"Then grieve the fact that you didn't know her."

"I've spent my whole life grieving that fact already."

"I think you may be in a bit of denial."

"That's what you keep saying." Maybe he should confide in Chaim. Only Chaim. Caution argued against it, but since when had he let cau-tion guide his path?

"I want to tell you something, Rabbi. But I want you to swear to secrecy. Can you do that?"

"Have I ever broken your confidence?"

"No, you haven't, but this you have to swear to. No matter what, you have to agree not to breathe a word. Do I have your word?"

The rabbi smiled. "Do I have to prick my finger?"

"I'm not kidding." Stephen leaned back against the desk. "I just need your confidence on this."

They held stares. "Then you have it."

"You swear?" Stephen asked.

"Swear by neither heaven nor—"

"Just swear it."

"I swear, then."

"You won't tell a soul?"

"Stephen, I won't tell a soul that you went back to Rachel Spritzer's apartment and discovered a floor safe in the basement." Chaim arched an eyebrow.

"You know?"

"Simple deduction. And a few filthy clothes." Chaim glanced at the coal-blackened blazer on the floor.

Stephen let his enthusiasm rise to the surface. He ran both hands through his hair. "Okay, you were right; it's a safe."

"Doesn't surprise me. I know Jews. Especially Jews from the era. I'm going to eat. Would you like something?" The rabbi turned and walked toward the kitchen.

Stephen hurried after him, incredulous at the man's ambivalence. "It's a floor safe, Rabbi! My mother's floor safe!" The dog jumped from the bed and pattered along behind him.

"I don't mean to be insensitive, Stephen. But I don't think you should do anything without proper legal representation. Rachel Spritzer went to great lengths to hide the Stone she donated to the museum."

"The Stone should be mine! I could contest the will."

"If you could prove you were her son, perhaps. But why was your mother so careful to hide it? There are those who would stop at nothing for something so valuable. Rachel was frightened. You have to be careful."

Chaim's wariness made Stephen pause. Telling him had been a mistake. Though the rabbi did have a point.

"Involving attorneys could take months. It's hopeless. How could I ever prove that I'm her son?"

"That would be for the courts." Chaim sighed. "Although you're probably right in the long run. She's donated everything to the museum."

"But not"—Stephen's mind spun—"not necessarily what is in the safe. Not if the safe wasn't listed among her assets. I can find that out. But trust me, if it was listed, the museum would have made the claim already. They obviously haven't."

"Perhaps because it's empty." Chaim pulled out the leftover veal and set it in the oven. "I know these may be hard days for you, but you must be careful."

Stephen decided then not to tell the rabbi about the inscription on the safe. If anything, he would have to divert attention away from the safe now.

"There might be another way," Chaim said.

"Another way to what?"

"To take possession of whatever is left in Rachel's apartment. Who's handling the estate?"

"The building's sold," Stephen said.

"Already? We were just there yesterday."

"A German investor."

Chaim studied Stephen with an amused expression. "Then buy the place from this German investor."

The suggestion hit Stephen like a bucket of ice water. Yes. He could offer the investor a quick turnaround profit. Once the building was in his name, he could open the safe.

He turned away, worried that the rabbi might note his eagerness. He had to downplay the whole thing.

"Maybe. Ah, you're probably right. I should just forget it. What do I have to gain? I've seen what's there, right?"

"I'm not suggesting that you forget it," Chaim said. "She was your mother. You need space and time to deal with that. And your true inheritance should be yours. But you must walk very carefully."

"You're right." Stephen clapped his hands and squinted at the oven. "Veal sounds great."

"That's my boy. Now. The reception at the Board of Realtors is formal?"

Stephen looked at him, not understanding.

"The reception you invited Sylvia and me to?" Chaim said. "Tomorrow night? It's a formal affair, right?"

That reception. It was this weekend? "Formal, yes, I think so."

They ate veal together.

Ten came before they retired. "Good night, Stephen. Sleep well."

"Good night. I will."

But he didn't. He hardly slept a wink. The dog, on the other hand, slept like a baby nestled against his shoulder.

12

Los Angeles
July 20, 1973
Friday Morning

THE SLEEPING MIND WORKS IN STRANGE WAYS WHEN HUNG UP somewhere between out-like-a-light and bright-eyed, Stephen had always believed. In this no-man's-land, the challenges of the next day's plans walk about like relentless trumpeters. IRS agents and bill collectors loiter. A few hastily spoken words of a friend echo and transform themselves into vile threats.

On this night, Stephen's no-man's-land was populated by his mother, a faceless German crook, Chaim Leveler, and a hole in the ground filled with black air. He himself was mysteriously absent. The rabbi spent most of the night walking around inside the safe, waving his arms like a leprechaun, insisting that danger lay ahead. Rachel Spritzer spent most of the time holding her one golden Stone up to the light, asking it to lead David home. The German stood guard at the boiler room, his rocket launcher aimed at the elevator. And the hole . . .

The hole was just an empty hole, apart from the munchkin rabbi.

Stephen awoke late, at eight. He stumbled out of bed, pulled on a pair of olive-green slacks and a white shirt. No time to shower. A shave was in order, but a bit of scruff wouldn't hurt. He had plans for this day.

The dog! Where was Spud? He ran out to the living room. The cocker spaniel sat by the front door, waiting patiently. "There you are." The rabbi must have heard her whine and let her out. What was Stephen going to feed her? "Come on, let's take a ride."

Stephen hopped into the Vega after Spud and fired the engine before realizing he'd forgotten to brush his teeth. "Wait here, dog. I have to brush my teeth." Spud eyed him smugly. "*You* should try it sometime." The dog turned away.

Stephen left the car purring, ran into the house, gave his teeth a quick scrub, and returned. The prospect of the deal he was set to propose ran through his veins as hot as any he could remember. Purchasing a building that held a secret treasure trove in the basement was nothing less than the stuff of fantasies. And yet that was precisely what he was about to do.

The German had purchased Rachel Spritzer's apartment building for four hundred ninety thousand dollars. With a little work, the building could easily go for six or seven hundred thousand. Maybe more. The bank might just finance the deal without a down payment, based on his portfolio. This would accomplish two things. One, he would still have the money he had promised to Dan. And two, he would have unfettered access to that safe.

Assuming the German would sell.

The whole plan was perhaps a tad impulsive, but really it involved little more than shifting a few funds around.

And if the German didn't want to sell?

He would. He just would.

He pulled up to the curb in front of the apartment. It seemed as familiar to him as his own home now, even though this was only his third visit.

"Okay, dog, here's the deal. I can either leave you here or let you out, but if you get out, no running around getting into trouble."

Spud whined and glanced through the windshield. These were her stomping grounds. She would probably just run off, which could be a good thing. For all Stephen knew, someone else had taken the dog in and was waiting for her to return.

"Come on, let's have a look."

He got out and walked up to the door. Spud trotted proudly alongside. Stephen pressed the intercom buzzer. Butterflies took flight in his belly.

He pushed the call button. "Hello? Anyone home?"

Nothing.

The doorknob twisted freely in his hand. The building was open? He hadn't locked the door behind him yesterday—maybe they hadn't noticed. They used the garage door for access.

Stephen glanced up the street before stepping into the garage with Spud. It was empty. He scanned the room. Like a tomb. Hallowed. His pulse quickened. Where would Rachel hide a key to the safe?

"Let's go," he whispered. They walked toward the elevator in tandem, the son and the dog. Stephen's shoes clacked loud on the concrete and he rose to his tiptoes. Next time, he would wear sneakers.

He winced when the elevator started its grinding ascent. The four-story climb took twice the time a climb up the stairs would take. When the doors finally clanged open, empty space greeted him. Silence rang in his ears.

"Hello?" A faint echo from the elevator. He poked his head into the flat. "Hello?"

Unless he was hiding to pounce on him, the German was gone. The closing, perhaps.

Spud stepped cautiously past the door, ears perked, mouth closed, testing the air with her nostrils.

"What is it?" Stephen whispered. The dog relaxed and trotted for the bedroom as she had yesterday.

The scent of licorice filled Stephen's nose. "Hello?" Empty. If the new owner was at the closing, then the transaction hadn't been completed, had it? The building was still technically for sale. As a Realtor, he had the right to inspect the place. Find a key, maybe. Open the safe.

He walked slowly into the living room, taken once again by the unspoken history here. He'd left the first time determined to leave this history behind him, but now, inexplicably, he felt the irresistible urge to seek it out. To embrace it. To hear his mother speak to him from beyond the grave.

He ran his fingers over a white doily and then gently picked it up. His mother had purchased this doily, perhaps in a small shop somewhere in Budapest. He set it down.

And there, that painting of a young girl smelling a rose. Why had it attracted Rachel? Had it been a careful purchase, or one made simply to fill a hole? The former, probably. Rachel struck him as a careful person.

He walked on the carpet in a daze. He looked for a brass or silver key in all the places people normally hid keys—kitchen cupboards, jars of pot-pourri, dresser drawers, bookcases—but really he was looking past it all to find his mother. Did she hum while she worked in the kitchen? What kind of food did she cook? Did her sweet breads and rich stews fill the apartment with their aroma? He inhaled deeply and tried to smell her over the scents of licorice and cherries.

The walls creaked. He jerked up. Wind? Or just the frame expanding with the warming sun? He returned to his search.

Rachel had left signs of a careful life everywhere. Silver bells and crystal butterflies lined a bookcase, perfectly positioned in small groupings. Intricately designed rugs, woven in rich reds and blues, lay precisely where he would have placed them. A painting of a yellow daisy growing out of a bleak, rocky landscape hung above the couch.

If the new owners had spent the night here, there was no sign of it. Why?

Stephen had finished a full round of the apartment and was tiptoe-ing through the master bedroom when he noticed an odd strip of mold-ing behind the window drapes. He stepped around the bed, drew the curtain back. A door? Here, to the left of the window, was a door. He turned the handle and eased the door open.

A sunroom. Stephen walked in.

White curtains were drawn on three windows. A single rocking chair sat beside a doily-covered oak lamp table. Dozens of framed photo-graphs lined the wall, mostly black-and-white. Hundreds. They were pictures of the war. Of concentration camps. Of people, some in prison clothes, others in street clothes.

It was a sanctuary. Rachel's special room.

History charged the air, electric enough to lift the hair on his arms when he moved.

A photograph to his right showed a mass grave filled with hundreds of emaciated bodies, tangled as they had fallen. The fuzzy image showed a woman, two children, and two men standing in their underwear with their backs to the pit, hugging themselves. One of the children was looking back into the grave. The caption above read, *Jews await execution in Belzec.*

Stephen's vision blurred. He tried to move his foot, but he stood rooted to the carpet. He'd seen similar pictures before but refused to engage them. He'd come to America to start over, not to wallow in this horrible chapter of history. But here . . .

Here in Rachel's shrine, this chapter of his mother's history—of his history—grabbed him by both arms, yanked him in, and would not let go. She was here, one of the faces in these pictures. He might be here.

His eyes moved to a picture of a young girl, maybe ten, mouth open and toothless. Round, innocent eyes. Legs and arms crossed, preserving her modesty. Hardly more than a skeleton. She was bald and she was naked.

The picture said she was Greta's daughter, Susan. *Medical labs.* He'd heard that the Nazis had conducted experiments on children, but he'd never seen them, not like this. What had they done to this child?

Stephen lifted both hands to his cheeks, as if that would somehow quell the nausea in his gut. These were Jews. His people. How could any sane human do this to another living person? He wanted to run from the room, but his legs refused to move. Part of him hated Rachel Spritzer for leaving this grotesque monument.

But no, it was also lovely, a lovely thing. It was a monument to love. By showing this picture of the toothless girl, Rachel was speaking to her through time. *I will not forget you, Susan. You are not ugly to me. You are beautiful, and I will cherish you forever.*

And Mother would surely say the same to him. I love you, David. I will cherish you forever. Tears filled his eyes. To think that he'd turned his back on the memories of his mother's own suffering . . .

He searched the walls for a picture that resembled the picture from the newspaper. He wanted to cry out, *Mommy, Mommy.* And the fact that he wanted to cry out brought a fresh flood of tears to his eyes.

Stephen's eyes stopped on an eight-by-ten frame that sat beside the lamp on the oak table. The black-and-white photo captured a woman with long black hair. Rachel? He stumbled forward on numb legs and lifted the photograph.

The woman seemed to stare through him. Round, melancholic eyes. Innocent lips. She was beautiful.

He turned the photo over and saw that there was no backing. He read the black cursive.

My dearest Esther, I found this picture in Slovakia after the war. It is your mother, Ruth, one year before your birth.

Not an hour passes without my begging God that you and David will find each other. I will never forget. You are the true Stones of David.

Stephen's heart bolted. *You are the true Stones of David?* He flipped the picture over. The woman's name was Ruth. Her daughter was Esther. Esther was also a Stone of David? But the daughter of Ruth, not Rachel Spritzer.

Esther and David were meant to find each other.

Stephen sank into the rocker and stared at Ruth's picture. For a moment he imagined that Ruth was actually Esther. Was Esther alive? A secret bound them all together. Ruth and Rachel and Esther and David. He stared into the eyes of the young Ruth, and he knew with unequivocal certainty that his life had just been irrevocably changed.

His own destiny stared him in the face. Nothing would ever matter as much as understanding what secrets lay behind these eyes. He vowed it silently.

The air felt thick. He wiped his eyes and drew long breaths.

The Stones are like the lost orphans. They will eventually find each other.

The safe.

A hum ran through the floorboards. Elevator?

Hands shaking, he pried the photograph out of the frame with his fingernails, slipped it into his shirt, shoved the empty frame under the end table, and hurried out of the room.

The key. He hadn't searched the room for a key.

Spud scrambled from under Rachel's bed, went rigid for a moment, and then raced from the room.

Stephen ran after the dog. "Spud! Get back here."

But the dog already stood on guard by the door. She uttered a low growl. "Down, girl!"

——⁓——

THE ELEVATOR doors slid open. Stephen leaned nonchalantly against the wall and took a settling breath. Two men dressed in dark suits stepped out and stopped at the sight of the dog.

"Well, it's about time," Stephen said. "Don't mind Spud. She doesn't bite."

They looked up at him, unfazed.

He unfolded his arms and straightened. "Hope you don't mind— the door was open, and I was looking for the owner." He reached out a hand. "Name's Stephen Friedman. I'm a Realtor. Sit, Spud."

The man ignored his hand.

Spud growled and bared her teeth. "No, Spud. Relax, girl."

Amazingly, Spud quieted and backed up.

"You're trespassing." Heavy German accent.

Stephen lowered his arm. "I'm sorry, maybe you don't understand. I'm here with an offer. I have a client who is willing to pay a substantially higher price than what you paid for this building. I realize it's a bit unusual, but—"

"We really have no interest in selling," the man said with an amused smirk. "You said the door was open?"

"Yes. I was looking for a Roth Braun."

"I can assure you Mr. Braun has no interest in selling. I apologize for the inconvenience, but you really should leave now. He will be here soon."

"Then I'll wait for him," Stephen said.

"You're not listening. Please leave. Now."

"I'm offering—"

"I don't care if you're offering twice what was paid; we're not interested."

Stephen stared at them, taken off guard by their dismissal. "You hear that, Spud? They aren't interested in the million dollars I was going to offer them." He had no intention of offering a million dollars, of course. But saying it might make them think twice. "May I ask what Mr. Braun's interest in the building is?"

"Actually, no; that would be completely inappropriate," the dark-haired man said. His friend looked on without expression. He was white enough to be an albino. Blond hair and eyebrows. Pale blue eyes that forced Stephen's stare away. They obviously weren't impressed.

"Is he going to tear it down?" Stephen asked.

The dark-haired man glanced at the blond, then back to Stephen, apparently amused. "Are all Americans as dense as you?"

Perhaps the man was more incensed than amused.

"I will now give you precisely thirty seconds to vacate the property, or I will personally show you the door," the German said.

Stephen lifted both hands in a sign of surrender. "Easy. I'm just a businessman interested in business. It's a simple matter of money. How could any sane man refuse to double his investment in a day? It makes me wonder what you're doing here. In America."

"That is none of your concern. Now, please"—the man bowed his head in an unsuccessful attempt at graciousness—"leave."

He wore thick gold rings on several fingers, one with an onyx carved in the shape of a lion. A heavy gold chain hung on his neck. And under his jacket? Stephen would be surprised if the man didn't wear a gun.

"Okay. I'm leaving." He turned to the stairs, paused, and turned back. "Does the owner have any interest in Rachel Spritzer?"

The man stepped forward, grabbed Stephen above his elbow, drew him roughly toward the stairs, and shoved him down the first two steps. "Now you're trying my patience. Get out!"

Pain flared up Stephen's arm. "Ouch! I'm going."

Spud barked and dodged a swift kick. She ran deftly past them and into the stairwell.

"I know you're going. And I'm going with you."

Stephen twisted his arm away and hurried down, stunned by their treatment of him. When had he ever been physically removed from a building by a bodyguard? *Ouch?* Had he actually said "ouch"?

"This is crazy. You're actually physically throwing me out of the building?"

"I'm protecting the interests of my employer. You, on the other hand, are breaking the law."

Braun's bodyguard pushed him across the garage floor, ignoring Spud, who'd found her courage again and was hopping to their left, barking furiously. The man pulled the front door open, swung his foot at Spud, who bolted out in a hasty retreat, and shoved Stephen through.

"The door was open—"

"Forgive the confusion. You won't find it open again." The door slammed in his face.

"Uh! You . . . *idiot!*" Stephen turned to find an elderly lady on the sidewalk watching him.

He forced a grin and shrugged. "Brothers."

She smiled knowingly and went on her way.

Stephen hurried for his car, trailed by an indignant dog. They climbed in and sat side by side, staring out the front window. He hadn't actually talked to Braun, but somehow he doubted the treatment would have been any different.

"What do you think, Spud? Maybe we overdid it a bit?"

He pulled out Ruth's picture and stared into her eyes for a long minute.

"Well, I don't think we did," he said. "I'm going to find a way in, Spud. One way or another, I'm going to find out what's in that basement."

The dog whimpered.

A black limousine drove by, took a left at the stop sign and rounded the apartment. Braun. Stephen slipped the picture between the seats and gripped the wheel with both hands.

Several thoughts flashed through his mind. His deal with Dan Stiller. The reception tonight. Chaim and Sylvia, whom he'd invited to the reception tonight.

All were distant distractions from the driving urge to get to the bottom of Rachel Spritzer's apartment complex. Literally.

Stephen decided then that he would cancel the rest of his plans for the day and apply his energy to one end and one end only: getting at that safe.

He started the engine and angled for La Brea.

—⁓—

"A REALTOR named . . ." Claude turned to Lars.

"Stephen Friedman," Lars said.

"Stephen Friedman. Don't worry, he won't be back."

"He was inside?"

"Yes. Up here, in fact. He claimed to have a client willing to pay a million dollars for the property."

"How did he get in? I said no one enters. Is that too complicated for you?" Roth wanted to hit one of them. Not because the man had come in, but because Claude and Lars had broken his trust. He immediately set the impulse aside.

"He said the front door was open," Claude said. "I can promise you, he won't be back."

On second thought, reprisal of some kind was in order. And the appearance of the Realtor confirmed that the game was in full swing.

Could it be the Jew?

He had to play the game perfectly now. One slip and all would be lost.

"If anyone else enters, kill them. We have too much riding on this to risk exposure."

"Killing a Realtor will draw attention," Lars said.

"Not the Realtor. Kill anyone else. The Realtor, bring to me."

Roth turned away and walked to the living room. He withdrew a white handkerchief and dabbed at the sweat that had gathered on his forehead. He couldn't remember ever feeling so terrified over the prospect of failure.

The Stones were here. They called out to him. But also, more than mere fortune. With calculating, deliberate moves, he would finish what Gerhard had started in Toruń.

"We have to move quickly. Start in the kitchen. I want every drawer emptied of every spoon and fork." He faced Claude and Lars, who waited with folded arms. "Every word she wrote, no matter how insignificant it seems, comes to me." He looked around at the remaining artwork and sniffed at the air. "They're here, I can smell them. Can you smell them?"

They exchanged glances. Fools, pawns, oblivious to the game. "I can smell Jew," Claude said, the corner of his mouth lifting slightly.

Roth ignored the bourgeois response and glanced out the window. He'd expected more activity around the building. The wench had possessed one of the Stones of David, for heaven's sake. He'd half-expected the museum to be out here with a wrecking ball, searching for the others. Their assumption that someone who'd gladly donated her entire estate would not cunningly hide a greater fortune betrayed them for the fools they were. They'd picked through the apartment and removed a number of valuables but conducted no thorough search. Like most men, they were psychically impaired.

All the better for him.

He stripped off the black silk jacket. His shirt was also silk. Black silk. He loved the way it felt on his skin, smooth and slick. He draped the jacket over a chair. They would blockade the entry door, bring in only food and what tools they needed, and live on the third floor while they worked.

"Take off your jackets," he said.

Claude and Lars stripped down to white undershirts.

"Place your guns on the table where we can get to them. Just as a precaution."

They did so.

"What about the sunroom?" Lars asked. The man's gray eyes had always fascinated Roth. You could look in his eyes and guess that he was ruthless, but at other times those eyes seemed as innocent as a child's.

"I will work in the sunroom," Roth said. Rachel Spritzer's own private museum had been a delightful surprise. The pictures excited Roth, gave him the unexpected thrill of reliving his formative years.

He turned and headed for the master bedroom.

13

Toruń
May 25, 1944

EVEN WITH DOUBLE RATIONS OF THE BROTH AND BREAD, MARTHA didn't know how her baby would survive another two months. She and Ruth had both lost weight in their arms and legs—everywhere but in their bellies, which had grown slowly to show the life curled up within.

Prisoners came and went, most bearing long expressions of desperation and hopelessness. News of the outside world filtered in with the new arrivals, but separating the rumors from the truth was nearly impossible.

Warplanes flew high above, presumably on bombing runs to the south. Rumors of the Russians advancing with their allies, advancing to crush the Germans, rippled through the camp but provided little hope. Here in Toruń, such possibilities could not rise above the resignation of five thousand women plodding on dry mud, clinging to a life few were sure they wanted anymore.

They said the Germans were gathering all the Hungarian Jews in the camp at Kistarcsa, outside Budapest, but Martha could hardly remember what her homeland looked like, much less cry over what was happening in the bleak landscape of her distant memory. The exceptions were her sister, Katcha, and Antonette, her mother. She pressed every prisoner from the south for news of the two women, but no one had any. How could they? Trainloads of Jews shuttled here and there, and they were supposed to remember a face or a name among them all?

Martha stood outside the barracks and stared at the gray sky. Heavy clouds stretched from horizon to horizon, dark like the mud under her feet. To her right, the gate to Toruń, where she'd seen eighteen women hanged with bags over their heads over the past month, stood exposed to the gathering storm. To her left, the commandant's house rose like a monument painted red with the blood of his victims.

Rebecca was the first she'd seen hanging from the gate, but always, every two days, or three at most, the camp awoke to another body, swinging like a sack of rocks. It wasn't enough for Braun to kill the women. He insisted on this inconceivable torture before the slaughter, of dining them and God only knew what else. The wails of some victims cut through the camp at midnight. But the cries would always end abruptly, cut off by the sudden snap of the noose.

Martha heard movement behind her. She turned to see Ruth walking toward her from the barracks, smiling. No other woman in the compound could smile as much as the young mother-to-be from Slovakia. Unfortunately, her optimism was lost on most of the others. At times even Martha felt a hint of contempt, perhaps a bit of jealousy as well. Ruth's talk of passion and joy sometimes struck Martha as offensive in this place of death.

Ruth slipped her arm around Martha's and pulled her close. "It's getting warmer," she said. "Summer will be here soon."

On the other hand, Ruth exhibited an unrelenting need for companionship. Since their meeting on the train, she had been more like a sister to Martha than a friend. When they stood side by side like this, as they often did before the evening roll call, Martha felt more alive, and more hopeful, than at any other time during the day.

"It's going to rain again," Martha said.

"Hmm. Look at the flowers out there," Ruth said, gazing at the field.

"They've painted the guard towers," Martha said. "Why would they paint the guard towers?"

"Perhaps they want to brighten the guards' mood."

Her optimism was incorrigible. Martha nearly laughed, but the gray skies held her back.

"Little David's been kicking me silly today," Ruth said. She put her hand on Martha's belly. "Yours?"

"Quiet. I think he has the days and nights mixed up. I could hardly sleep last night. Anyway, how do you know yours is a David?"

"Then she's an Esther, and yours is a David. Or they are both Esthers."

"Or both Davids."

"But it would be better if one is a David and one is an Esther."

"Why?"

Ruth smiled wide. "So they can fall in love and be married, of course. Wouldn't that be something?"

Martha had to chuckle. "You're impossible. Women are being hung from the gate, and your mind is skipping through the daisies, planning weddings."

Ruth's smile faded. She reached up and swept a strand of hair from Martha's cheek. "If you have a daughter, she will be very beautiful, like you. She'll run through fields of daisies and marry my beautiful David."

"Aren't you forgetting something?"

"That dead babies can't grow up to be married men and women?"

"Yes."

Ruth looked out at the field, shifting to one of her rare, somber moods. "You're right. That's the problem with this world. But do David and Esther know that? They're warm and snug in our bellies, jumping for joy, oblivious to the trains and the camps. We should take a lesson from them."

"We're not oblivious to the stink of death, though."

"No. But we aren't oblivious to the joy that awaits us either."

"Joy? You mean the possibility of a noose around our necks? Or a train ride back to Auschwitz?"

"No, I mean what awaits us when we are born into the next life."

Martha sighed. "Yes, of course, how silly of me. The next life. After we've been killed."

"Or after we have lived long and full lives. Death is the one thing that happens to every person. So what if our passing is a little strenuous? What awaits will be no less delightful."

Ruth had never spoken so frankly about death, and Martha wasn't sure she liked it much.

A guard approached them from the commandant's hill. Ruth looked his way, silenced for a moment. Braun had asked both of them to his house only once since that first meeting—a ridiculous social affair during which they sat on his couch and talked nonsense. Ruth had been called up on three other occasions, by herself.

"He likes you," Martha said, still watching the guard.

"I'm not sure I can go again." Emotion crowded Ruth's voice.

"You have to. But please tell me you won't let him touch you."

"There's a letter opener on his desk. I would stab him in the heart before I let him touch me."

"Maybe you should do it anyway."

"I've been tempted."

Ruth turned to Martha. "I would like to ask you something. If anything were to happen to me after my child is born, will you take him as your own?"

"Of course. I would think of nothing else."

"And if anything happens to you, I will care for your child." Ruth's eyes searched hers, concerned, which alarmed Martha.

"What is it, Ruth? Do you know something?"

"No. No, of course not. I swear it, Martha. I will care for your child as if it were my own."

Martha nodded. "And I will take care of yours."

"At all costs. Forever. Swear it."

"At all costs, forever. I swear it."

"As do I," Ruth said.

The guard stopped twenty feet away. "You. The short one. The commandant wants to see you."

Ruth squeezed Martha's hand. "Thank you."

"Be strong," Martha whispered.

The admonition was more for herself than her friend.

14

C HAIM LEVELER SCANNED THE RECEPTION HALL AGAIN, BUT Stephen was nowhere to be seen. He hadn't seen or heard from the boy since they'd retired last evening. The Realtors' semiannual reception had started an hour ago, and still no sign. This wasn't entirely unlike Stephen, but given the circumstances of the last two days, Chaim worried.

Three hundred voices of realty professionals and their significant others filled the room with a steady murmur. Guests dressed in black jackets and trendy maxis surrounded a few dozen tables, each decorated with miniature homes—whether edible or not, the rabbi wasn't sure. The crab cakes and truffles certainly were edible, and quite good too.

"Hello, Rabbi."

He turned to see Sylvia, dressed in a long black gown and smiling softly. "My, you look stunning, dear." He took her hand and kissed it. "Have you seen Stephen?"

"No. He's not here yet?"

"Not that I've seen. He's distracted. I think this discovery of his mother is getting to him." He'd given his word not to breathe a word about the safe, not even to Sylvia. "Not that I blame him."

"He's not doing anything stupid, is he?"

Chaim looked at her, surprised. She'd touched on his fear exactly, but to say it so plainly seemed insensitive. "No, no. Why would you say that?"

"Stephen is unpredictable and impulsive. I wouldn't put anything past him. You talk to Gerik again?"

"Yes," Chaim said.

"And he's worried about Stephen's safety?"

"You know Gerik. Sure he's concerned, but he also sees this as a private matter. And he thinks Stephen should follow his heart to whatever resolution awaits him."

"Well, if any danger does exist, Stephen is the type to find it."

"Listen to us. It's probably nothing." Chaim smiled. "We're seeing ghosts. Stephen is a grown man, not a child. Maybe Gerik is right—let him follow his heart."

Sylvia sighed. "Probably right. I'm a bit uptight. All this talk about a serial killer has the office in knots."

"Serial killer? What are you talking about?"

"You should turn on the television more often, Rabbi. Two women killed in two nights, each found with their wrists slit."

"That's reason to assume it was a serial killer?" Chaim asked. "It's a big city—"

"Both women were Jewish. Both were left in identical states. A red scarf was draped over the face of both women. These are deliberate killings."

"My, my." The rabbi shook his head slowly.

"The mayor isn't too thrilled that the information was leaked to the press. Last thing we need is panic among Jewish women."

"Does it concern you?" he asked.

"What? That I'm Jewish?" She scanned the floor. "Honestly, I hadn't thought about it."

"Well, I'm sure a good party is just what you need to get your mind off work."

Chaim patted her hand and took a step before stopping short. She followed his gaze. Stephen angled toward them from the main entrance. He wore a white shirt without a jacket. No tie. His dark, thinning hair had been hastily slicked back.

Sylvia watched him approach. "Distracted, you said?"

Stephen zigzagged his way around curious stares, mounted the steps into the hall, and hurried to them, winded. A light sheen of sweat coated his unshaved face.

He cracked a boyish grin. "Hey. Boy. Sorry I'm late. I've been tied up doing some"—he paused and shifted his eyes—"research."

Chaim stared.

"I feel a bit underdressed," Stephen said. "It was either that or miss the whole thing." He looked around. "Whole gang's here."

"Daniel Stiller is looking for you," Chaim said. "Something about the Santa Monica property. Where have you been?"

"Stiller . . ." Stephen stared off in a daze.

"You okay?" Sylvia asked.

"Right. Fine. I just lost track of time. Do I look okay? I tried to freshen up a bit in the restroom."

"A jacket wouldn't hurt," Sylvia said. "But hey, who's looking? Nothing wrong with the . . . earthy look."

"You think someone has a jacket I could borrow?" He attempted to smooth his rumpled shirt.

"I doubt it," Chaim said. They stood in silence for a moment. He'd never seen the lad so frazzled. It was hardly his business, but Chaim felt compelled to ask the question again. "So, where were you?"

Stephen looked from him to Sylvia and then back. He glanced around, bright-eyed now. He took them both by their arms and eased them around so their backs were to the main hall.

"Did Chaim tell you, Sylvia?"

"Tell me what?"

"About the safe. That's good, Rabbi. I knew you were a man of your word. Promise me you won't tell a soul, Sylvia." He glanced over his shoulder. Evidently, the coast was still clear.

"How can I promise you what—"

"Just promise me."

"Fine. I promise," Sylvia said.

"It *is* a safe. And she has a room in her house filled with pictures of the camps. She had to be a camp survivor. I found a note on a picture—there's a girl she referred to as a Stone of David. Her name's Esther. I think she may still be alive. My foster father used to call me his Stone of David."

He looked at them as if expecting this information dump to fill their minds with amazement. Chaim heard it all, but he'd been so distracted by Stephen's near-rabid performance that he'd missed the point. He caught Sylvia's eye. She took Stephen by the arm.

"Stephen, I don't have a clue what you just said, but I think you need some rest. Maybe we should go."

"What do you mean, you don't have a clue? Aren't you listening?" Another quick look over his shoulder. He whispered harshly. "It's a *safe!* And I swear the people who bought the building know something's there. Don't you see? I'm an orphan from the war. *The orphans will find each other.* She wants me to find the safe. For all we know, it just might have the other four Stones."

He stopped midgesture, looked from Sylvia to Chaim, and lowered his arms. "You don't see it, do you?"

Chaim finally found his voice. "We see that you are quite taken with this thing, my boy. But this is neither the time nor the place to show the world your interest."

"You're right. You're right. I don't know what came over me. Sorry."

"Don't be," Sylvia said.

He closed his eyes. "I must look like a fool."

"Don't be silly. A crazed maniac, maybe, but not a fool." She smiled.

Stephen grinned. "Okay. Sorry. Not another word about it tonight. I swear."

"Honestly, you have to be careful," Chaim said.

"Not to worry, Rabbi." He patted Chaim on the shoulder. "How's the food?"

"The crab cakes are among the best I've tasted."

"You've both had a chance to meet some new people?"

"Not yet," Sylvia said. "But I'm sure there are plenty of Realtors who'll willingly serve an attorney her drink. Would you mind?"

"Not at all," Stephen said.

But Stephen didn't move to get Sylvia her drink.

"Listen." Stephen stroked his chin and glanced around furtively. "I'm not sure this was a good idea. I shouldn't have come in the first place, and the thought of having to mingle is giving me the shivers."

"Please, Stephen, we didn't mean to suggest that—"

"No, Rabbi." He held up his hands. "I really, really think I need to go. I'm not dressed right." He winked and put a hand on Chaim's shoulder. "Do me a favor, will you? If you run into Dan Stiller again, tell him I'll get in touch with him in the morning."

"Actually, I was thinking of leaving myself. It—"

"No. Absolutely not. I forbid it! You will stay and enjoy yourself. I have a few errands to run, and then I'll be home."

"Errands? It's nine o'clock."

Stephen grinned deliberately. "Exactly. Need to buy some shampoo and a razor. Thank you for coming, Sylvia. I would love to stay and chat, but the shower is bellowing my name. Stay and have some fun."

"Don't worry about me. I'm just getting started."

He cocked his finger at her like a gun. "That's the spirit. Show the rabbi how an attorney parties, will you?" He began to back away. "Good night."

He turned and hurried toward a side door, leaving Chaim and Sylvia staring after him with raised brows.

———

STEPHEN RAN out of the building, more relieved than he could remember feeling in a long time. He hadn't been roped into a conversation with a single one of his peers—luck was definitely on his side. It was going to be a good night. Even the dog seemed eager, perched on the edge of the passenger's seat.

"Don't worry, Rabbi," Stephen muttered. "If you knew what I know . . ."

Which was? That he had indeed done some research, if stalking Rachel Spritzer's apartment building from every conceivable angle and setting every last cell in his brain to the task of getting at that safe could be classified as research. As a result, he'd stumbled upon information only a fool could ignore: the contents of the safe did not belong to the museum.

At least that's the way he read the provision buried in the will.

He'd left the apartment and visited Caldwell Realty, where he'd persuaded a secretary named Sally to let him take a peek at the documents. No harm—they would soon be part of the public record in a transaction like this anyway. He found the portions of Rachel Spritzer's will that dealt with the apartment. According to the document, in addition to the building itself, Rachel Spritzer had donated to the museum all of her earthly possessions "currently located in the fourth-floor apartment of #5 Thirty-second Street . . . including but not limited to . . ." The document contained an inventory of her most valuable possessions.

The contents of the safe weren't in the fourth-floor apartment. They were in the basement. And they weren't technically part of the building. The safe itself was, but not the contents.

True, the specific mention of her residence may have simply been intended to address her living quarters in general, but as far as Stephen was concerned, that was open to debate. Which could mean there *was* something in that safe Rachel Spritzer didn't want the museum to possess. He was no attorney, but considering everything else, the implications read like absolute fact to Stephen.

He'd also taken the time to flesh out the man who'd bought the building on such short notice. Roth Braun. A German investor with no ties to the United States that he could find. Not one. He had a name in Germany, owned a bunch of businesses that read like Mafia cover-ups to Stephen, especially in light of his earlier exchange with Braun's henchmen. Still, the man looked clean on paper. Maybe he really had purchased the building as a legitimate investment.

Not a chance. Braun knew something. Specifically, something about Rachel Spritzer. It struck Stephen that the man could be the very danger his mother alluded to in her note. All the more reason to get into that safe.

Stephen had spent three hours thinking through a dozen ways to get into the building. He watched as a woman, apparently someone from the city, approached the front door, spoke briefly to the dark-haired German, had him sign something, and then left. An inspector, maybe, getting a waiver.

His challenge was to get in without them knowing he was in. No matter how he broke down the problem, this meant the front door was out of the question. A dozen times he told himself that he was charting dangerous waters. And a dozen times the photograph of Ruth reached into his soul, demanding he liberate the Stones of David. The authorities were out, absolutely out. He had no claim against the Germans. Retaining an attorney was even more impossible. If Braun learned about the safe, he and the treasure would be long gone before any court could even hear a case.

Stephen's only option was to move alone, and quickly. He felt sick—or was it giddy?—with the impossibilities of the situation.

And then one thought healed his sickness.

A plan.

An improbable, highly creative plan that no one would suspect of anyone but a fool. Improbable enough to actually work.

He returned to the apartment building, drove around it three times, each time gathering his resolve, and finally settled on his course. A visit to the hardware store ate up the remaining daylight and the first hour of darkness. But the time proved invaluable. He refined options and details by careful calculation until the plan was perfect.

Skipping out of the reception without talking to Dan Stiller may not have been wise, but they still had ample time to submit their proposal to the city. Next Wednesday was still a long ways off. He had to get this small matter of history and destiny and several hundred million dollars off his chest before he could really concentrate on the Santa Monica property anyway.

Chaim and Sylvia no doubt believed him a tad whacked-out, but he'd covered well enough. They couldn't possibly understand the true significance of the safe.

Stephen glanced at his watch. A little over two hours before midnight. Perfect.

15

Los Angeles
July 20, 1973
Friday Night

SURPRISINGLY, LA BREA AVENUE SEEMED TO HAVE MORE TRAFFIC near midnight than midday. Stephen parked the Vega on a side street two blocks south of his mother's apartment. He pulled a backpack from the back seat, checked to see that no one was watching, and hefted the bag over his shoulders. *Natural. Look natural.* Just an ordinary Joe taking a midnight stroll with a pack strapped to his back.

"You stay put, Spud. I'll be back before you know it."

The dog jumped out before Stephen could shut the door. "Spud!" But the dog ran up the street and disappeared. This was getting to be a bad habit.

Stephen locked the car and turned north, searching for the dog on his way. Surely she would come back. He felt oddly lost without the dog's carefree presence.

The sidewalk was deserted except for a woman walking directly toward him, half a block up. Where had she come from? *Avoid eye contact. Natural.* They passed each other without incident. Had she seen his car?

He cut east at the next street and then turned left into an alley that approached the rear of the abandoned complex across the street from Rachel's building. Darkness swallowed him. He hurried his pace. So far, so good, but still no sign of Spud. Maybe just as well for the time being.

Stephen stopped at the end of the alley and poked his head around the corner. The windows of what he'd decided to call "Building B" were patched up with plywood. Graffiti covered the back wall. How many pimps and drug pushers frequented these shadows each night? He hoped not to encounter any. Beyond Building B, across the street, stood Rachel's apartment. If he could get into Building B, he might be able to find a window with a view of her apartment. He glanced at his watch—11:30. Half an hour to burn. He looked down the empty alley and then stepped lightly toward the back door.

Something clattered noisily on the asphalt and he jumped. His foot had hit a bottle. Enough of this. He ran for the building, pulled up beside a rear service entrance, and twisted the knob. To his surprise, it opened. He slipped in, shut the door, and heaved a sigh of relief.

His breathing sounded like billows in the hollow chamber. The lines of walls slowly grew out of the darkness. A long hall and stairs. Couldn't use the light yet.

He mounted the stairs and felt his way up one flight, then two, then three. Fourth floor. He pushed on the door exiting the stairwell and stepped cautiously through it.

Moonlight shone through a single window on the opposite wall. The rooms had been gutted—sections of framing lay in tangled heaps in every direction. But the floor seemed sound enough. He picked his way across the room to the window.

There it was, illuminated by a bright moon—Rachel's apartment. Stephen's pulse surged. The lights in her fourth-floor suite were still on. The lights of her master bedroom. The sunroom.

He instinctively pulled back from the window. Rachel's curtains were drawn. Made sense—the men who'd thrown him out didn't seem the kind to walk around in their underwear with the drapes wide open.

Stephen slid the backpack off and settled to one knee. They were up there all right, picking through her belongings. How dare they? But on the bright side, if they were preoccupied with the fourth floor, they wouldn't be in the basement.

If.

Thank God he'd taken the picture of Ruth from the sunroom. He straightened, struck by a terrible thought. The picture! Where had he put it?

He remembered immediately and relaxed. He'd left it on his desk.

For a brief moment, he considered retracing his steps, racing home, retrieving the photo, and returning. What if the rabbi entered his room and found it? He could trust Chaim. After all, it was only a picture.

Stephen studied his mother's building. The real trick was to get in and out without dropping any clues. Leaving a trail to the boiler room would only proclaim that it possessed something noteworthy. In the unlikely event that he failed tonight, he couldn't afford to tip his hand. He was smarter than that.

Eleven thirty-five. His fingers trembled with anticipation. There was nothing magical about midnight. It had just seemed a good time. The neighborhood was already quiet; maybe he should just go now.

No. He had to follow the plan, and the plan was midnight.

Was it illegal, this plan of his? Maybe. Maybe not.

On second thought, absolutely. But at times, principle should supersede the law, and this was one of those times.

The sum of the matter was this: if Rachel had intended the museum to have the contents of the safe, she would have specified as much in her will. The fact that she hadn't meant its contents were for someone else. Someone like him. That's why she'd inscribed the safe with words that would have meaning only to an orphan branded with a Stone of David.

An element of danger trailed Rachel, a secret that put her son's life at risk. She had hoped that her son would recognize the caption in the paper—"the Stones are like the lost orphans"—and figure out the rest. As he was doing.

As Chaim would say: *If you want to have what others do not have, you must be willing to do what others are unwilling to do.* If ever there was a time to prove such an axiom, it was tonight.

One hundred million dollars—more money than he'd ever dreamed about. The idea made his mind hurt. He could walk down Sepulveda slipping hundred-dollar bills to the down-and-out and watch their eyes light up. He could buy an island with a yacht parked in the slip down by the shore.

On the other hand, his passion for this safe was as much about principle, about his mother and her secret, and about a little girl named Esther who'd been lost to Ruth. Put together—the safe, the Stones, Rachel, Esther—the sum was too much to ignore. As a Stone of David, he had an obligation. A calling.

It occurred to him that his liberation of this treasure was, in some convoluted way, not terribly unlike the liberation of a concentration camp by the Allied soldiers. He was redeeming what belonged to the Jews. Restoring their inheritance. His inheritance. This would be his part in the war. Stephen's mind reeled with a dozen thoughts, some completely reasonable, others admittedly less.

Desperate times; desperate measures.

Watch. Eleven forty. Time was crawling.

Something thumped softly across the room. Stephen started, nearly choking on his heart. He pressed himself against the wall and gazed into the shadows.

A dog bounded silently over the rubble, grinning wide, tongue flopping. Spud! She jumped up and stretched to lick his face. "Where'd you go? Okay, enough. Enough!" Stephen hugged the dog. "Boy, am I glad to see you."

No, he wasn't. What was he going to do with her now?

"She likes you," a woman's voice said.

Stephen bolted up, knocking the dog to the ground. "What?"

"I said, she likes you." A petite woman in her twenties stepped out of the shadows. She wore torn bell-bottom jeans with a light-colored blouse and beads. Hundreds of beads: on her wrists, on her neck, in her braided hair.

"What are you doing up here?" she asked.

"I was . . . I was just looking around."

"Is that right?"

What was he supposed to say? Nothing came to mind.

"The last time I saw anyone wearing those kind of duds up here was three months ago when they put this building up for sale. But nobody's buying. You know why? Because it belongs to us."

"Oh."

She stared at him, uncertain, then a smile slowly formed on her lips. "Well, the dog likes you, so maybe I do too. You can call me Melissa."

"Okay." She was a hippie type. Stephen had only one thing on his mind now. Get past this and pretend she'd never seen him. This wasn't in the plan. "Groovy," he said.

"Groovy." Melissa walked around him, wearing a whimsical smile, smelling like jasmine tea. "Groovy. Well, Mr. Groovy, you are in the wrong building. This building belongs to the Brotherhood of Bohemia. What's in the backpack?"

"Nothing."

"Mr. Groovy, whose bulging backpack has nothing in it, and who doesn't like to talk. That about cover it?"

He just nodded, then glanced out the window over his shoulder. Street still empty. Almost midnight.

Melissa suddenly started to chuckle, and Stephen smiled with her.

"What's so funny?"

"You."

Her laughter grew until it echoed around the room. He stepped forward and tried to wave her down. "Could you hold it down? The whole place will hear you!" Across the street, the curtains were still drawn.

"There's no one in the building right now but us, baby." She controlled her laughter. "I think you just might do. You could play the city slicker who wants to be groovy but doesn't have a clue."

He had no idea what she meant.

"Okay, you can stay for a bit. But I've gotta cruise—city's just coming alive for us bohemians. Wanna join us?"

"No thanks. I've got some stuff to do."

She looked out the window. "They moved in a few days ago. Friends of yours?"

"Who?"

"The people you're looking at. You know, Rachel's place."

"You . . . you knew Rachel?"

"Not really. She was friendly, and she asked me to take care of Brandy here." Melissa bent and rubbed the dog's back. "But that's about it. You knew her?"

"No."

Melissa nuzzled the dog playfully, cooing. She jumped up. "Gotta go. Come on, girl." She hurried off. Spud—no, Brandy, the dog's name was Brandy—gave Stephen a long, indecisive gaze, then bounded after the girl.

It took ten minutes for Stephen to recover from the intrusion. He wasn't sure how he felt about Melissa's attachment to the dog. A constant companion like little Brandy, although something he never would have sought, appealed to him. But there Brandy went, bounding after the girl.

Stephen surveyed the street one more time. Not a soul had walked by in ten minutes. Time for Mr. Groovy to boogie.

16

STEPHEN MADE HIS WAY DOWN THE STAIRS, STOPPING ON EVERY floor to listen. Apart from his own pounding heart, he heard nothing. Melissa and Brandy were gone.

Every Special Forces movie he'd ever watched barked the same mantra: *Get in quick, and get out.* Made sense. In his case: Get in quick, secure the fortune, and get out. Without leaving a calling card, of course. Or, better yet, leave a calling card with the wrong address.

Stephen huddled at the base of the gutted building for a full minute, trying to overcome an acute case of hesitation. Once he went to work there would be no backing out, no explanation that any cop would buy.

A hundred million dollars.

Esther.

He headed toward the apartment. *Natural. Look natural.* But when his foot hit the lawn, he couldn't resist hunching over and scurrying for the apartment's dark shadows, natural or not. He squatted at the wall and looked back. Coast clear.

Keeping low, Stephen rounded the corner and walked to the metal garage door. As he saw things, the garage was the best way in, because it faced the side street rather than the main thoroughfare, and also because it was hidden from view. The most brilliant break-in artists always found the weak holes, however unexpected. Besides, the windows were high and covered with wrought iron—no easier to deal with than the garage door.

He fell to his knees, unzipped the backpack, and yanked out a roll of heavy, dark gray plastic. Gray, same color as the building's stucco. The plastic unfurled noisily with a whip of his wrists. He shoved his hand into the pack, pulled on a pair of gloves, withdrew a roll of duct tape, and quickly taped the plastic onto the garage door over his head, so that it covered him like a lean-to. Working under the crackling plastic, he was sure half the neighborhood could hear him. It was possible that from the street he looked like a gray ghost, flailing under the plastic sheeting in the moonlight. No, he'd made sure the plastic was thick, hopefully thick enough to block the light. Of course, the plastic was thick enough to prevent him from noticing whether a crowd had gathered to watch the specter.

The roll of tape slipped out of his sweaty fingers. He drew back the plastic and peered toward the street just to make sure. No one.

He fumbled for the roll and completed his disguise. Now he crouched under the plastic lean-to, taped above him and on both sides. The idea was to blend in, but he couldn't shake the suspicion that he was doing more poking out than blending in.

Cutting torch. He'd used one once, in Russia many years ago, a monster consisting of twin bottles on a dolly. The largest part of the setup he'd purchased today was the torch itself, a foot-long silver tube with a ninety-degree cutting tip. Green and red hoses fed into two football-sized canisters in his backpack. One oxygen, one acetylene. He fired up the device in an alley after buying it—seemed simple enough despite the clerk's warning that it wasn't a toy. No, of course not.

Stephen cracked the acetylene valve and lit the cutting tip with a lighter. Yellow light filled his hideout. Safety glasses. He reached into the bag, came out with a set of dark glasses, and tried to fix the band around his head with one hand. No go. Sweat snaked past his left eye. He raised his right hand to nudge the goggles into place.

The plastic to his left sizzled. He jumped back and inadvertently dropped the torch. Flame licked at his legs and he cried out, kicking at the torch. The plastic to his right pulled free, exposing him to the world.

Stephen dived for the pack and twisted the canister's knob. The flame died. He sat on his knees, shaking. He'd burned a hole in the plastic and singed his leg hair.

It took him a minute to calm down, resecure the plastic camouflage, and set up for a second, informed attempt. Goggles on, nerves under control, flame down. With dark goggles on, he found he couldn't see to light the thing, and his nerves were anything but under control. Bringing focus to bear, he finally managed to light the torch, pull his glasses into place, and set up for the burn.

He took a deep breath. This was insane.

The words of his foster father blazed through his mind. He'd spoken them a hundred times during Stephen's adolescence: *Try to see trouble as you would see a brick wall, Stephen. Then try not to run smack into it at every turn. Seriously, son, I worry for your life at times.*

He felt like a fifteen-year-old boy at the moment, running straight for a brick wall.

Then again, there was Chaim: *If you want to have what others do not have, you must be willing to do what others are not willing to do.*

Like run straight at the brick wall.

He cranked the oxygen, adjusted the flame until it was bright blue, and tested the pressure trigger. The miniature jet flared to life. Stephen leaned forward on his knees and committed an irrevocably criminal act.

He cut into the building. That was the *breaking* part of *breaking and entering*.

But he was smart about his breaking. Cutting too close to the plastic would melt the tape. He cut a foot in, slicing right through the thin sheet metal as if it were butter. With any luck, he didn't look like a glowing Christmas bulb from the street. He shielded the light with his body as much as possible.

If Braun was in the garage at the moment, watching red sparks spray over his floor, Stephen would be toast. And if the metal fell inward onto the concrete, it might wake the world. But if he could cut this hole without setting off any alarms, the plastic would hide the hole while he did his real business.

Halfway through the long arc, Stephen concluded that his idea wasn't so brilliant after all. No doubt he *did* look like a glowworm. No doubt the metal *would* fall in.

As it turned out, the sheet did fall inward, despite his attempt to pry it toward him with the torch's cutting tip. But the sound it made wasn't so much a *clang* as a *whap*.

Stephen yanked off his goggles and held his breath. A dome-shaped hole led into the dark garage. No Braun. Only the black limousine parked on the right-hand side.

He wrapped a rag around the hot torch, shoved it into his pack, and pulled the bundle into Rachel's garage behind him. The plastic settled into place, masking the ragged opening.

He let his eyes adjust to the deeper darkness. If they came down now, he would roll under the Cadillac. Or maybe he'd just dive back out the hole. Out the hole, he decided, definitely out the hole.

Now for the car. He had to make it look like some local hoodlum had seen the car and broken in to steal it. Sleight of hand. Get their attention on the garage so the real damage in the basement would go unnoticed.

He pulled out a screwdriver and approached the Cadillac's driver-side door. It was unlocked. And the key was on the front seat. His first real stroke of pure fortune.

He left the car door wide open for his return later, cut across to the garage, and eased through the door. The stairwell was an echo chamber. He tiptoed down into the basement.

A buzz grew louder in his mind. He'd made it into Rachel's basement. His plan was unfolding in brilliant fashion. Had his pulse eased even a beat or two since breaking and entering, it would have surged now, but his heart already was maxed out.

No windows down here. He hit the light, acquired the boiler room, turned the light off, and angled for the door. He found it with his fore-head in ten strides. Good to remember that—ten strides.

He opened the door, closed it behind him, flipped on the light. New gas water heater, black potbellied boiler, empty fifty-five-gallon drum. And under the drum . . .

The safe.

Stephen stared, mesmerized. The room was black and gray and

smelled musty from concrete and dust and water. But the bland colors were inviting and the musty smell intoxicating. He'd let his mind walk into this small room a hundred times over the last forty-eight hours, and to actually be here again . . . the feelings of comfort and accomplishment surprised him.

For several long seconds, Stephen stood immobilized with anticipation. His world was spinning in a new direction, and this room was its axis.

He crossed the floor and tugged at the drum. It scraped loudly against the concrete. Could they hear that? He had to get the torch out first. Get the torch out, pull the drum off, slice through the safe's metal lid, extract the treasure, flee.

He grabbed at his backpack and then abandoned it in favor of the drum again. He had to see the safe, just to be absolutely sure that it hadn't been opened by the idiots upstairs. The drum slid with another wake-the-dead scrape. Stephen tilted it on edge and froze.

Exactly as he remembered. Undisturbed beyond his own work. An irresistible sense of urgency swarmed him. He released the drum and yanked the backpack from his shoulder. The drum clanged to the concrete. The fact that he was now making enough noise to wake Braun from a coma occurred to him as a distant abstraction. The man was four stories above him anyway.

Stephen dragged the drum out of the way, pulled out his tools, donned the protective goggles, and lit the cutting torch with the confidence of an experienced journeyman. No problem. *Whoosh* goes the acetylene, *pop* goes the oxygen, and we're in business. He could cut through Fort Knox with a big enough one of these, right?

His unsteady fingers betrayed his frayed nerves.

He dropped to one knee and lowered the cutting tip to the lock. If he could cut out the bolt, hopefully the lid would lift out. The torch eased into the hard steel with a blast of oxygen. Not exactly like cutting through butter, but the metal melted away and fell inside.

He jerked back, struck by a horrifying thought. What if the glowing steel fragments melted the gold on the Stones of David? Too late. Surely Rachel had protected whatever she'd hidden in the safe.

Drawing the full molten circle around the lock took Stephen several minutes, time enough to heighten his fears that he was ruining the safe's contents. He finished the cut, turned the torch off, and pulled off the goggles. A ragged but complete gap ringed the two-inch lock.

He flipped the torch over and tapped the circle. It fell in and landed with a dull *thunk*. Stephen reached for the hole and jerked back from the heat before he made contact with the metal. He hooked the cutting tip into the hole and pulled up, but the lid refused to budge.

"Come on . . ."

Stephen jumped to his feet and jerked back as hard as he could. The lid suddenly released, sending him back two steps and then to his rear end. He stared at the safe, lid dislodged, half covering a hole in the concrete.

He'd done it.

He was afraid to look.

Slowly he rose, hardly aware of the dull pain in his tailbone. He bent over the hole but saw only darkness. He tested the metal for heat, felt it quite cool opposite the cut, and shoved the lid aside. A hole, eighteen inches wide and maybe two feet deep, opened up before his eyes.

And at the bottom of the safe, an object.

His movements seemed too slow. The buzzing settled in his ears. There was something in the safe. There was a shallow metal cookie box down there. And there was a picture taped to the top of the box. Several black burn holes spotted the picture.

Ruth's picture. Only it said "Esther" on it.

Stephen stared into her eyes. Esther was a Stone of David. But was there more? *See, there's a tin can under that picture, and in that tin can is something your mother left for you. A hundred million dollars' worth of something.* He could hardly breathe.

Far above Stephen's head, a voice yelled.

Stephen jerked his head up. They'd found his hole in the garage door!

He plunged his hand into the safe and grabbed the box, but immediately a warning bell clanged in his head. If the Germans were in the garage at this moment, there was a decent chance they would discover him—bad enough. But what would happen if they discovered him *with* the box under his arm or shoved into his pack?

For the first time that night, true-blue panic flooded Stephen's veins. He reacted without conscious thought, like a finely tuned machine masterfully created for a single purpose.

To hide the treasure.

He dropped the box back into the hole, shoved the lid over the top, kicked at it until it clanked into place, and then spun the drum back over the whole mess.

The car. He had to make them think someone had broken in for the car. If they found him down here, they would want to know why a man had broken into the building with a cutting torch and made straight for the boiler room.

It was all he could do to ignore the whispers in his head that demanded he take the box now. There was a fortune in that box, for heaven's sake!

Not a chance. Not that dumb.

He donned the backpack, grabbed the cutting torch, and scanned the floor. To his eye, it looked undisturbed. At this juncture, he was more concerned with the safe's well-being than his own. If they found the safe—end of story. If they found him, he still had a chance.

Stephen turned off the light, slipped out of the room, then poked his head back in and hit the switch one last time just to be sure he'd left no clue. Reason should have him fleeing for safety already, he realized. But he was beyond reason. He slapped off the light and closed the door.

Now what? Instinct vacated him. Footsteps sounded on the concrete over his head. He had to get out of the basement. Anywhere but down here with the safe.

Stephen ran for the stairwell and took the steps two at a time. The hum of the elevator told him they were using it rather than the stairs. Maybe he could wait them out here. He pressed up against the wall behind the door into the garage.

No. He had to get closer to the car—away from the stairs.

He stepped up to the door and cracked it. Two large forms dressed in T-shirts stood by the large hole in the garage door, backs to him. How far could he get in his tennis shoes before they heard him? The front door had been chained—no exit there. Apart from the Cadillac, thirty yards away, the garage offered no cover.

The sound of his heart, pounding like a tom-tom, might give him away before his footsteps did. He took a careful breath, squeezed into the garage, and eased the door closed.

He moved quietly on the edges of his soft-soled shoes, rolling from heel to toe. A shadow in the night, gliding toward the car. He couldn't bring himself to look up, as if doing so might alert them. He had to reach the car. Every step was one closer to freedom.

This was idiotic! He was out in the open! At any moment they would glance back and see the thief strolling across their garage, armed to the teeth with his cutting torch. He almost turned to retreat.

Then again, they hadn't seen him yet. If they'd seen him, they'd be yelling—

"Hey!"

Stephen jerked up. "Hey!" he yelled back.

The two bouncers he'd met earlier stared at him. Maybe if he distracted them with some clever move, like torching one of the car's tires, he could buy himself enough time to sprint between them and dive through his hole to freedom.

The smaller of the two, if "small" could be used in reference to either man, walked toward him. In a moment of lucidity, it struck Stephen that this man was no ordinary thug. No insults, no demands to know what he was doing in their garage, no cautious approach or gun. The man pulled out a cigarette and lit it as he walked. He stopped by the car and leaned on the hood. His friend walked up casually beside him. Neither spoke.

"You're leaning on my car," Stephen said.

The larger man, the blond, spoke quietly into a radio. German.

"Get *off* my car. If you don't get off the car, I'm going to call the police," Stephen said. "I don't know who you think you rented it from, but this limousine belongs to me. My employer. She's my wife." That was stupid. "I only came to take what does not belong to you."

They appeared not to have heard him. A voice crackled on the radio.

"I have to talk to your boss. I know this may look a bit out of the ordinary, but it's imperative that I talk to Roth Braun."

They just stared at him. The man with the radio spoke into it again.

They were probably discussing how to dispose of his body. "Do you recognize me?" Stephen demanded. "I'm the guy who was here this morning, claiming to be a Realtor. Well, I must confess, I'm not a Realtor. But what I am will definitely interest Roth Braun."

The quiet blond stepped forward and indicated the elevator across the room. "Please step into the elevator."

Stephen hesitated. This was unquestionably one of those life-or-death junctures.

The man on the hood tossed his cigarette and stood up. "Move."

Stephen turned and walked toward the elevator.

17

ROTH BRAUN SAT AT RACHEL SPRITZER'S DINNER TABLE DRESSED in a black silk shirt. A heavy gold chain hung around his neck. Stephen stood before the man, unable to hold his eyes. The blond German had blue eyes too, but his were soft, distracted. Braun's were cold, still. Like death.

Stephen's backpack sat on the floor, contents dumped out and thoroughly examined. Piles of kitchenware were stacked neatly on the dinette. The knickknacks so carefully arranged by Rachel Spritzer had been taken from the walls and shelves along with the paintings. They were conducting a methodic search of the apartment.

"What's your name?" Braun asked.

"Parks," Stephen said, and cleared a croak from his voice. "Jerry Parks."

Braun looked at the blond man. "You said his name was Friedman?"

"That's what he told us this morning."

Back to Stephen, eyes bland. "Well?"

"Do you mind if I have a drink?" Stephen asked. "Surely the old woman left some scotch around here."

"You burn a hole in the side of my building and ask me for a drink?" A slight grin curved Braun's wet lips. "Sure, why not? Lars?"

The blond went to the cupboard and returned with a bottle and a glass. He poured Stephen a finger of amber liquid and then stepped back.

"Scotch," Braun said.

Stephen never touched the stuff, and he barely managed to throw it back without gagging. He set the glass on the table, mind scrambling. One look at Braun, and he knew this man wouldn't hesitate to do him bodily harm. But he hadn't betrayed the boiler room, had he? The safe was . . . safe.

He glanced at his knapsack. "I know this looks a bit strange to you." Insane was more like it. Stephen forced a tentative smile. "I mean, it's not every day someone lies about his identity, offers a million dollars for a gutted building, gets thrown out, and then returns at midnight to burn a hole in the garage door, right?"

Braun's right eyebrow arched.

"Well, it makes perfect sense when you know what I know." Stephen walked to his right and stared around at the bare walls. He was about to make a very big gamble. "Trust me, it does."

"Trust doesn't come naturally to me," Braun said.

Stephen had abandoned his theft story during his climb, somewhere around the third floor. Depending on who Braun really was, he would either turn him over to the police or worse.

"For starters, I'm not a Realtor and I'm certainly not a thief," he said. "Do I honestly strike you as being desperate enough to risk my life for a Cadillac? I'm interested in the building, not the car."

"And what about a rundown building interests you?"

"You'll have to ask my employer. Maybe the same thing that interests you."

Braun looked amused. Stephen cleared his throat and pushed ahead. "I mean, you have to admit, burning a hole in a garage door might be strange, but refusing an offer of one million dollars for this heap is just as strange, don't you think?"

The German studied him for a moment. "Claude."

The dark-haired man walked forward. His hand flashed out and struck Stephen on the cheek with enough force to drop an ox. Stephen fell to his seat.

"You broke into my building, Mr. Parks," Braun said. "I believe it would be within the law to shoot you."

Stephen struggled to his feet. "Then I've succeeded, haven't I?" The night's emotion suddenly surged in him. "Stop being so dense." *Too much, Stephen, way too much.*

Braun took the insult without any visible reaction, which for some reason unnerved Stephen more than if he'd whipped out a gun. Stephen felt as if he might fall if he didn't sit. He put a hand on a chair to steady himself. "My employer will pay you two hundred thousand dollars for a three-day lease of the building."

His mind worked furiously. He had to get their attention completely off the basement. If he rented the top floor, he could find a way to the basement unnoticed. "Actually, two hundred thousand for a three-day lease of the top two floors."

Braun smiled softly. "You burned a hole in my garage door to tell me this? Why don't you call my Realtor?"

Stephen hesitated. "Your Realtor doesn't do property management. His work on this deal is done."

"I'm not interested."

"That's . . . that's ridiculous! Two days, then."

"Ridiculous? I would say that offering two hundred thousand for two days is ridiculous."

If Braun took him up on the offer, he might actually pay. The Stones of David were in that cookie tin down in the safe—they had to be. He could take them and be on his way. Actually, he needed only fifteen minutes, but he had to consider what impression he would leave if the offer failed. He had to persuade them there was something on the upper floor that would require a two-day search.

"I think he wants to search this flat," Stephen said. "Something of sentimental value—your guess is as good as mine. Maybe the pictures. Humor him."

"Pictures?"

"The ones in the sunroom. I saw them the last time I was here."

"Out of the question."

"There's another hundred thousand in it for me. I'll give you half of my take. That's two hundred and fifty—"

"No." Braun stood, almost as tall as the man he called Lars, but broader in the shoulders. "Take our guest down to the basement and show him our hospitality," he said, turning.

Stephen stepped back. The basement? They were going to hurt him. "If I'm not back by two, my employer will call the police," he said. He meant to sound matter-of-fact, but his pitch sounded more scared-to-death.

"I doubt it," Braun said, turning back.

"He said you might say that. He also said you were even less likely to want the police involved. You touch me again, and I swear I'll have the police crawling through this building like bees in a hive. My employer assures me his motivations were purely sentimental. Somehow, I doubt yours are."

For several long moments they faced off. A thin smile finally curved Braun's mouth.

"Claude, Lars, please excuse us."

The two men left and descended the stairs.

"Jerry Parks?" The man walked up to him. There was enough power in his arms to snap Stephen's neck with a single twist. He was breathing heavily, deliberately, and Stephen got the impression that he was enjoying himself.

Braun walked around him. Circled him slowly, arms clasped behind his back. He stopped behind Stephen, lingered for a few seconds, then stepped easily to Stephen's left.

The man seemed delighted and doing his best to hide it. *Whoever he was, Roth Braun was a man possessed by evil,* Stephen thought.

"There's nothing to be found here except some old photographs of Jews who deserved to die," he eventually said.

A strange brew of emotions bubbled in Stephen's chest. The picture of the toothless young girl in Rachel Spritzer's sunroom filled his mind.

He looked back at Braun. "You won't know that until you've taken a wrecking ball to these walls," he said, then added, "Up here."

"You're dancing on your own grave." Roth spoke in a low, gravelly voice. "I can smell it on you. Fear. Sorrow. Desperation. Hope. The most powerful forces known to man. You stink of them all."

Stephen barely managed the fear that gripped his mind. Roth's heart was as black as his shirt.

"If you ever set foot on my lawn again, I will track you down in your home and burn you along with it. Tell your employer to search for pictures of dead Jews somewhere else. These are mine."

Braun turned and walked toward the master bedroom. "Claude will see you out."

The tremble that overtook Stephen's limbs should have been triggered by relief. Braun was setting him free. But the shaking was full of dread. Fear, sorrow, desperation, hope. As Braun had said.

Susan. Toothless Susan. She might just as easily have been Ruth's daughter, Esther. For all he knew, Esther had ended up in the same medical lab, and this beast Braun took some kind of demented pleasure in it all.

Stephen scooped up his backpack and hurried to the door. He wanted out nearly as much as he wanted that safe in the basement. He met Claude in the stairwell and the man escorted him to the hole he'd burned in the garage door.

The moment the plastic fell into place behind him, Stephen began to run.

He couldn't go home. What if they followed him? Could he dare risk exposing Chaim to these people?

Stephen ran east, away from the neighborhood, but the moment he was out of Claude's sight, he doubled back through the alley toward Building B, yanked open the same back door he'd used earlier, and climbed the stairs to the fourth floor. He sat down by the window that overlooked Rachel's apartment. The sunroom was right there, across the street, nearly at eye level. He lowered his head between his knees and began to cry.

Understanding didn't seem important. Emotion shouted down reason. Anguish, horror, anger. In a strange way, he felt that he had to right what had been wronged for little Susan, the victim of his mother's oppressors. He had to become what the Jews couldn't become in their cages. For Susan's sake, his mother's sake, Esther's sake, he had to take back what was theirs.

He had to possess that tin box left for him in the safe.

My little Stone of David.

If he'd been eager to get to the treasure before, he was now desperate for it. His urgency made no sense; his desire had become a compulsion. How he'd gone from reasonable Realtor to manic desperado in the space of three days, he had no clue.

He stood, paced, bit his fingernail, and stared at that building across the street.

Stephen had once heard that over half of the homeless suffered from some sort of mental delusion. Many were once-successful people who'd vacated reason for a small spot in one abandoned building that overlooked another.

He finally slumped in the corner and rested his head against the wall. The last thing Stephen remembered thinking was that he was losing his mind.

18

Toruń
July 21, 1944
Just before Dawn

SHE HEARD MOANING AND WHISPERS AND THE SOUND OF spattering feet, but these were common fragments in many of Martha's dreams. But when whispers hissed into her left ear and hands began to jerk her body, she knew this was no dream.

"Martha! Ruth's giving birth; wake up! Hurry, hurry, wake up!"

She bolted up in the darkness, rolled out of bed, and began to run before her feet hit the floor. "Ruth?"

Three steps along, she realized she was running the wrong way. She spun.

Ruth lay in her bed, knees bent, moaning softly. Half a dozen women were huddled around her.

"Water!" Golda stood up and barked the order. "Bring a bucket from the showers!"

Martha slid up close to Rachel and knelt by Ruth's head.

"Give Ruth room," Golda bossed. "Stand back, some of you. Let her breathe, for heaven's sake. Who's getting water?"

"I am," someone said. The door banged behind the voice as someone ran to the showers for water.

"And blankets. Someone else, hurry."

"Martha!" Ruth suddenly buckled with a spasm. "The pain . . . Martha!"

Martha grabbed Ruth's hand. "It's okay, dear. I'm right here. Breathe. Breathe."

Ruth rolled her eyes and looked at Martha. The early morning moon shone through the windows and gently reflected the sweat glistening on her face.

"Martha." She smiled. "Martha."

"Shh, shh. Save your strength." She turned to Golda. "We need more light."

Normally, light was prohibited. Golda hesitated, then said, "Get some candles, Rachel." Rachel ran for three small candles they saved for special occasions. This indeed qualified. Golda shooed the women away from the bunk. "Stand back. You'd think none of you had ever seen a woman give birth before. And keep yourselves quiet, or the guards will hear."

"Let the guards hear," Martha said. "What do they expect, a nice calm Sabbath affair?"

"No, but they may want to take her to the clinic. Believe me, we don't want her to give birth in the clinic."

Martha hadn't considered the possibility that the camp doctor would not share the commandant's feelings about Ruth giving birth. He could easily kill the child and claim it was dead at birth!

"Okay, then we have to keep quiet," she said.

"We are quiet," Rachel objected. "But she's in pain; you can't just muzzle—"

"Shut up, all of you!" Ruth gasped.

They stared at her, silenced. The scene was both terrifying and wonderful at the same moment, Martha thought. She herself would soon be in this position, lying on her back begging God for mercy.

The women went to work like a flock of hens intent on the coop's only chick. Rachel lit the candles. Golda slid blankets under Ruth. Martha rubbed Ruth's back and spoke softly in her ear. They set the bucket of water at the foot of the bed.

Some of the others spoke in hushed tones or watched from a distance. But even the most jaded women could not completely ignore the bustle about Ruth's bunk.

A baby was being born. New life was coming into the world.

Here, perhaps more than any other place on earth, the wonder of it felt monumental. Martha knew that some of the women despised her and Ruth because the commandant had favored them. Or because they intended to bring their babies into this horrible war. Some even murmured that an abortion, however crude, would be better than a delivery.

For three months, Ruth had talked to them about joy and passion, scolding them for their long faces as she rubbed her belly. She'd upset more than one woman along the way, but she'd lightened the hearts of many others. There was not one woman in the barracks who didn't have some stake in this baby.

The women piled up on the nearby bunks and peered at the scene as if it were a theatrical play unfolding before their eyes. An hour later, well after Ruth's water had saturated the blankets, Martha ran through the barracks for dry ones. She saw that only one woman remained in her bunk at the far end of the barracks—Latvina, a twenty-year-old from Russia who'd been beaten the day before for spilling a bucket of mud in the brick factory.

"Is she having the baby?" Latvina asked.

Martha spun back. "Yes!"

"It's . . . alive?"

The simple question frightened her. "I think so. Lie down and get your rest; we'll bring the baby to you later." Then she ran for the blankets, suddenly panicked for not being at Ruth's side. Why hadn't she let someone else get the blankets?

"Blankets!" She held them over her head.

"Let her through!" Golda barked. "Let Martha through!"

The women parted like the Red Sea, and Martha edged through the narrow aisle, brushing half of them with her own pregnant belly. She gave Rachel the blankets and knelt beside the bed.

Tears ran down Ruth's face, and Martha grabbed her elbow in alarm. "Ruth? Ruth, what's happening?"

Ruth opened her eyes and smiled through her tears. "I'm having a baby, Martha." She gripped her belly with both hands and cried it out, an impossible blending of pain and gratitude. "I . . . am having . . . a baby!"

"A baby." Martha put her hand on top of Ruth's and smiled with relief. "Yes, you are having a baby." She faced the others, flooded with joy. "She is having a baby," she cried through a sudden burst of laughter.

Several dozen women stared at her, some smiling wide, others lost in their own thoughts.

Ruth's body began to quiver, and Martha turned back. Her friend's mouth was open in silent agony. And then it wasn't silent at all. She began to scream, long and loud. Loud enough for the whole camp to hear.

The final push lasted only thirty seconds, with Golda and Rachel easing the new life into the world, and Ruth wringing Martha's hands until they were white.

It happened almost unexpectedly. First there was only Ruth, screaming on the bed. And then there was Ruth and a baby, cradled in Rachel's arms, covered in fluid.

The room fell silent under the gaze of a hundred women stretching for a clear view of the birth. Then one question cut through the silence, braved by someone too far away to see. Latvina.

"Is it alive?"

As if in answer, the baby's cry sliced through the room.

Pandemonium swept the barracks, dozens of voices piled on top of each other.

"It's a girl!" Rachel announced, working quickly. She wiped away most of the fluid and handed the child to Martha, who carefully laid her in her mother's waiting arms.

Ruth was crying again, this time with loving eyes on the new life in her arms. She held the baby tenderly and began to shake with sobs.

Martha wept with her, unable to speak. Behind them, the women had quieted to sniffles and soft sobs. The barracks was held captive to the emotion bound up in the miracle of this new life. For a few minutes, no one spoke.

"Do you have a name?" Rachel asked.

Ruth caught her breath, wiped her eyes, and drew a finger down the tiny girl's cheek. "Her name will be Esther. She—"

The name passed through the room on the lips of the women, covering Ruth's next words.

"Hush!" Golda ordered. "Please, have some respect."

The women grew quiet.

"What is it, Ruth?" Golda asked.

"Let every woman here look at my child and see that there is hope. She is a star in the sky, pointing the way." She started to cry again, but stopped herself. "What price can you place on this treasure? Esther is the hope of our people. The seed of Israel."

A young woman pushed her way through the others. Latvina.

"May I hold her?"

Golda held out her hand. "This is no time—"

"No, it's okay," Ruth said.

Latvina stepped forward and gingerly lifted the child. She smiled, kissed little Esther on the forehead, and began to sing a soft lullaby in Russian. This young woman who perhaps wondered if she would ever complete her womanhood by bearing a child held tiny Esther as if she were the mother herself.

Then another woman, Margaret, wanted to hold her, and Ruth again overturned Golda's objection. Margaret held the child delicately. She'd lost her two-year-old daughter at Auschwitz before being shipped here to work. A surreal calm settled on the barracks in the dim glow of first light. The candles flickered silently as the six or seven women closest to Ruth took turns holding the baby. Hushed tones of awe and wonder rippled through the onlookers. Quiet tears of hope and love.

Martha silently questioned the wisdom of exposing the child to so many so soon, but one look at Ruth's beaming face, and she knew it was the right thing. Allowing these women to hold this moving, breathing hope was life-giving. Its own kind of birth.

The baby came to Golda, who hesitated at first but then reluctantly took the child. The woman stared into Esther's tiny, wrinkled face. Her own face slowly knotted, and a tear made its way down her right cheek. "Hope," she whispered, and kissed the baby on the head. "Ruth's hope."

"Our hope," Ruth said.

Golda stepped forward and passed Esther into Martha's arms. "Israel's hope."

19

STEPHEN AWOKE TO A HOT SHAFT OF SUNLIGHT ON HIS RIGHT cheek. A warm, musty-smelling towel licked his cheek. For a moment, nothing else registered except this most peculiar sensation and the ache in his neck.

The dog. It had to be the dog.

He pushed himself to his elbow and stared into the mug of Brandy, who stood over him grinning wide and wagging her tail. Behind the dog stood Melissa, now clad in a halter top and gauchos. Beside her were two men, both dressed in corduroys and army jackets. Hippies.

"Welcome to the world of the living, Mr. Groovy," Melissa said.

The man on her left reminded Stephen of Shaggy from the *Scooby Doo* cartoon, only with longer hair. The other was squatty with a touch of Asian in his face. All three looked at him as if he were a specimen to be studied, but he doubted this motley crew would threaten a flea.

"Stephen," he said. "My name's Stephen."

"Excuse me. Stephen. I thought I told you this building belongs to us."

Stephen looked around. He was lying on what had once apparently been carpet, worn thin and so packed with dirt that it now resembled concrete. Portions of an old wall clung to steel supporting posts, but someone had taken an ax or a chain saw to most of the rest. He could see straight through the building to an empty elevator shaft thirty yards away. A pile of twenty or thirty old tires leaned against one wall. The room smelled like mud.

He stood unsteadily, trying to remember why he hadn't gone home.

Then he remembered. He turned to the window, ignoring the pain in his neck. The morning sunlight bathed Rachel's building across the street. The night's events crowded his mind.

"Hey, dude. Did you hear the lady? We're not offering a lease on this spot, dig?"

He turned back and faced Shaggy. "I was just resting."

"You running?"

"No."

"He's interested in Rachel Spritzer's building," Melissa said.

The gangly man looked out the window. "That so?" He walked up and peered across the street. "Why's that?"

"I'm a Realtor," Stephen said.

"That so? And why would a Realtor sleep in a dump like this, watching a building that's already sold?"

"Why would an intelligent man like yourself take leave of his senses and claim to own a building like this?" Stephen asked.

The man's eyebrow arched. He grinned. "What makes you think I'm intelligent?"

Stephen hesitated. "Your choice of jacket?"

Melissa chuckled.

The gangly man winked. "We got us a Realtor with spunk, dudes." He stuck out his hand. "Name's Sweeney."

Stephen shook the hand. "Nice to know you, Sweeney."

"You've met Melissa, and that's Brian. And for the record, intelligence can be overrated. I should know. I not only attended UCLA, I graduated with honors. Believe it or not, under this skin I'm really an architect, although I haven't actually worked as one in the fake world. Melissa's old man runs a law firm downtown, and Brian's just hanging with us for the day."

He walked back to his friends, crossed his arms, and turned around. "So what are you really doing here?"

Stephen wasn't sure he knew. He'd broken into the apartment last night and come out empty-handed. But he *had* come out. And he knew some things now. He was sure that Braun knew about the Stones of David. Nothing else explained his intense and unreasonable interest in the building. He was also quite sure that Braun *didn't* know about the safe.

And he was sure the safe wasn't empty.

"I'm not sure," he said.

They held stares.

"Why are you here?" Stephen asked. "You throw it all away?"

"No, my man. I'm finding what I couldn't find in the books. Life, love, and the pursuit of happiness. The second bohemian revolution."

"Sounds interesting." Brandy was sniffing through a pile of wood ten feet away. Stephen suddenly felt tightness in his chest, and he wasn't sure why. He looked back out the window.

"It has its downsides," Sweeney said, "but in the end, we're all just children chasing after the rainbow."

"Maybe that's why I'm here, then," Stephen said. "Chasing the rainbow."

"Looks like some idiot tried to break into Rachel's building last night. Cut a hole in the garage. You know anything about that?"

Stephen blinked. "You're kidding. Cut a hole?"

"That's what it looks like. Cutting torch or something."

"How stupid is that?"

"Definitely not the intelligent way to approach life's problems. Some druggies will try anything for a fix."

"Idiots," Stephen said.

"What do you say, kids? Should we let Mr. Groovy hang?"

Melissa winked at Stephen. "Sure. Why not?"

Brian just shrugged.

Sweeney spread his hands. "There you go. You can hang. But don't tell anyone about this place—it's quiet and far enough out of the main drag to stay that way. We on?"

"Sure."

"Gotta split."

Stephen watched them go. Brandy eyed him cockeyed for a few seconds. "Hey, Brandy," he whispered.

The dog trotted over to him and licked his hand eagerly.

Melissa whistled. "Come on, puppy. Let's leave him in peace."

"No—"

The dog galloped for the hippies, stopped at the stairs for one last look, and then disappeared.

Stephen stared at the stairwell until the sound of their footsteps faded. The door slammed far below. Gone. He was alone in the world—even the dog had left him again.

He sighed and faced the window once more. The image of the tin box with Ruth's picture, which he was now thinking of as Esther's picture, loomed in his mind. Like mother, like daughter. The woman he'd been destined for.

He stared at the sunroom across the street, transfixed by the drawn curtains, wondering what Roth Braun was doing in secret over there.

Who are you, Esther?

The perplexing obsession that had taken him out of his game yesterday taunted him again. Now, in retrospect, it felt rather childish. He really had to get back to being normal. The thought of trying to explain why he'd spent the night in an abandoned building made him cringe.

But with each passing second, Rachel Spritzer's apartment continued to draw him, like a wraith beckoning a man to his appointed death; like a siren seducing a fool to his destruction.

Only it wasn't a wraith or a siren; it was a tin box with a picture of Esther. Stephen sat heavily against the wall.

That and the Stones of David, which, incidentally, were worth millions.

He closed his eyes and swallowed. Maybe he had gone over the edge last night, but he couldn't just dismiss his connection to the Stones of David.

His mind drifted. If he was right, no one knew how valuable that safe really was. He was faced with the kind of opportunity that presented itself to one lucky soul maybe once every century. Like stumbling onto a lottery ticket worth ten million dollars. Only this was far more significant.

How far to the Spritzer building? Thirty yards. Then straight down about another thirty yards in the corner of the boiler room.

He should've grabbed the tin box last night. Stephen gritted his teeth. No, they would have found it on him. But he could have at least opened the box and stuffed its contents in his pockets, right? No, too risky.

With any luck, he'd stalled Braun with the bit about the upper floors. How long before the creep made his way into the basement? Then again, even if he did search the basement, there was no guarantee he would find the safe. If Stephen was lucky, he had a couple of days. Maybe three.

Stephen stood slowly, determined to fight off waves of gloom. He looked around, dazed. The thought of going home to the rabbi made him queasy.

A thought struck him. The picture of Ruth was still on his desk at Chaim's house. He really should have brought it with him, really should get it and keep it with him. Besides the note from his mother, it was his only tangible link to his past. And perhaps to his future.

He would go home, get that picture, and then decide on a reasonable course of action.

Stephen turned and headed for the stairs. Maybe he could show the picture to Gerik. The old Jew knew everything about everybody from the war. But could he trust Gerik with more than the antique dealer already knew? Not a chance. He couldn't trust anyone. Even if he could, he didn't want to. This was solely his business. Besides, you trust one person with your once-in-a-lifetime, and it becomes someone else's once-in-a-lifetime.

On the other hand, what if the antique dealer actually knew Ruth? Or Esther? Unlikely, but possible. Stephen stepped up his pace to a jog.

The Vega sat where he'd parked it. If anyone saw the haggard man climbing in, they might guess he was stealing it. Stephen eased the car into traffic. At least he hadn't forgotten how to drive. How to comb his hair, perhaps, and how to sleep in his own bed, but out here on the streets he was incognito. On a mission. To do nothing more than retrieve a photograph from his own desk, true enough, but at least he was making progress again.

The Beatles insisted he let it be, let it be. Stephen ejected the tape from his eight-track and threw it on the floor of the passenger seat. Whispered words of wisdom, please. They had no idea.

His next bit of progress was to get into his bedroom unseen. Facing Chaim's scrutiny at this juncture was as unappealing as chewing quinine tablets.

The plan was simple. He was getting pretty good at sneaking into buildings. If Chaim wasn't home, he would just walk in the front door, clean up a bit, take the picture, and leave—five minutes max. If the rabbi *was* home, then Stephen would climb in through his bedroom window, which he was quite sure he'd left open. The trick would be to get in without the neighbors seeing his butt hanging out the window.

He parked the car a block from the house. Chaim's old Peugeot was in the drive.

Stephen sat in silence for a good minute before stealthily climbing out of the car. He ducked into the backyard and crept as naturally as possible along the wall toward his window. He reconsidered the plan—walking in and explaining himself to the rabbi would be so much simpler. On the other hand, the thought of baring his soul really was unnerving. What was he going to say? *Oh, good morning, Rabbi. Yes, well, I look like a vagabond because I've decided to become one. To kick things off in the right spirit, I torched a hole in the German's garage door last night and then spent the night in the dump across the street.*

He reached the window, glanced around, and pushed it up. He'd forgotten about the screen, but a hard punch put his hand right through it. A few more, and the mesh sat in tatters. Another quick look, a kind of pull-up dive, and Stephen spilled into his room, no worse off than a bruised hip bone, compliments of the windowsill.

He had to move quickly. The unframed photograph sat on his desk next to several phone messages left in Chaim's handwriting. He couldn't read Ruth's piercing eyes, a mysterious blend of resilience and tenderness. She was perhaps the most beautiful woman he'd ever seen.

He shoved the photo into his shirt and immediately withdrew it. His sweat would ruin it. Besides, he was going to take a shower. He tiptoed for the bathroom. No. Running water might alert the rabbi. Maybe he should skip the shower. He really didn't have time anyway.

Stephen stood before the mirror, photograph in hand, and looked at himself. His hair stood on end, and his face was coated with dust. He quickly patted his hair and reached for the faucet, but stopped before twisting the knob. The house had noisy pipes that were known to even groan on occasion.

He really should just walk out into the living room and tell Chaim he was home. He'd gone out with some friends last night, partied until dawn, and come home for a shower. Fun, fun, fun. And the hole in the screen? Well, a bird must have crashed through.

Stephen grunted. This was ridiculous. He had to get out.

Using some water from the tank behind the toilet, he managed to clean his face. He took a stab at fixing his hair and brushed his teeth without using water. Three minutes in the bathroom, and he suddenly felt sure the rabbi would walk in on him at any moment. He wrapped his treasured picture in a towel, stuffed it under his shirt, and climbed back out the window.

⁓

"I DON'T know what he's up to," Lars said, "but his name *is* Stephen Friedman, and he *is* a Realtor. He lives up north with an old Jew."

"Another Jew," Roth said.

"Both father and mother dead. Has connections with the DA through a friend. A Jewish girl named Sylvia Potok."

"Married?"

"Stephen, no. The woman, I don't know."

Roth suddenly wanted off the subject. It wasn't an issue that Lars or the others should concern themselves with.

"He should be easy enough to deal with if he becomes a problem," Lars said.

Three more men had arrived from Germany this morning to join the deconstruction project. They were carefully removing the plaster from the walls in the kitchen and would work their way through the entire floor. The task would take them a couple of days, coincidentally the term of the Realtor's suggested lease. If either the journal or the other four Stones were in this house, they would find it.

But Roth had already found what he had come for. Stephen Friedman.

The boy had come home. Exactly as Rachel Spritzer had wanted. The game. The game was on.

Roth had spent the first part of the night in the sunroom, desperate to coax secrets from the pictures. So much pain. But like hope and fear, pain and pleasure yielded the most power when they could be found together.

Afterward he satisfied himself by selecting another Jewish woman, this one from Pasadena. Toruń had come to Los Angeles. And soon, if the powers of the air were smiling on him, he would take Los Angeles back to Toruń.

"We move on the grave site tonight and the museum tomorrow night," he said. "How much will the grave cost us?"

"Half a million U.S. dollars to exhume the body, leave us alone with it for an hour, and return the grave to normal by morning. The guards at the museum, on the other hand, can't be bought."

He had expected this. "We only want to look at the contents. Surely we can find someone there who will accept a million dollars for a few hours alone with some old trinkets. We don't want to see the Stone, just her belongings." He paused. "Offer two million if you have to. If all else fails, we'll go in with gas."

Lars didn't respond.

"I want access to every last item from her estate, every scrap of paper, every photograph, and I want it within the next forty-eight hours. Frankly, I don't care what it costs."

"Understood."

"And the next time Gerhard calls, tell him I'm occupied. I will not speak to him again."

"Of course."

Roth was an unusually patient man, but he'd never been in a position quite like this, with such high stakes and on foreign soil. He stood and slowly paced.

In under a week, he would finish what his father should have finished thirty years ago.

The fact that his plans were proceeding exactly as he'd envisioned was almost too much to bear. His success made him feel warm. He wanted to look at the pictures again.

20

FROM THE STREET, GERIK'S ANTIQUE SHOP LOOKED LIKE NOTHING other than one more flea-infested hole that might sell used clothes, half of which had been soiled and never properly cleaned. But step past the bell that clanged upon entry, and even an amateur would know this shop was unique.

The store ran long and narrow, crowded by hundreds of antiques that sat and hung and leaned and balanced in every conceivable space. The walls could be plastered with mud or coated in gold and no one would know, because there was no wall to see. Instead, there were Queen Anne chairs and ornate mirrors and huge brass plates and myriad paintings. A large cherry four-poster bed purportedly once owned by Thomas Jefferson himself hung from the ceiling.

Stephen stood at the door and peered into the shadows for a glimpse of Gerik Dlugosz, "Gary" to all who frequented his store. A middle-aged woman with a splotchy red face and a blue silk blouse glanced up at him from some silver vases. She was looking at the towel wrapped under his arm, he just knew it. *What does that man have under his arm, pray tell? It looks valuable. It looks secretive. I wonder if he'll show it to me.*

Stephen hurried up the left aisle, past long glass cases stuffed with coins and copper figurines and sprawling collections of silverware. If it was old and valuable, it belonged here. The floor creaked with each step. You'd think that with all the money Gerik made, he could invest in a new place.

"Stephen?"

Stephen instinctively gripped his wrapped picture and jerked at the sound of Gerik's voice.

The thin man walked toward him with an outstretched hand. A scraggly gray beard hung off his chin. "So good to see you again." He put an inviting hand on Stephen's shoulder and steered him to the side. "And how are you holding up?"

"Fine. Good."

"Excellent. Excellent." The proprietor stopped by a case and ran curious eyes over Stephen. "You've been to Rachel's apartment, then?"

"Yes."

"And?"

"Nothing much. The museum had already been through."

"Yes, of course. I am very sorry, Stephen. I wish I could help you. You've contacted an attorney?"

"No."

"No. I don't blame you. You should follow your own heart until things become clear."

They stood in silence.

"Maybe I could help you in some other way," Gerik said.

"No, nothing." Stephen was feeling hot under the neck. It had been a mistake to come. "I just came by for a visit."

"Is that so?" Gerik smiled softly. "I don't believe you. But I'm willing to pretend. So then, let's visit."

A mistake. Definitely a mistake. The shop had four or five other customers at the moment, and Stephen was sure they were all at least curious about him, if not downright fixated on him. His hair was a mess, his clothes wrinkled and dirty, his face haggard, and he clung to a bundle under his arm as if it were his last worldly possession. He relaxed and leaned on the counter, determined to appear somewhat normal.

"Business good?" he asked.

"Always."

Stephen looked at an old pocket watch in the case. A handwritten tag hanging off it read 3000. Nothing else. Surely that couldn't be the price. Twin horse heads graced either side of the silver piece. He dared a glance at one of the other customers and saw that the man wasn't staring at him after all. But if he knew what Stephen knew, his eyes would be popping out of his skull. *Fess up, boy, where are the other four Stones? You have no right to them. They are for a serious collector with millions to spend.*

"Three thousand," Stephen said. "What does that mean?" Question sounded dumb, but he had to say something before making a retreat.

"It means that someone will give me three thousand dollars for a watch I paid five hundred dollars for," Gerik said.

Stephen looked up, surprised. "Three thousand dollars? It's worth that much?"

"It's worth what someone will pay for it. What's the value of a diamond? Whatever someone is willing to pay for a pretty stone that makes him feel important."

"And someone will want that old watch enough to pay three thousand dollars? Amazing."

"They aren't buying an old watch, my boy. They're buying an idea. The value of an idea is determined by how appealing the idea is to someone. If you want something desperately, you will pay desperately. Isn't that true?"

"Yes. Yes, I suppose so."

"I sell ideas. Actually, if you think about it, everything is really no more than idea. The past is nothing more than a memory, which is one kind of idea. The future is still a hope, another kind of idea. The present is fleeting and becomes a memory before you can put your hands on it. All ideas. I sell ideas."

"That's a bit cynical, isn't it? Am I just an idea?"

"No. But what I think of you is." Gerik grinned. "And, of course, there's the greatest of ideas," he said with a twinkle in his eyes. "Love. You could even say that I sell love. Obsession. A good thing."

Stephen chuckled nervously and looked at the three-thousand-dollar watch. "Sure—love. I would say that's stretching things a bit."

"Is it? Last week, I sold a brass masquerade mask with red feathers to a woman from Hollywood. It is said the mask was worn by a wealthy French nobleman known for his extravagant parties. She'd been seeking that mask for seven years, and I was fortunate enough to track it down for her. I honestly think she might have parted with her husband for it. She loved it as much as she loved anything. Another collector offered me ten thousand dollars for the mask. She paid me twenty-five. What was it worth? Twenty-five."

"Most people associate love with other people," Stephen said.

"And I associate it with any object of desire. People who buy from me are in love with what they purchase. Many are obsessed. I'm not sure some wouldn't risk their lives for a particular obsession. Which isn't all that crazy—some ideas are actually worth dying for." Gerik winked. "I think Rachel was such a person."

Stephen looked at him, taken off guard. He couldn't think of a response.

"Life is hardly worth living without an obsession. God himself is obsessed."

Stephen stared on dumbly. What was this man talking about?

"With his creation. With humans. With the love of humans. You think he created with nonchalance? Let's throw some mud against the sky and see if any of it sticks? Not a chance. We are created for love, for obsession. So we do indeed obsess, though usually not over the right idea." He hesitated and eyed Stephen's shirt again.

"I had a rough night." The words about this obsession business echoed through Stephen's head. "Is that . . . Judaism?"

"What? That we are created to obsess? Sure, why not? What do you have there?"

Stephen shifted nervously. "This? Nothing. Really. Just some stuff I picked up. Some, you know, personal effects that I picked up from my place and wrapped here. In this towel. For safekeeping. You know." *You babbling fool!* He looked around again. "This is a beautiful place, Gerik. A wonderful . . . little place. You should be proud of what you've done here in this . . . place."

"Thank you." The man was eyeing him without a break now. "Would you like to clean up in the back?"

"Me? Why would I want to clean up? I'm fine. I just picked up some things, and I wanted to stop by and see, you know, all this things." *This things?* "I'm fine, really."

"Fine."

"Good."

Stephen felt terribly exposed. As if he were in one of those dream sequences in which he walked out onto a stage, only to realize that he was naked. He was chewing on his fingernail without remembering exactly when he'd lifted his finger to do so.

"Okay, so I'm not completely good," Stephen finally said. The antiques dealer arched an eyebrow. "Do you mind if I have a word with you?"

"Not at all," Gerik said.

Stephen glanced around. "Not here."

Gerik hesitated, then turned and walked deeper into the store, where the furniture hung lower and the shadows were darker. He stopped and turned around.

"This is private?" Stephen asked.

"We might as well be in a vault," the old man assured him.

"Our voices might carry."

"No one can hear us."

"No, but voices can travel."

"I've practically lived in this room for twenty years, and I can assure you—"

"Please, Gerik."

Stephen looked back at the man browsing thirty feet away and saw that they'd attracted his attention.

"I'm sorry, where are my manners? Please, I'm not thinking clearly. Follow me."

They walked past the last of the stacked furniture way in the back and stepped into an office cluttered with books and papers. Gerik closed the door, picked up a pipe, and lit it. A blue cloud billowed over his head. Stephen held the wrapped photograph against his chest now.

"You found something at the apartment," Gerik said.

Stephen didn't respond.

"May I see it?"

"This?"

"You did want to show me, didn't you?"

"I guess so, yes." He began to unwrap the picture, suddenly unsure if he wanted to show it. "I . . . came across this." The picture of Ruth stared up at him, mesmerizing.

He hadn't noticed it before, but her hair was swept back so that it exposed her left ear. That would be her right ear if the photo had reversed her image. A nice ear. A stunning ear actually, one that looked as if it had been painted on with a skilled—

"And?"

Stephen looked up and blinked.

"I . . . I found this photograph and thought maybe you could take a look at it."

Gerik held out his hand. The towel fell to the floor. Stephen gave him the picture. "Her name's Esther."

Gerik puffed on the pipe and studied the image. He turned the picture over. "It says her name is Ruth."

"Right. I mean Ruth."

"Taken before or during the war." He read the note on the back. "Stone of David," he said, and glanced up at Stephen. "Taken before the war. Esther would be your age, if she survived."

"Exactly," Stephen said. "That's exactly my point!"

"It is?"

Was it?

"You found this in her apartment?"

Stephen cleared his throat. "It was with some other pictures of . . . of victims. Maybe I shouldn't have taken it, but I just . . . it was quite moving."

"Of course you should have taken it. She would have wanted you to have it. Most of the world wants to forget the Holocaust, you know."

Gerik knew nothing about the safe; he was speaking from his heart only. He set his pipe down and examined the edges of the photograph with a trained eye.

"Did Rachel tell you anything else? About Ruth."

"No, nothing," Gerik said. "She asked about the Stones, of course. Do you know what one Stone of David is worth?"

"Millions."

"Like I said earlier, it's worth what someone will pay for it, which means twenty million as of this morning."

"Someone offered twenty million to the museum?"

"A group of Jewish moguls who insist the relic belongs in Israel. I'm not sure I disagree. But Christians also lay claim to the Stones, as you may know. The seed of Adam to strike Lucifer on the head, in the line of David. Christ. I know of collectors in Rome who would pay well over one hundred million for the collection. Perhaps even two hundred."

Stephen felt his heart thump a little harder. "Hmm." He was chewing his fingernail again.

Gerik handed the picture back and Stephen took it carefully. "Thank you."

"I doubt they'll be found in our lifetime," Gerik said.

"No? Why not?"

"Because they were part of some Nazi's war spoils. No one knows which officer took them, but it's rumored that they were pillaged from a wealthy Polish collector's home in Warsaw. If the Nazi survived the war-crimes trials, he won't be eager to show off his loot, I can promise you that."

"Maybe Rachel had all five."

"Unlikely."

Stephen went rigid. Did Gerik know something definitive, or was he just guessing?

"Think so?"

"Why give one Stone and not five?"

"Exactly! That's exactly what—no, that makes sense."

"I really should get back to the store. Half of my inventory could be gone by now." Gerik walked toward the door, and Stephen followed him.

"You're right to treasure the picture, Stephen," the old man said, turning back. "Wherever she is now, little Esther is worth more than all the

Stones of David together. Now, there would be an obsession worth dying for, don't you think?"

Stephen felt his face blush, and he shifted his gaze. "I don't know. It's just a picture."

"No. It's an idea. A memory. Perhaps a hope, but not simply a picture. I'm sorry I can't help you find her."

"That's not—"

"Of course it is. If I'm not mistaken, you're quite taken by her, which is understandable. I'm a Jew. I was there. She deserves your obsession, dead or alive. Your obsession gives her life value." Gerik smiled politely and left.

Stephen didn't remember actually leaving the antique shop. He drifted rather than walked. The old man was right about some things and wrong about some things. Right about Esther deserving someone's obsession, wrong about the Stones not being found.

Unless they weren't in the tin box.

He wasn't willing to dwell on that possibility.

He drove to Rachel's apartment. Still there. Still alone on the lot, towering in the midday sun while the busy beavers scurried through the upper floor, chewing, chewing, chewing. He drove around it once, then twice, doubling back three blocks away so as not to be too obvious. Too many passes of a blue Chevy Vega, and someone might raise an eyebrow. Or a gun.

Shades were pulled. The hole in the garage door had been sealed with boards. They wouldn't leave the bottom floor unguarded this time, not a chance.

That's right. This time. He had no choice but to go again.

They probably had men or dogs or machine guns rigged to go off upon unauthorized entry. This time it would take more than a torch and a lighter to get in.

Fifteen minutes. Fifteen minutes alone in the basement, and he would be finished.

He finally parked the Vega on a side street and crept back up the stairs to his hiding spot on the fourth floor of Building B. He had to think this through. There was a way. There had to be a way.

He leaned against the wall beside the window and slid to his seat. There was always a way. This one hid in the dark corners of his mind and refused to step into the light, but Stephen knew he could eventually coax it out. With enough patience, with enough focus, the right plan would present itself.

He unfolded Ruth's picture and gazed into her eyes. "Speak to me, Esther. Tell me."

21

Los Angeles
July 21, 1973
Saturday Evening

SYLVIA SAT AT HER DESK STUDYING THE PHOTOGRAPHS IN THE file. Forty in all, taken from every conceivable angle. They were duplicates from homicide, a precaution that the DA insisted on.

"I want a parallel file compiled now, and I want you to build that file with every last bit of evidence that you can scrounge from every detective on this case. Baby-sit them if you have to, but I need that file to be up-to-the-minute."

It was Sylvia's first high-profile case. No telling how long before they apprehended the killer, or when it would eventually go to trial, assuming he lived that long. But if and when the time came to prosecute, the DA would be ready. Sylvia would make sure of it.

Three nights; three victims; same MO.

She stared at the bodies. Blood pooled around each. Enough to conclude that whoever had killed the women had wanted them to bleed out.

Why?

The last victim had struggled more than the first two, according to the preliminary investigative reports. Bruises on the wrists.

The sight sickened her. She'd become an attorney to protect the rights of victims, not analyze their brutal deaths.

Jewish women across the city were double bolting their doors or moving in with relatives. The fact that the case had gone public was a good thing, despite the fear it caused. Better fear than death.

And what about you, Sylvia? She glanced at the office door. The rest of the staff had already gone home. How easy would it be for a killer to break into the DA's office?

But really. What were the chances that she would be singled out? Besides, all three had been killed in their homes.

Still, the quiet was disconcerting.

The phone rang shrilly and she jumped. She snatched up the receiver.

"Hello?"

"I'm worried, Sylvia." It was Chaim. "Very worried. This isn't like Stephen. Something's wrong."

She reoriented her attention from the killer to Stephen.

"Sylvia?"

"I'm thinking, Rabbi." She sighed. "He's probably out on a hot date. What did you expect with all of your love talk?"

"A hot date is the farthest thing from his mind. I would have thought at least he'd call."

"Maybe he did and the line was busy. Maybe he has something he wants to surprise you with. Maybe he's at that Santa Monica property."

"He tore out his own window screen, for heaven's sake!"

That silenced her for a moment. "Like I said, he can be irrational at times."

"Impulsive, not irrational," he said.

He had a point.

"Really, Sylvia, I'm worried, and this conversation isn't helping me."

"Look, I'm sure he's fine. He may be reeling from this news about his mother, and God knows he can do some crazy things when he puts his mind to it, but he's not an idiot."

"This from the same woman who insisted that if anyone could find danger, Stephen could?"

"Well, maybe I was wrong."

"And maybe you weren't."

"He's smart, Rabbi. Like you said, he really is. Let him follow his heart."

"Now you sound like Gerik."

"Would you like me to come over? I could bring some Chinese."

"Would you? Yes, I would like that."

———w———

STEPHEN HAD reviewed the situation a hundred times. Maybe a thousand, counting all the subconscious assessments. The long of it was that he was in a vicious circle of dilemmas; the short of it was that the dilemmas ended at an impasse. He just couldn't see a way out.

Still he paced in front of the window and rehashed his problem.

His head hurt, and he wasn't sure he was thinking so effectively anymore. Nevertheless, he was thinking: he was thinking that Gerik was much smarter than he'd imagined. His words of wisdom had set Stephen free.

He was thinking he had wasted the day pacing and driving and avoiding the house.

He was thinking he was avoiding the house because he didn't want to answer to Chaim.

He was thinking involving Chaim could be dangerous for the rabbi.

He was thinking Roth Braun knew the Stones were in Rachel's house and would kill for them.

He was thinking he would either go home tonight or get a motel room. He might be a tad whacked-out, but he wasn't loony enough to sleep here again.

He was thinking he really should go to the police.

Then again, he knew a few things too: he knew he couldn't go to the police because he, not Braun, was the one committing crimes here.

He knew the Stones of David were in the basement over there.

He knew the Stones in the basement were his.

He knew there had to be a way into that basement to take the Stones that were his.

Stephen peered out the window. A city worker walked up to Rachel's building. His heart skipped a beat, but then he saw that she was only reading the meter on the back wall. Maybe he could take her place and demand to read the meters in the basement. Were there any meters in the basement? He couldn't remember. Of course, they would see his face and end it right there. He had no reason to doubt their threats.

He resumed his pacing.

He also knew that nothing he knew was really for certain, except the fact that he couldn't go to the police.

There had to be a way into the building.

He did know how *not* to get into the building. Not with a cutting torch.

Not with a truck through the garage door.

Not on a hang glider to the rooftop.

Not via a helicopter pounding above their heads.

Not through the front door.

Not in a huge wooden horse, or in a cake, or in a massive scrumptious pizza delivered for the Wolfmeister.

Not through the front door. Said that already.

Not on a rocket . . .

Stephen stopped. Not through the front door. Why was that again? Why not?

His heart bolted. Could it work? He jumped to the window again. The meter reader was down the street now, climbing into a black Datsun. Why not?

He resumed pacing, frantically now. It was bold. It was daring. It was the kind of thing no one could possibly expect.

It was lunacy!

Which made it perfect.

He glanced at his watch. Almost seven. Almost dark. That was even better.

But where would he get an outfit at this hour? His mind revved into overdrive. It was Saturday night.

He knew something else. He knew that every Saturday night, Marjorie Stillwater played bingo.

———

THE CHURCH Chaim attended was a small interdenominational affair, a study in cultural diversity. Black, white, Korean, Jewish—you name it—

a hodgepodge of seekers who'd found their answer in Christianity. The old church building had a steeple on the outside and exactly thirty pews on the inside. Two hundred or so managed to squeeze into the sanctuary every Sunday.

They were a friendly lot, a little too friendly for Stephen's tastes. Hugs and kisses and smiles, smiles, smiles. They seemed genuine enough, but to an outsider like Stephen, who didn't want to care about God, much less Christianity, their sincerity came across as a pressing invitation to join them. Fine for the meek and mild, not so fine for the headstrong.

Stephen had attended services on three separate occasions, and each time he'd left feeling both welcomed and repelled by the oddity of it all. The fact that he suspected some truth in Chaim's assertions that Jesus of Nazareth was more than a man only complicated the matter.

He'd always seen religion as a function of some folks' need for meaning and a moral compass. Whatever it was, it was not an object of personal faith. Father had led him and his foster brothers through the seven feasts, spring and fall, with an emphasis on Passover, and Stephen had dutifully followed the course expected of all non-Orthodox Jewish boys until he'd come to the United States.

He'd found in Chaim a different kind of religion altogether. His was born less out of tradition than simple faith. The rabbi still was attracted to much of Judaism, but he also believed the Messiah had already come. He'd put his faith in Jesus of Nazareth, and he talked regularly about falling madly in love with him. Christianity: faith, love, and lots of wet kisses on the cheek from old ladies who wore wigs.

Actually, *one old lady* would be more truthful, and *one* wet kiss even more so. He'd met Marjorie Stillwater within a few minutes of entering the church the first time, and he'd spent at least half the service watching her. Her big, flowing, blond wig had slipped to one side, and no one but him seemed to notice or care.

One of the pastor's teachings suddenly returned to Stephen. He'd heard it on his second—or was it his third?—visit. The pastor recounted a story Jesus had apparently told, about a man who was walking in someone else's field one day, found a treasure, and basically went ballistic.

That was the way the pastor had put it. Ballistic. In the parable, the man hadn't told the landowner about the treasure on his land. No, he was far too focused on the treasure to do any such decent thing. Instead, he'd hidden it again, snuck out and sold all that he owned, approached the owner, and bought the field without telling the man about the treasure. A tad deceptive, to be sure. Surprising that Jesus would tell such a story. All things considered, one might think he was trying to say that man's passion for God needs to look more like desperation than reason.

Stephen nibbled on a fingernail and made a connection. His own ordeal with his mother's building wasn't so different from the man's ordeal with the field, was it? Stephen might not be after the kingdom of God, but then neither was the man in the story. They really weren't so different, he and this man. Neither was a Christian, both were after a treasure, and both were singularly focused on the task.

The thought gave him some courage.

Stephen had been to Marjorie's tiny house six blocks from the Santa Monica Pier only once, but he'd seen enough to know precisely what he had to do now.

He slowed the Vega to a crawl in front of the house. Light glowed through the living-room curtains, but he couldn't tell if she was home. He had to either get her out of the house or verify that she already was. Pay phone.

He found a phone three blocks over, searched the directory for her number, and made the call. The plan was simple enough—if she answered, he would call Marjorie to the church for an emergency. *Come quick, Miss Stillwater! Don't have time to explain, just get down here as fast as you can. It's life or death.* Click. That would send her scrambling.

But ten rings later, she hadn't answered, which meant she was probably at bingo, exactly as he'd suspected. Perfect. Bingo ended . . . when?

Probably not before eight o'clock. That gave him almost an hour. Very perfect.

Stephen drove to within a block of Marjorie's house and approached her front porch on foot. He was getting in the habit of parking his car a block away from all his destinations these days, a noteworthy but not necessarily incriminating fact. He walked straight, without daring to look left or right. Nothing that would make him look suspicious to neighbors. Just nephew Stephen coming for a visit.

The trusting old woman had locked her keys inside and used a spare from under the third flowerpot when Stephen had visited. The flowerless pot sat where he remembered it, full of dirt that had spilled to the wood porch more than a few times, judging by the stains. Stephen bent, withdrew the key, unlocked her door, and returned the key.

And if she was still here?

He stepped in. "Marjorie?"

Her bedroom door stood open to a dark interior. Stephen closed the front door. "Marjorie?"

The tiny house rang of silence. She was gone. Which meant she would be back sooner or later. With his luck, probably sooner. Stephen hurried into the bedroom, found the sliding doors that presumably led into her closet, and slid the door open.

Two dozen dresses hung organized by color—reds and blues and purples. He had absolutely no business being here, staring at Marjorie Stillwater's dresses. They smelled like talcum powder.

Stephen ran his hand lightly down the row of hangers, parting each dress for a better view. This was how women shopped at Sears. For hours, inexhaustibly running their hands down the rows and around the carousels, imagining what, only God could really know. He'd gone shopping once with Sylvia and was exhausted after the first rack.

A business suit of some kind would be best, but Marjorie just wasn't a business-suit kind of person. He wasn't sure he cared for her selection of colors. Lots of purples. Dresses might be too . . . feminine. A pantsuit would be better. At least it had pants and a jacket thing. Question was, did Marjorie own any pantsuits? He continued down

the row and stopped three outfits from the end at a lime-green polyester pantsuit, freshly pressed. Maybe she'd bought the outfit in a
moment of youthful extravagance and not yet worked up the courage
to actually wear it.

He wrestled the suit jacket from its hanger and held it up to his
shoulders. Marjorie wasn't thin, and he wasn't large—should work. The
idea was preposterous, but that was exactly the point. No one would
suspect this woman could possibly be Stephen Friedman. Dressing as a
man in disguise would be nearly impossible without the help of someone who knew what he was doing. Arriving as a woman, on the other
hand . . .

Still, he wasn't thrilled with the prospect of donning Marjorie's lime-
green pantsuit. He walked to her dresser and started rummaging through
the drawers for the rest of his outfit. What else? Nylons—definitely nylons.
Couldn't walk in with hairy ankles. Maybe socks would work. Depended
on the shoes.

He bounded over to the closet again, dropped to his knees, and
scanned her shoes. High heels, mostly. They'd never fit. Working women
did wear men's shoes on occasion, didn't they? Shoes that looked like
men's? He stared down at the tassels on his own black leather shoes and
tried to imagine them with Marjorie's lime-green pants.

He really had no choice but to split the difference—he'd go for the
nylons and wear his own shoes. It wasn't unbelievable that a woman in
his occupation might wear comfortable shoes on the job.

Stephen hauled his bundle into the bathroom and plopped it down
on the floor. Flared lime-green polyester pants, matching suit jacket,
lavender shirt with paisleys, white pantyhose or nylons (he wasn't sure
what this particular variety was called), white gloves, and the crowning
element of this disguise—the reason Marjorie had been a brilliant selection—a blond wig.

He dropped his pants and pulled on one leg of the nylons. Tight,
but they were supposed to be tight. The hair on his legs was still visible,
but the pants would take care of that. He stood and hopped into the second leg.

This particular method of donning nylons proved to be less brilliant than he'd imagined. He had his leg halfway in before it occurred to him that things were going wrong. He started to fall forward, hopped once, tried to free his leg, and succeeded only in catapulting himself headlong toward the wall.

After betraying him so boldly, his masculine prowess came to his aid. He performed a duck/roll/flip and hit the wall with his back instead of his head. The whole house shook with the impact. A shelf full of knick-knacks slipped off the wall and crashed over his head before he could get his arms up to protect himself.

Stephen lay on the floor, one leg still half-caught in the nylons, and took quick stock of the situation. Silence. No one banging on the door, demanding to know who was in there trying to get into a pair of pantyhose.

A broken plate lay in pieces a foot from his head—not unheard of with all the earthquakes that rolled through these parts. All in all, he'd averted any real setback.

Stephen rolled to his back and tugged on the second leg of the nylons. He felt as if he was being strangled from the ankles up. Why women quietly suffered in these contraptions, he couldn't imagine.

The rest of the outfit slid on with ease—lime-green pants, lavender paisley shirt, lime-green jacket. His own shoes. No need for a bra, not with the jacket. See, that was smart too; judging by his battle with the pantyhose, he might very well hang himself trying to don a bra. Stephen slipped his shoes back on and stood in front of a full-length mirror behind the door.

Lime green was clearly not his color, but the lavender blouse actually brought a glow to his face. He tugged at the jacket sleeves and managed to extend them another inch, enough to cover what hair the gloves would miss.

The weakest link in the disguise was clearly the length of the pants, which flared wide and hung short, six inches above his ankles. Three-quarter-length pants—he was sure he'd seen a model or two wearing an outfit something like this. They might even pass for gauchos. His

TED DEKKER

black shoes looked a bit out of fashion—maybe he would leave them in the car.

Now for the second reason Marjorie Stillwater was a brilliant solution—makeup. Even if he had bought a new outfit at Woolworth's, he needed makeup and the dressing room to apply it.

He walked into the bedroom and glanced at the dresser clock. Seven thirty. Plenty of time.

He fished in her shower, found a razor, and shaved his face as clean as the dull blade would allow. Patted his skin dry with a towel. Face powder, lots of face powder. A touch of reddish stuff he found in her third drawer that he thought might be rouge or perhaps blush. He examined himself in the mirror.

More. More makeup.

Five minutes later, he pulled on the blond wig and stood back for a view. His image was actually quite frightening, with all the hair and the red lipstick. He looked like a stick of celery with blond leaves. But apart from the heavy eyebrows, there wasn't a hint of man on him. The heavy eyebrows and the square jaw. And the shoes.

On the other hand, he imagined he might look quite sexy to someone who didn't know. He would kick off his shoes before entering and walk light on his feet. In the dim light, he would easily pass for a city inspector. He cleared his throat and tried out a fitting voice.

"Hello?" Too low. Sounded nothing like a lime-green celery stick.

He tried again, leaning on his falsetto. "Hello. My name is Wanda."

A door slammed. She was home early!

For one eternal second, Stephen froze. The bathroom drawers were open, his clothes were in a pile behind him, the fallen shelf and its broken plate lay scattered to his left. He tore himself from terror's grip and flew about the room, scrambling to hide his tracks. The broken plate went in the laundry hamper; the fallen shelf went under the sink with a little brass elephant that had plunged with it; the lipstick went back in the third drawer down. Or was it the second?

No time. He scooped up his clothes and ran for the bedroom, slapping off the lights as he passed. He evaluated the bedroom window. Short of burning holes in garage doors, diving out windows was one of the best ways to enter and leave other people's buildings unawares.

Unless they were covered with wrought iron.

So Stephen did what any man in his situation would do: he dropped to his hands beside the bed and rolled under the mattress in one smooth motion. Immediately, two problems presented themselves. One, his feet were sticking out of the bottom. This he remedied with an instinctive jerk/curl. His left knee slammed into the box spring, bumping the whole bed a few inches into the air. He reacted to the sharp pain up his leg by dropping his knee. The box spring *thumped* softly back to the frame.

The second problem he saw while the bed was momentarily elevated: he'd dropped his clothes upon rolling under the bed. They sat in a mound just beyond the bed skirt. He snatched them into darkness not a moment too soon.

The lights popped on. "Hello?"

Stephen held his breath in the stillness, but his heart was echoing down here.

Apparently satisfied, Marjorie hummed a few notes and walked into the bathroom. He couldn't see her, which meant she couldn't see him. He should slip out now.

Stephen began to execute his turn, but Marjorie walked back into the bedroom, still humming. At least she hadn't discovered the evidence in the hamper. Or, for that matter, the shelf missing from her wall.

She tossed something on the bed and headed back for the bathroom. Stephen waited a few seconds and resumed his turn toward the foot of the bed, where he would roll/spring/run stealthily from the bedroom.

But Marjorie, who'd graduated from humming to opera, came back before he could get even halfway around. She sat heavily on the edge of the bed, opera voice now gaining volume.

Stephen knew that beds with poor frames and cheap springs bowed under weight, but he had an awful premonition that *bow* would be far too gracious a term to describe—

Marjorie catapulted herself into the air and slammed into the bed with a shrill, high-pitched vibrato. The mattress pounded into his chest, and he grunted. Her virtuoso halted abruptly. After a few moments of silence, she humphed, shifted her weight for comfort, and turned off the light.

Turned off the light? It was what—seven thirty? Who went to bed at seven thirty? This was not good. A celery stick with blond leaves pinned in the darkness under the body of a woman who went to bed before the sun did.

Stephen considered his predicament. Not even Gerik with all his talk of obsession would approve of this.

Did I say go stark-raving mad? he would ask the jury. *No, I said we were created to obsess. Not to don women's clothing and crawl under strangers' beds.*

Stephen waited ten minutes before a soft snore put him at ease. He put both palms flat on the springs and carefully pushed up. Like a bench press. How much? Felt like two hundred if it was an ounce. Dead, heavy, sagging weight that—

Marjorie rolled over, and Stephen slid three inches to his right, masked by the motion. That was it! Move when she moved.

He waited a minute and then pushed up again. She lay like a log, so he pushed harder. She shifted, and he slid another inch or two. It was working. Five pushes later, he was free.

Stephen tucked his own clothes under one arm and crawled from the room on his remaining limbs like a thieving monkey.

The moment he stepped on the porch, he regretted his decision to park the car a block down. There were streetlights out here! He would be strutting his stuff down the sidewalk, exposed for the whole neighborhood to see. On the other hand, it would be an opportunity to practice. He needed a crash course on walking confidently, like a woman. This was nothing less than an unexpected gift.

Stephen headed out to the sidewalk. He tried several gaits and decided the short-step one, with cocked arms and a limp wrist, did the trick as well as any.

A whistle cut through the air. He jumped. A man leaned against the streetlight across the road, staring at him. Her. Stephen hurried for the Vega.

By the time he slid behind the wheel, Stephen was feeling quite buoyant. He was on a roll. His plan was going to work; he had a feeling about this. The dashboard clock read a quarter of eight—a bit late for a city inspector, but time wasn't something he had to play with.

22

HE MADE TWO STOPS ON HIS WAY TO THE APARTMENT AND ARRIVED at eight thirty, later than expected, but he had the angle covered.

Stephen grabbed a black leather doctor's bag, took a deep breath, adjusted his wig in the rearview mirror, and stepped out. From here on out, it was purely professional. Confident. Purposeful. He turned and strutted up the sidewalk, up the steps to the porch, and pushed the doorbell.

He cleared his throat and tested the voice he'd used for the duration of the ride. Sounded thoroughly male, but with a good half hour's practice he managed to capture a decidedly female quality.

He quickly reached into the bag, withdrew a round plastic lemon, and squirted a shot of juice into his mouth. He'd bought the lemon juice with his other supplies, thinking it might help his voice.

Chains rattled. Startled, he tossed the lemon over the rail and did his best to ignore the waves of heat washing over his skull. From now on, he was a her. Remember that. Her, her, her.

The door parted a crack; the one called Claude stood in the gap. "Yes?"

"Alicia Ferguson with the city," Stephen said in his practiced falsetto. "I'm here for the pest inspection."

Claude's eyes swept down his body. Her body. They stopped at her shoes. Stephen glanced down. He'd forgotten to take them off. They looked absurd, sticking out all black and gangly.

"Feet kill me on this job," Stephen said. "I can't afford to care about fashion."

"It's night," Claude said. "I was told nothing about an inspection. We can't accept any visitors at this hour."

"I'm afraid you don't have a choice; 5031CBB isn't something we debate. I'll need to come in and run a few tests, and then I'll be out of your hair."

Five minutes alone in the basement was all he needed.

"We were told nothing of this."

"Doesn't surprise me," Stephen said. "I spend half the day explaining myself to owners, which is one reason I'm so late today." He pulled a sheaf of paperwork from the bag. "Had a guy on Thirty-fourth who made me call the authorities in. Set me back two hours." He flipped open the pages. "Here it is, city ordinance 5031CBB. *The city shall at its election inspect any building suspected for pest contamination within seven days of the sale of such property.* It goes on, but that's the gist of it. Ten, fifteen minutes is all I should need."

Claude eyed the paperwork suspiciously and pulled a walkie-talkie off his hip. He spoke to someone in German. A dog barked in the garage. Two dogs.

Claude lowered his radio. "I'm sorry. You can't enter at this time. Come back on Monday."

"I don't think you're hearing me, sir. I will inspect the building now. If you refuse me, I will be back with the police and several colleagues."

"It's after eight o'clock. Why are you working so late?"

"I thought I told you why. I had another stubborn foreigner who forced me to call in the police. I don't have a choice on this; they give me ten properties, I have to finish ten properties. Any less and it affects my bonus, and I'm not about to let you cost me any money." Claude just stared and Stephen wondered if he'd heard. He spread his hands, careful to appear as delicate as possible. "Fine. I'll be back in a few minutes with the LAPD."

He turned to go. Claude spoke quickly into the radio. A static-filled response came back.

"Where do you need to run your tests?" Claude demanded.

"Five basic pest groups," Stephen said. "I'll have to take a look."

Another quick exchange on the radio.

Claude pushed the door open. "Please be quick. We will be leaving soon."

"Is that so? Don't wait on my account. Go ahead and leave—I'll be happy to lock up."

"Just hurry your tests. Please."

Stephen stepped in and looked around the huge garage. Two large dobermans growled at him from a spot halfway across the room, where they'd been tethered to a metal pole.

To the right, the stairs.

"Okay, why don't you leave me to run a few tests," he said. "Say, fifteen minutes?"

"I would rather watch."

"Well, I would rather be home in bed, off these poor feet. I'll tell you what, Claude, why don't you sit down here and let me do what they pay me—"

"How do you know my name?"

Stephen blinked. "You are Claude, aren't you? Associate to a Mr. Roth Braun, I think the paperwork said."

Claude hesitated. "Yes."

"Well, Claude, if you don't mind, I'd rather do what I do without you breathing over my shoulders. Now, where are there pipes in this rats' nest?"

"Everywhere—"

"Does this thing have a basement?"

"Yes."

"Then I suppose I'll start there. How do I get down?"

Claude motioned at the staircase.

Stephen gripped his bag and walked without further hesitation. Any luck, and Claude would stay put. No further hints necessary.

He reached the door and stepped into the stairwell. No Claude. A tremble coursed through him. He was going to make it! Just stay here, big boy. He ran down to the first landing. Just stay—

The door pushed open; Claude stood above him. Stephen felt his heart drop to his heels. If he'd had a gun, he might have pulled it and winged the guy then.

"Don't you have something better to do?"

Claude descended the stairs without responding.

"Fine," Stephen said, turning back up the stairs. He wasn't about to lead the man anywhere near the safe. He'd have to regroup above.

He mounted the steps and walked up briskly, mind racing. This wasn't the plan. "If you're going to insist on badgering me, I'll come back tomorrow with more help. This is absolutely ridiculous. I have to say, I've never . . ."

Cool air flooded the crown of his head. His hair suddenly felt liberated.

Stephen jerked around and saw that a few loose hairs from the wig had caught on a splintered wooden beam above. It swung by the strands, six inches from his matted hair.

For a moment they stood in silence, struck by the sight of the blond furry ball swinging in space above Stephen's dark head of hair. Their eyes met.

Stephen threw the bag at Claude, hurled himself up the stairs, and slammed past him while he clutched the bag. The German yelled, stumbled, and came after him. Had Stephen elected to wear the heels, he would be dead now. But he had a head start, and he was dressed in pants. He flew across the garage, a streak of green.

The front door was still open. Stephen crashed through it and fled toward his Vega.

Claude stopped on the porch and yelled something in German, but Stephen could hardly make out the words, much less the meaning.

He threw the car into drive before his door was properly closed and squealed for La Brea. It took him two blocks to fully realize what had just happened.

He'd survived. This was good.

He'd failed. This was bad.

ROTH BRAUN DESCENDED THE STEPS ONE AT A TIME, FEELING destiny and purpose course through his veins like liquid gold. The man had played his cards as expected.

With this latest charade, the Jew had given away more than he had intended: he was after the basement. From the beginning he had been interested in the basement.

It was why he drew attention to the top floor. It was why he'd broken into the garage and then emerged out of thin air from below. It was why he had tried to descend the stairs then reverse course when Claude insisted on following.

The Jew's heart was in the basement.

He stepped into the garage and stared at the dogs. Their eyes shone yellow in the dim light, but they didn't move. They sensed something in him. They perceived his power, like a high-pitched sound inaudible to the human ear.

He *tsked* and was rewarded with their soft whines.

Roth opened the door to the stairwell and walked down, not bothering to turn on the lights.

In the basement he elected to flip the light switch. His breath sounded hollow and welcoming in the concrete chamber. The Jew had been here—he could feel the emotions in the air. Excitement. Fear. Hope.

The scent of the room reminded him of the basement in his father's house at Toruń. Mildew and dirt. Not so different from a grave.

This was an unexpected little treat, wasn't it? Here in America, so far from home, yet home after all.

Roth Braun felt compelled to sing. He shut the door behind him, stared at the gray room with its sealed steel doors and sang the German war anthem. His voice echoed with vibrato and he pumped his fist and sang louder, the whole song, just as he had as a child.

Gratified, he twisted his head, stretched his neck, and walked toward the door directly opposite him.

It was his third time in the boiler room. The other rooms were made of concrete and had no furnishings, so if anything had been hidden in the basement, it would likely be in the utility room. The previous two visits had been cursory, but this time he would look for evidence of the Jew.

The potbellied stove looked undisturbed. No sign of anything that . . .

Roth caught himself. The drum behind it had been moved. He could sense it as much as see it, although a thin line of dust a centimeter from the base confirmed the same.

Roth stepped forward and pulled the drum aside. A steel lid sat in the floor. It had been scraped clean.

A floor safe.

Rage overcame him. The Jew had beat him to it. In this delicate game, Roth had been outmaneuvered. By a Jew.

Just as his father had been.

The feelings that had warmed him while singing the anthem were gone. He tightened his fists and closed his eyes. Control.

Not all was lost, of course. The Jew hadn't been down here on his last unbelievable visit as a city employee. Claude had assured him of that much. Whatever Stephen had found earlier was still here, or he wouldn't have risked so much to come back for it.

Roth bent down, pulled the steel lid to one side and stared into the hole. He withdrew the tin box and stared at the picture of a woman whom he immediately recognized.

Seeing her here, on this box in America, offended him. The fact that they'd managed to smuggle even a picture of her out was an insult to his father. To him.

Roth demonstrated considerable restraint in not tearing the picture from the lid. Instead he pried the cover off with a controlled hand. Inside, a piece of cloth wrapped around Rachel's treasure.

But was it his father's treasure?

He set the tin box down and carefully unwrapped the cloth.

Heat gathered at the top of his skull and rushed down his head, making him momentarily dizzy.

The journal.

No Stones, but that didn't really surprise him. A relic as valuable as the Stones of David would never present itself so easily.

The journal was treasure enough for now. It was true then. She had smuggled the journal out with the Stones. The journal that could incriminate not only Gerhard, but dozens of others. She'd hid it all these years knowing that if Gerhard were executed for crimes, her hope of finding her son would be dashed.

She was a smart one.

Roth lifted the old leather cover and gazed at the contents. Every woman that Gerhard had ever killed was listed, by date of execution. Details of the ritual and a small smudge of their blood by each name.

With the journal was a letter. The letter told the rest of the story. Rachel's story.

Roth sank to his knees and began to weep with gratitude. There was so much hope here. So much fear and desperation and longing. So much power. His resolve to finish what he'd started when he'd bought this building crashed through him like a waterfall.

Gerhard wanted the journal because it threatened his very life. But Roth knew that the journal would call to Stephen. Roth hadn't come to Los Angeles for the Stones, no. Nor the journal.

Roth had come for Stephen.

He spent an hour with the treasure, soaking in its meaning, plotting his next move. This was good. This was very good. It confirmed everything he'd guessed. He was perhaps the most fortunate man alive at this moment. But fortune had little to do with his success. He was here because he had earned his good fate and been patient in the working for it.

Thirty long years.

He set the journal back into the cookie tin as he'd found it, replaced the box in the safe, pulled the lid over the hole, and slid the drum back into place.

Stephen must find the treasure, and he must find it on his own, in a way that elevated his hope to the highest heavens.

He stood to his feet. A celebration was in order.

Roth walked from the basement, determined to find not one, but two women this night.

24

THE BIRTH OF LITTLE ESTHER HAD FILLED MARTHA'S BARRACKS with a surreal hope that lingered against all odds. The rumors of mass gassings at Auschwitz came so regularly now that none of the women doubted them any longer. Hungary had been all but emptied of its Jews, they said, and most of them had vanished into the camp at Auschwitz. Only the strongest were occasionally spared and sometimes sent north, to Stutthof. Martha could hardly bear to think of what had happened to her mother and sister. Part of her insisted that she couldn't afford to think about them—she had to think about one thing only: giving birth to the child within her. Any day now, maybe even tonight. A few days at the most.

Her heart hammered every time she thought about going into labor. Imagine, not one baby in the barracks, but two! Esther and David. Or if she had a baby girl, Esther and Esther. Two stars of hope.

Ruth and Martha hurried from the factory and walked quickly to the barracks, where Rachel had been given charge of the baby today. The commandant had allowed Ruth to stay with Esther for ten days before issuing the order that she return to work.

"She's going to be famished," Ruth said breathlessly. "It's been eight hours since I fed her. He's a beast!"

"Of course he is," Martha said. "But he's been good to you. And Esther is alive." She looked up at a group of women passing the other way. "Half the women in this camp grumble about how you're favored."

"Not in our barracks."

"No, not those who know you, but they all see you walking up to his house every day with Esther. It drives them mad. They think he likes you."

"Then they should try to spend some time with him! He insists I go; what am I supposed to do, slap him in the face? I have Esther to think about now. He hasn't touched me. Do they know that?"

"I've told them. Keep your voice down."

Streams of women crisscrossed the camp, making their way back to their barracks or the bathrooms before the roll call. Here in Toruń, roughly five thousand women, over half of them Jews, clung to the hope that they might be spared, yet they all knew a single order could change everything. The Russians were advancing from the east. If they could just hang on a little longer, surely the nightmare would end. Little Esther had been spared and allowed a new life outside her mother's womb—perhaps they, too, would be spared.

Martha imagined an army advancing over the fields to the east, coming to liberate them. What a day that would be. She and Ruth holding their tiny babies bundled in blankets, being whisked away to begin a new life. They rounded the showers and angled for the barracks where Rachel waited with baby Esther. Fifty yards. Ruth quickened her pace.

"This waiting is making me crazy," Martha said.

Ruth faced Martha, eyes bright. "Oh, Martha, you will be so excited. It's a miracle. You can feel the new life coming from you, and nothing else in the world matters."

Martha laughed. "Except for the pain."

"No, the pain tries to distract you, but the baby is stronger than the pain, Martha! A baby! You're giving birth to a baby, and the whole world stops for that." Ruth touched Martha's belly. "Can't you feel it?"

"Yes. Honestly, I'm terrified."

Ruth took her hand and squeezed it. "I was too. I was so scared that I couldn't breathe right. You were telling me to breathe, and while part of me was thrilled with what was happening, the other part was terrified." She smiled wide, as if her confession had been a secret.

But Martha knew her friend too well. Ruth, the courageous one who spoke the truth with chin held high, needed comfort and assurance as much as any woman in the camp. She was like a little girl in some ways— wise and confident, as long as Martha was by her side to hold her hand.

Ruth began to skip.

"Stop it, Ruth. Do you want to rub salt in their wounds?"

"They could use a touch of salt now and then. The red scarf hasn't touched one of their beds since Esther was born. Don't they see that? They should be grateful for my skipping and all my trips up the hill. Little Esther and I stand between them and that monster. He does like her, you know. It horrifies me to think about it, but that pig is actually fond of my baby."

She hurried the last twenty meters, threw open the door, and ran in with Martha on her heels. "Rachel?"

Ruth pulled up three paces in, and Martha nearly ran her over. Down the aisle between the bunks Rachel faced them, holding the baby in her arms, tears streaming down her cheeks.

"What's wrong?" Ruth ran for her baby. "What did they do?" she demanded.

Something had happened to Esther? Martha felt her heart bolt. She ran after Ruth, who carefully took the bundle from Rachel.

"Is she okay? Please, tell me she's okay."

Rachel's lips were quivering. She still said nothing. Ruth peeled the blanket from her baby's face. The child cried. So she was alive!

"Shh, shh. It's okay now. Mommy's here." Ruth cradled the child and rocked her gently. "What is it, Rachel? She's hungry?"

Rachel didn't respond. Why should she? It was a rhetorical question. Several others entered the barracks behind them.

Ruth pulled her shirt up and let the baby suckle. The child quieted and began to eat noisily. "You see, Rachel? She's fine. What is it?"

Someone gasped behind them. "The scarf!"

Martha looked past Rachel and saw the scarf immediately. The bright red material was draped on a lower bed, six or seven bunks down the aisle.

The first thing Martha thought was that Ruth had been wrong about the commandant.

The second thing was the realization that the red cloth lay terribly close to her own bed.

On her bed.

She blinked, unable to process the meaning. This silk scarf angled across the corner of her bed. This splash of red against the drab gray blanket. There was a mistake, of course. That bunk was her bunk. She was about to give birth to her baby. The commandant had promised it.

The barracks filled with more women. Questions—What is it? What's going on? Why is everyone standing here?—then silence.

Martha stared, still stunned.

Ruth's baby suckled quietly beside her.

"Ruth?" Martha faced her, suddenly very worried. "What . . . ?"

"I'm sorry," Rachel said, weeping. "The guard, he came in and asked me which was Martha's bed. I didn't know; I swear, I didn't know. He put the scarf there and then left." She fell to her knees and gripped Martha's dress. "I'm so sorry, Martha. I'm so sorry."

"Stop it!" Ruth snapped. "Stop your blubbering, Rachel."

Golda pushed through the gathered women. "What's going on?" Then she saw the red scarf and her lips formed a grim line.

All of this ran through Martha's mind: Rachel's weeping, Ruth's anger, Golda's silence. They all meant the same thing.

She would be hanged tonight, before her child was born.

Her legs started to give way, and she reached out to break her fall, but Rachel and Golda both held her up. She wanted to scream, but she was suddenly hyperventilating. The others were silent, and she hated them for it. A breathy moan escaped her lips.

They would come for her at six thirty, in ten minutes. But the baby! No, he couldn't do this! It was inhuman! Why had he placed this cloth on her bed? Didn't he love little David as he loved little Esther?

"Ruth." She touched her belly. "Ruth!" Her voice sounded distant, inhuman. She could see her friend still staring at the scarf, baby cradled in her arms.

"Hold Esther, Rachel," she heard Ruth say.

"Where are you going?"

"To the commandant."

"No!" Golda objected. "You can't just go—"

"He's going to kill her!"

"And if you go, he may kill you as well."

"It's my life!" Ruth yelled.

"Stop it!" Martha cried. Her limbs trembled, but she couldn't bear these women screaming at each other. She sat heavily on the nearest bunk. "Please, don't argue. Ruth, you know you can't go up there. You have to think of Esther."

Ruth stared at her, face flushed. She looked at the scarf then back at Martha. Slowly, she relaxed.

"I know this is a horrible thing," Golda said, "but he's killed dozens of women this way already."

"She's pregnant!" Ruth snapped. "He gave his word!"

"We have to accept it."

Martha knew she was right, but the truth did nothing to temper a sudden urge to claw the woman's eyes from her face. How many pregnant women had the commandant hanged from his gallows? How many within a day of their child's birth?

"No," Ruth said. "We don't have to accept it."

She walked up the aisle, took the scarf in her hands. "He told me once that the woman presented to him wearing the red scarf was the Jews' sacrificial lamb. She would die for the whole camp, to appease his wrath."

What she did next could not have been anticipated by any of them. She walked to her own bed, lay the red cloth across the corner, and smoothed it.

"Now the scarf is on my bed. I will go."

What was she saying? A sliver of hope sliced through Martha's heart. Ruth would make an argument for Martha's life? What if the commandant would listen? There was some hope in that, wasn't there?

"What do you mean, you will go?" Golda asked.

Ruth looked at Martha and then at her own baby. Tears misted her eyes, and she raised her hand to her lips.

Then Martha understood. "No! No, Ruth!"

Her friend wasn't listening. Ruth returned to Rachel, took her child lovingly. Kissed the baby on her forehead and then on her lips, tears dripping on the infant's cheek. She sniffed softly and then swallowed back her tears.

"I love you, dear Esther. I love you so much."

Martha was horrified by this display. She staggered to her feet. "Ruth—"

Ruth put a finger on her lips. "Shh. Listen to me, Martha."

"What are you doing? You can't take the scarf!"

"Listen to me! This is the only—"

"No!" Martha sobbed. She couldn't hear this. The panic she'd felt only a moment ago felt small next to the notion that Ruth would follow through with her plan.

"No, you can't—"

"Listen to me!" Ruth shouted. "They'll be coming soon."

Martha blinked.

"I'm sorry, I don't mean to shout." Tears slipped from Ruth's eyes again. "This is the only way to save both of our babies, Martha."

"He will never allow it."

"Your child will die with you," Ruth cried. "How can we allow that? Your child has as much right to live as I do. Should both of you die so that I can live?"

"Yes! I was chosen, not you."

"And now I choose."

"You don't even know if he will accept your choice."

"He will. I know him. He will, and he will let you live and have your baby." She kissed her infant again, several times, all about the face. "Promise me, Martha. Raise her as your own."

She handed the child to Martha, who took her, fingers numb. "Ruth . . ."

The women stared at the scene, dumbstruck. Not even Golda found the courage to object. Martha didn't know what to say. She didn't want this to be happening any more than she wanted to die herself. She should stop Ruth. Push the baby back into her arms and run up the hill to demand that Braun hang her.

She could do none of these.

For an endless minute, Ruth and Martha stared into each other's eyes. Then Ruth's show of bravery slowly began to fold. Her lips began to curve downward and quiver. Her breathing came quicker and sounded forced. She was trying to be courageous, but she couldn't stand against this terrible onslaught of fear and sorrow on her own.

This was Ruth, the young woman with more courage than the whole camp put together. But this was Ruth, the girl who'd edged her way through the train to find Martha's comfort in a time of loneliness.

Martha gave the baby to Rachel and wrapped her arms around Ruth's shoulders. The younger woman hugged Martha's pregnant belly, buried her face in her neck, and began to sob.

The pain in Martha's heart threatened to tear a hole through her chest. She wanted to die. She had to say something, anything that would stop Ruth from what she was going to do.

Golda's cheeks glistened with tears, and she made no attempt to wipe them away.

"Please, Ruth. Please . . ."

The door banged open. "Get back! What is going on?"

Martha began to panic. "Please, Ruth."

The women parted, and there stood the guard, the same young blond who'd come on several occasions to lead away women. She was accustomed to some emotion, but this scene made her hesitate.

"Whose bed is that?" she demanded, pointing her stick at the red scarf.

"If you have a boy, tell him to marry my Esther," Ruth whispered. She faced the guard and wiped her tears. "That's my bed."

She retrieved the scarf and glided down the hall, past Martha's clinging hands, passed her baby with one last kiss and one last sob, and past the guard, out the door.

Martha slumped to the bed, curled into a ball, and began to cry uncontrollably.

25

THINK, THINK, THINK. HE'D PRACTICALLY THOUGHT HIMSELF TO
death these last five days.

Stephen had returned to the hiding place in Building B two nights
before, stripped off the green pantsuit, donned his old dirty slacks, paced,
and made an important decision.

He would not go home tonight.

He would rent a motel room.

And so he had. An old, flea-infested room seven blocks down on La
Brea. Sunday, he'd made another important decision.

He would not rent a motel room that night.

He would sleep here overlooking Rachel's apartment on the off
chance that the German entourage would vacate the building for a spell.
Monday, he would go home. After he found a way into that basement.
But Monday had come, and he had neither found a way into the basement
nor gone home.

He'd lost his mind to this thing, and he no longer cared.

Braun had made a threat, and Stephen had dared to defy him. For
the first time, he feared for Chaim's life. He couldn't go home. As long as
he stayed out of reach, Braun couldn't hurt him or endanger Chaim.

Besides, Stephen didn't want to go home.

On the other hand, he had to at least let Chaim know that all was
well, even if it wasn't. He'd made a phone call from a booth on La Brea.
The conversation lasted less than a minute.

Where are you? Are you okay? What are you doing?

I'm in a . . . motel. I'm okay. I'm taking a few days to think things through. Are you okay?

Of course I'm okay. When will you be home?

Soon. Don't worry. Please don't worry.

But he knew from Chaim's tone that the rabbi was worried, so he added the warning. *Be careful, Rabbi. Promise you'll be careful.*

Stephen looked around the ten-by-ten living space he'd pulled together while thinking. He'd scavenged wood and some tires from the piles around the room and built up a semblance of walls to cordon off his area. Two walls, each stabilized by nothing more than its own weight, leaned against trusses and angled from the floor to the building's outer wall. A few tires added stability. It was a lean-to of sorts.

Some might think he'd flipped his lid. Sylvia, for example. The rabbi even. But it wasn't madness that drove him. He was no more mad than the rest of God's children, chasing after their rainbows.

See, Stephen, even that sounded a bit mad. Your reasons for not being mad are mad.

In a bohemian kind of way, what he was doing made perfect sense. He was pursuing an idea that really mattered. The safe was his pot at the end of the rainbow. Until some dramatic breakthrough would put his hands on that safe, he would carefully block out any part of the world that took his attention off the goal. Did that sound like madness? Of course not. The greatest achievements in history were accomplished by men willing to do what others were not willing to do.

The antique dealer, Gerik, had said that man was created to obsess. The rabbi had said that the only thing worse than not getting what you desperately want is not desperately wanting anything at all. Well then?

Stephen straightened from his work over the left wall. What was that diatribe the rabbi had once delivered at the breakfast table?

You can have nothing to die for until you first have something to live for. The Holocaust did that for Jews. It revealed the incomparable value of another idea. Life. Love! Love, Stephen. We should be daily ravaged by love. The Nazis hated us. If from this we do not learn to love, we dishonor the lives of six million Jews.

"That's right, Rabbi," he muttered. "So then I will desperately want and I will love. This is my labor of love."

He nudged a two-by-four into place—an extra brace required because the wall swayed every time he touched it—and stood back.

"Lovely," he mumbled.

Another preposterous idea had been brewing over the last twenty-four hours, and with each passing hour its preposterousness faded. The notion that Joel Sparks could be his salvation seemed counterintuitive, given the man's less-than-honorable character. But Stephen was in pursuit of love, not necessarily reason.

Stephen reached into his backpack, carefully pulled out the eight-by-ten photograph of Ruth, and looked into her eyes. In his mind's eye, this woman was Esther. As Gerik had said, the daughter of this woman would today be about the age of her mother in the picture. She would look like her mother, perhaps.

This was Esther. This was the woman he was meant to find. She was an orphan, a true Stone of David, and her picture was in the safe, on top of the tin box that Stephen would soon have.

He had stared at Esther's picture for hours in these last three days.

He was meant for her.

Honestly, he thought he might be falling in love with the woman in this picture. Her daughter, Esther. Chaim would call it infatuation, but Stephen knew the difference.

"You have ruined me," he whispered lovingly, and he kissed the picture lightly.

He stood and looked around. The two haphazardly erected walls bordered the window that overlooked Rachel's apartment. A piece of plywood layered with some insulation made a bed in the left corner. Three cans of beans and two cans of corn stood in a neat pile in the right corner. A crate with a candle, some matches, a spoon, a can opener, and a comb he hadn't yet used sat dead center.

He'd slept on his bed here last night, if *slept* could be broadly defined. *Moaned* and *rolled about* and *stared* at the sagging ceiling might be more accurate word choices. He tried to walk the beach yesterday, figuring a bit of sun and a change of scenery might do him some good. The walk lasted fifteen minutes. He'd fled the crowds in a near panic, desperate to be alone to think things through, as if he hadn't done enough of that.

Think, think, think. The thinking was driving him loopy.

On the bright side, the short exposure to the real world had stimulated his appetite. The idea of going to a restaurant unnerved him, so he made one stop at a grocery store, gathered a handful of necessities, endured the checkout line, and retreated to safety here.

Stephen approached the wall to the left of the window, dropped to his knees, and carefully taped the corners of the photograph to the dry-wall with duct tape. He stepped back, sat cross-legged, rested his elbows on his knees, and stared at the picture.

Was there another woman in the world as beautiful? Was it even physi-cally possible for the world to produce not one, but two women as stun-ning as the woman who gazed at him from this black-and-white photograph? The sweep of her hair; the subtle curve of her jaw; soft, steady eyes. He could swear the photo had been touched up with a skilled brush. No nose could be that perfect, no lips so symmetrical. But he knew that no artist had retouched this photo. This was Ruth, who was Esther, who was perfect.

Stephen closed his eyes and swallowed. Time was running out. He had to make contact with Joel Sparks. Illegal, insane, impossible.

But he had to do this. For Ruth's sake. For his mother's sake.

He opened his eyes and stared at the picture. For Esther's sake.

Stephen grunted and rose quickly to his feet.

─────

GREAT WESTERN Bank was bustling with a late-morning crowd when Stephen walked through its doors just before noon. To say he felt con-spicuous sporting two days' growth of stubble and a rumpled shirt was only half-true. The crowd, not his appearance, was to blame for his anxiety.

The white Converse tennis shoes he'd bought to replace his imprac-tical wing tips stood out like fluorescent bulbs. Maybe he should have

dirtied them a bit. Still, he was doing nothing illegal. He really had no reason to be nervous.

Wait. What if Sweeney and gang returned to the fourth floor and stole
his picture of Ruth? Some vagabond could ransack his shrine and disappear
without a trace. He should have brought the picture with him. Too late.

Stephen made a halfhearted attempt to smooth his shirt and walked
straight for the closest banker's desk. A middle-aged woman with a ball of
blond hair, meticulously shaped by curlers, looked up. A gold nameplate
on her desk read "Nancy Smith." Her eyes scanned him from head to toe.

"May I help you?" she asked, her politeness all but forced.

Stephen slid into a chair, glanced around, and leaned forward. "I
would like to make a withdrawal," he said.

"You need to go to one of the tellers for a withdrawal—"

"No, I need to withdraw a lot of money."

Her face slowly turned white. "I . . . we don't keep money in our
desks."

"Of course not. But you have it in the vault. I need a hundred thousand. Surely you keep that much on hand."

Her eyes shifted with a look of panic. What was her problem? He
knew that banks didn't like to shell out large sums of cash without prior
arrangements, but her reaction was uncalled for. It wasn't like he was
holding her up.

"I'm . . ." She swallowed. "Please . . ."

Understanding came in a flash. "You think I'm trying to rob you?"

Her look was answer enough.

He found it within him to laugh kindly. "Don't be ridiculous," he
said. "I have money in this bank, and I need to withdraw some of it."

"You do?"

"Yes." Her eyes dropped to his shirt, and he pulled the tails to
straighten the wrinkles. "I'm sorry, I . . . I got mugged in the alley, and
the . . . people got my shirt dirty." He felt his face flush, and he grinned.
"Druggies. They'll do anything for a fix these days."

She just looked at him.

"I need a hundred thousand dollars," he said.

"Wait here, please."

She stood and walked toward the manager's office. Stephen hunched down and watched her speak to a balding bank manager. Both looked out at him, and he looked away until he sensed someone approach.

"My name is Bruce Spencer; I'm the bank manager. Can I help you?"

"Do you have cash in your vault?"

The manager grinned. "We're a bank—we always have money."

"Then you can help me. I have an account with your bank—just over eight hundred thousand. I need a hundred thousand in twenties. Can you do that?"

The man's left eye twitched. "That's a lot of money."

True enough. Any normal investor would have put it to work in more aggressive ways than what a bank could offer. But Stephen's rearing on foreign soil had given him this incongruous conservative streak when it came to saving money.

"Which is why I have it in your vault rather than stuffed under my mattress." He pulled out the check he'd prepared and handed it to the man. "If you don't mind, Mr. Spencer, I'm in a bit of a hurry."

Spencer glanced at the check. "Are you in some kind of trouble?"

"Do I look like I'm in some kind of trouble?"

"Frankly, yes."

"There you go, then. I'm in a spot of trouble, and I need some money. Isn't that what money's for?"

"That's a lot of money," Spencer repeated.

"I think we've already established that." He had no reason to treat the manager with condescension, but he was growing impatient.

The manager handed the check to Nancy. "Please verify the funds and get Mr. Friedman his money." Then to Stephen, "This will take a few minutes, I'm sure you understand. Most large withdrawals are arranged in advance."

"I'll wait. No problem. But please don't take all day. I am in a hurry."

Stephen walked out twenty minutes later, sweat leaking down his back, big bag of cash under his right arm. So far so good.

26

JOEL SPARKS WAS A DEVELOPER IN PASADENA KNOWN FOR HIS low-income housing developments. But a closely held rumor suggested that Sparks had more than casual Mafia ties. The possibility had nearly paralyzed Dan Stiller two years earlier, when Stephen had proposed Joel bail them out of their deal gone bad. After all, the Mafia bit was only a rumor, Stephen had insisted. But judging by the way the man carried himself, Stephen thought the rumor might have some credence.

He drove north, nibbling on a nail, knowing that he was about to plunge into very deep waters.

Then again, there was no guarantee the man was even available on this particular Monday afternoon.

Sparks's large white mansion stood against a hill in north Pasadena, surrounded by palms and a sweeping red-brick driveway. Stephen leaned out his window and punched the call button at the main gate.

"Yes?"

"Uh . . . yes, Stephen Friedman here to see Joel Sparks."

The intercom remained silent. He pushed the button again.

"Hello?"

"You have an appointment?"

Not good.

"Uh . . . well, yes. Better, I have business he won't be able to refuse."

The wait was longer this time, but just as Stephen was again reaching for the call button, the gates began to swing inward.

Okay, baby. Calm and collected. He drove up to the house, parked the

Vega, and walked up the steps to the front door. The cash would stay in his trunk for now. One step at a time.

A bodyguard who passed himself off as a butler led Stephen over marble floors to a spacious office. Details registered in his mind but didn't stay—the paintings on the walls, the crystal chandelier, the floor-to-ceiling cases of leather-bound books. Then his attention was consumed by the large man at the sliding glass doors, back to Stephen, phone plastered to his ear.

"Of course, don't I always?"

The butler-bodyguard closed a door behind Stephen, and Joel Sparks turned. His deep-set eyes tried to hide behind pronounced cheekbones. He smiled, but to Stephen it looked more like a grimace. He had nasty written all over him. Amazing he wasn't locked up yet.

Or was Stephen just imagining things?

"Good. I'll call as soon as I hear." He set down the phone. "Well, well. If it isn't the man who sold me that overpriced piece of junk on Wilson." He stepped forward and offered his hand. "How's business these days?"

"Good." Stephen took the hand. "Yeah, good."

"Really? You're driving a Vega and you're dressed like a schmuck. Can't be that good. Have a seat."

Stephen sat on a black leather couch. "Yeah, I know. I didn't have time to change."

"What can I do for you?"

Right to business. Just like any deal. Stephen crossed his legs, then set his foot back down.

"I need a favor."

"You owe me a favor. What makes you think I'm in the mood to give you even more credit?"

"This one will make up for both."

Sparks leaned against his desk. "I'm listening."

"Let's say you left something important in a building, but when you went back to get it, the owners wouldn't let you in."

"And?"

"How would you go about getting it?"

Sparks's plastic smile softened. "I'm not sure I understand. I deal in real estate, not the law. I think you have the wrong party. Come back with a building to sell me at half price, and we'll do business." He reached for a call button on his desk.

"It's worth a lot to me," Stephen said, "this thing that I left behind. Family heirloom that dates back to the war."

Sparks withdrew his hand and studied Stephen for a few long seconds. "Just out of curiosity, how much is it worth to you . . . this heirloom? I may know a good lawyer."

"I'm not sure. A lot of cash."

"How much cash?"

"You tell me."

"Tell you what? You're the one with the heirloom, not me. Lawyers don't come cheap these days."

"Twenty?"

"Twenty thousand."

"Twenty thousand cash."

"Tell you what, I'll mention this to a lawyer I know, and maybe he'll give you a call."

"I need to retrieve the heirloom tonight."

Sparks sighed. "Then I'm afraid I can't help you. Try the yellow pages."

"How about fifty?"

"Exactly what kind of heirloom are we talking about here? You walk into my office looking like you fell off a cliff, offer me fifty thousand dollars in cash to break into a building, and I have to wonder if you're on the wrong side of the law. I don't mess with the law."

"Of course not. I'm just trying to get something that belongs to me without having to go through a lengthy process. I may not look like it now, but I've done quite well for myself these last few years. Some things are more important than money. I'll pay you fifty thousand in cash to distract the owners long enough for me to take what's mine. Totally copacetic. No harm, no foul."

"Paying for something like this could be illegal."

"Why? I'm not stealing anything."

"You have fifty thousand cash?"

"In the car."

Sparks took a deep breath. "Well, God knows I could always use fifty thousand cash, but this is just not something I do."

"It so happens that these guys have guns. They're in an abandoned apartment complex—five of them now, I think. German Mafia types. Considering the circumstances, how about seventy-five thousand?"

"I'm not sure you realize what you're asking."

"I pay you, and I'm the one incriminated in any crime, right? But this isn't even a crime per se. I've got seventy-five thousand dollars in a bag that says you know someone who can help me out."

"What's the heirloom?"

"Some photographs."

Sparks stood and walked toward the sliding glass door that led out to a pool. He stood, hands on hips, doing what mafioso types do best, making a judgment call. Stephen could practically hear his thoughts. *Do I trust this punk with my true identity? Do I let him into the inner circle of the unlawful? Do I tell him that I look like a bat because I am one, feeding at night on the weak and the lonely, like this poor sap?*

Then Stephen thought to himself *I'm already in your circle, mafioso. I've lost my mind and I'm chasing after a rainbow, and I've gone too far to turn back now. Take your best shot, baby.*

"If you double back on me, I will destroy you." Sparks turned around, lips drawn tight. His transformation from aboveboard businessman to underworld criminal was complete. "Do you understand me?"

"Absolutely."

"Something goes wrong—someone gets hurt and you even sneeze— I guarantee, you'll spend your life regretting it."

The sincerity of Sparks's tone sent a chill down Stephen's back. He could hardly have hoped for more. If the man who stood before him now couldn't distract the Germans for a few minutes while Stephen retrieved his treasure, it couldn't be done.

He smiled. "Nothing will go wrong."

"Bring me a hundred thousand and we'll talk."

"A hundred?"

"Not a penny less."

Stephen stood. "Okay. I have it in the car."

———~~~———

TWO DAYS and nothing but one short, cryptic phone call from Stephen. Chaim had taken nineteen messages for Stephen, eight from a desperate Dan Stiller. The rest were from a variety of sources, mostly related to real estate.

The rabbi stood and walked into the kitchen. He decided against a glass of orange juice, breathed a prayer, and headed for the phone.

His initial alarm slowly had been replaced by curiosity. Stephen was no doubt disturbed by the discovery of his mother and her death, but if Chaim was right, this recent strange behavior wasn't connected to remorse. Stephen was after what he believed was his. He was maybe even after the Stones of David, and, apparently, he believed he could get them.

Gerik answered on the third ring.

"Hello, Chaim! So pleased you called."

"Hello, Gerik. Have you heard from Stephen lately?"

"Not since last Friday. He's missing?"

"You saw him Friday?"

Gerik relayed his encounter with Stephen and the photograph without the slightest hint of concern.

"This doesn't worry you?" Chaim asked.

"What? That a young Jew has discovered something worth throwing his life into? Not in the least."

"The something is a *picture*—"

"Hardly, Chaim. That something is a girl named Esther who may or may not have survived the death camps. His passion is for Esther and everything she represents. Grace in the face of horrible suffering. Love. Let him run. Let him redeem her. Let him obsess. God knows, we could use a few hundred thousand more like him."

"Yes, of course, let him obsess. Have you ever considered the dangers of obsession? Just because you love someone doesn't mean you have the right to break the law in their name."

"I don't think Stephen is planning on breaking the law, do you?"

"I truly can't say. But I'm worried. He has a tendency for this, Gerik. He's done it before."

"He's gone after his mother's inheritance before?"

"No. But there's more here. He's a war child, an abandoned orphan, an immigrant without a true home. He compensates for his loneliness with some of his antics. But at times like this, I fear he retreats into isolation, searching for meaning. For belonging. Family. He becomes the lost child again, and he doesn't follow reason."

"Maybe becoming a child again isn't so bad," Gerik said. "He needs time to work through this, Chaim. Let him search for his identity. Let him feel his need to belong to someone. We all might consider the same with God."

Chaim took a deep breath and nodded. "I think he may be after more than his identity. There are the Stones of David."

"If he is so fortunate to have stumbled on information leading to the other Stones, he should go after them. Especially if they are his rightful inheritance."

Chaim didn't necessarily disagree. "Rachel's note mentioned danger. I'm thinking of calling the police."

"The police would put an end to whatever hope Stephen has for finding what he's searching for. Surely you know that."

"The police could save his life."

"How many times have you told me your Christ taught that man should abandon this kingdom for the next?"

"These are Stones, not the kingdom of God. The passionate dedication that Christ requires of his followers can destroy a man if misdirected."

"But this isn't really about the Stones," Gerik said. "It's about love. Isn't the kingdom of God about love?"

"Yes."

"There you go, then."

"I'm still worried."

"Then you don't trust him," Gerik said.

"Exactly. I don't trust him. Passion has a way of making people do stupid things. Especially people like Stephen."

There was kindness in Gerik's laughter. "Yes, passion is dangerous, but it's also a requirement for good living."

"This isn't God he's pursuing, Gerik."

The antique dealer turned somber. "Then help him, Chaim. Be with him to keep him from falling over himself. But don't kill his passion."

Chaim let the man's suggestion settle in. "Maybe."

"Perhaps we should all be so obsessive of love."

Chaim didn't answer.

27

Los Angeles
July 23, 1973
Monday Night

STEPHEN MET FIVE OF SPARKS'S THUGS IN THE ALLEY AT NINE AND led the black-clad men to the fourth floor of Building B as agreed. The leader, Bert, was a burly man with a pitted face who looked as though he'd grown up on a diet of thumbtacks.

The other four were no more congenial. Three had each survived a tour in Vietnam. This pleased Stephen more than he would ever admit. They were his salvation, and he welcomed them with a giddiness he didn't know he was capable of.

"What's this?" Bert asked, motioning to Stephen's makeshift hiding place.

"This place? I don't know. Looks like a . . . hangout. I found it here."

"Someone lives here. What if they come back?"

"No one lives here," Stephen said. "It's been abandoned."

"Doesn't look abandoned to me. Picture on the wall, food cans in the corner. No way." Bert eyed Stephen. "You do this?"

"You take me for an idiot? Why would I do this? Forget it. Doesn't matter anyway. You do your thing, and I watch from here like we planned. If someone comes, it's my problem, not yours."

"I don't like it," one of the others said. "You should wait somewhere else."

"Fine. I'll find another window." He had no intention of doing any such thing. The fact that these thugs were tromping all through his place was annoying enough without them ordering him around in his own home. Who did they think they were?

"Let's get going," he said.

Bert lifted his binoculars and peered across the street. "Top floor's lit, the rest are dark. Looks simple enough. You're sure there's only two dogs?"

"Does it make a difference? You're using a stun grenade—that should knock them all out."

"Everything matters. Joey, you think you could get the gas canister through one of those windows from here?"

Joey eyed the top floor. "Should be easy enough. But a ground-level shot will be just as easy. That puts me in position when we go in."

Bert nodded and lowered the glasses. "Okay, everyone follows the plan. We gas the top floor, knock out the dogs in the garage, and hold the stairwell and the elevator for seven minutes from the all-clear. That means you"—he jabbed a finger at Stephen—"have exactly seven minutes from the time we signal three short flashes to get your butt across the street, into the basement, collect these . . . heirlooms of yours, and get out. Two long flashes, and we abort. Clear? You see two, and we're out of here, no questions, no refunds."

"What if I fall or get delayed somehow? I know we agreed on seven minutes, but—"

"Seven means seven. What you do in those seven minutes is up to you. Any longer and we'll have cops swarming the place, especially if whoever's in there starts firing off unsilenced rounds."

They'd been over this several times already. Their entry would be relatively painless, but there was no telling what the Germans would do if they got off the fourth floor before the gas knocked them out. If one of the neighbors called in gunshots, it would take the nearest precinct seven minutes to show, less if a squad car happened to be nearby—a risk they would have to accept. If a cop did show before the seven minutes were up, they would blow a hole in the back of the garage and vanish into the night. Stephen would be on his own.

That was the plan, and Stephen thought it was stupendous. The way he figured it, three minutes would be all he really needed to drop into the basement, move the barrel, scoop up the tin box, and do his own vanishing act.

"Let's do this," Bert said. He caught Stephen's attention, brought two fingers to his eyes, and then pointed them at the building. "Don't take your eyes off the target."

"Not a chance."

"Seven minutes."

"Seven minutes."

They pounded down the stairs, and Stephen took up his position at the window. He lifted the binoculars and strained to see shapes beyond the drawn curtains. Nothing. If someone pulled back a curtain and saw a man staring at them through binoculars from across the street . . .

He lowered the glasses and edged to his left. A dark shadow crossed the street to the right—that would be Joey with the grenade launcher. Stephen's pulse pounded. He scanned the neighborhood for pedestrians. All clear.

Could this actually work? What if the gas canister from Joey's launcher bounced off the window? No, these guys knew what they were doing. They were in the zone, man. They would crash the party and put Braun out of business.

The other four men broke for the side of the building and slid into the shadows below one of the ground-floor windows. He could hardly believe this was happening. Should've done this three days ago.

The curtains suddenly parted at one of the fourth-floor windows. Stephen jerked back. They'd been spotted!

No, not necessarily. Maybe the Germans had only heard something. Stephen sneaked another peek. A man stood at the window, studying the street. Come on, Joey! Light them up! Do it, do it now!

But Joey was out of sight, and the south side of the building remained dark. The man in the window didn't seem satisfied. Stephen dismissed a sudden temptation to stick his head out the window and direct their attack.

A dull *thump* sounded, followed by a crashing window. Joey had fired. And hit.

The curtain dropped shut. Stephen leaped to the center of the window and strained for a view of the attack. Another crash, this one from ground level. A definite *whump!* Maybe more than definite. Maybe thundering. The stun grenade. The cops were probably already on their way.

Stephen watched five men hoist themselves into the window and disappear. Still no sign of anything from the top floor. Maybe they were all unconscious. Or racing down the stairwell bearing arms.

"Come on," he growled. "Come on!"

"What's up, Groovy?"

Stephen spun. Sweeney and Melissa!

"Lotsa commotion out there tonight," Sweeney said. "You in on it?"

"What are you doing here?" Stephen demanded.

"I asked first."

Stephen whirled back to the window. What had he missed? He had to watch for the flashes! Nothing seemed to be happening.

The bohemians had walked up beside him and peered out. "You looking at anything in particular or just gazing at that missed opportunity over there?" Sweeney asked.

Stephen turned sideways, keeping the building in his peripheral. He could feel sweat snake past his right temple.

"I need some privacy right now."

Melissa looked at his flimsy walls. "You want us to knock before entering, is that it? Come on, dude, let's knock." She led Sweeney out of Stephen's square with a straight face and lifted her fist to knock. "Oops, no door, Groovy. I would knock on the wall, but it might fall if I do."

This could not be happening.

ROTH BRAUN was seated on what was left of Rachel Spritzer's leather sofa when the canister crashed through the dining-room window, rolled to a stop under the table, and hissed white gas.

A sliver of fear immobilized him momentarily before his training took over, returning to him his full power of control.

The Jew had returned. This was good.

He bolted from the couch. "Gas!"

The effects were surprisingly quick—three men seated at the table were on their knees already, gasping for air. Roth was far enough away to escape its initial effects. Surely it wasn't lethal. Or had he misjudged the man?

A dull *thump* shook the floors below them.

Lars ran from the master bedroom, stared at the scene with wide eyes, and stepped aside just in time to avoid Roth's rush.

"A blanket!" Roth said. "Hurry!"

They'd shredded the bed to its springs. Lars grabbed a blanket from the floor and threw it at Roth, who quickly stuffed it into the crack at the bottom of the door.

"It'll seep around the door," Lars said.

"Give me an ax." Braun shoved the closet doors leaning against the wall to the floor. "The stairwell's behind this wall."

Axes were one thing they weren't short on, and they'd already taken the plaster off the bedroom side of the wall. They wouldn't find anything by tearing down the walls—the treasure was in the basement. But Stephen had to believe that he was in a race against time to retrieve the treasure. So Roth would keep up the charade. He would play the game until Stephen found his own way in. There was no point in crushing the Jew's hopes until they had been elevated to a point of fanaticism.

Roth caught the ax with his left hand and broke a two-by-four with his first swing.

"They will be coming up the stairs." He cursed himself for leaving the masks on the third floor and swung again. The ax shattered two timbers this time.

Roth grinned and swung again. This time, the entire wall sagged. Nothing was so satisfying as the game. They were coming to the finish line, neck and neck.

"Come on, Jew!" Roth bellowed, swinging again. "Come on!"

Another three quick chops, and a three-foot portion splintered off and fell out.

Roth dropped the ax, shoved his head into the stairwell, saw a clear path, and crawled out. He dropped to the third-floor landing, followed by Lars. The attackers were still below, waiting for the gas to complete its work. He slammed through the door and ran for a cache of supplies in the first bedroom.

"The ventilation system. Flood the building with tear gas."

Lars tore through a large black duffle bag, yanked out two gas masks, and tossed one to Roth. Gas masks secure, they each grabbed three small canisters. Lars snatched up a rifle.

"Gas first," Roth snapped. He shoved a crowbar at Lars. "Use the return vents." He ran into the hall, turned the thermostat to manual vent, dropped the canisters, and crammed his crowbar under a large return vent above his head. The grill popped off in two attempts. He could hear Lars doing the same in the adjacent hall.

Roth popped the tabs on all three canisters and dropped them into the vent. Perhaps the men below already had gas masks in place, but with any luck they would wait to don the gear until they secured the stairwell. Masks limited field of vision.

It would take no more than a minute for the gas to work its way through the building. Without another word, they collected their weapons and reentered the stairwell.

Roth motioned Lars to cover. The blond German swung his rifle over the rail. "Clear."

So, they were still in the garage? Or was this the work of a lone fool, firing off a canister of gas with the intent to crawl up after half an hour to collect his treasure?

"No killing," he ordered. "Not now."

He descended the stairs to the second-floor landing and covered for Lars. They took up positions on the first landing, weapons trained on the door to the garage. If anyone cracked that door, Roth would put a bullet in his gut.

—*∿*—

THE FIRST *clunk* came while Melissa's hand was still raised, and for a moment Stephen thought she'd stomped her foot to imitate a knocking sound. The noise came again, distant.

All three of them looked out the window together. The sound was hardly more than a knock, but there it came again. Stephen froze. Someone was taking a hammer or an ax to one of the walls in Rachel Spritzer's apartment.

"What's that?" Sweeney asked.

They'd entered his hiding place without knocking again.

"I . . . I don't know." Stephen was desperate. He turned and held up both hands to ward them off. "Please! I have to do something here."

"What's up, man? Something's going down and—"

"Just leave!" Stephen shouted.

They flinched.

He flung his arm toward the door. "Can't you take a hint? Leave!"

"Now you've gone and hurt my feelings, man," Sweeney said. "What gives you the right? And after we extended our hospitality to you?"

"Is that what you call this? Hospitality? You're hurting my feelings by being here. I'm telling you, I have something real important to do, and you can't be here!"

"Then maybe you should apologize," Melissa said, crossing her arms.

Stephen stared at her, mouth open. The whole scene felt surreal. He glanced back at the building. No flashes, right? He would have seen the light from the corner of his eye. Nothing but black on the garage level. What was keeping Bert? They should have given the all-clear by now. He swung back.

"I'm sorry!" He was frantic, and he knew that they knew he was frantic. "Believe me, I'm so sorry."

"For kicking us out of your little shrine here."

"Yes! For kicking you out of—"

"What was that?" Sweeney asked.

Stephen turned back to the window. "What?"

"I thought I just saw some flashes."

"You did? How many?"

"I don't know. Two, I think. Maybe it was three."

"Well, was it two or three?" Stephen demanded.

"I don't know. Lighten up."

Stephen turned on Sweeney. "It was either two or three, it couldn't be both! And they were either long flashes or short flashes. Two long flashes or three short ones. Tell me!" he yelled.

Sweeney stared back, shocked.

"Sorry. I'm sorry for that. Look, I just need to know exactly what you saw. You have no idea how important it is to me."

"That your signal?" Melissa asked. "That's why you're looking over there. You're waiting for a signal from someone inside. You've been holding out on us."

"You're right, I have. And I'm sorry, okay. Just tell me what—"

"I think it was three short," Sweeney said. "But I saw only two."

"Then why is it three?"

"Because the two flashes I saw were short. You said three short or two long right? These were short, so there must have been three. I just saw the last two."

He had seven minutes! He'd already wasted at least one. Stephen bolted for the stairs.

"Hey, someone's climbing out the window down there," Sweeney said.

Stephen slid to a stop. "What?"

"No, two! Check that, make it three . . . five! Five people dressed in black just dived out that window down there."

Stephen ran for the window. Sure enough, Bert and gang were out of the building, along the wall, bent over.

Two long flashes blazed from one of their flashlights.

"What?"

"Are they okay?" Melissa asked.

"What happened?" Stephen asked, disbelieving. "What are they doing?"

The men ran to the east, crouched low. They rounded a building and were gone. Stephen faced the apartment, still not comprehending exactly what had just happened. There had been three short flashes followed by two long flashes. The team had entered, secured, and then been beaten back by Braun somehow.

But how?

It didn't matter how. The fact was, they were gone.

The desperation came quickly, pummeling him like a breaking wave.

He spun from the window, suddenly panicked. He should go anyway! He should run over there, dive through the window, zip into the basement, and grab the tin box! For all he knew, Sparks could have told his men to shut it down before he got in.

But Braun had managed to beat back five trained soldiers. He was either a lot smarter or a lot stronger than Stephen previously assumed.

He slowly lowered himself to the crate. The world faded. Five days of pent-up frustration flooded his chest. It was time to give up. It was time to go home and explain everything to the rabbi. To crawl out of this hole and rediscover the land of the living. Tears blurred his eyes, and he fought to contain himself.

"You okay, man?" Sweeney asked.

No, man, I'm dying here. Can't you see that? Of course I'm okay. I'm a successful Realtor with eight hundred thousand dollars in the bank. Make that seven.

Melissa put her hand on his shoulder. "It's okay, honey. We all have bad days."

He lowered his head and tried to shake off the emotion. The attempt failed miserably. Silence swallowed them for a few minutes.

"Man, you have it bad, don't you?"

Stephen cocked his head to see Sweeney sitting cross-legged in the corner of his hiding place.

"I have what bad?"

"The desires. You've got a case of the desires, and you have it bad. Maybe that's good."

Stephen didn't bother with a response.

"That's what I'm looking for, you know. It's why I left the world behind and took on the bohemian ideals. I don't know what about Rachel Spritzer's place has you like this, but you've given yourself to it. Know what happens when you abandon yourself to something like that?"

"No, tell me."

"It either ruins you or makes you. Drugs, for example. There's something that you give yourself to, and it ruins you. But give yourself to love, and it makes you."

"Whatever."

Sweeney stood. "Come on, Melissa, let's leave Groovy to figure things out. He's got me all inspired again."

"Take care, Stephen," she said. They looked at him from his doorway that wasn't, and he knew that somewhere in his breaking down he'd earned their respect. Somehow, the realization comforted him. His new family was embracing him.

They left, and Stephen curled up on his bed.

"TEAR IT apart!" Roth thundered. "Every wall, every post, every carpet, the whole building, from top to bottom, starting with the third floor. We begin now!"

"It's midnight," Balzer said.

Roth glared at the man.

"We're still recovering," Balzer said.

The gas had rendered them unconscious for an hour before its effects faded. From what they could tell, four or five men had orchestrated the attack and been driven out by the tear gas. One of them had dropped a magazine of 627 rounds in their quick exit, most likely from an M-16. A stun grenade had killed one dog and knocked the other out.

The attackers had used a grenade launcher for the gas canister. Whoever they were, they didn't lack resources.

Roth was pleased with the Jew's efforts. It was critical that he find his own way in. Then, and only then, could Roth make his next move. If Stephen suspected at any point that he was being played for a fool, he would be compromised. He might even quit.

And what if the Jew actually outwitted him as his mother had outwitted Gerhard?

Roth would have to take that risk.

Suddenly angered, he lifted his pistol and shot Balzer through the head.

"Balzer was ill," Roth said. "We don't have time for illness. Is anyone else ill?"

No one challenged him.

"Good. I want this building stripped to the basement in two days."

He faced Lars. "What was the name of the woman at the district attorney's office?"

"Which woman?"

"The friend of the Realtor."

Lars hesitated. "I don't . . . maybe Sylvia. Yes. Sylvia Potok."

"I need her address," Roth said.

28

RUTH'S FIRST MOMENT OF REDEMPTION CAME WHEN SHE STEPPED
through the door to Braun's house on the hill.

She'd been here at least a dozen times, and always she was greeted
with a coy smirk, a look that said, *Aren't you fortunate to be in my presence?* Tonight, the commandant stood by his dinner table, dressed in full
dashing uniform, and his look went from coy to shocked in the space of
two seconds. Ruth took a tiny measure of comfort in his surprise.

The guard shut the door behind her, and she faced Braun with as
much courage as she could muster. Bitterness and fury had marched her
up the hill, but now, looking at him blinking in his silly uniform, she felt
more ill than angry.

"What are you doing here?" he demanded. His eyes shifted to the
red scarf hanging from her arm. "I didn't send for you."

"You sent for a woman who is pregnant. Of course you would. Why
waste a rope on one when you can hang two with the same rope?"

He stared at her, unmoving. "You think this is a joke?"

"Is it?"

Behind him, the table was set with two place settings of Dutch china,
crystal glasses, white serviettes rolled in silver rings, and a single red rose.

Braun walked around the table, fingers dragging lightly on the silk
tablecloth. "I sent for Martha, not you. There has been a mistake. I'll send
a guard—"

"I took the scarf." She said it with her usual confidence, as if her visit
was just another contest of wills. But she knew this one was different.

"You don't have the right." His face darkened. "I sent for Martha."

"You insist on your sacrificial lambs. What kind of sacrifice does an unwilling victim make? I'm here willingly. Or don't you have the courage to match mine?" She walked toward the table and met his eyes. "We'll see who has more courage tonight, a small Jewish girl with a gun to her head, or a big, strapping Nazi thug."

Ruth stepped past the commandant, lifted the lid on the white porcelain dish. Steam rose, scented of chicken and celery with a touch of ginger. She paused, gripped by the incredible sensations that ran through her mind with this single, delightful odor. She hadn't smelled real food in many months, but this . . . this tantalizing scent seemed to spread right through her. And another scent—fresh bread from the kitchen. Fresh, hot, sweet. The back of her tongue tightened and immediately flooded her mouth with saliva. The rose that stood eighteen inches from her eyes was fragrant too. And it seemed redder than the roses she remembered in Slovakia. Such beauty blossoming from a stalk of thorns. The commandant said something, but she didn't hear it.

What was coming over her? All her own words of new birth and hope and passion were now, at this very moment, being tested. In a way, she was coming alive, wasn't she?

But what if it all was just talk? What if there was no true virtue or meaning in this madness of hers?

She swallowed and looked up at the commandant. "Shall we eat? It smells . . . delightful."

He glared at her, but his shock seemed to have lost its edge. "I could have you both shot for this."

"You could have had us both shot months ago. But you're tired of shooting Jews; you told me that yourself. The challenge is gone, remember? So now I give you a new challenge. Accept a sacrifice in the place of another. You may be the only one in the entire war to have done so."

"You're worthless to me like this!"

She wasn't sure what he could mean by that.

"How can you abandon your own child?" he demanded.

"How can you kill Martha's child?"

"She is a Jew!" he shouted.

"So am I!"

To Braun, the war was a game in which he played god. Anything that elevated his status moved him closer to winning. Anything that diminished that status compromised his power. The fact that the Russians were advancing three hundred miles to the east hardly mattered. His game was here, in Toruń, and in Toruń he was winning.

Ruth pulled out the chair she assumed was hers and sat.

"You really believe that I will hang you and let the others live?" Braun demanded. "That's your understanding of how I work?"

She immediately lost her appetite. It was his use of the word "others." He meant Esther and Martha and Martha's child, and she knew that he was fully capable of hanging her and then marching straight over to the barracks to murder Martha and the children. Esther would be most difficult for him, because he regarded himself as Esther's benefactor. She was his proof that he was still human, merciful.

"I expect you to honor the rules of the game," Ruth said. "You may be a murderer, but you still have honor, don't you?" It was a bold-faced lie, but she knew he believed it.

The commandant pulled out his chair, sat, crossed his legs, and studied her carefully. "You never cease to amaze me," he said. "Honestly, I don't understand you. Are you positive that you're Jewish?"

"Yes." Fear began to work its fingers into her mind. He was going along with this. She knew he would, but she expected more of a fight. Maybe a quick gunshot to her head in a fit of anger. The thought of being hanged by a rope—

"Okay, then. Have it your way. But I'll have to kill your daughter. We can't have a baby here without its mother. Maybe I'll send it to Auschwitz in a potato sack."

Ruth was suddenly moving without a clear understanding of what she was doing. She jumped to her feet. The hot porcelain dish with the ginger chicken was in her hands, and then she was hurling it against the back wall. It smashed into the wood with a horrendous crash.

"No!" She knew this wasn't the way to deal with him. For a moment, she'd taken control of the game, but now he'd trumped her. "Don't you dare touch her! Ever!"

He chuckled. Ruth stood, fists shaking at her sides. Her noble sacrifice felt foolish now. She had to control herself. For Esther's sake.

"You have the spirit of twenty men," Braun said. "But you should know by now that you can't tell me what I can or can't do. If I decide to kill your baby, I will. And if I decide she goes to Auschwitz in a potato sack, she goes. Your pathetic sacrifice means nothing."

Ruth sat hard. She took a deep breath and set her hands, palms down, on the table. "I'm sorry. You struck a raw nerve," she said, and then she swallowed to rid her voice of its tremor.

He was smiling, but she noticed that his upper lip was beaded with sweat. "Understandable," he said.

"Thank you."

Think, Ruth. Say what you came to tell him now, before he ends this game.

"But you shouldn't kill my daughter or Martha. In fact, you should honor them. It follows the cleverness of your method here. You extend hope and then dash it. The problem with butchers like Himmler is that they don't extend any hope. They simply take life, and take life, and take life, until the whole mess becomes meaningless. You've said that yourself."

His smile softened. "And?"

"If after my sacrifice you kill Martha or Esther, you will crush the hope of the others completely. They'll know you no longer play by the rules. The scarf will come, and they won't care. You'll become nothing more than yet one more cog in this killing machine."

He regarded her with a long stare. The truth of her words struck her, and she hesitated, but she would say anything now to keep Esther and Martha alive.

"But if you honor them, you will flood the barracks with hope. The next time your scarf settles on one of their beds, they will be crushed. Killing the body is much easier than crushing the spirit."

"All of this at the expense of your own life?" he said.

Her stomach turned. "Yes."

"You really do love them, don't you?"

"Yes."

"I can't guarantee that they will live."

"Then you aren't as powerful as you think you are."

Braun pushed back from the table, stood, gave her a long look, and walked to the window that overlooked the compound. Abandoned to silence once again, she considered what it would feel like to be hanged by the neck. Would the world go black immediately, or would she choke to death? Would her legs jerk?

Dear God, she was abandoning her baby! Her face flushed hot and she suddenly stood. How could she do such a thing to the beautiful, innocent life she'd given birth to only ten days earlier?

No, but there was Martha and Martha's child. If Martha were standing here right now, two lives would be lost for certain. This was the only chance Martha's child had.

Braun turned from the window, face fixed in a frown. "Have it your way, then." He walked to the phone.

"Then make me a promise," Ruth said.

"You've ruined my plans for the evening," he said. "I'm not interested in giving the others hope. I had my heart set on taking Martha's. You're right about the power of hope. Desperation. Desire. I live for it. But you've disturbed me."

"Promise me that you will let them live," she said.

He picked up the field phone and spoke in a soft voice. "Now. Yes, now." He set the phone back in its cradle.

"Promise me." The tears sprang from her eyes before she knew that she was going to cry. The room swam, and she didn't know what to do. Braun watched her, then walked to a dresser and opened a drawer.

Ruth looked away and closed her eyes. She had run out of smart arguments. The guards were coming up the hill. She'd committed herself to death, and she didn't know what to do.

Except cry. She thought that crying now would be okay, because she'd already been strong enough. What did it matter if she died with tears in her eyes? No one would see except for a few guards, who had probably placed bets on how long she would jerk about on the end of the rope. Either way, she would be dead within the hour.

She let the tears stream, but she didn't make a peep. No, that was too much in front of this monster. And she wouldn't beg anymore, no matter how much she wanted to. Braun would not respond well to a begging woman.

"Look at me."

Braun stood three feet from her. In one hand he held a sharp, thin knife. In the other he held a crystal wine glass. He looked like a demon.

"I will do as you request on one condition."

A wedge of hope. She felt suffocated.

"Anything," she said. A sob. "Anything, I swear, anything."

"I will let them live, Ruth. But I need some of your blood. I want you to give me some of your blood. Willingly."

"My blood?"

"Just a small cut on your wrist."

His request made no sense.

"I need it to verify your child's blood line."

Ruth was beyond caring about his reasoning. She believed him. And with her belief came a flood of hope unlike any she'd felt in a very long time.

She stood, trembling from head to foot. He was blurry from her tears, but she held out her arm, wrist up. "Cut me," she said. "Just save my baby. I beg you to save my baby."

He took her hand gently. Rubbed her palm with his finger, fascinated by her skin. It was the first time he had touched her. "I will. I swear I will let your baby live. And I will let you live as well."

Electricity shot through her veins. Could he mean it?

She felt the cold edge of the blade on her wrist.

"I swear you will survive this war."

He jerked the knife. The blade stung. She gasped. The cut was deeper than she had expected.

Braun twisted her wrist and watched the blood dribble into the glass beneath. His eyes were wild and his lips were parted.

Ruth felt a pang of fear.

He dropped her arm and lifted the glass to his nose. Sniffed it like a delicate flower. For a moment she thought he was going to taste it.

Braun looked at her as if suddenly realizing that she was still in the room. They exchanged stares. Then he smiled.

"There is one force in this universe that rules them all," he said. "It is the power behind war and love and life and death. It is hope. Desire. It is passion. It is what enables a mother to give her life for a child. It is what sends man on his search for God. It is what set Lucifer on his ambitious course. It is heaven and it is hell. The desires and affections of man are in the crosshairs."

She was too shocked to move.

"Like Lucifer, I have entered the fray, my dear."

A knock sounded on the door.

He lifted the glass and swirled the blood like a red wine. Then Gerhard Braun lifted the glass to his lips, tilted it back, and drank it to the last drop. When he lowered his arm, his eyes were closed, his breathing ragged, his lips red.

The blood drained from Ruth's head. "You made a promise . . ."

The door opened.

"Which I have no intention of keeping," Braun said. He set the glass on the table. "Hang her. Now."

Boots clumped.

Ruth's throat had frozen shut with horror. They pulled a black bag over her head and quickly bound her arms behind her back. She gave in to their handling completely.

They pushed her forward, down the stairs she'd climbed so many times. Maybe he would let Esther live. Maybe hanging her would be enough for him.

Father, give my baby hope!

She blinked in the pitch darkness and tried to push the picture of the front gate from her mind. The musty cloth pressed into her nostrils. Did they force this same cloth over all of their victims' heads? She imagined the other women who'd taken this walk, how they must have felt all alone in complete darkness, certain only that their lives were about to end. Did they cry? Was it dried tears that she smelled?

Her breathing quickened.

"Step up!"

She stepped up—a chair or a crate. She could feel the rope as they worked it over her head. The adrenaline came in waves, hot to her skin, slicing through her nerves like a million tiny razor blades, each one urging her to run, run away. But there was nowhere to run.

"Dear God in heaven, I beg you to save the children."

Whoever was working on the rope paused for moment, and then cinched it tight.

"Don't let my death be in vain. Save the children." Her voice rose in pitch and in volume. "Give them love and hope."

MARTHA AWOKE before dawn, disorientated in the dark. A baby lay against her belly.

Ruth's baby.

Ruth!

Dread swept through her chest and she moaned. She could look now if she wanted to. She could climb out of bed, sneak over to the window and have a clear view of the gate to Toruń.

But she couldn't.

She lay still for ten minutes before the need to know compelled her to throw off the covers and hurry for the window. She would have to be strong now; the babies depended on her alone. Part of being strong was facing the truth. Knowing. She had to know.

She edged her head into the window slowly.

Then she knew.

The body hung in silence a hundred yards away. There was a black hood over Ruth's head. Her arms and legs hung limply. So innocent and still there across the yard.

Martha clenched her jaw and swallowed the knot in her throat. No more crying. She now had one objective only. Keep the babies alive. Nothing else mattered. Her life mattered only because the children needed her to survive. The war's end mattered only because such an end would set the children free.

The price that had been paid for the child in her womb demanded her unfailing devotion.

Martha stared at Ruth's body and vowed to live so that Ruth's death would not be in vain.

29

Los Angeles
July 24, 1973
Tuesday, Early Morning

STEPHEN DREAMED OF LEECHES CRAWLING THROUGH HIS TOES and woke to find the dog licking his bare feet. Brandy matched his stare, whined, and crept up the bed to nuzzle his neck before lying down beside him.

It was the most touching moment in Stephen's recent memory. The dog had returned. He was loved. The world had not ended, despite his conclusion of several hours past.

He drifted back into an exhausted sleep—three days without a decent nap had worn him onionskin thin. He'd gone up to the giant, he'd fought with all of his strength, and he'd been sent home packing. Goliath had not fallen.

Someone shook him. Goliath was mocking him, egging him on for a fifth round.

"Stephen."

Goliath knew his name.

"Wake up, dude."

Stephen jerked up. "What?" Brandy lay across the room on Melissa's lap. Sweeney sat cross-legged beside his bed.

"What's up?"

"Sorry to wake you from such a blissful sleep, but I have something I think we should talk about."

Stephen sat up, groggy. "What's up?"

"I just told you what's up."

"I mean, what do you want to talk about? What time is it?"

"It's time to face the dragon, baby." Sweeney grinned.

What was this guy talking about? This was the problem with bohemians—they were too idealistic to be useful. Poetry was fine, but you couldn't wear it, eat it, or sleep in it.

He wanted to reach out and slap the man for waking him.

"How much is it worth to you to get into that building?" Sweeney asked.

"What do you mean?"

"I mean, how much would you pay?"

Stephen sat up, suddenly awake. "Could you get in?"

"Maybe. Depends. But let's say I did have a way in. I mean, an absolutely guaranteed way in. What would it be worth to you?"

"Just tell me if you have a way in!"

"You think I'd wake you up from such serenity to toss around esoteric hypotheticals?"

"I doubt it's beyond you."

"See, there you go, hurting my feelings again. Just go with me, baby. Give me a figure."

"Okay. A thousand dollars."

Sweeney looked long and hard. "That's it? This whole thing is only worth a thousand dollars to you?"

"You have a thousand dollars now?" Stephen asked.

"I don't want a thousand dollars now."

"So why are you asking?"

Sweeney waved a hand. "Forget it, man. I don't know how to get into the building anyway."

"What do you mean, you don't have a way in? You just sat there and told me you did!"

"What does it matter—it's hardly worth a thing to you, right? A thousand bucks—please, man."

"Okay, ten thousand," Stephen said.

"I have a way in, you know. I really do." Sweeney grinned. "But I was under the impression that this thing really meant a lot to you. I'm hearing numbers like a thousand and ten thousand, and I'm thinking that I was wrong."

Sweeney wasn't bluffing, was he? He actually might have a way in. Stephen scrambled to his knees. "You get me in there, and I'll pay you whatever you want."

Sweeney looked over at Melissa, who was watching quietly. "Hear that, babe? Now we're getting somewhere. But that's not the way it works, Groovy. I need to know what it's worth to *you*. It's not what I want that matters here. It's how much you want whatever's over there that matters. How much will you pay?"

"Twenty thousand."

Sweeney just stared at him.

"Fifty thousand—if you get me in."

"Not enough."

"For crying out loud, then! How much *is* enough?"

"Your desire's bigger than that, Groovy. I've seen it in your eyes. You would sell your soul for whatever's in that building."

Stephen settled to his haunches and looked at the smiling bohemian. A bright moon hung in the window. The traffic from La Brea hummed faintly, even though the sun wasn't up.

"You're asking me what I'll pay you, not what it's worth," he said.

"They're synonymous. You'll pay whatever it's worth. It's worth what you'll pay for it. What price are you willing to pay for this obsession of yours? That's what I want to know."

Stephen looked up at Ruth's picture. The moon cast a soft hue over her face.

"That's an unfair question."

"So few are really willing to put their money where their mouths are, isn't that the truth? That's what sets the greatest apart. Gandhi. Jesus. They gave their lives. All I'm asking for is money."

Stephen wasn't sure if he wanted to hit the man or cry on his shoulder. He had promised Dan Stiller five hundred thousand. He'd spent a hundred on Sparks. He had two hundred to spare.

"A hundred thousand," he said.

"Not enough. Guaranteed access to the building."

"Two hundred."

Sweeney hesitated. "That's it? You would walk away from here if it cost you more?"

"No! I didn't say that!"

"Then stop messing around!" Sweeney yelled.

His fury startled Stephen. Tears welled in his eyes.

"Put your gut into it, man!"

"Five hundred!" Stephen cried. Dan would have to forgive him.

"Stop it, Sweeney!" Melissa said. "That's enough. You're torturing him!"

"This is exactly what he needs. It's what we all need." He reached out and rubbed Stephen on the shoulder. "You did well, my man. You did well."

The man stood up and walked to the window. "How will you pay me?"

Stephen cleared his throat. "You're serious?"

"As a heart attack."

"How do you want it?"

"Cash?"

"The bank doesn't like to give me cash, but I think I can arrange it."

"Just curious—how much money do you have in the bank?"

"Seven hundred thousand."

"See, that leaves you with two hundred thousand. Minus expenses."

"Expenses?"

"We'll need some equipment. Shouldn't cost more than a few thousand. I want twenty thousand in cash, and the rest in a cashier's check made out to the charity of your choice."

"What?" Stephen rose slowly to his feet.

Sweeney shrugged. "I don't really have use for money. Twenty thousand will keep me for a couple of years, high on the hog."

"Then why—" He looked at Melissa; she was smiling.

"You're paying every dime, my friend. If this is worth five hundred thousand, then someone's gonna pay five hundred thousand, and that someone is you. Let's just say I'm legitimizing your desire. Either you'll pay, or you won't. And there's one more thing. You pay even if you don't find what you're looking for. I get you in, that's all."

"But you have to guarantee me access."

"If I can't get you in, I'll tear up the check."

An image of the floor safe with the tin box sitting inside filled Stephen's mind. "Okay, when do we go? How's this work? Can you show me now?"

"First things first. I need the money."

"No, I don't think you get it. We can't wait! I'll get your money, I swear, but the people over there are after the same thing I am. They're tearing down the walls as we speak. For all I know, they might already have it! We have to move."

"This isn't an overnight thing," Sweeney said, eyebrow cocked.

"How long?"

"Two days. Maybe longer. Depends."

"Two days? Come on!"

"Two days. At least."

Stephen paced. "Then we have to start now. I'll get you a check as soon as the bank opens. I'll bump the amount to forty thousand if you'll show me now."

Sweeney looked at Melissa. "Okay. You can keep the extra dough, but you renege, and I go to the police and expose what you're doing down here."

"I'm not going to renege," Stephen said firmly.

Sweeney's eyes twinkled like an excited child's. "You wanna see?"

"Yes! Yes, I want to see!"

"Come on."

⁓

THEY HURRIED down the three flights of stairs to the ground floor in near darkness. "Wait here," Sweeney instructed. He returned thirty seconds later holding a makeshift torch. "We'll need light down there," he said.

"Down? I have a flashlight in my bag upstairs," Stephen said.

"Too small." He struck a match and set rags ablaze. Flames licked at the cloth and filled the stairwell with dancing light. "Besides, this is much more exciting, don't you think? Come on!"

He flew down the basement stairs, leading a ribbon of oily smoke. "This building was planned in tandem with the other one," Sweeney said, pushing into the basement. "Same basic layout, same foundation, same utilities. If you ask me, they're both trash, but they haven't caved in yet; I guess that's all some people want."

Stephen recalled that Sweeney studied architecture at UCLA. Stephen's blood pressure surged. They'd entered a basement almost identical to Rachel's. He stopped, fixed on one of the doors directly opposite the stairs.

That was the boiler room. The rest of the basement suddenly faded. Sweeney was saying something, but it sounded distant. They were actually in the basement! This was his mother's basement, and that was the boiler room, and in there was the safe!

Stephen tore for the room, slammed into the door, gripped the knob and yanked it open. Dark.

"Hurry!"

"Stephen—"

"Bring the light!" He motioned frantically and stepped in.

Flame light spread into the room from behind. "What is it?" Melissa asked.

Stephen blinked. No drums. The Germans—

"You see something?" Sweeney asked.

"I . . ." The door was missing from the boiler room. The water heater had been ripped out. "Is this the same?" No, of course it wasn't. What was he thinking? This was the boiler room in Building B. A mixture of relief and disappointment washed over him. "Boy. For a moment there I thought this was Rachel's."

He faced Sweeney and Melissa. Brandy trotted into the room, tested the air with a raised nose. All three looked at Stephen.

"It's in the boiler room?" Sweeney asked. "What you want is in the boiler room across the street?"

No use denying what he'd made painfully obvious. "Yeah. I'm sorry, I just kinda flipped out."

"Boy, are you going to love me," Sweeney said with a big smile.

"Why?"

"I said I could get you into the building. What I didn't tell you was that I could get you into the basement."

"You mean just the basement?"

"You'll see. Come on." He turned, walked out, and stopped in the middle of the basement as if undecided where to lead them next.

"By the way, just out of curiosity"—Sweeney faced him—"I know this thing of yours is a closely guarded secret, but so is what I'm about to show you. So first, what exactly are you after over there?"

A compulsion to tell them surprised Stephen. "A box," he said. Surely, anyone who wanted to donate four hundred eighty thousand dollars to a charity wasn't the kind who would steal to feed their greed.

"And what's in the box? Just curious. Are we talking the Ring here? My precious?"

Stephen stared at Sweeney and then at Melissa. He liked them. He liked these two people very much—at this moment, maybe more than he had ever liked anybody his entire life. That was strange, considering the fact that he hardly knew them. The sentiment choked him up a little and he just stared at them, swimming in this fondness.

"You okay?" Melissa asked.

He nodded. "You guys are pretty neat, you know."

She walked over and rubbed his back. "We think you're neat too. That's why we want to help you. We weren't going to ask for money—that was Sweeney's idea." She flashed Sweeney a glare. "He insisted it would make the whole experience more rewarding for you."

"And it will," Sweeney said. "You're feeling it already, aren't you, Groovy? The more you pay for the diamond, the more you love it. I can feel a whole lot of love in this room right now. You understand what I'm saying?"

Stephen nodded. He wanted to hug them both. "To be honest, I don't know for certain what's in the box," he said. "But I'm sure it came from

Nazi Germany, and I know it belongs to a girl named Esther, the daughter of the woman in the picture upstairs. If she's alive."

"Oh, how sweet," Melissa said, rubbing his back again. "You're doing this for love."

"What's in it could be worth a hundred million dollars," Stephen said, but saying it to these two, the detail seemed insignificant. Silly.

Still, the added detail earned him a moment of silence.

"Even so," Melissa said, "you're doing this for love. I can see it in your eyes." She walked over to Sweeney. "All this talk is making my knees weak, baby."

He took her under one arm and kissed her on the lips. "Love, baby. It's all about love."

They looked over at Stephen, smiling like two jack-o'-lanterns. He let out a short sob-laugh, the kind that mothers cry at weddings, the kind of sound he'd once sworn only a woman could make.

"Ready, Groovy? We don't have all night. I'd hate to get caught down there with a burned-out torch."

"I was born ready."

Sweeney winked and walked for a door. They were in a dingy basement in the middle of the night, headed wherever "down there" was, talking gushy and conquering the world. Sweeney was going to march him into the basement, right to the safe.

They entered a room blackened by coal.

Sweeney had said that it would take two days, but that was because he'd wanted the money up front. Without that caveat to hold them up, they would probably have the box by daybreak.

"What's this?" Stephen asked, looking around.

"This is it, man."

Black lumps lay scattered on the floor or stacked in small piles. "The coal room."

Sweeney walked to one end and kicked at the floor. "No. just watch."

Stephen hurried over. "What?"

"Hold this, honey." Sweeney handed the torch to Melissa, dropped to one knee, and yanked on a steel lid. The metal slab slid free with a loud grate and a clang. A two-foot black hole gaped in the floor.

"I give you a drain," Sweeney said proudly, hand extended in majestic presentation.

"A drain?" Stephen looked up. "Where does this lead?"

"Follow me."

Sweeney plopped to his seat, swung his legs into the hole, mounted what Stephen could now see were iron rungs, and climbed down. "You might want to roll up your pants," he called. "It's a bit wet down here." The announcement was followed by a splash.

Stephen stood in dumbfounded stillness. The dog barked, and he flinched.

"It's okay, puppy," Melissa said, rubbing the dog's head. She turned to Stephen and gave the light to him. "Hand this to me when I get set."

Stephen handed her the torch when she was halfway in and stared down at the glowing hole. There was definitely water in there.

"Come on, dude! We don't have all night."

He thought about rolling up his pants, but neither of them had, so he crawled in after them. Brandy stuck her head into the drain and whined, but she made no attempt to take the plunge.

"Hold on, girl; we'll be back."

Stephen lowered himself gingerly into the sewer drain and turned to face Sweeney and Melissa. The concrete tunnel ran past them into darkness—round, about six feet in diameter. Brown slime covered the walls. He looked down at his feet, but they weren't visible in the murky water. Or whatever it was.

"Don't worry, the city has upgraded," Sweeney said. "This drain isn't in use. They moved the street twenty years ago when they rezoned the neighborhood to accommodate the hordes of people who wanted to live by the sea in bliss. Part of the drain was rerouted, but this section was just cut off. This manhole is the only service entrance. Code. You can't have a drain that's inaccessible, even if it's out of use. A piece of bureaucratic brilliance hard at work."

"How do you know all this? This is the only entrance?"

"I designed two buildings to replace these two as part of an assignment for a design class. So you see, this building has sentimental value to me. I'm not here by accident. I chose it."

"But there's only one manhole?"

"It's all that's left of the old sewer system. Come on, let me show you."

Sweeney turned and plowed up the drain, bent slightly to keep the slime out of his hair. Stephen slogged after them. His mind was still suspended between the romance of their moment up on dry ground and the less-appealing sogginess here. There had to be another service entrance that led up into Rachel Spritzer's apartment.

"Ladies and gentlemen, we have arrived." Sweeney spun around and spread his arms.

"Where?" Stephen looked up. Nothing but slime. "What is it?"

"Another drain," Sweeney said, shoving the torch to his left. A round hole no more than eight inches in diameter exited the side of the sewer.

Stephen looked at the hole, glanced back at a smiling Sweeney, and stared at the hole again, hoping this was not Sweeney's answer. His mind fell free of any romantic threads that had kept it in suspension.

"What's this? It's a hole," he said.

"Well said. A hole that leads into the basement of Rachel Spritzer's apartment."

"But it's tiny. I don't see—"

"It's tiny now." Sweeney had not lost his smile. "When we're done with it, it'll be big."

"How?"

Sweeney lifted up his forefinger. "One word, my bohemian understudy. Jackhammer. Or is that two words?"

"Jackhammer."

"Hammer by Jack. Exactly."

"You're telling me that I just shelled out five hundred thousand dollars for you to point out a tiny hole that you expect me to take a jackhammer to?"

Sweeney's smile faded. He lowered his finger. "It's more than a tiny hole. It's the sewer. It's a way into the basement! It's love and passion and the pot at the end of your rainbow."

"It's crazy!" Stephen's voice echoed down the tunnel.

"What did you expect, Groovy? A rocket ride? I said two days."

"No, I didn't expect a rocket ride, although for five hundred thousand maybe I should have. You think we're dealing with idiots up there? You saw how they sent those soldiers packing. The sound of a jackhammer pounding away down here will echo up every drain in the building. Every sink, every toilet, every shower, booming like machine guns. And even if they are deaf, the whole building could fall in on us!"

Sweeney stared at him in silence, smile gone.

"I told you he might not dig it," Melissa said. "No pun intended."

"This can work, man," Sweeney said. "Where's your suck-it-up, I-gotta-have-it-at-any-cost desperation? I *know* these buildings. There's only seven feet of earth and some concrete between us and where that drain takes a turn for the boiler room. That turn is buried in twelve inches of foundation directly below the coal room. I'll admit, there are a few challenges—like the sound thing—but five hundred thousand dollars says that won't stop us."

Stephen ran a hand through his hair and slopped through the muck in a half circle. Maybe he had expected a rocket ride and maybe he was overreacting to the disappointment. He wanted the safe, and he wanted it tonight.

"How do we deal with the sound?"

"Baffles."

"Brilliant. Baffles," he said cynically. "Why don't we tie some earplugs to a rock and throw it through one of their windows? Who wouldn't turn down a free set of earplugs?"

Melissa giggled. Sweeney looked hurt.

"Sorry," Stephen said. "I . . . I just wasn't expecting this." He stared at the hole. Seven feet. He'd never operated a jackhammer, but surely it could cut its way through seven feet in a day, depending on how much concrete they ran into. Maybe they could baffle the drain. Maybe with all their own hammering, the Germans wouldn't hear. And if they did, they might have trouble identifying the source. Or they could be distracted.

The idea began to take root. Imagine breaking in through the bottom of the safe itself. Like breaking into Fort Knox and taking a hundred million dollars' worth of bullion, only this would be legal. At least the taking part would be legal. The breaking-in part could be a problem.

Stephen grunted.

"I'm telling you, Groovy. This is a lot smarter than going in dressed as a woman."

"You know about that?"

Sweeney winked. "You looked marvelous, although I'll admit it was a bit dark and we were a ways down the street. We saw your exit. The Vega gave you away."

"You know my car?"

"Melissa figured that one out."

"Man. You think anyone else saw me?"

"If they did, they couldn't have put it all together. Your secret's safe with us."

Stephen stared at the hole. This idea might actually be the smartest thing he'd tried yet, though that didn't necessarily put it in the brilliant category. He leaned over and peered into the hole. Couldn't see the end.

"Seven feet. Man, wouldn't that be something if we pulled it off. Come up under them like that. Ha!"

"I said I could get you into the building, and I can. That much we definitely will pull off. Whether or not they will be standing over the hole with guns is another issue altogether."

It could work. Stephen stroked the stubble on his chin. It really could. In fact, in its own way, it *was* brilliant. Braun would *never* expect it.

"Okay," Stephen said, turning from the small drain. Nervous anticipation swept through his nerves. "How do we get power down here?"

"Groovy," Sweeney said.

30

Los Angeles
July 24, 1973
Tuesday Afternoon

ELECTRIC JACKHAMMERS DON'T FALL OUT OF THE SKY UPON request. This is what Stephen learned Tuesday morning.

Nor do cashier's checks for four hundred eighty thousand dollars, but the fact that Stephen had the bank make it out to the Los Angeles Museum of the Holocaust seemed to earn him some respect. "I'm having a stellar year," he told them. "I need the tax break this donation will give me." Donating such a large sum to the same museum his mother had selected seemed fitting.

He walked out at nine thirty with thirty thousand in cash—twenty for Sweeney, ten for operating expenses—and the cashier's check, to be sent posthaste to the museum.

The jackhammer, on the other hand, proved more difficult. They weren't available at the local five-and-dime, and the only rental company that had an electric one ready to go was all the way out in Riverside. By the time Stephen finally made it to the shop, rented the beast, and returned home, noon bells were ringing. Half a day and they hadn't even started. Meanwhile, Braun was tearing through the walls next door.

Stephen parked in the alley behind the abandoned building and climbed out. Sweeney approached and threw open the back door.

"You get it?"

"Got it. The manager assured me it would cut through concrete like butter. You get the extension cords?"

"Ready to go, man. Lights blazing, just waiting on you."

Stephen popped the trunk, and they gazed upon the mammoth rig together. Bold black letters that had once read "Sledge Master" were worn thin in some spots and off in others. Streaks of crusted tar ran down one side. The bit looked as though it had eaten one too many nails.

"He said the gas one would be better 'cause it's heavier," Stephen said.

"He doesn't know that we're digging up, not down—carburetor wouldn't work at that angle. Besides, without ventilation, the exhaust would kill us."

"You sure we have enough power?"

"I blew a fuse not three minutes ago testing it. Sparky's live. Let me give you a hand with this."

They hauled the tool out of the trunk, each on one end. "You have any idea how this works?" Sweeney asked, squinting in the noon sun.

"No. Don't you?"

"Seems awful heavy. I can't imagine what the gas one must weigh."

"But you do know how these work, right?"

"What I do know is that we're standing still, and my arms are about to drop off. It vibrates, right?" He chuckled. "Just pulling your leg, man. I could operate this monster in my sleep."

"This isn't funny, Sweeney!" Stephen felt a trickle of desperation leak into his mind. What if it didn't work? He stumbled backward for the door and stepped through. "Just how many times have you worked one of these?"

"Awake or in my sleep?"

Stephen stopped. "You're kidding, right?"

"Relax, dude. How hard can it be? We plug it in and chop away."

The desperation swept in like a wave. "If this doesn't work, I swear I'm going to strangle you."

"Watch the steps."

They struggled down the stairs, into the basement, and into the coal room. Both were sweating steadily by the time they set down the jackhammer.

Melissa scrambled up the ladder and stuck out her head. "You get it? Wow, that thing's huge!"

"Get the rope, honey."

She came back up with a coil of rope, which they tied around the handle. "I'll guide it from below," she said.

"Not a chance. This thing drops, and it'll crush you like a ripe tomato," Sweeney said.

"And we're supposed to dig up with it?" Stephen asked.

"Have faith."

They were doomed.

They managed to lower the jackhammer into the hole and lug it up the tunnel, which Sweeney had strung with several lights while he was gone. Stephen felt his frustration grow with each step. "I swear, Sweeney. There's no way this is going to work. Maybe I should let you do this while I try something else."

"Something else like what?"

"I don't know, but we're running out of time."

"Did I ever tell you I graduated from UCLA with honors?"

"Meaning what?"

"Meaning I'm not an idiot."

They came to the hole, and Stephen looked up at a contraption that hung from the sewer's ceiling.

"What's that?"

"That's my genius at work." They propped the jackhammer against the wall.

Stephen examined Sweeney's creation. The rig was pieced together with ropes, pulleys, and springs, all anchored into the concrete above by three large screws. It looked like a huge spider dangling from a web.

"I'm not a mechanical engineer, but I did take several engineering classes," Sweeney said. "The way I figure it, those three anchor bolts I've secured into the concrete will hold a hundred pounds without a problem. Maybe twice that. But we'll have a lot of vibration, and the last thing we need is for the whole thing to come crashing down with one of us under it."

"Ripe tomato."

"Exactly. The beast will hang on two ropes that pass through these pulleys and then attach to this spring, which will absorb most of the vibration. Presto. In my sleep."

A grin crept across Stephen's face.

"And you doubted me," Sweeney said.

"Okay. Never again. Let's try it."

"First, we try the jackhammer."

The extension cord was strung from the ceiling with the lights. Melissa plugged the jackhammer in and eyed them. "Who goes first?"

"I will," Stephen said, stepping forward. His confidence was making a comeback. He dragged the machine upright and examined the two levers, one right, one left. Seemed simple enough. A single knob switched the power on. This done, he stood the jackhammer at an angle in the water, braced himself, and pulled the right-hand lever.

Nothing.

Panicked, he grabbed the left-hand lever.

An awful scream filled the tunnel, and the jackhammer started to jump. The power was fierce, like a bull desperate to buck its rider. Stephen hung on for dear life. The beast bounced away from him, jerking madly down the slippery floor.

Sweeney was yelling something, but the noise swallowed his words. Didn't matter, Stephen knew what he should do. He should let go. But if he let go, the whole machine might fall down, land in the water, and fry its circuits.

It was quick thinking, not panic, that made Stephen hang on to the jackhammer gone berserk. He slipped and splashed in a scramble to keep up with the apparatus, which continued to race away from him.

It died suddenly, and he nearly over ran it. Shrieking laughter echoed down the tunnel from behind. He spun and saw that the cord had come unplugged.

"Quiet!" he yelled.

Melissa lifted a hand over her mouth. "I'm sorry, it's just . . . my goodness."

"They'll hear us!" Stephen yelled.

Of course, that was ridiculous. They were about to pound a hole up their noses with a machine that screamed like a banshee. A little laughter was nothing.

Stephen suddenly began to cackle. Melissa removed her hand and laughed out loud. Sweeney howled. For a solid minute, they were incapacitated with relentless laughter in the bowels of the earth.

"It works," Stephen finally said.

This sent Melissa off again, so much so that Stephen and Sweeney both eventually suggested she'd laughed enough. What would they do if she had a hernia down here? Call an ambulance?

It took them another twenty minutes to hoist the jackhammer into place and fill the pipe with as much insulation as they could stuff up it. The baffling wouldn't stop noise from traveling through the ground, but at least it wouldn't pound through the pipes.

They still had one major test. The hammer was designed to operate with gravity doing the hard labor, like a sledgehammer. Pound at a rock hard enough and long enough, and it would break down. But with the weight now suspended from the ceiling, and only Stephen's or Sweeney's strength to bear on the hammer, would the device exert enough force to break up the concrete?

"Ready?"

"Go for it," Sweeney said.

Stephen braced his lower body against the wall behind him, leaned into the jackhammer, and pulled the lever. The tunnel filled with that awful scream and the machine pounded furiously. Stephen had to clench his jaw to keep his teeth from clacking.

"Come on, baby!" he grunted.

First a chip. Then a tiny chunk. Then a very small slab dislodged and splashed into the water. Stephen let up on the lever. His ears rang. All three stared at the damage. It wasn't much, but it was something.

"Yeehaa!" Sweeney bellowed. "Am I a genius, or am I a genius?"

"I need earplugs," Stephen said.

Sweeney grabbed some insulation, tore off a piece, and stuffed it into his ears. Thirty seconds later, they all had pink fuzzballs sticking from their ears. Stephen pulled on the gloves Sweeney had purchased with the rest of the supplies, and set himself up again.

"Ready?"

"I am," Stephen said and pulled the lever.

The progress was slow, and he had to swap out with Sweeney every ten minutes to realign his jarred bones, but slowly the jackhammer chipped away a two-foot circle of concrete around the small drainpipe. Melissa periodically went up to the fourth floor to see if the Germans were peering out the windows or putting their ears to the sidewalk, seeking the source of any noise they heard. The afternoon passed without any sign of them.

The first foot took ten minutes—nothing but gravel packing.

The next foot took three hours.

Stephen let off the lever and squatted, exhausted. His sopped shirt clung to his chest. He pulled off the goggles and painter's mask Sweeney had insisted they wear, and looked up at the hole. Maybe fourteen inches. They'd cut through the sewer wall and were into some rock.

"We're not going to make it," he said.

Sweeney looked into the hole. "Sure we are."

"You're the genius; do the math. You said seven feet."

"If I remember right. Could have been nine."

"Seven times three is twenty-one hours of straight digging. I don't think I can last that long. And I doubt the hammer will either. I think it's already slowing down."

"Not a chance. We'll have to start letting it cool down every now and then, but—"

"And there's another problem. You said the last foot would be solid concrete. Even if we get that far, the last bit will be three hours of straight banging on the foundation. The whole building will echo like a gong."

"Not necessarily."

"Necessarily."

"You're way too moody, man. Have I let you down yet? I told you I could get you in, and I intend to."

The likely outcome of his situation suddenly struck Stephen. He was in a drainpipe under an apartment complex, digging his way into the basement to break into a safe. San Quentin was full of people who'd executed far better plans.

"Okay, here's the truth," Sweeney said. "The digging will get much easier as soon as we hit the gravel base. These buildings are set on footers that run deep, but here in the center it's all gravel, designed to give with the earthquakes. Digging through the gravel will be quiet, but you're right about the noise when we hit the concrete. We'll have to set up a distraction."

"A distraction."

"You're repeating me. Once we break through, you nab the box and we immediately fill the hole with quick-setting concrete. No one ever knows we were even in there."

Stephen was surprised by Sweeney's forethought. He stood up. "You can do that with quick-set? How long will it take to dry?"

"Couple hours. Won't matter, we'll scatter coal over it—unless someone sweeps the room within a couple of hours, we're home free." He grinned. "See?"

"They have dogs in the garage."

"I'm not sure the dogs survived your friends."

"Okay." Stephen paced. His body quivered, and he doubted it had anything to do with the jackhammer. "This could really work."

"Of course. That's why we're doing it. Why don't you catch a couple hours of sleep? We may be in there by noon tomorrow, and we're definitely going to need you awake."

"Noon, huh?" He could hardly stand the wait. "Why can't we press through tonight? If the gravel is that easy, we could be in by morning!"

"Maybe, but we can't start beating on their floor in the middle of the night when the whole world's asleep. They'll hear us for sure. We need a distraction."

"You could blast music from the sidewalk. You know, just a couple of hippies playing their music too loud."

"I don't have a stereo."

"I'll buy you one."

"Not loud enough."

"You want louder?"

"You want a ring of guys with guns standing over the hole when we come out?"

Stephen paced again. This one small problem could be a spoiler. Maybe he could call Sparks and ask his boys to create a distraction. Not a chance.

Another idea dropped into his mind, a gift from the God who favored the oppressed. He stopped and turned slowly to Sweeney.

"I've got it."

31

Los Angeles
July 24, 1973
Tuesday Night

T HE BOY WAS CLOSE. STEPHEN WAS VERY CLOSE. THIS MIGHT BE Roth's last night of hunting.

Tonight he would plan a special surprise for Stephen. He'd decided that the friend named Sylvia would be his next victim. She wasn't exactly a blood relative of Stephen's, but she was a Jew and she was a woman.

He'd considered killing the old man and spent two hours watching Chaim Leveler's house earlier that evening. But breaking protocol could adversely affect the cosmic order of power, so he rejected the idea.

Few people understood that the powers of the air were carefully balanced and even the slightest change could upset this perfection. Rituals had to be performed with precision. If you decided to harvest the souls of Jews, but then switched to Russians, for example, you might lose all of the benefit derived from taking Jews.

This was Gerhard's downfall. He'd broken the rules of his own ritual by allowing Martha and the children to live after selecting them with the scarf.

As a result he'd lost all of his power. A single decision made in a moment of weakness had robbed him of power. Now the only way to restore that power was to kill those who should have been killed in the first place. Gerhard would be vindicated. His power restored.

Then Roth could take that power and kill him.

Roth's present indulgences, on the other hand, weren't a matter of precision. He was simply adding to his pleasure. He was showing the powers of the air that he was the kind of vessel that deserved the might they would pour into him when it was all over, in a matter of days now.

Then again, he could use the woman Sylvia as a pawn against the Stephen. Yes, yes, he could do that. Roth smiled, pleased with himself for thinking so broadly about the challenges that lay before him.

He parked the car in the alley behind her apartment complex. He'd killed eight women since coming to Los Angeles. Eight in six nights. He would decide when he saw her whether she would be the ninth. A part of him was tempted to delay killing so that when he took Stephen, his thirst for blood would be ripe.

Another interesting thought.

Roth pulled out another red silk scarf and pressed it to his nose as he always did. Inhaled. He draped it over his neck and tucked it into his shirt. If anyone saw him strolling the alley with a red scarf, they might connect him immediately to the other killings, and the thought excited him.

He wouldn't be caught, naturally. He might have to change his plans for the night, but they would never catch him.

Roth pulled his black gloves on and stepped into the dark alley.

———

SYLVIA HAD spent the evening as she had spent the last three evenings— returning to her apartment late from work, eating a meat loaf TV dinner and talking to Chaim about Stephen and the Red Scarf Killer, as they were calling him, before retiring at about eleven.

Chaim had left five messages and then called her from a hotel. He was nearly frantic about something Stephen had told him about danger. And he'd seen a black car parked down his street, so he'd packed up and moved into a hotel room for the night.

Sylvia's first response was one of alarm. The rabbi was overreacting. Stephen was a grown adult, not a child.

If anyone had something to be concerned about, it was Sylvia, she said. The killer was still selecting only single Jewish women. He'd upped his nightly quotient to two.

"Then you must come, Sylvia! Spend the night here with me."

"In the Howard Johnson's?"

"In another room, of course. I insist."

"Please, Rabbi. You're taking all of this too far. What is the likelihood that I would be selected by a serial killer in a city this size? He's never broken into an apartment. I have neighbors on all sides here. And I lock my doors with dead bolts."

"Then come for my benefit. Maybe I am overreacting, but that doesn't change the fact that I'm frightened."

She'd spoken to him for nearly half an hour, and when she finally hung up she wondered if her refusal to go was insensitive. She peered out of her window, but saw nothing but an empty alley and the glow of distant city lights.

The one-bedroom apartment was silent. Kitchen with breakfast bar to her right. Bedroom to her left. What if the killer had sneaked in before she'd returned home?

After a moment of contemplation, she satisfied the ghosts of concern by checking the lock, the closet, even the cupboards in the kitchen.

No killer. Of course not.

She brushed her teeth, washed off her makeup, slipped into a yellow-and-blue-flowered cotton nightgown, and rolled into bed. Bathroom light, on. Kitchen light, on.

Soon thoughts of an intruder were replaced by thoughts of Chaim, wringing his hands in the Howard Johnson's. She should have gone over, she thought. At least to reassure him.

Sleep came quickly.

The first foreign sound came even more quickly. A scratch from deep inside of Sylvia's dream.

She made nothing of it, though it did wake her momentarily. The glowing clock face by her bed read almost 2:00 a.m. She'd been asleep that long?

She rolled, and pulled in her second pillow. Sleep was one of the most wonderful sensations. Blissful sleep.

The sound again. A creak this time.

In the space of two heartbeats, Sylvia's world changed from sweet dreams of sleep to blood-stopping terror. Her eyes snapped open and she caught her breath.

She could hear nothing but silence.

Don't be ridiculous. You hear a single sound and you jump out of your skin. It's nothing. Nothing . . .

"Hello, Sylvia."

The words were whispered behind her, low, so low that she wasn't absolutely sure she'd heard them.

"If you make even a very small sound, I will bury this knife in your temple. Can you hear me?" Still whispering very low.

This time she could not mistake the words, try as she did. Someone was behind her. Someone who knew her name. Someone who had a knife.

Sylvia could not move. Her heart crashed violently. Repeatedly.

"Are you awake? You're awake. Your breathing's changed."

She could hear his heavy breathing now.

"Turn over. Let me see you."

She couldn't. *Dear God, help me!*

A cold blade touched her cheek. She clenched her eyes tight and suppressed a whimper.

"Now, now, no need to ruin things with your fear. I'm not going to kill you. Not necessarily. Unless you make noise; then I will kill you." He paused. "Roll over."

Slowly, as if rolling through thick tar, she turned.

He stood tall over the bed. A black shirt, white face. Built like a bull-dog with short cropped hair above grinning face.

There was a red scarf around his neck and a large silver knife in his gloved hand.

"Sit up," he said.

She sat up without thinking, because her mind was filled with other thoughts. She was going to die. She knew she was going to die because this was the same serial killer who'd killed eight single Jewish women in six nights.

She was a single Jewish woman and it was the seventh night. She was going to die.

The man stood looking at her for a long time, pleased with himself—or with what he was doing, or with her, she didn't know which—but pleased.

He sat down on a chair he'd brought in from the kitchen. He'd been here that long? Maybe he'd climbed the fire escape and broken the window. But why hadn't she heard him? Maybe the neighbors had heard him and called the police already.

"So, I understand that you are a female friend of Stephen's; is that so?"

Stephen? This man knew about Stephen?

"You may speak now," the killer said. "No yelling or loud noises, but you will answer my questions."

"Stephen?" she whispered.

"Stephen Friedman, yes? The Jew. You know him?" German accent.

"Yes."

"Good. What can you tell me about him?"

This killer, for whom the whole city was looking, was interested in Stephen? Maybe the man wasn't going to kill her.

"Then should I just kill you? If you don't answer me, I'll have no choice."

"He's a friend. He's a Realtor."

"Yes, I know. But what drives him? Is he religious?"

"He's . . . he's Jewish."

"But is he a man of faith? You know the difference, don't you? Does he put his hope in powers beyond him, or is he just another self-motivated fool who can't see beyond the night?"

The room felt cold. *You have to be strong. Think of a way out. Keep him happy. Maybe if you keep him happy, he won't kill you.*

"He's not really a man of Jewish faith," she said.

"Then maybe Christian, like the old man he lives with? Does he realize that the power of life is in the blood? That's why the Christians drink the blood of Christ. The power is always in the blood. It's why

I have to cut my victims. It's why I drink their blood. Do you know this?"

"No." She had to keep him talking. He was absorbed by this train of thought, so she had to let him follow it long enough for her to think of a way out of this madness.

"No, of course not. He isn't easily discouraged; that's good."

Stephen again.

"No."

How did this man know Stephen? A disgruntled client? A Jew-hater certainly. But why?

"Do you want to know why I'm doing it? Why I killed all of those Jews?"

She didn't, but she couldn't bring herself to say no.

"Because it makes me strong. Pure. What most Aryan purists won't tell you is that the Jews have more power than any other race—that's a spiritual matter we don't have time to go into. Hitler's solution was to eradicate them. Not a bad plan, but shortsighted. Better to take their power." He sat slightly hunched over. Unbreaking stare.

"Have you ever tasted another person's blood, Sylvia?"

"No."

"Its flavor changes with the donor's mood. Anguish, Sylvia. The greater the anguish, the sweeter the blood."

His talk made her sick. She'd recovered enough to speak in a reasonably normal voice.

"Why are you telling me all of this?"

"Because it excites me."

"Then you're a sick man," she said.

He chuckled. "You remind me of Ruth. She was a strong woman too. So strong, you Jews." He shuddered. "I'm tempted."

Tempted to kill her. Sylvia said nothing.

"I'm playing him like a mouse, Sylvia. He doesn't know, of course. He thinks that he's outwitting me. That's good; I need him to feel like he's outwitting me. It raises his hopes. But in the end I will finish what my father started."

For a long time he just looked at her. She knew she should be saying something, distracting him, stalling him. Instead she held very still and silently cried for him to leave.

She would alert the police. Stephen. Chaim. The serial killer was sitting in her room.

"What's your name?" she asked.

The killer suddenly stood. "Turn around."

She instinctively pulled her sheets tight.

"Face the wall. Now."

"You promised—"

"And if you don't do exactly as I say, I may change my promise."

She faced the wall away from him.

The sound of cloth flapped behind her. He'd pulled the scarf off of his neck and snapped it open. It whooshed over her head and then smothered her face.

She wanted to tear it free, but resisted the impulse.

His gloved hand pulled the cloth down into her mouth. He tied it tight behind her head. She could breathe through her nostrils, but her mouth was effectively gagged.

"Step off the bed."

She followed his order and stood shaking.

He jerked her arms back and bound them together with string. Then he ripped tape from a roll and strapped her wrists. Her hands felt as if they were in a plaster cast.

"Lie down on your back."

Again she did as he instructed. It took him a minute at most to tie her legs to the bed posts and her neck to the headboard. Another strap of tape went over her mouth.

He wasn't taking any chances of her escaping, but that was good, she kept telling herself. That meant he was going to let her live. She lay still and let him finish his work.

When he was done, he stood beside the bed and looked down at her. The moments stretched in a long vacuous silence. He grinned.

"Forgive me, but I've changed my mind," he said.

Then he reached down and flicked his knife across her left wrist. Pain flashed up her arm.

He'd cut her!

"Good-bye, Jew."

His fist came out of nowhere and crashed into her temple.

The room went dark.

32

Toruń
January 25, 1945
Night

EVEN FROM HER SMALL ROOM IN THE BASEMENT OF THE commandant's quarters, Martha could hear the faint thunder of the Russian artillery to the east. Braun had been beside himself for a week now, taken to muttering from time to time, scurrying from room to room and always to the room down the hall from her own, "the vault," as he called it, which he kept bolted and locked at all times.

Her door was closed now, but he'd stomped past not ten minutes ago, and she hadn't heard him return. He was in his vault. She sat on her bed, staring at the door, willing it to remain closed. Little Esther slept peacefully in a bundle of wool blankets behind her.

His demands had become more absurd as of late. Wash the floor, wash it again, scrub the walls, scrub them again. Scrub them again. He seemed intent on making her life as difficult as possible. She'd given birth four days after Ruth's hanging, and it was a boy after all. She named him David. The barracks had been flooded with hope, perhaps even more than after Esther's birth. See, the commandant wasn't completely evil. He had allowed Martha and Esther and now little David to live because of Ruth's sacrifice.

For five wonderful days, Martha had nursed and coddled the two babies, Esther and David, giving herself completely to the mandate before her. Save the children. At all costs, save the children.

Then a guard came and told her that she was to leave the barracks and be Braun's personal servant. She was to bring Esther. And David? No, not the boy. The boy would stay with Rachel. Bring only Esther.

She'd kissed her son and left in tears, clinging to Esther.

That night, not knowing what the commandant intended for her, Martha had served dinner to Braun and a woman, Emily, whom she recognized from one of the other barracks. Was he going to hang her in Emily's stead? What would happen to her precious David?

The commandant had dismissed Martha at the end of the meal, but she listened with her ear to the door. Emily had squealed with joy, then gasped in horror not two minutes later. What Braun could have said to cause such a reaction, Martha could hardly guess.

The woman's body hung from the gates the next morning. Then, with full view of the body out the picture window, Martha served Braun breakfast while he made his intentions for her utterly clear. She was alive only because of Ruth's sacrifice. She was to care for Esther, but under no circumstances would she be allowed to see her own child, David, even though David would also be allowed to live. He owed this to Ruth.

It was Braun's twisted method of punishment. Of extending hope while maintaining the power and will to withdraw it at any moment. *Please me here, and I will allow your son to live there.*

She'd served him for five months. Or was it six? And no, she was serving Esther, not the commandant. He beat her with his stick on occasion for not cleaning well enough or quickly enough or burning a batch of buns, but otherwise he never touched her.

His footsteps clumped back down the hall. Martha instinctively put her hand on the baby and slowed her breathing. How many nights had she imagined sneaking upstairs to Braun's bedroom and sticking a knife in his throat? If it weren't for the babies, she might have done it.

The door swung open and the commandant stood in the door frame, face drawn, collar unbuttoned and skewed. He stared at her like a man who wanted consolation. She turned her face away.

"We've received orders to evacuate the prisoners," he said.

She looked back and stood, stunned by the news.

"Those who are able to march will be gone in the hour. The weak and the sick will stay."

Why was he telling her this?

"I have been ordered to stay," he said. "You will stay as well."

Her heart hammered. "David?"

"Rachel will stay. So will your son."

If he'd said that David was going, she might have flown at him. The Russians could break through any week and liberate the camp—surely Braun knew his days as a god were numbered. By the haggard look on his face, he did know.

"Follow me," he said and turned for the stairs.

Martha checked Esther, saw that she was still sleeping, and hurried up the stairs after the commandant. He stood at the picture window overlooking the winter-locked camp. Long lines of prisoners filed through the windblown snow toward the front gate. The wind chill had to be well below zero.

"How far are they going?" Martha asked.

Braun sighed. "Seventy kilometers. Let's put it this way: I am extending your life by making you stay."

The women weren't dressed for a one-kilometer march through the snow, much less seventy. They walked proudly, as if to their freedom, but half of them didn't even have coats or proper shoes. Martha doubted that this was Braun's idea, but it would have fitted his methods perfectly. Give them hope, make them think the day of their deliverance had finally arrived, then march them to their deaths.

The door to her old barracks suddenly opened, and out came a troop of women led by Golda. Golda! Martha stepped closer to the window and searched for Rachel's face. She would be the one holding a bundle, her little David. Others whom she recognized followed.

"It would have been easier to send them all to Auschwitz last month," Braun said bitterly. "I told them that. They are too concerned with covering their tracks. Now even Major Hoppe will be leaving. And who stays behind to cover their backsides?"

The last woman spilled from Martha's old barracks—no Rachel.

"It's inhuman," Martha spat. "For such a proud race, don't the Germans even know how to surrender with honor?" Her words surprised her. It was a bold accusation, something Ruth would say.

Braun only shrugged into his coat and opened the door to a blistering wind. The door slammed shut.

Where would they keep the ones who stayed behind? Maybe the commandant would allow her to see David. Maybe even to care for him!

Martha stared, enraged, at the lines of women marching steadily from the camp. But David was still alive. Esther was sleeping peacefully in the basement. They were her concern. For their sakes and for Ruth's, she couldn't allow herself to do anything stupid in her grief over these other women. Grief was useless anyway. Just because she had a warm bed and plenty of food while the rest marched to their deaths didn't mean she had the power to change any of it. She would put what little power she had into protecting the hope of David and Esther.

She turned from the window, ran down the stairs, and was about to enter her room when she noticed that the padlock to Braun's vault lay open.

Open? He never left the lock unlatched! She glanced into her room, saw that the baby hadn't moved, and stood frozen by indecision. Silence filled the house, empty except for her and Esther. Outside, five thousand women blindly marched to their deaths. What kind of courage would it take for her to step into this room and see what the commandant had hidden for so long?

In the distance, a large gun boomed like thunder.

Martha walked quickly to the door, unlatched the lock, and shoved the door open before she could stop herself. The room was dark. If Braun caught her, she would pay a dreadful price.

She found the light switch and eased it up. Twin incandescent bulbs popped to life, baring a sight that made no sense to her at first. She saw the paintings first—a dozen, maybe two—stacked against one wall. Degas, Cézanne, and Renoir—she recognized them from her father's art books. A fortune. Behind her, the house slept on.

She stepped in and glanced around. To her left stood a writing desk with neat stacks of passports, ledgers, a few books, a typewriter, and a quill pen.

The floor was littered with piles of artifacts. A suit of armor that looked very old, with a large shield and sword, the type she imagined a gladiator might wear. There were piles of china and more paintings and spears and several chests. Shelves lined two of the walls, and on the shelves, carefully sorted relics, gold and silver and bronze. An entire wall of Jewish artifacts.

Museum pieces. Spoils of war! Martha clamped her mouth shut and swallowed. Such wealth! Braun had been busy before his assignment to Toruń.

She stepped up to a shelf and lifted a gold candlestick. If she wasn't mistaken, this very piece came from a collection she'd seen in Hungary, although she couldn't remember which. How was that possible? Had he been in Hungary before coming here?

She caught sight of a small, very old mahogany box, perhaps thirty centimeters square, beside the candlestick. She found it familiar but couldn't say why. She set down the candlestick and lifted the lid. Five golden spheres lay embedded in purple velvet. They varied in size and shape, each a few centimeters in diameter, flat like river-washed stones. Each had a five-pointed star stamped on its surface.

Martha's heart nearly seized in her chest. She knew these! They were the Stones of David! Her father had known the collector, who had secured these very stones just before the war—he'd taken Martha to see them several years ago. Pure gold gilded to the five stones David had chosen to slay Goliath, they said. Over the course of history they'd gone missing for hundreds of years at a time.

She reached out and picked one of them up between her thumb and forefinger. This one Stone in her hand was worth many millions of forints, pounds, dollars—take your pick. The entire collection was worth more than her father's entire estate, he'd told her.

What if she were to slip it into her pocket? Not the entire collection, of course, just the one Stone. With all the relics in this room, Braun surely didn't inspect this box often. He might never notice.

She cupped her left hand around her right to steady it. On the other hand, these five Stones could be the most valuable artifacts in the entire collection. For all she knew, Braun inspected them every day.

She set the stone back in its velvet housing, stepped back, and gazed around, pulse throbbing. A treasure trove worth hundreds of millions. She lifted the lid to one of the trunks. Brilliant jewels. Ancient gold coins. How many museums had he raided for these? And how many of these had been confiscated from Jews? She stared at a diamond necklace with large rubies displayed in a glass case. It alone might be worth several million. And the coins?

Martha took a deep breath and let it out slowly. *What do you think you'll do? Pack all of this in a purse, grab the babies, climb over the fence, and hike to the Baltic Sea?*

She closed the box that held the Stones of David.

But one small Stone . . . What if she were to find a way to keep it in Jewish hands? The reward alone could take care of the children for a very long time.

David and Esther were the true Stones of David. Israel. The seed of Abraham. Ironic that one of the most valuable icons in Jewish history should now be in the hands of their enemy.

She was about to turn when she saw a leather book behind the box. She wasn't sure what made her pick it up and open it. It was a journal, and it contained the names of hundreds of women.

Slowly the meaning of this book came to her. What she held in her hands was a trophy of Gerhard Braun's serial killings. She wanted to throw up.

This was a record of his red-scarf game. Only it wasn't a game. It was a ritual, very different from the mass murders at other camps.

Martha replaced the journal, slipped from the vault, set the latch back exactly as she'd found it, and tiptoed to her room.

She decided then that, at the right time, she would take the journal.

And maybe one of the Stones.

Toruń
February 28, 1945
Night

THE WAR WAS COMING TO AN END. YOUNG ROTH BRAUN KNEW
that, even though the radio announcers insisted it wasn't. He knew
it because he'd heard father talking about it. The Russians were coming,
Gerhard said.

Roth had been to Toruń six times since he'd first seen the woman hanging from the gate. If his mother had been more cooperative, he would
have gone at least ten or twelve times, but she insisted that his spending
time at a labor camp, away from her, was too risky. But with bombs falling
on Berlin, her perspective changed.

Each visit had lasted a week. Once ten days, when the supply routes
had been clogged by a bomb. Before each visit, he'd spend a month dreaming of what his days at the camp would be like. There were no other boys.
No games, nothing to do really, except to watch the camp and dream about
what Father did to the women.

There was nothing else in the world he wanted more than to serve the
power, and thereby gain more power.

The Jew servant, Martha, lived in the basement with the baby, Esther,
and Roth was on his third visit when he first began to think about killing
the baby.

He grew more powerful every time Father let him drink the blood
and chant the oaths late at night. Gerhard spoke until dawn about how
many leaders in the Third Reich secretly followed Adolf Hitler in his fas-
cination with the occult. But it was a privileged membership, a secret soci-
ety, reserved for the superior even among Germans.

Roth decided on his third visit that he would be one of those superior people. He could hardly think of anything else. He was bursting at the seams to reveal his plans to his friends in Berlin, despite his promise not to tell.

He finally broke down one afternoon and told Hanz that he drank the blood of Jews when he visited the labor camp where his father was the commandant. Hanz had laughed and Roth had beaten his face with his fist. When his hand began to hurt, he grabbed a rock and pounded the boy until he stopped moving.

That night, after lying awake for two hours, still exhilarated from beating Hanz, he decided he would definitely kill Martha's baby. For one thing, she was just a Jew. For another thing, he was sure that there was more to Gerhard's ritual than drinking blood. His father was actually responsible for killing the women. That was a big part of it.

Every night until he returned to Toruń, Roth tossed and turned, dreaming of how he would sacrifice the baby and drink her blood. The fact that Father had allowed the child to live in his house made no sense to him.

Father had told him how he'd selected Martha and her baby to be hanged, and how Ruth had taken her place. But in Roth's mind, Martha had been chosen to die. If she lived, she would be the only Jew chosen by Gerhard to actually survive.

The only Jew to outwit his father. To take back all the power that he'd harvested all these years. This one woman and her child could be the undoing of his father. And, by extension, of Roth.

He despised Martha. She was a Jew—even without the scarf, why would Father allow her to live? He had a weak spot for the baby, and Roth thought it was because Gerhard had had a weak spot for her mother—Ruth.

By killing the baby, Roth would gain power and save his father from his own weakness.

On his fourth visit, he plotted and watched and waited for the opportunity. If his father learned of his plans, he would probably forbid it, saying that he was too young. If he just did it, he was sure Gerhard would see the wisdom of it and praise him.

The closest he got to killing the baby on that visit was when he sneaked down the hall late one night and peeked into the Jew's room. But the servant was asleep with the baby in her arms—he would never be able to take it without waking her. He'd returned to Berlin determined to rethink his strategy.

Three weeks later he returned to Toruń. Three nights had passed and he couldn't wait any longer. He would either kill the baby tonight or be caught trying. Roth was agitated; Gerhard hadn't brought a woman up to the house for three nights.

At dinner, he asked his father why.

"Tomorrow night," Gerhard said. He'd nearly finished a whole bottle of wine. "You have to learn to pace yourself. Control, boy. Control."

Roth thought about that.

"If I wanted to show some of my power, would you let me?"

His father seemed confused by the question. "How?"

"Why can't I have a servant?"

"Well . . . you can, boy."

"Then I want Martha," he said.

"No, not Martha. She has a debt to pay to me."

"What better way to show her your power than making her obey your son?"

Gerhard laughed. "Well, then, since you asked, Martha can be your servant tomorrow."

"Tonight," Roth said.

"Tonight? What can she do for you tonight?"

"Cut some wood. It's cold, and I would like a fire."

Gerhard seemed amused. "So tonight it is, then! She's in the kitchen; call her out."

"Not now. Later, when she's already settled for the night. That will show who the boss is."

His father grinned. "I can see you will make a very good soldier."

Roth waited two hours. His father had drunk himself into a warm stupor in his bedroom, and the house was quiet. He told Father that he would have his fire now. Gerhard laughed and waved him on.

The stairs creaked as he descended into the basement where Martha had gone to bed for the night. He stopped in front of her room and lifted his fist. Should he knock?

The thrill of what he was about to do shook his body. He knew why, of course. He was feeling the power of true hope. The kind of desire that had made Lucifer denounce God. He had the power of Satan in him because he'd stolen the hope of Father's Jews with him. It really did work, just as Gerhard had said.

He knocked, because it seemed like the right thing to do.

The door opened a few seconds later, and Martha stared at him, dressed in a dirty night dress.

"I am cold, and I want a fire," he said. "Go outside and chop some firewood and build me a fire."

She stared at him, confused.

"You have to obey me. I am your master."

"You're just a boy. It's not very cold. It's already late."

"If you question me, then my father will take your baby away from you. I have his authority now."

She looked too shocked to react, and Roth felt the thrill of his power over her. Martha started to say something but thought better of it. She grabbed the tattered German coat Gerhard had given her, stepped into the hall, and pulled the door closed behind her.

Roth marched up the stairs ahead of her. He didn't want to give her any ideas. It was bad enough that his hands were shaking like leaves in anticipation already. He put them in his pockets, hoping she hadn't noticed. The pocketknife he'd sharpened felt cold against his fingers.

As soon as he heard the back door close, Roth tiptoed back down the stairs. He pushed the door to Martha's room open.

The baby lay on the bed, like a lump of laundry.

He could hear her breathing. He could hear himself breathing. The room was nearly dark. Quiet. Peaceful. In a way he couldn't explain, he felt sorry for the baby.

Standing there in the doorway, Roth was suddenly horrified. Could he really kill a baby? What kind of power did that require, really?

It didn't matter. He'd dreamed of this moment and told himself that he'd probably be scared. But it was the power of Lucifer in him that would overpower the weakness he felt.

Roth stepped toward the bed.

He couldn't hear the sound of wood chopping outside, probably because he was in the basement. But he had to hurry.

He stepped to the bed and pulled the wool cover down. The baby lay on her side, facing the wall, breathing steadily.

Roth pulled out the pocketknife and pried the blade out.

There was great power in this baby's life. Esther and others like her were the hope of the Jews. And as Gerhard said, the greatest power in the universe is hope. Without it, no one could become like God.

Killing the baby was Satan's hope.

Saving the baby was God's hope.

In the end, hope was the fuel that empowered both sides, and right now Lucifer was winning.

This was the war.

But standing over the child, Roth couldn't ignore the fact that his heart was hammering with more than hope. What if she cried out? What if he couldn't cut her skin with the blade? Or what if he became too frightened to actually do it?

Give me strength.

He immediately felt a surge of confidence. Father never should have let the child live in the first place. Gerhard should have killed Ruth and Martha and both of the children. Now Roth would finish the job, or at least this part of the job.

He lifted the baby's small wrist and turned it so that he could cut the veins. A terrible shaking overtook Roth's body. He suddenly felt like throwing up.

But he knew that this was only his weakness. It would pass.

He rested the blade against the baby's wrists and whispered another prayer.

Please give me strength to become like you.

"What are you doing?"

Roth whipped around at the sound of the servant's voice. Martha stood in the doorway, eyes white in the dim light. Roth's heart bolted into his throat.

"What are you doing?" Her voice was higher. Louder.

Roth couldn't move.

Martha saw the knife in his hand. She screamed and flew at him like a ghost. Her voice was so loud, so piercing, that Roth thought she might actually be a ghost.

He jumped to the side at the last moment. Her fist beat on his shoulder, but she turned her attention to the baby and scooped it up in her arms.

Cut them! Cut them both now, while her attention is on the baby!

Roth swung his knife at Martha's head. It stuck her arm, but he couldn't tell if he'd cut her. He had to go for her throat. Or the baby's . . .

"What is this?"

Father loomed in the doorway, scowling. He glanced from Roth, who stood with the knife, ready to strike again, and the Jew, who sheltered the baby.

"What is going on?"

"I'm killing the baby, Father."

Silence filled the room. The Jew began to sob softly.

"Get out of here!"

At first Roth thought that Father was yelling at Martha. Leave the baby for my son to kill and get out of here!

But then he saw that Gerhard was glaring at him. Why was he so angry? And in front of the Jew!

Gerhard stretched his arm toward the stairs behind him. "Get out of here!"

"Father—"

"Now!"

Roth felt himself blush.

"You can't let them live," he said. "If you do, they'll be the only ones who escape you. They have to die. Why can't I kill one?"

"Out!" his father screamed.

Roth stared at him, stunned by the anger. Surely his father understood that they had to die.

"I said *out*," Gerhard snapped.

Roth hurried past his father and ran up the stairs. A pile of wood sat by the stove. Maybe it had already been cut. He walked to the window overlooking the camp and stared into the darkness.

He decided then that he hated his father.

If Martha and her child lived, he would hunt them down and kill them. He had to. They had been sentenced by the scarf.

34

Los Angeles
July 25, 1973
Wednesday Morning

C HAIM WASN'T SURE WHY THE BLACK CAR HAD ALARMED HIM so much. Perhaps because of those three words spoken by Stephen two days ago: *Be careful, Rabbi.*

What if there really was danger? What if someone else was after what Stephen was after? And what if he, Chaim Leveler, was about to be squeezed in the middle?

And what if there was someone in that black car, watching him? Or watching to see if Stephen came home?

He'd called Sylvia at eight in the morning. No answer. He'd called her office. She was likely running late and on her way to work.

It was time to put an end to this craziness. If he couldn't find Stephen himself, he would go to the police.

Chaim approached Rachel Spritzer's old apartment complex, whispering prayers for Stephen's safety. Chaim had no indication that the lad was anywhere near here, but his fixation on the place made perfect sense. It was, after all, his mother's home. And Stephen had found a safe.

He drove from the north, toward the front of the building. A repair crew was working on the corner today. One man with a yellow hard hat wielded a gas-powered jackhammer in an area cordoned off with orange caution signs. What a racket that thing made.

He crept past the house—no sign of life. For all he knew, Stephen was actually in some trouble. Kidnapped, or worse. He couldn't ignore the possibility any longer.

The construction worker looked at him as he passed, smiled, and returned a wave. A bit odd to see that these days.

The building adjacent to Rachel Spritzer's was another abandoned apartment building. Was it remotely possible that Stephen was in there, watching him drive by at this very moment? He'd said that he was in a hotel, but Chaim wouldn't put this past him.

Chaim *humphed* and parked the car by the alley behind the building. He climbed out and headed for a back door on the off chance it was open. Even here, the jackhammer rattled his ears.

The door stood ajar. He stepped in and let his eyes adjust to the dim light.

"Stephen?"

No answer.

"Stephen!"

His voiced bounced around with the jackhammer. A quick look upstairs wouldn't hurt—he'd come this far. He mounted the steps and made his way up through the floors, calling out Stephen's name at each stop.

Last floor. He poked up his head, saw that it was stripped and vacant, and started back down. What was that across the room there? A picture on the wall next to the window. Someone had been here, maybe not so long ago. The window overlooked Rachel's apartment.

Curious, Chaim climbed up and walked across the room. What he saw stopped him. The photograph was of Ruth, the picture Stephen left in his room for a day before breaking in through his window. A bed lay in the corner, and next to it cans of food—half opened, half still sealed. Beans, corn, cranberry sauce. The area was cordoned off with tires and sections of broken wall.

Chaim had found Stephen's . . . place.

"My, my," he muttered. "My, my, my, my. What have you gone and done, my boy?"

What had come over his Stephen? The boy was obsessed with this treasure.

He turned and called out loudly. "Stephen?"

Still no answer. Wherever Stephen was, it looked as though he intended to return. Chaim walked into the space and turned around in a slow circle, imagining what it would be like to sleep here for a few days. Whatever had taken hold of Stephen, he'd lost himself in this thing. And so quickly!

Chaim looked out the window at Rachel's apartment. Was it possible that the Stones of David really were hidden in there?

"Hello?"

He jerked around. A young woman looked at him from the stairs.

"May I help you?"

"Yes, hello. Yes. Do you know Stephen?"

"Stephen?" She was a petite girl, pretty, with bright eyes and dark braided hair heavy with beads. "There's a lot of Stephens around."

He walked out of the square. "I'm looking for a Stephen who is tall. Thin. Dark hair. A Realtor." He pointed back at the shrine. "This is his place. I am his friend."

She glanced at the picture of Ruth. "Is that so? For all I now you're an old kook looking for a scam."

"Really?" He cocked his right eyebrow. "I strike you as an old kook. Funny, but I've never actually been called that before. I just want to talk to him. He lives with me, you see. If I can't find him, I will have to report him missing to the police. They'll want to search this building."

She stared at him evenly, expression now flat.

"Can you at least tell me if he's okay?"

"He's fine. What's your name?"

"Chaim Leveler. Stephen calls me Rabbi, even though I'm not."

"You only want to talk?"

She knew where he was! "Definitely. Just to know that he's safe."

"You swear not to tell anybody about this place?"

"Of course not."

"Swear it."

For the second time in a week, he broke his vow not to swear. "I swear it."

"Follow me. He isn't going to like this."

"THERE IT is again," Lars said. "The sound is different. Faster."

Except for Roth, they all stood with ears pressed against the bared apartment wall, listening intently to the sound of a strange thumping that didn't match the racket outside.

Lars straightened. "He's digging under us."

They'd heard the hum through most of the night, but it was morning before Lars suggested that it might not be traffic. Then the thumping in the street had broken the silence—a lone worker breaking up the side-walk. After an hour, the worker had made no progress, and they knew that something was wrong.

Roth crossed to the window and peered down at the construction worker again. It did make sense—what better way to cover up a jack-hammer underneath the building than to run a second jackhammer on the street.

If so, the Realtor's gall was unprecedented. Roth grinned. *Come to me, Stephen. I've been waiting so long. So very, very long.*

Roth descended the stairs. His men followed. He shoved the basement door open and stepped into the concrete room. A steady thumping echoed softly through the entire structure. He faced the east wall, then the west. It was impossible to pinpoint the source of the sound.

Lars ran his fingers along one wall, listening. "It could be from the street, but I don't think so. It's too loud. I think he's actually planning to break in through the floor."

"Idiot!" Claude said. "He'll come up to a rifle in his mouth."

"No," Roth said. "We can't be sure where he'll come up. Even if we could, he'll drop back down and be gone if he sees us. I want him, and I want him alive."

He walked to the doors lining the basement and opened them one by one. He could feel the vibration run through his feet—stronger on the east side away from the boiler room, if his imagination wasn't playing tricks on him.

The worker on the street was a cover-up. Unless the wrong person happened by, no one would know he wasn't who he seemed to be.

Who would have imagined this, tunneling of all things? Then again, if Roth was in his position, he might have done the same. There must be an old sewer or something below the foundation.

"It is critical that we allow him to enter," he said, turning back. "One man stays in the stairwell—Claude. The rest of you, finish upstairs. The moment he breaks through, key your radio three times. Watch him. Take no other action." Roth frowned and then grunted. "Let the mole dig."

35

"N THERE?" CHAIM SHOUTED. A HORRENDOUS CLAMOR RANG FROM
the hole in the ground.

"It's wet down there, Rabbi. You sure you want to do this?" the girl
asked.

"Stephen's down in that hole? Is he a prisoner?"

She laughed. "I suppose that's a matter of perspective. Come on."

The dog that had come home with Stephen last week braved the
noise to lick his hand. It whined and backed up several steps.

"It's okay, puppy," the girl said. "We're almost done."

The dog retreated out the door, tail between her legs.

The girl lowered herself into the hole and disappeared.

Chaim took a deep breath and swung his legs into the sewer. "My,
my, my. What have you done?"

The tunnel glowed under a string of lights. Muddy water covered his
leather shoes. Chaim covered his ears and waded toward the pounding.

At first all he saw was a rear end and legs protruding from a hole in
the tunnel's wall. The person was operating a jackhammer or something
inside the hole, up at an angle. A strange contraption dangled free from
the ceiling.

The girl slapped the person's backside. The hammering stopped.

Chaim didn't recognize the man who pulled himself out of the hole.
White dust covered a mask and glasses. He looked freshly buttered and
rolled in flour. The man saw Chaim, rubbed the lenses, and then pushed
them to his forehead.

"Rabbi?"

He heard the voice and knew immediately. "Stephen! I didn't recognize you. What on earth are you doing down here?"

Stephen looked at the girl.

"He said he was going to call the police if I didn't bring him down," she said.

Stephen looked back into the hole, stricken.

"You're tunneling up?" Chaim asked.

Stephen didn't answer.

"Isn't this city property you're tearing up?"

"We're going to fix it," Stephen said.

Looking at the boy now, Chaim knew that he could not hope to stop him. He wasn't even sure he should try. In fact, he probably *would* do more service to Stephen if he helped him, as Gerik had suggested.

"That's Rachel Spritzer's basement up there, isn't it?"

"Um . . . yes."

"The Stones of David? They really are inside?"

"Well . . . I think so."

"And the front door is no longer open to you?"

"No."

"My, my, my." Chaim shook his head. "I do love your spirit. Could you get arrested for doing this?"

"I . . . I don't think we will. The new owners don't want anything to do with the police. They're after the Stones too."

"I see."

"How . . . how did you find me?"

"Detective work." Chaim tapped his head. "My powers of deduction. I think to myself, where would Stephen seek love and happiness, and I narrow it down to two possibilities. One, in Sylvia's arms, or two, the sewer under Rachel Spritzer's apartment. I checked with Sylvia, and her arms were empty, so I rushed here."

The girl chuckled. A crooked grin twisted Stephen's mouth.

"How can I help?" Chaim asked.

"You're serious?"

"This is about a girl named Esther, isn't it? Love. And about your inheritance. I'm not sure I can operate that monster, but anything else, you name it."

A thought seemed to flip a light switch behind Stephen's eyes. No longer concerned with any threat presented by Chaim's sudden appearance, he stuck his head in the hole and pulled out a large jackhammer. The handle thumped to the ground, and Melissa helped him lean it against the wall. He grabbed a flashlight and dived back into the hole, all but disappearing this time.

"My name's Melissa," the girl said, hand extended.

"Pleased to know you, Melissa. How deep is the hole?"

"Seven feet, about."

"How far to go?"

"I'm surprised he hasn't broken through yet."

Stephen slid out, ignoring the dirt that encrusted his stomach. "I'm eight inches through the floor. If Sweeney's right, that leaves four inches." His eyes darted around. "The drill. Hand me the drill."

Chaim stood back and watched them. Melissa unhooked a large red drill from the ceiling and handed it to Stephen. "How long is this bit?" the boy asked. "Six inches? That should work, right?" His frantic pace would impair his judgment.

He virtually threw himself back into the hole and wiggled up till only his muddy tennis shoes stuck out. His voice echoed back after a moment.

"What's he saying?" Melissa asked.

Chaim stuck his head in. "What?"

"Plug it in," Stephen said. "Power!"

"He says to plug it in," Chaim told Melissa.

"Oh. Suppose that would help." She switched the jackhammer's cord for the drill's and then swatted his shoe.

"What's he doing?" Chaim asked.

"Playing it safe. Despite the distraction, there's a possibility that whoever's in there has heard us. He's drilling a small hole to check it out before he breaks in."

Stephen's feet suddenly wiggled in farther. For a moment they remained still.

"I think he's in." Melissa looked into the hole. "Stephen?"

He suddenly scrambled backward, as if he'd met a brood of vipers. He piled out and stripped off his glasses.

"We got a problem. They're in the basement!"

"They're inside? How do you know?" Melissa demanded.

Stephen took two splashing steps through the water and wheeled back. "Oh, man. Oh, man, this isn't good."

"How do you know?"

"I heard someone cough, that's how I know. And the light's on. You have to get Sweeney."

"You want him to stop?"

"We have to figure this out." He paced, desperate. Chaim felt his own pulse quicken. "Get him!" Stephen snapped.

Melissa ran down the tunnel and up the ladder.

Stephen flexed his jaw and slowly beat his head against the concrete wall. "They heard us. They're in the basement."

"There has to be something you can do," Chaim said.

"They probably have it already."

"Can I go in? The front door?"

Stephen ignored him. He dived back into the hole, pulled himself way in, lay still for a moment, and then slid back out.

"They're definitely in there."

"I'm sorry—"

"Please." Stephen held up a hand and closed his eyes. "Just let me think."

THEY STOOD in silence, feet planted in six inches of water. Sweeney, Stephen, Melissa, and the rabbi. Stephen clenched his teeth, furious. He fought a terrible urge to run across the street and slam through the front door. Maybe the dogs were dead; maybe he could bluff his way in; maybe he could race down the stairs, grab the box, and lock himself in the coal room while Sweeney finished the digging. Another five minutes of hard hammering would surely crack open the hole.

"We have to get them out of the basement," Sweeney said.

"Smoke 'em out," Melissa said.

Stephen glared at her. "Well, sure, that's just brilliant. We could build a fire down here and let the smoke seep through the little hole I drilled."

"Lighten up."

He lowered his head and kneaded his skull.

"There's got to be a way," Sweeney insisted. "Why don't we burn down the building?" They looked at him. "Strike that."

"You need to get them out of that building, correct?" Chaim asked.

"Yes. At least out of the basement."

"For how long?"

"There's about four inches of concrete, but without any support behind, it's going to crack pretty quickly. Maybe fifteen minutes."

"Plus time to repair the damage?" Chaim pressed.

"Forget that—"

"No, hear him out," Sweeney said. "What's on your mind, old man?"

"Maybe nothing, but it might start you thinking. The city has very specific evacuation policies for fires. If a fire breaks out in any building, they immediately evacuate not only that building, but any building next to it. It's the law. They have to verify safety before allowing the occupants back into their homes."

"So what are you saying?" Sweeney asked. "We start a fire?"

"No, we could never do that. But I know the fire department, and I know that if this building were to catch fire, the city would force the evacuation of all the buildings—"

"That's it!" Stephen said. "That's it! Right?" His eyes were like saucers.

Sweeney smiled. "Actually . . ."

Stephen broke for the manhole.

"Stephen? Where are you going?" the rabbi demanded.

"To start a fire," he yelled. "Come on!"

G ET THE GUNS," ROTH SAID. "EVERYTHING, IN THE CAR. NOW!"
Claude ran for the stairs. Three fire engines had screeched to a halt
in front of the building across the street. Thick black smoke boiled out
of the windows on the upper floor. He could see no flames, only
smoke.

The construction worker had run out to the street, heaved the jackhammer and the signs into the back of a car with the help of an older
man, and then careened around the corner.

Still no sign of a breakthrough in the basement.

"He's burned himself out," Lars said. "The fool stumbled over a gas can
or something—"

"Quiet," Roth snapped.

The game had escalated. It was more than he'd hoped for. The others had no clue what was happening, but they weren't meant to. This was
between him and the Jew.

Naturally there was the possibility of failure, but that was part of the
exhilaration—success was still a hope.

Lucifer's hope.

In reality, the possibility of failure was very small. Roth was far too
powerful. He just had to bring that power to play in a reasoned, methodical way, as he had last night.

He would be out of the country before anyone figured out that he
was connected to the killings. This thought made Roth feel warm.

The streets filled with running people. Firemen quickly strung a hose, yelling at the gathering crowd to stay back. How likely was it that something had caught fire and was forcing the Jew to shut down?

A fist pounded on the front door. "Fire Marshal. Open up!"

Roth took a deep breath and turned from the building. He glanced at the car. Claude slammed the trunk on the last of the equipment they'd retrieved from the third floor and nodded. Roth walked to the door and pulled it open.

A fireman stood in a yellow slicker. "I'm sorry, but you'll have to evacuate this building."

He looked past the fireman and gazed at the fire. "Is everything under control? What happened?"

"We need everyone out. Don't worry, it won't touch this building."

"Then we'll stay here." He began to close the door.

The man leaned forward, barring the door open. "I'm sorry, but you have to leave. City ordinance. No more than half an hour, with any luck. Let's go."

Roth motioned Claude out with a nod. "You won't be entering the building?"

"Just to clear it." The man waited while they filed out. "Anyone else inside?"

"No."

"Wait here." The man ran for the stairwell and disappeared.

"Spread out along the street," Roth ordered his men. "Keep your eyes open. No one enters without my knowing."

The fireman ran out, slammed the door, and stretched a piece of wide yellow tape over to seal it. "This one's clear. Stay back on the street. We'll let you know when it's safe. Unauthorized entry is a crime, understand?"

Roth ignored him and looked at the burning building. Three police cruisers had joined the party. Stephen was up to something.

Think, Roth. Outthink the Jew.

———

"GO, GO!" Sweeney yelled down the manhole. "They're out!"

Stephen turned to the rabbi. "Cut the lights!"

The string of lights went out. He scrambled into the hole, put his full weight into the jackhammer, and squeezed the lever. The machine shook furiously in his hands. Four inches. With any luck, the Germans wouldn't hear the sound now that they had evacuated. Not that it mattered. With a little more luck, the slab he was pounding on would break free along the circle of holes he'd drilled while they waited for the fire trucks to respond.

They were taking three calculated risks, any of which could sink them. The most obvious was the whole arson bit. They'd laid down slabs of old asbestos on the top two floors, piled the slabs with tires, and lit the stacks on fire. Unless the fire department responded slowly, the smoldering tires would be extinguished and the building cleared in short order, though hopefully not too short. The stunt might cost them a slap on the wrist, but they already had their story in place. Sweeney wanted to see how much smoke tires made. He'd taken precautions. If there was a law against burning tires, he was totally unaware of it.

The second risk was possibly being discovered by the fire marshal down in the manhole, operating a jackhammer. To this end, Sweeney had closed the door to the coal room and presumably pulled the mound of insulation over the cover as planned.

The third risk was beyond them entirely. Stephen wasn't positive how many men Braun actually had over there. What if he'd hidden one away in the coal room with a gun?

He would find out soon enough.

So close. So, so close after so much effort. Stephen redoubled his pressure on the jackhammer. "Come on, baby, break. Break!"

He'd drilled twenty holes—surely that had weakened the slab. Sweeney had assured him there was no rebar in the floor, said they would've run into it by now if there was. Man, if there was rebar, they were dead. He would kill—

The jackhammer suddenly surged forward. He released the trigger. Chunks of large concrete lay over the bit. Above, a gray circle of light.

The breakthrough was so sudden, so complete, that Stephen wasn't sure it had actually happened.

"Guys?"

Stephen jerked his head up, slammed it into the ceiling and ducked back down, hardly aware of the pain. He lowered himself back into the sewer. Pitch black.

"Guys?"

"Here," said Sweeney.

"We're in!"

"We're in?"

"We're in!"

Stephen tugged at the jackhammer and jumped out of the way as it hurtled out of the drain.

Splash.

"What was that?" Sweeney asked.

"The jackhammer."

Stephen clambered back up the hole, saw that the broken concrete would need to be removed for him to climb past, and dragged the two largest pieces back down the hole.

Splash, splash.

"What was that?"

"Concrete."

He crawled up again, scooting all the way on knees and elbows. Shoved more debris past him, down the hole. Someone grunted.

"Sorry."

The slab had broken free along the line of holes he'd drilled. "Perfect. Perfect, perfect." He reached up, gripped the floor's edge, and pulled his head out.

The basement.

The sweet, sweet, beautiful basement. Silent and bare past the open door. No guns, no Germans. He could hardly stand such a sight.

Something bumped his foot. "Go, go!" Sweeney called up.

Stephen climbed out of the hole and stood. The door into this room stood open; it had a dead bolt on the inside, which was strange. Maybe it had been a study or hideout once. The bulb out in the basement glared. The cement on the floor was shiny. He ran to the door, poked his head out, and then stepped into the main room. The door to the boiler room was closed.

"Please, please," he breathed. What if they had found it? He couldn't think like that. Not now.

"Take my hand," Sweeney whispered behind him. Stephen glanced back to see Sweeney kneeling over the hole, helping one of the others. He looked up at Stephen. "Hurry, man! We have to do this and get out!"

Stephen walked to the boiler room, cracked the door, peeked into the dark. His heart pumped like that jackhammer, breaking up his confidence. What if the tin was gone?

He hit the light switch, and the lone incandescent bulb snapped to life. The boiler was open. He'd left it closed. The drums looked as if they might have been shifted.

Braun had been here!

Stephen leaped for the boiler, grabbed the empty drum behind with both hands, and sent it crashing to the side. There lay the top of the safe, covered in dirt.

Stephen let out a soft, involuntary cry. For a moment, he felt ruined by relief. Then he dropped to his knees, swept the dirt off, and yanked the lid. Esther's face stared up at him, serene.

He shoved both hands into the safe, latched his fingers around the tin box, and pulled it out.

Surprisingly light. What would four gilded Stones wrapped in cloth weigh? Less than the tin box perhaps. Maybe more. Maybe much more.

He spun around and ran into the rabbi, who had come in unnoticed.

"It's here?"

Stephen clutched the box with white fingers. "Yes."

The rabbi looked from the box to Stephen.

"I have it," Stephen said.

"Yes. Yes, I see that." A slight smile formed on Chaim's face.

Stephen rushed past him into the main room, driven by the adrenaline in his blood, not the thoughts in his head. There were no thoughts in his head. He had the box, that was all. The box was in his hands.

"Are you going to open it?" Chaim asked.

He whirled around, caught off guard by the question. "Here? Not here!"

Sweeney and Melissa stood by the coal room, staring. "That's it?" Sweeney asked.

For a moment, they all stared at it. Why? What were they trying to prove with their gawking? Sweeney had already mixed the quick-setting concrete, which sat in a bucket behind him. They should be moving, not gawking.

Sweeney stuck out his hand. "As much as I would love to sit around and look at your five-hundred-thousand-dollar box, the clock is ticking. It's been a pleasure, Groovy. If I don't see you in prison, I'll try to look you up." He grinned. "The concrete's already half-set, so as soon as I wedge the wood in place, you pour. Got it?"

Stephen's legs were numb. He nodded.

"You sure you're all right?"

"'Course." He cleared his throat.

"And you might want to stash the contents of that box in your pockets. It's a bit obvious."

It was Stephen's idea that he should be the one to stay behind, fill the hole, and escape through the garage. After all, it was his treasure, and someone had to do it. The notion struck him as a bit ambitious now.

Melissa kissed him on the cheek. "See you around, Stephen."

"Okay," Sweeney said. "Come on, Rabbi."

"I'll stay with Stephen," Chaim said.

"You have to get out, you know? Two will be harder than one."

"And three will be harder than two escaping from the smoking building. I think I should stay with Stephen."

"Okay, Stephen?"

"Okay."

Sweeney winked, followed Melissa down the tunnel, and wedged a piece of plywood behind him, forming a floor of sorts for the quick mix. He knocked on it from below. "Okay, all set. Good luck."

Stephen kept looking down at the box in his hands. It was an old cookie box, roughly twelve by eight inches. Orange wafers ran around the sides. No tape to seal it. Ruth's picture looked up at him in a surreal silence. He shook it gently once—something thumped softly inside. A knot filled his throat.

Chaim watched Stephen, and then, without a word, dumped the concrete into the hole. He smoothed it as best he could with the bottom of the bucket, and then shoved loose coal over the mess.

Stephen would have helped, but he couldn't bring himself to put down the box. He watched in silence, contemplating Sweeney's advice that he leave the box behind. A box was just a box. He could take the picture off and take out the Stones and leave the box.

Chaim finished in less than a minute. It wouldn't support a man's weight for another half hour, but the coal masked the job well. If Sweeney was as successful at hiding the manhole on his end, their tunnel might never be discovered.

All Stephen and Chaim had to do now was get out.

———ᨙ———

SOMETHING WAS wrong. Roth had never been so sure of his instincts before. It was the fire—something was wrong about the fire. So much smoke and yet no flames.

He paced the sidewalk, eyes peeled for any sign of a fireman, a policeman, a city inspector, anyone who might look like the Jew or the construction worker. For that matter, he wouldn't have to look like the Jew—Friedman wasn't beyond dressing as a woman. Anyone who approached the building would be suspect.

Ten minutes after their evacuation, he learned why there were no flames. Tires. They were saying that someone had set tires on fire.

The Jew had set the tires on fire knowing it would force an evacuation, resumed his digging, and was now in the building.

Roth ran toward the front doors.

He pulled up. What was he thinking? The authorities had eyes everywhere.

He hurried back to Lars. Panic spread through his limbs, enough to make him want to scream. "They may have tunneled through the floor under cover of the fire. Have Ulrich set fire to one of the cars down the street—I need their eyes away from me. Do you understand what I'm telling you?"

"Start a fire? How?"

"I don't care how!" he yelled, then quickly turned in the event he'd attracted attention. "I don't even care if he's caught. Tell him to stuff a rag into the gas tank and set it on fire. Just do it!" His head swam with emotions he had never experienced before. He might be having a breakdown right here on the street. Control. He had to regain control.

"Hurry!"

"RABBI!" STEPHEN WHISPERED.

Chaim turned from the door that led into the stairwell.

"Maybe I should take them out."

"We have to hurry!" the rabbi said.

"I know, but maybe Sweeney's right. I should hide them somewhere else so that if they take the box, I'll still have the Stones. I think we still have time; it's only been ten minutes—didn't you say we had at least twenty?"

The rabbi looked at the door, then back. "Where would you put them?"

"In my pockets. Or my shoes."

Chaim walked back. "Okay." He looked at the box. "Open it."

"Okay," Stephen said.

He couldn't move his fingers though. They hadn't moved in five minutes.

The rabbi's hand reached out and touched the photograph. "She's very beautiful. Please, Stephen."

"Okay."

He gingerly set the box on the ground, knelt down, wiped his palms on his pants, and pried his fingers under one end of the lid. It came loose with a soft popping sound. Stephen felt such a terrible desperation in that moment that he nearly slammed the lid closed. Desire, of course; yes, desire. But fear as well. Terror!

What if the Stones of David weren't in this box?

He slid the lid over and let it clatter to the floor. Inside was a red bundle. Silk. He scooped it out with trembling hand. Beautiful, soft silk that felt like cream in his hands.

He looked down, thinking there could be more at the bottom of the box. There was. A worn journal. He scooped it out, leafed through it quickly, and handed it to Chaim.

Carefully, he unraveled the silk scarf. It felt empty. Panic crept up his throat. He shook the scarf. A folded letter fell to the floor.

No Stones.

Stephen sank to his haunches, horrified. He could hardly breathe. A red scarf and a folded letter. There had to be more. The safe! The safe had a false bottom!

He leaped to his feet, tore into the boiler room, and plunged his hand into the safe. His knuckles crammed against a hard bottom. He struck at it furiously, but it sounded dull. No false bottom.

Stephen stared into the hole and began to breathe hard, as if he were locked in an overheated sauna, desperate to get out.

"Stephen?"

The truth was unbearable. A mountain on his shoulders, crushing with its dead weight. There was no treasure. The children were the Stones of David. Esther. Ruth's picture flashed through his mind.

"Stephen!"

Chaim was at the door. Stephen turned slowly, senses dulled. The rabbi looked at him, face white. The letter shook in his right hand.

Stephen stood unsteadily. "What?"

"I . . . you should read this." The rabbi held it out.

"It's a letter," Stephen said. "To Esther?"

"Yes. To Esther and David. From Martha."

"Martha?"

"I think you should read it."

Stephen walked forward and took the letter. Written in cursive. The ink was old, and the creases in the paper were worn nearly through.

My dearest son, David, and Esther, for whom you were born:

I've searched the world and cannot find you. I can only pray that someday one of you will find this letter and know the truth.

I have married a good man, Rudy Spritzer, and I call myself Rachel now in honor of the woman who cared for you, David, in the camp. There I was known as Martha. I was able to give birth to you at the labor camp Toruń only because of the sacrifice of Ruth, who had given birth to Esther just weeks earlier. I was chosen by the red scarf to die, but Ruth took the scarf for herself.

The commandant wouldn't let me care for you, David, but I cared for Esther. He took you both before the camp was liberated. I searched for five years and then came to the United States when I learned that many orphans had immigrated. I discovered only that the commandant left my dear David in an orphanage near Ketrzyn and took Esther into Germany.

Please forgive me, but I couldn't let him know that I had taken the journal, or he would hunt me down. It contains enough information to send him to his grave. But you must understand, I could not allow them to prosecute the commandant. He alone may have knowledge of your whereabouts.

I couldn't seek you out publicly, for fear that they would come for you as well. You will know you belong to me and to Ruth because I have marked both of you with half of David's Stone. I tried to find you through the mark—I'm so sorry I could not.

I have prayed every day that God will draw you to me and to each other as he draws a man seeking the pearl of great price. May he fill you with the hope we entrusted in you. You must find each other. Then you will know the real treasure, which makes the Stones look like toys for children. I am sorry, so sorry, dearest children. You are the true Stones of David, and I pray every day that if I cannot find you, you will find each other in good health.

As for the Stones, their hiding place will go to the grave with Ruth and me. Find each other and find God.

Martha
Sept. 1958

"Esther," Stephen said quietly. Tears welled in his eyes, and he was forced to swallow. "Dear God, I have to find her."

He owed his life to a woman named Ruth, and by extension to her daughter. *Esther* was the treasure. Not some ancient Stones covered in gold, but a child of the war. A woman. Esther, for whom he was born.

He couldn't explain what happened next, except to think that a week of madness had finally broken him down to a pulp. Stephen dropped to his knees, covered his face, and yielded to sobs. They started with soft shakes and grew to rob his breath completely. He bobbed on his knees, wanting to shake the emotion that ravaged his body, but it only tightened its grip on his throat and chest.

The photographs from Martha's sunroom flashed across his mind. Girls and boys, wives and mothers and daughters, husbands and fathers and sons. They had died, and he had lived—because of one named Ruth. He owed his every breath to another Jew. And for twenty years, he'd betrayed the memory of their deaths by ignoring their pain.

Chaim tried to comfort him, tried to suggest they must leave, but Stephen sank to the ground, letter clenched in his fist. For a few unbearable moments, he imagined that the picture of the little bald girl from the medical clinic was him. He was there, in Poland. Every day, the Germans carried him down to a room that smelled like alcohol, and they injected different parts of his body with cancer cells. That's how he lost his hair and his teeth.

But he wasn't dead from cancer. He was alive because someone else had died to give him life. Ruth. Esther.

Chaim was shaking Stephen violently. "Someone's coming!"

Stephen scrambled for orientation. "The letter!"

A door slammed somewhere.

Stephen struggled to his feet. They had to get out! He quickly shoved the letter into the ash tray below the boiler.

"You're leaving it?"

"What if they find it on me? We'll come back for it. Hurry!" He ran out, scooped up the tin box with the journal and the scarf, and turned for the door.

"No. Not this time."

Braun stood at the entrance to the stairwell, pistol in his fist. He walked straight for Stephen. The German's gun hand flashed out, and Stephen felt sharp pain shoot through his skull. Something crashed to the concrete. A tin box.

He hit the floor hard and lost consciousness.

38

STEPHEN HAD NO IDEA HOW LONG HE'D BEEN UNCONSCIOUS. He lay in a heap on the basement floor, stripped to his undershirt and briefs. His head pounded, and he lay still for a few minutes, listening to several men talking in German. Slowly, the details of the letter again filled his mind. He had to find Esther.

Stephen straightened his leg. The talking ceased immediately. Thirty seconds later, Braun stood above him.

"Have a seat."

Hands hauled him up from behind. They set him in a chair.

"Where's the rabbi?" Stephen asked.

"The rabbi?" Braun chuckled. "He's no rabbi. Which is a disappointment to me." Braun wore an unbuttoned Nazi SS jacket, revealing a black silk shirt beneath. His slacks and shoes were the same he'd worn before. The red scarf was draped over his left shoulder. He strolled to Stephen's right, drawing on a cigarette.

"I would have killed his worthless soul already, but for the moment he's more useful to me alive. The old ones always go quickly, my father used to say."

Stephen felt a chill snake down his spine. The large blond they called Lars stood by the stairwell, staring without emotion. Claude stood in front of the boiler room.

"Do you like my jacket?" Braun asked. "It was my father's. I wear it sometimes, when I make deals with Jews."

He held up the tin's lid and stared at Ruth's picture. "I want you to tell me where you put the Stones, Mr. Friedman. We found the floor safe. I must say, your juvenile bluffs successfully diverted our attention from the basement. We tore the upper floors to pieces, and all the while you had the safe covered by a drum in the basement. How did you get in?"

"What do you mean?"

"I mean, an hour ago you weren't in, and now you are. How did you get in?"

They hadn't discovered the covered tunnel yet. "Through the garage door."

Roth slapped Stephen hard across the cheek. "I don't have time for lies, Jew."

Stephen caught his balance, put his hand to his tingling face. "We . . . we knew the fire would force your evacuation. In the confusion, we forced the garage door open and walked in. I was dressed like a fireman."

"Where are the clothes?"

"We tossed them outside."

Judging Roth Braun by his expression was impossible. He showed no emotion. "And the jackhammer?"

"We were digging a hole from a sewer that connects the buildings, but the motor burned up. The fire was a last resort." Stephen took a deep breath. "There are no Stones," he said. "Only the scarf."

"And the journal." Braun raised it in one hand and took a drag on the cigarette with the other. "Do you know who this scarf belongs to?"

"Rachel Spritzer."

"You mean Martha. She was my father's personal servant at Toruń. She stole this scarf from my father. I know it well. It was very special to him." He lifted the picture of Ruth, caught Stephen's eye, and sniffed the photograph as if testing her perfume.

Stephen felt sick.

"This is Ruth," Braun said. "Amazing how Esther resembles her."

Stephen's hands were free; he could rush the man and take the picture. But it would only prove that he knew about Esther. He couldn't tip his hand. Braun didn't know about the letter yet.

"You do know Esther?" the German asked, gaze studied.

Stephen didn't respond.

"Ruth's daughter." Braun's lips twitched. "My father sent her into the Alps after the war, to a small village named Greifsman." His eyes twinkled. "She's very beautiful."

She *was* alive! "He . . . I don't understand . . ."

"Why is she alive? Let's just say that Esther is our bargaining chip, in the event we ever found Martha. But her value has now expired, hasn't it?"

Braun grinned. "And you're Martha's son, David. My father made the mistake of allowing you to live as well. He wanted Martha's missing son to haunt her till her death. A good instinct, but fundamentally flawed. After all, you were chosen by the scarf."

"I don't know what you're talking about," Stephen said. He had to distract Braun from this line of thinking. "I knew Rachel Spritzer from an antique shop I used to frequent," he lied. "She purchased some things there. She talked about her Stones of David, but I always thought she meant her children, until I saw that she had donated one to the museum. I looked around and stumbled onto the floor safe. You know the rest."

"Another one of your inventive stories? My father took the Stones of David as spoils from a collection in Hungary, and I'm sure he would like to have them back. But this"—he held up the journal—"interests us the most. If you've seen the contents I'm sure you know why."

It occurred to Stephen that Braun was incriminating himself—something he would never risk if he intended to let Stephen live. A moan seeped from under the door to the coal room.

Chaim.

"I think the Stones were in this box with the journal," Braun said. "I'm willing to wager the old man's life on it. We can begin now, one finger at a time, or you can tell me what you did with them and make this painless."

"There are no Stones! Do whatever you want, but there was only the scarf."

The letter would prove there were no Stones here, but did he dare tell him about the letter?

"Fine." Braun turned to Claude, who stood by the door to the coal room. "Start with a thumb."

Stephen bolted to his feet. "Stop!" He had to stall. "Okay, listen. The scarf must mean something. She left it for a reason. It leads to the Stones. Ask yourself how."

Braun hesitated. "Nothing comes to mind."

"Think about it. She wanted me to find the scarf. Why?" Stephen felt toothless, standing up to this monster while wearing nothing but Fruit of the Loom briefs and a torn T-shirt, but he would bite at any hope. "Because you're right. I am David. The scarf saved my life. She drew me in to find the scarf."

"Cut off his thumb," Braun said to Claude, who turned to enter the room where Chaim moaned.

"Wait, there's a letter! It's in the boiler."

Braun held up his hand to Claude. He glanced through the door into the boiler room.

"Well?"

Claude ran in and emerged a moment later bearing the smudged letter.

Braun took the letter, eyed Stephen, and then read it quickly. His left eye twitched once as he neared the end. Stephen sagged into the chair. Braun would now assume the Stones were hidden somewhere else. *The Stones' hiding place will go to the grave with Ruth and me.*

―∽∾―

ROTH WAS having a hard time controlling his exuberance. He was playing the boy like a fiddle. He'd convinced the Jew that he was after the Stones of David as well as the journal. And that Esther was still alive in Germany.

He turned his back to Stephen and reread the letter. The old man called Stephen's name softly once, and Claude thumped the door. "Shut up!" An eerie silence filled the basement.

Roth planted his feet wide and rolled his neck.

"The Stones aren't here," Roth said softly.

He took several deep breaths. He was so taken by his own game that he almost missed the significance of the last line. He'd missed it when he'd first read the letter several days earlier. Now it jumped out at him.

"What could she have possibly . . ." He read the last line out loud. "As for the treasure, its hiding place will go to the grave with Ruth and me."

The implication was what? That Ruth, not only Martha, had known something about the Stones' hiding place.

He turned around and would have grinned wickedly if not for his practiced control.

"Strip him!"

The others hesitated, not expecting the sudden order.

Roth walked to the Jew. "I said *strip* him!" He grabbed the neck of Stephen's T-shirt and jerked it down. The cotton fabric ripped, leaving half of Stephen's chest exposed.

Lars and Ulrich grabbed Stephen and pulled him to his feet.

Roth stared at Stephen's chest. He extended his hand and touched the scar. Traced it.

"David," Roth said. "Isn't it ironic that after all these years, your very survival continues to play into our hands? You've led us to this letter, which says more than Martha meant—I can promise you that. I have to pay our beloved Esther a visit now, so I'm afraid we won't be seeing each other again, but I want you to remember my face. I assure you, I look like my father. Your mother went to her grave with his face stamped in her mind. Why should you go any differently?"

He dropped the letter and walked to the door. "Lars, Ulrich, come with me." He opened the door and turned back to Claude. "Kill the old man and dispose of his body. Keep this other stinking Jew alive until I call. If he tries to escape the basement, kill him. I trust you can manage that."

The instructions were for Stephen's benefit, naturally. The game wasn't over—not yet.

Claude dipped his head, indicating that he'd understood. If he didn't, he would pay with his own life.

THEY WERE going to kill Chaim?

"Cover the stairs," Claude said to Carl. Stephen jerked his head around—Claude was screwing a silencer onto his pistol.

Stephen responded instinctively rather than with any kind of coherent plan. He leaped to his feet, hurled the chair at Claude with a furious grunt, and rushed the man before the chair struck.

Claude absorbed most of the flying chair with his left forearm, but one of the legs struck him square in the forehead. Stephen slammed into the chair, shoving Claude hard against the wall. The German batted at him with a thick hand, struck him on the shoulder, and pushed him into the coal room door.

Stephen grabbed the handle, jerked the door open, and spun inside. He slammed the door, once on Claude's hand, and again after the man sensibly withdrew it. Stephen crammed his palm into the dead bolt he'd seen earlier. It banged home.

Stephen took a step back, trembling from head to foot. He couldn't see—the room was pitch black. Fists pounded on the door. Bitter curses.

"Hello?"

Chaim's voice. From his left. The pounding stopped, and it occurred to Stephen that a bullet could pop through the door as if it were paper.

He dived to his left.

Phwet! Stephen hit the rabbi and both crashed to the floor. *Phwet! Phwet!* Bullets punched round holes of light in the door.

"Uhhh!"

"Down!" Stephen snapped. "Stay down!"

He jerked his eyes back to the door. They seemed to be shooting randomly, hoping for a hit, but it wouldn't take much to blow off the latch. In ten seconds they would be through.

"The tunnel!" Stephen coughed. The quick-drying cement they'd used set up in thirty minutes, but how long before it solidified?

Stephen rolled to his feet and tore for the center of the room. Somehow the spitting bullets missed him as he kicked at the coal they'd scattered over the tunnel. A circle darkened by coal quickly took shape.

"Chaim—"

"Hurry!" The rabbi was beside him, already stomping.

The shooting stopped momentarily, then started again, just below the dead bolt.

"Jump!" Stephen shouted. "Hard!"

He slammed both feet down and was rewarded with a teeth-rattling jolt. It had hardened.

"Together. One, two, three!" He jumped again, but the rabbi's leap came after his. Two more holes popped in the door, up toward the latch.

"Together. Together! One, two, three."

They both leaped; they both slammed into the fresh concrete together; they both fell when the concrete caved.

"Out!" Stephen pushed the rabbi, who quickly crawled out.

Streams of light blazed through the holes in the door. Stephen shoved his hands into the tunnel, grabbed chunks of concrete and wood, and threw them out.

A shot blew away the door latch. But the dead bolt above still held. Someone kicked at the door and swore again.

The tunnel couldn't possibly be clear of all the material Sweeney had used to prop up the concrete, but Stephen had pulled out the large slabs and the plywood. They were out of time.

"Follow me."

He went in headfirst, like a tentative child taking his first daring ride down a slide. His hands struck two-by-fours, and smaller chunks of crumbling cement littered the hole. He shoved them down, ahead of him, praying they wouldn't jam.

Wiggling and squirming, he slid down, plowing the refuse until it splashed into the sewer ahead. He didn't try to slow his exit, but he did tuck and roll the moment his head cleared the tunnel. The sudden cold of sewer water sent waves of relief through him. He wanted to cheer.

The rabbi was spared the bath; he fell on top of Stephen like a huge sack of potatoes. The impact knocked the breath from Stephen's lungs, but the fact was lost to the whine of bullets. Claude was shooting down the hole.

"Hurry!" Chaim gasped.

They ran through the blackness. The shooting stopped, and Stephen knew the German was coming down after them. He hoped Sweeney hadn't heaped bricks on the manhole cover.

Stephen managed to find the ladder, scrambled up first. He heaved on the grate, but it refused to budge. Behind them, Claude swore. He was feeling his way out of the tunnel they'd dug. Stephen pushed again. Not a chance.

"Move it! Move it," the rabbi whispered.

"It's stuck! Shh, quiet!" But even the *shh* carried down the sewer like air brakes.

A huge splash. Claude was in. Stephen swallowed. This was it, then. They were trapped. He gathered all of his strength and crammed his back against the lid above. Nothing.

Far away, a dog barked.

"Brandy?" Stephen's whisper echoed down the tunnel. His question was answered by a sudden sloshing and another big splash, followed by another curse.

Now the dog was barking furiously.

The manhole cover suddenly slid off. Stephen stared up into the round eyes of Sweeney. Brandy attacked his face with a wet tongue.

"No, Brandy. Hurry, get me out!" he cried.

Sweeney and Melissa grabbed his arms and yanked him out of the hole. Brandy stood back, head cocked.

"The rabbi, hurry!"

Up came Chaim.

The sewer filled with splashing and yells. Stephen shoved the cover back over the hole. "How was it braced?"

Sweeney got behind a large timber that he'd found and pushed it back over the cover.

"Good night, what happened?" Sweeney asked.

The cover bounced up.

"More! He's strong."

"There is no more," Sweeney said.

Stephen looked around quickly. The cover rose a full two inches off the hole—he could see the German's gun hand. Without thinking, Stephen jumped up on the timber. The lid clanged back into place.

"Find something." The lid rocked crazily. "Hurry!"

Instead, Sweeney jumped up with him. This time the cover slammed home with confidence. "That'll give him something to think about," Sweeney said. "You're lucky we came back to check out the damage."

"My car's on the street," Stephen said to Chaim. "Spare key's in the gas well. Take Melissa and wait for us."

Chaim needed no encouragement. They left with Brandy bouncing behind.

The timber below them shifted, and Sweeney crouched like a surfer. "That guy's a bull!"

"There's more than one," Stephen said. "We have to get out of here. Four guys with guns could be crossing the street already."

"What went wrong?"

"Long story."

"Did you get it?"

Stephen hesitated. "Sort of."

"You don't have any pants on," Sweeney said.

"I about had my tail shot off. No time for pants."

Sweeney stared at him dumbly.

"Make sure you don't kick the wood off the cover when we push off," Stephen said. "Ready? You go first; I'm right behind. Go!"

Sweeney jumped off and sprinted from the room. Stephen followed on his heels. Behind them, the cover scraped concrete. A single bullet chipped the wall before they made the stairwell. They cleared the building, tore up the alley, and ran straight for Stephen's car, a happening hippie in blue bell-bottoms and a scruffy Realtor in white underwear.

Not until Chaim pulled the car into traffic on La Brea did Stephen feel his pulse ease. But the madness wasn't over, was it? In so many ways, it was just beginning.

For the first time, he knew what was happening; now he just had to follow through. A whole new world had just been opened up to him. He was being drawn by the pearl of great price. The pearl was Esther, for whom he was born.

———∽∿∽———

STEPHEN PACED in the living room, peering repeatedly out the windows on either side of the house. They'd let Sweeney and Melissa off ten blocks down La Brea and returned home the long route. An hour had passed since their narrow escape, but Stephen's nerves still felt taut like piano wires.

They'd called the police who'd dispatched a cruiser to check out Rachel Spritzer's apartment.

"Rabbi—"

"I'm sorry I didn't help you sooner, Stephen. I was afraid you were pulling back into yourself. But I see that you've been reaching out more than withdrawing. You're finding your own identity."

Stephen nibbled at his index fingernail. "I don't think I can hang out here for the police."

"They'll want to take a statement. We were shot at and nearly killed!"

Stephen looked in his eyes. "She's alive, Chaim."

"Who is?"

"Esther."

"She's alive and in a German town called Greifsman." He swallowed. "He's going to kill her. I have to stop him. He said the red scarf had selected—"

"Red scarf?" the rabbi interrupted, paling.

"The red scarf. You saw it. The letter—"

"He's the one behind the killings!"

"That's what the letter said. His father was the commandant in the camp where my mother was held."

"No, now. The killings in Los Angeles."

"What killings?"

"You haven't heard? Of course you haven't!" Chaim quickly filled him in.

"There's no direct link," Stephen said. "Either way, he's gone now. I have to get to Germany, rabbi."

Chaim looked at him blankly.

"Braun's going to kill her, did you hear me? I have to beat him there."

"And maybe that's what he wants."

"Then he would have taken me with him. Or killed me when he had the chance."

"This is very dangerous, Stephen." The rabbi hurried to the phone, dialed a number. "You can't just run off to Germany. Do you even have a passport?"

"Yes. Who are you calling?"

"Sylvia. She's working on the Red Scarf case."

Stephen stared out the window as Chaim spoke on the phone. The possibility that Roth Braun was a killer failed to upstage the revelations of Martha's letter.

"Thank you," Chaim said into the phone. He dialed a second number.

On the other hand, this serial-killer business was extremely important. It meant that Esther was about to die. At least that's how Stephen saw it.

He bumped his forehead with his fist. The emotion that had consumed him for the last few days now felt like a hot branding iron on the brain.

Chaim dropped the receiver in its cradle. "She's not at work. No answer at home."

"I'm going, Rabbi."

They stood in silence for a moment. "Why would Braun want to kill her now, assuming he's known all along where she lives? Does she know where the Stones are?"

"No. I don't know. The letter says that their hiding place would go to the grave with Martha and Ruth."

"And they're both dead."

"Right."

"So what does Braun know?"

"I don't know. But I know he's going after Esther."

"Well, this is terribly dangerous."

"No, this is my life!" Stephen was yelling now. He might burst into tears at any moment. "I have to do this. I can't explain why any more than I can explain why I tunneled into the apartment, but I have to go."

"The police—"

"I can't afford to be questioned by the police. If Roth Braun is the man they're looking for, then the danger for Los Angeles is gone. Let them try to find him, although I can guarantee you that he's already in the air. It'll take time to coordinate any action with the German police."

His words echoed in the small house.

"I have to go now."

"Then I'll go with you."

"No. Stay and fill the police in. Tell Sylvia. Do whatever you need, but please give me a chance to get out of the country."

"They'll want to know—"

"Then tell them. Just don't tell them where I've gone. I'm not the criminal here. They can't hold me, can they?"

"Vandalism."

Stephen knew Chaim had a point, and it infuriated him. He gathered himself.

"I have to go, rabbi," he said quietly. "Please, hear me. I have to go."

Chaim sighed and finally nodded. "Okay. Find her, but please remember what I said, Stephen."

The phone rang. Chaim snatched it up. The police.

In a moment the rabbi set the phone back down and faced Stephen wearing a frown. "You were right—no sign of Braun; no evidence of a crime. Other than a hole in the basement. They want a statement from both of us."

"I'll give mine when I get back."

The rabbi seemed to accept this.

"Obsession is a dangerous business, Stephen. You can't lose sight of virtue or morality for the sake of passion. Just because your intentions are noble, you have no right to break the law. Certainly not to kill or to—"

"I'm not going to kill anyone. I'm going to rescue Esther. God has answered my mother's prayers."

39

Toruń
May 8, 1945
Dinnertime

THE COMMANDANT'S EYES WERE RED AND WATERY FROM LACK OF sleep. He leaned over the table and sipped at a spoon of the corn chowder Martha had prepared for supper at his request. The china was set on a white cloth, and the commandant was dressed in the uniform he reserved for social events—black, pressed, and starched. For nine months she'd waited on the commandant, while the war slowly ground to a halt throughout the world. Auschwitz had been liberated, Belsen liberated, even Buchenwald in Germany itself liberated. But here in Toruń, just a few miles from Stutthof, the Germans had dug in and were fighting a fierce battle over these last camps. Why? And how could Braun sit so calmly while even now Russian planes flew overhead, armed with bombs for Stutthof?

Martha had long ago lost her fear of Gerhard Braun.

"It's over," she said.

"It will never be over," he answered, not bothering to look up. "You're alive today. Does that mean you'll be alive tomorrow?"

Martha looked away. His threats hardly even registered anymore. Several other facts, however, did resister, like glaring lights in her eyes. The first was that David was still alive. She hadn't seen him for nine months, but she knew he survived in the barracks below. The second was that in a matter of days, whatever end awaited them all would come.

And the third was a growing hope—yes, hope—that she could actually affect that end. How many nights had she laid awake, her mind filled with fantasies of revenge, plotting to use Braun's treasures to her advantage? Her only living mission was to save the children; perhaps she could do so with the help of the spoils hidden in the vault.

The only question was how? Anytime now, Braun would evacuate the vault and be gone.

Paper covered the picture window now, obstructing the view of the camp below where her little David lived. Most of the Russian bombs had descended on the main camp at Stutthof, but Toruń had suffered several raids as well. Braun had sent most of the remaining prisoners north to the Baltic nearly two weeks ago to be evacuated by sea, he said. All but a hundred, mostly wounded or sick, were gone. Rachel was among those who remained. Rachel and David. Rachel and David and Martha and Esther, pawns in his game, kept only to make Braun feel powerful.

If only there was a way to speak sense into this pig! "You have no reason to keep us," Martha said. "And you have no reason to kill us. What will any of this prove?"

Braun set his spoon into the empty bowl, dabbed his lips with a serviette, and ran his tongue over his teeth. She wanted to cut off his red lips with a knife. A fantasy as foolish as taking his treasure.

"Don't be a fool," he said softly. "I have more reasons than you can possibly know to kill you." He stood and picked up his hat. "As it turns out, I also have several compelling reasons not to kill you. Killing you would end your misery, and I have no interest in ending your misery. Also, the Allies are evidently frowning on the indiscriminate killing of prisoners—I'll be gone when they come, but I wouldn't want to leave any evidence to fuel their fires."

Martha, confused, watched him walk to the door. It was the part about her misery that sounded wrong. How would her liberation lead to extended misery—except in the memories she would take with her? Such relatively insignificant misery was beneath Braun. He meant to do more.

"I will be leaving in the morning, but the guards at the perimeter will remain. Don't think you can walk out of here."

He reached the door, put on his hat, and turned the handle. "Oh, and I've decided to take the children with me."

Martha's mouth dropped open. "No! No, you can't!" She took three steps toward him and stopped. "You . . . you can't!"

"But I am. What's more, I can promise you that you'll never find them."

Martha ran to him, fell to her knees, and grabbed his hand before considering the consequences of such an action. "No, I beg you!" she cried. "I beg you; they are children! They mean nothing to you!"

He looked at her as a scientist might look at a lab experiment, pleased by such an unusual reaction from her.

"Please, let me keep my child," Martha whispered.

"You don't think that I'd seriously allow Ruth's ridiculous obsession with hope to actually find life outside this camp, do you? There is no hope for the Jews."

He jerked his hand free and stepped out into the darkness. "If you make any attempt to escape, I would be delighted to shoot all three of you. Except Esther. I've taken a liking to the little girl."

"As has your son," Martha said bitterly.

His head snapped up. He glared. The night Roth had tried to kill Esther had been the last time Martha had seen him.

She pushed him, knowing the danger of it. "He's stronger than you."

Gerhard spat. "He's a child who doesn't know that the war is over. Yesterday's indulgences are today's death sentences. If I didn't know you better, I might think you were asking to be killed."

"I have no reason to live without my David."

"Which is the point. You'll live with the horror of this camp your whole life. Roth doesn't understand that death is sometimes the easy way out."

Gerhard made a disgusted, dismissing motion with his right hand and shut the door with a *thump.*

Martha jumped to her feet and ran for the stairs, mindless. Her right foot was already down two steps before the first clear thought forced her attention. She had to get David! The commandant was leaving, and she had to get her baby before then. She spun around, ran for the door, but pulled up without opening it.

What was she thinking? Even if she could get David, she could never escape with two children under her arms. Even alone, she would be killed.

She threw both fists toward the floor, jerked to the window and screamed through gritted teeth, like an animal. For several long seconds she just stood there, tensed from head to foot, trembling with fury. The thought of losing Esther and David was like the thought of dying. Maybe worse. What did he have to gain from this? Nothing!

But she knew that her scream would do nothing for either David or Esther. She forced herself to take a deep breath. Maybe she could still prevent him from taking the children. Or maybe he didn't really mean to carry out this threat. He was playing with her, one last sick joke before running off with this loot of his.

She blinked. The Stones of David. The journal.

Martha walked to the kitchen and then back working quickly through ideas. There *was* no way to save the children. Nothing would prevent Braun from taking them.

She stopped by the kitchen table and stared at the far wall without seeing, never so hopeless since seeing the red scarf on her bed nine months earlier. Whatever Braun planned to do with the children could not be good. He might kill them outside the camp, leaving her with lingering hope and uncertainty.

"No, Martha," she muttered, wiping her eyes. "You have to be strong. You have to be strong."

She returned to an idea she'd massaged for dozens of hours late in the nights. A thread, however thin, of hope for the children.

She ran down the stairs, suddenly consumed with accomplishing this one task before Braun returned. Esther slept in peace—her night started at five, something the commandant had insisted on. He wanted the child asleep before he sat down for a quiet evening meal. Martha had wanted to dump poison in his quiet evening meal when he'd first made the demand, but tonight she was grateful.

First, the vault.

How long would Braun be gone? It could be five minutes, or it could be several hours. She ran back upstairs to his bedroom, to a beautifully engraved, white jewelry box on his nightstand, under which she'd discovered the key to the vault three months earlier while cleaning. Tilting back the box, she snatched up the key and flew to the basement. Most of her plan would require stealth, in the late-night hours after Braun was asleep. This first part, however, she could not do without disturbing the peace.

The idea had first mushroomed in her mind as she contemplated how renowned the Stones of David were. Certainly they were far more important to the world than two Jewish children, even if in her mind David and Esther were the true Stones. If her children were ever to be lost, they would be forgotten forever with untold thousands following the war. But the Stones would always stand as icons, sought by the whole world.

What if she could somehow link both children to the Stones of David? Draw them by association to each other and to her? Rachel's confession in the barracks over a year earlier had haunted Martha. What if she could mark Esther and David as Rachel had done? And what if later she could make it clear in private circles that she was looking for a girl named Esther and a boy named David, both bearing this mark?

She unlocked the door with unsteady hands and stepped into the cool, dark room. It looked just as it had the first time she'd come in. But the journal was gone.

Gone?

Martha hurried to the box and opened it. There, on top of the five stones, lay the leather journal.

She emerged from the vault three minutes later with two green ammunition containers the size of shoe boxes under her right arm. Sweat slicked her palms, but she didn't falter. Not once. She locked the door, slid the boxes under her bed, and returned the key to its place under the commandant's jewelry box.

Returning to the living room window, she peered past a tear in the paper. No sign of him yet. She had to put the mark on Esther before he returned, or her crying would cause a terrible scene. And she would cry. Poor baby, she would cry.

Martha hurried to her room and reached under her thin mattress for the twisted piece of metal. She'd formed the symbol a week ago, using one paper clip, cut and folded back on itself to show the brand she intended.

It would never work! She paused, reconsidering, trying to think of a better way.

There was no time.

The child slept on her back. Martha looked at her supple, innocent body and started to cry silently. She tied the crude brand to the end of a wooden ladle and then bared little Esther's chest. Should she wake her?

Dear God, this was madness! How could she burn a child? She nearly abandoned the plan then, but this was the only way she knew to extend the very hope Ruth had died for. The thought gave her the strength to slowly heat the metal over a candle flame until it was red hot.

She had to clear her eyes of tears twice so she could see. "I'm sorry, dear Esther," she whispered, and then she pressed the metal into the baby's flesh, hard.

Esther did cry. She screamed through Martha's fingers. But thankfully, before the child fully realized she was under assault, the damage was done.

Martha hugged the child tight and rocked her. "Shh, shh, I'm so sorry. I don't mean to hurt you. Shh, shh, you must be quiet."

She dabbed the deep burn with an ointment she'd confiscated from Braun's personal medicine cabinet and then placed a bandage over it. Esther might tear it off, but Martha knew the burn must be hidden from Braun, at least for as long as he had both children.

Surely he wouldn't keep both—it wasn't in his character. He would rid himself of David; why would he keep David? No reason to keep a Jewish boy. The only reason he'd allowed the boy to live was for the sake of his game. He would rid himself of her son within a day or two, maybe sooner.

Martha's thoughts brought her no comfort. Had she burned in vain the child she had promised to care for as her own? Fresh tears streamed down her cheeks, and she lay down with the child, soothing her slowly back to sleep. Exhausted by the pain and tears, Esther finally settled.

She would have to wait now, lying here in bed, cold with sweat. Wait. And doubt.

The door upstairs banged an hour later, and Martha bolted up. Boots clomped on the wood floor, then down the stairs. Many boots, maybe four pair or more. They walked by her door, straight to the vault.

Panicked, she slid from the bed, dropped to her knees, shoved the ammunition boxes all the way under her bed, and then pushed some dirty clothes after it, knowing this cover-up was hopeless. If the commandant discovered anything missing from the vault, he would tear through the entire house, starting with her room, until he found it.

This wasn't just a few coins she'd relieved him of. The journal could destroy him. Dear God, what was she thinking?

They walked by nineteen times, and each time Martha lost a kilo in sweat. And then they didn't return. The house grew quiet. A sudden, terrifying thought struck her: What if he meant to take the children tonight?

She jerked upright. He'd said in the morning, but what if he meant *by* the morning? What if he'd left already to collect David, with the intention of returning for Esther?

Martha threw off the covers and tiptoed up the stairs in her bare feet. Water, if he asked. She was getting a glass of water.

She peeked down the hall and saw his bedroom door closed. A thin line of light ran along the base of the door. She retreated, her bare feet whispering across the concrete. He'd emptied the vault, presumably without noticing anything missing. What kind of good fortune had extended her this grace?

And to what end? She wouldn't be leaving here with the children, much less the treasure. It was nearly midnight, at least eleven. Her plan would be for nothing if she didn't get down to David. She *had* to get to her son. How could she possibly explain this to Rachel?

Martha slipped to her seat and sat in the dark hall, sunk by a terrible hopelessness. What would Ruth do in a situation like this? Ruth would pray. She would cry out to God for his favor and his hope. She would believe that God would preserve the Stones of David. She would believe that God would protect the children without being compelled to explain why he hadn't protected countless others in this horrifying war.

Martha whispered her prayers to God and then assured herself that he would indeed preserve the true Stones of David. Her tears slowly dried, and her resolve returned. She finally took a deep breath and set about to do what she must.

She pulled out the ammunition boxes, rolled them in a blanket, and ascended the stairs. The light was out beneath the commandant's door. So then, what was she waiting for? Ruth had given her life for hope; it was time for Martha to risk hers.

She would need a shovel, and although she had an idea where she could get one, she wasn't sure. This part of the plan she might have to abandon. She had one of the Stones at any rate, stashed in her underclothes. If all else failed, she could call to the children after the war using this one Stone.

Martha took a deep breath and slipped out the back door.

40

Germany
July 27, 1973
Friday

STEPHEN STOOD BY THE VOLKSWAGEN BUS HE'D RENTED IN Hamburg and stared down at the small town of Greifsman. A bird chirped from a grove of trees to his right; the sky was blue and the air was cool. It felt surreal to be here, so far from home, yet so close.

Several children played in the village square; a tall bell tower marked the church around which two or three hundred homes crowded. The village wasn't unlike any small Russian town, a far cry from the sprawling cities of America. For every minute of the past forty-eight hours, he'd imagined this moment, driving into Greifsman and running into Esther's arms, two soul mates finally and miraculously reunited. He'd stared at Ruth's picture for hours, considering every conceivable eventuality.

But the three-dimensional reality dashed his fantasies. If she wasn't here, he was lost. If she was here but refused to go with him, he was lost. If she was here and agreed to go with him, and Braun was also here, they were both lost. For all he knew, she was already dead. Or alive and happily married with twelve children. Even one child. Spoke no English. A dozen other possibilities.

Stephen had contacted Chaim upon his arrival in Germany. The rabbi had terrified him with new details.

Sylvia was dead.

Dead?

Dead.

The news still seemed impossible.

Chaim had gone looking for her after giving the police a statement on the fire. She never had shown up at work.

He found her bound in her apartment on blood-soaked sheets. Gagged with a red scarf. Lifeless.

Chaim blurted the news through tears, demanding that Stephen return immediately. This changed everything. Stephen couldn't return, of course. Another woman's life was at stake.

Esther. Her face was burned into Stephen's head, begging, dying for his help. His love.

They'd already made contact with the German authorities, but Stephen was right—these things took time.

Now standing over the village called Greifsman, Stephen was suddenly sure that the next hour would turn out badly.

In a moment of overwhelming resolve, however, he ran for the Volkswagen, climbed in, and fired up the van. Lack of sleep had made him emotional. He looked over at the picture of Ruth on the passenger's seat. This was insane.

He muscled the gearshift forward, released the clutch, and jerked with the bus. The gravel road was steep, and he found himself wondering how they managed in the winter. Maybe there was another road, although the man at the rental agency had assured him this was the only way to Greifsman, if he absolutely insisted on visiting. No one visited Greifsman. It was nothing but a pile of rubble in the middle of nowhere.

Stephen accelerated and shifted into a higher gear. He would blaze into town; he would search; he would find; he would leave.

Honestly, he wasn't sure he actually wanted to find her. Yes, as odd as that sounded, he really wasn't too thrilled about the prospect of searching for someone who was likely married or dead. And he wasn't just telling himself that to keep his hopes from boiling over. Or was he? Either way, he couldn't race through the streets yelling her name, now, could he? The residents might come out of the houses with pitchforks.

No, it would be a calm, collected affair. A simple question here, a suggestion there. He would compare faces against Ruth's picture, show it to others. If he wore his collar up, Braun might not even know he was in town.

He glanced at the picture and took a settling breath. "God help me."

Everyone who saw him drive up the cobblestone street into Greifsman stared. They didn't run out and clap their hands and dance in the streets as if he were the liberating army; they simply stared at him, as if they'd seen this before. The return of the gunslinger. Maybe the car rental man back in the airport knew a few things.

Stephen parked the van by the square and looked around. A bread shop, a butcher, the distant sound of children singing. School. An old man with a wrinkled face sat on a bench ten yards ahead, watching him with casual interest.

Okay, Stephen. Calm, collected, methodical. You've come this far.

He took the photograph, exited the van, and walked straight to the old man.

"Excuse me."

The man cracked a toothless smile and nodded.

"Excuse me, you speak English?"

"Anglesh," the man said.

Apparently not. He held up the picture. "Du yu no vwherr I ken fined dis wooman? Estar?" What was he thinking? He cleared his throat and spoke in normal English. "Do you know where I can find this woman?"

"Nein." The man shook his head and wagged one hand.

"Thank you." He walked up the street where a group of children watched him, smiling.

He held up the picture. "Esther? Anyone know this girl?"

A girl of eight or nine giggled. The rest ran off, squealing with delight.

He walked on, feeling more self-conscious than he had upon exiting the van. Several women were crossing the street to his left. "Excuse me." They ignored him and continued. "Excuse me, does anyone speak English? I'm looking for Esther."

They whispered to each other and moved on without paying him more than a sideways glance. Stephen stopped on the sidewalk, suddenly worried. What if she really wasn't here? Braun might have purposefully thrown Stephen off. He swallowed and hurried toward the bread shop. A woman with a plaid dress covered by a white apron walked out holding a large bag, gave him a quick glance, and moved away quickly. Not a good prospect. He stepped into the shop.

He stumbled out thirty seconds later. Not one of the seven people inside seemed to speak English. Not one showed any recognition when he showed them the picture. She wasn't here! And the people were treating him like a piece of trash that had blown in on the wind.

The calm, collected approach wasn't working.

Stephen ran to the corner and thrust the picture above his head. "Hey!" he yelled. "English! Who speaks English?" His voice rang out over the street. There were several cars, a dozen bicycles, and at least forty people in his field of vision. The bustle paused with his cry. A hundred eyes turned his way.

He had their attention.

"Please, I'm looking for Esther! The girl in this photograph." He pointed at the photo. "Can anyone tell me where I can find her?"

The pause lasted two seconds, and then as one they resumed their bustle, as if he didn't exist here on the corner, bellowing like a fool.

"Hey!"

This time, they ignored him entirely. They were hiding something! Of course! Why would so many people ignore him? Germans were well-known for their friendliness, even more so in the country. If one of them had responded kindly, tried to explain—but no. The whole village was conspiring against him.

The obsession he'd lived with in Los Angeles drove him forward now. Stephen ran down the sidewalk, waving the picture in front of startled villagers. "See her? This is Ruth. Esther's mother. Tell me where she is. Tell me!"

A middle-aged woman scolded him in high-pitched outrage. The only word he caught with certainty was "idiot."

He honestly didn't care whether she thought he was an idiot. If she had any idea what he'd gone through to be here, she would be running around frantically with him.

He showed the picture to at least fifty people, ignoring their blatant denial, gaining steam as he progressed, as much out of anger as hopelessness now. The main street ran for about a hundred yards, and he hurried all the way to its end, begging, yelling, whispering, any and every approach that came to mind. "Show me some respect, for heaven's sake. Look at the picture!"

Except for the occasional vacant or sympathetic stare and several angry lectures, the villagers continued to ignore him. He was doomed. No, he refused to be doomed.

Stephen pulled up and faced the street, beyond himself. "You lying hoard of insensitive—" He jumped up and beat at the air. "Speak to me!"

"They wouldn't tell you if they did know," a voice said behind him. Stephen whirled. A young man leaned against the wall, stroking a black goatee.

"You speak English," Stephen said.

"So do half the people in this town. The younger ones."

"Then why—"

"This town is controlled by the . . . what do you call it? Like German Mafia. Do you want these people to be killed? Only a fool would tell you anything, whether they know or not. And only a fool would run around town yelling at them and jumping in the air. You'll be dead by sunset."

Stephen stared at him.

The man turned away.

"No, wait." Stephen stepped up and grabbed his arm. "Do you know her?" he whispered.

The man stopped. "Let go of my arm."

Stephen did.

"Are you deaf? Do you want a sniper to pop my head like a pumpkin?"

"No."

"Then don't ask again." He walked off. "No, I don't know her," he said so Stephen could hear.

No? No? Stephen scanned the roofs of the buildings, half expecting to see the glimmer of a rifle. Snipers in this tiny village? It had to be a figure of speech.

He hurried for a side street, suddenly feeling like a fool. Okay, so maybe calm and collected would have been better after all. But now he had a problem of incalculable proportions. He had to believe Esther lived here, in this village. He really had no alternative. If no one would tell him where to find Esther, then he would have to find her himself.

Stephen stopped and looked back toward the town square. How many people lived in this place? One thousand? Three thousand? Couldn't be more than three thousand. How long would it take to search thirty streets? He would go door-to-door if he had to. If Esther was here, he would recognize her; he was sure of that.

On the other hand, some of them would surely recognize him from his circus act on Main Street—maybe even report him to the snipers. Half the town had probably seen or heard of him by now. He had to be more discreet. But he also had to hurry; if Braun hadn't taken her already, he couldn't be far behind.

He considered retreating to the van, but one glance at the picture and he discarded the thought. He hid the photograph under his shirt, shoved his hands into his pockets, and walked on. He bought a floppy black hat from a street vendor, hoping it might alter his appearance at least some.

He entered a lazy cobblestone street that ran in front of the towering church. Half a dozen people sat or stood outside as many shops. Someone laughed, but he didn't turn to see if it was directed at him. He glanced as nonchalantly as possible at each face. None of them was Esther. None of them was even a woman.

Another thought struck him. Maybe Esther would find *him*. If it was true that they were soul mates, wouldn't she recognize something special in him? Maybe he should be less concerned about being recognized by the Mafia types and more concerned with letting everyone in the village get a good look at him. He would leave the rest in God's hands, if indeed God was interested.

He glanced up at the church across the street. A woman stood at the side of the building, by the entrance to an alley, arms crossed. She was staring at him.

Stephen stopped. Was . . . was it her?

The same dark hair, the same finely curved cheekbones. Eyes that drilled him with a bright stare. She wore an equally bright blue dress.

He was holding his breath.

He glanced up the street—no one was watching him. Except her. She was still looking at him. His mouth was open, he knew that, but he wasn't thinking clearly enough to close it. Worse, he couldn't move his feet. He just stood there, forty yards away, ogling her as if she were an apparition who'd come to sweep him off to heaven.

This didn't seem to faze her. She continued staring. Or was she glaring?

Stephen regained his composure and headed across the street, straight for her. She let him come. He stopped ten feet from her. This was Esther, the perfect image of Ruth. The same hair, flowing gracefully past smooth cheeks. The same disarming eyes and the same small nose. She was petite, no more than a couple of inches over five feet.

"What are you staring at?" she asked.

"What?"

"You're staring at me as if you were looking at a ghost. Haven't you ever seen a woman before?"

"Of course." His voice cracked, but he didn't bother to correct it. She was reacting out of shock at finally seeing him. Hiding her own need for him with this charade.

"Then stop staring as if you haven't," she said.

He blinked. "You speak English."

"Obviously."

"Do you have twelve children?"

It was her turn to blink. "Do I look like I've had twelve children?"

"No! Sorry." His face flushed. "You're just so beautiful, I had to know . . ."

"If I've had twelve children?"

"Are you married?"

"No."

It was too much for Stephen. He rushed to her and threw his arms around her neck before she could move.

"My name is Stephen. David. I've looked everywhere for you!"

She was stiff like a mannequin. He was overwhelming her. *Get ahold of yourself, Stephen. She's a tender twig; you'll snap her in two. This is no way to introduce yourself.*

He started to pull back and was aided by a shove from her.

She stepped away, horrified and angry. "What on earth do you think you're doing?" she said, eyes darting up the street.

"I'm sorry. I don't know what came over me. You're . . . you're Esther, right?"

"I don't know what you're talking about."

This couldn't be! Was she terrified out here on the street? Of course!

"Maybe we should go to the alley," he said.

She reached out and slapped him. "What do you take me for?"

For the first time, he wondered if he'd made a terrible mistake.

"What do you mean, prancing around the village, making a fool of yourself?" she demanded.

Stephen stepped back. "You saw me?"

"Half the village saw you. If there's an Esther who lives here, I don't know her. Now leave, before you get yourself killed."

She glanced over his shoulder, gave him a parting glare, and walked away.

41

WHO THE MAN WAS, SHE HAD NO IDEA, BUT IF HE CONTINUED with these antics, neither of them would live out the day. She feared as much for him as she did for herself. Perhaps more.

That's why she'd slapped him.

Yes, that's why. Hard enough to really hurt. Tears came to her eyes now as she walked briskly from him. How he knew, she couldn't guess. He'd called her beautiful. She couldn't remember the last time a man had told her she was beautiful. It wasn't permitted.

But this bold fool from America named Stephen David didn't know that. He had maybe seen her somewhere and really thought she was pretty. Now he was coming after her in full daylight. Is this how Americans courted their women?

And yet she found herself undeniably attracted to the tall man with haphazard dark hair. He'd told her she was beautiful. Did he really believe she was beautiful? Was *he* beautiful? He did not fit her preconceived notion of American men. And yet, he could be missing his ears and she might think him beautiful. He desired her.

"Stop it," she whispered harshly. "What do you take yourself for? A whore?" Fresh tears filled her eyes. She bit her bottom lip. Some realities in life couldn't be changed.

The first: no man could love her.

The second: she could love no man, because she certainly could never love the man who'd imprisoned her here.

The third: she was trapped. If she set one foot outside this pathetic village, Braun would kill the only person who meant anything to her.

She rounded the corner and glanced back. No sight of the American. She stopped for a moment, swallowed, and then hurried down the street. Her memories flitted to Hansen. She was eighteen, and he was a strong young man with bright blue eyes and a wide smile. Braun had killed that budding desire. Literally. She'd cried for two straight weeks. Her first and last true love. Braun's decree could not have been more clear. The men stayed away from her after that. And she from them.

Her earliest memories took her back to age six, when she first began to realize that she was different from the other children. She had no mother, no father, only uncles. And her uncles were mean men who cursed often.

When she was eight, the other children seemed to turn on her. She remembered the day on the playground clearly. Freddy had called her a whore in front of all the other children. She didn't even know what a whore was. No one had stood up to him.

She learned the truth of her life when she was twelve—why she had no memory of her parents and lived with mean uncles and aunts.

She caught the eye of Armond across the street, keeping his eternal watch over her. She squared her shoulders.

What would they all say if the American ran up to her again and pronounced his undying love? Was she lovable? Was she not a woman? The American seemed to think so.

She secretly wished that Stephen David would do just that. That he would chase her at a full sprint and fall to his knees and cry out his adoration for all the village to hear.

But that was a foolish fantasy. And a dangerous one.

"Please leave," she whispered. "Leave this town."

⁓

STEPHEN LOOKED around. Three men angled toward him, intentions clear. They were coming to the aid of a woman who'd been attacked by a foreigner.

He stepped into the alley, took several long steps until he was sure he was out of their sight, and ran. What had he just done?

The alley ended. He veered to his right and slowed to a walk. How could she not be Esther? What was the probability that a woman who so closely resembled Ruth just happened to live in the very village Braun had named?

On the other hand, Stephen wasn't a student of faces. In the past twenty-four hours, a hundred women who resembled Ruth had made his heart jump. He had seen her face in the clouds, in the rocks, even in the Volkswagen emblem on the van's steering wheel.

Stephen began to run again, terrified by the possibility that he had just let Esther go. He had to at least warn her about Braun. Where could she have gone?

The answer came quickly when she walked out onto the same street, fifty yards ahead. He instinctively threw himself into a doorway. Somehow skipping up to her for another hug didn't strike him as the most effective way to gain her confidence.

He poked his head around the corner and looked both ways. The men had either given up their pursuit or had opted to follow her to safety. The girl who wasn't Esther was walking away, deeper into the village.

He stepped onto the sidewalk, lowered his head, and followed. The floppy black hat was a beacon now; he pulled it off and tossed it in a doorway. Ten paces later, he braved a glance. She wasn't walking as if she was concerned. Even if she wasn't Esther, she was one of the most beautiful women he'd ever laid eyes on. Of course, that was probably because he'd imagined she *was* Esther, and his mind had been ruined by . . .

She began to turn. He leaped to his right, behind a garbage bin, and dropped to a crouch. Someone chuckled, and he turned toward the sound. It had come from an older gentleman seated in a doorway. The man waved, and Stephen waved back, embarrassed.

He sneaked a peek. She was entering another alley, headed back toward the church! Stephen stood, immobilized by indecision. If he ran down the street she'd emerged from a moment ago, he might be able to intercept her.

He ran. If she was Esther, Braun hadn't arrived yet. The thought propelled him into a sprint, legs pumping like a world-class runner. The old man's cackle chased him down the street and around the corner. He ignored a dozen alarmed villagers, took a sharp left at the next corner, and blasted for the alley from which he knew she would emerge.

He slid to a stop at the corner, took one deep breath, and jumped out. Another second and he might have landed on top of her. She jumped back and shrieked.

The leap had been a bit much, he immediately saw. A nonchalant, suave entrance would have accomplished the same thing with far more subtlety.

She held a hand to her chest. "What are you doing, you idiot! Get away from me!"

He held up a finger. "Shh!" Looking into her eyes again, he was sure she was Esther. He felt as though he'd searched for those eyes his entire life.

"Why are you attacking me?"

Her accusation shocked him. "I wouldn't dream of hurting you. How can you say that? I'm here to save you!"

"Throwing yourself at me and then stalking me in broad daylight is your idea of saving me? They'll kill you for sure now."

"Stop it!" he yelled. Footsteps pounded behind him. They'd heard her cry and were coming. Stephen pulled out the photograph and spoke quickly. "Help me, I'm begging you. This is Ruth, Esther's mother. She gave her life for me in the concentration camp at Toruń. There isn't time—Braun's on his way here now. For Esther."

The woman stared. Running feet entered the alley.

"Please," Stephen said quietly. "I swear I thought you were Esther, otherwise I wouldn't have done that. Please, I have to help her."

A rough male voice spoke in German behind Stephen.

The woman hesitated. "I'm okay," she told the man.

The footsteps left.

"Thank you." He was still holding the photograph out to her.

Her eyes searched his for several moments and then lowered to the photograph.

"I wish I could help you," she said. "But I can't."

"You must!"

She stood defiant, but he thought her eyes were misty.

"I don't know who Esther is," she said, "but I do know they will kill you if you continue. Braun's well-known here. He doesn't value life."

"And he's on his way here now."

She stepped around him and hurried for the street.

Stephen walked after her. "Please—"

"You must leave before you get both of us killed."

He ignored the glares of onlookers and hurried to catch her.

"I'm telling you the truth. My name is David. I go by Stephen. I was born in Toruń. My mother's name was Martha. Do you know any of this?"

She veered up the stairs to the church doors. Her jaw was firm, but he saw a tear escape her eye, and the realization nearly crushed him. What had Braun done to make her so terrified?

He followed her into an arching foyer with stained glass high above. "I just came from Los Angeles. Braun was there looking for the Stones of David. Doesn't any of this mean anything to you?"

She spun. "You have no idea!" Her eyes blazed, but she could not hold back another tear that ran down her face. She was Esther after all! She had to be.

"Look at it!" he said, shoving the picture forward. "This is your mother! She gave her life!"

Esther looked at the photo. But her eyes stayed on the image. Surely she saw her own features in it.

"You are Esther!" He turned the photograph over. "Read it!"

Her eyes dropped to the writing.

My dearest Esther, I found this picture in Slovakia after the war. It is your mother, Ruth, one year before your birth.

Not an hour passes without my begging God that you and David will find each other. I will never forget. You are the true Stones of David.

"No. It can't be."

Her lips quivered. Stephen resisted an impulse to take her into his arms again.

Dear Esther, I am so sorry. What have they done to you?

She shook her head. "You have the wrong person."

Stephen grabbed his collar and ripped his shirt open, exposing the scar on his chest, daring her to deny it.

She stared, unable to move her eyes. Her face softened, and the tears began to run unrestricted. She lifted a trembling hand over her heart and slowly, as if in a dream, pulled the neckline of her dress down just enough to reveal the skin below her collarbone. There, burned into her flesh, was an identical scar.

"Esther," he said.

Her eyes rose to meet his. "Yes."

He stepped forward and put his hand on her shoulder. Anything else seemed inappropriate. She slowly rested her forehead on his chest and began to cry.

42

A YEAR HAD PASSED SINCE ROTH LAST VISITED THE VILLAGE. HIS MEN usually did the honors. From the road, the town looked unchanged.

Gerhard had his journal, but the Stones of David were still missing. With the threat posed by the journal behind Gerhard, Roth had little trouble stirring up his father's passion for the Stones.

Gerhard hadn't been so delighted in thirty years. Roth was pleased. And he had a plan.

When he'd received the phone call nearly two hours ago saying the Jew had arrived, Roth had nearly wept for joy.

Stephen had come, as surely as Roth had known in his remarkable judgment he would. The Jew would chase this fantasy of his to hell and back if necessary. Why not? After all, Christ had.

Little did Stephen know.

The danger of playing the game so close to the wire was both thrilling and unnerving to Roth. What if the Jew outwitted him as Martha had outwitted his father? Or worse, what if the Jew had already left?

"Straight to her house, Lars."

"If she's not there?"

"Then we'll find her at the church," he said. "Just hurry."

The car surged forward, down the steep grade.

He lifted his father's old red scarf, pressed it against his nose, and inhaled deeply. It smelled like Ruth, he thought. Like Esther. He glanced over his shoulder. Esther was about to get a wake-up call.

"Faster."

"Any faster, and we'll be off the side," Lars shot back.

Roth took a deep breath. The thought of what lay ahead tested even him.

———

STEPHEN WATCHED Esther pace behind the last pew, content to study her fiery brown eyes and her blue dress, which flowed lazily with each turn.

Esther. This was Esther. This stunning creature who paced before him was really Esther. He could still hardly believe she was Ruth's daughter.

They'd burned forty minutes in the church, far more than he knew was reasonable considering their predicament. But he was asking her to leave the only home she knew on a moment's notice. Half an hour ago, he was jumping out at her from the alleys; now, he was asking her to head to the hills with him. Unlike her confession, this wasn't something he could force.

He'd walked among the pews and discreetly watched her weigh the choice before her. There wasn't a shred of doubt in Stephen's mind: he was born for this woman. And he would win her love or die trying. No other woman could compare, not even in the smallest way—he was sure of this, though he hardly knew her at all.

Yet he did know some things. She had the spirit of an eagle caged by evil. If ever there was a victim of cruelty, it was her; and yet she endured it with her chin level. Because of this alone, he was utterly in love with her. He would set her free.

And there was more. The flip of her wrist, the darting of her eyes, the smell of her skin, the sound of her voice. She had the skin of a dove. She was his soul mate, created for him. And he for her.

His pearl of great price, as Martha had put it.

His obsession had taken flesh, and he would embrace it. Protect it. Its name was Esther. Gerik was surely right—man was created to obsess.

Despite the danger that now faced them, he could barely keep his mind on the task at hand. Perhaps because the task always had been love. It made sense that he was now as concerned about love as he was about staying alive or finding the Stones of David. Of course, staying alive was a prerequisite to winning Esther's love.

He knew she couldn't possibly feel the same about him. After all, she hardly knew him. But he thought maybe she was warming to him. Her apprehension was understandable. Once they got out of this mess, he'd give her time and space to grow to love him. He'd romance her properly. Candlelight, roses, moonlight strolls on the beach—the lot. She wouldn't be able to resist . . .

He looked over and stopped. She was gone! His heart jumped into his throat.

"Esther?"

"Yes?"

Her voice drifted in from the foyer. He vaulted the pew and ran in. "Don't you ever do that again!"

"Do what?" She stood before a large mirror, looking at her scar. "I walked ten paces. Just because I leave the room doesn't mean I've fled."

"I crossed the ocean to find you."

"And if I would have known about you, I would have done the same," she said.

This was good, right?

"I've been lost my whole life," Stephen said. "Until now."

She didn't respond, but her eyes spoke clearly enough. She was as lonely as he, just as desperate. The only difference was that she hadn't dwelt on the matter for a week as he had.

She looked back at the mirror. Even watching her now, his knees felt weak. He felt completely unreasonable and soft. Really, his whole life had been moving inexorably toward this day.

"Please don't go anywhere without telling me," he said. "Braun's out there somewhere."

"Stephen."

"Yes?"

"Will you come here?"

He walked over, feeling awkward. "Have you decided whether you'll come with me?"

"Yes," she said matter-of-factly.

He stopped. "Yes?"

She looked over at him. "Yes."

"So you'll come with me?"

"I said yes."

"Then we should go now."

She eyed him, amused. "Will you come here for a moment?"

He stepped up next to her in front of the mirror.

"May I see your scar?" she asked.

He exposed the burn on the left side of his chest.

"Come over here, on this side."

His hand that held the shirt open was trembling. He released it. "Please, Esther. If we don't get out now, we may never get out."

"Please," she said softly.

A strange faintness drained Stephen. Her words were a lovely, sedating drug. Just a simple word, *please*, yet he felt he might crumple where he stood!

Stephen swallowed. "Okay."

She guided him to her right side, so they stood shoulder to shoulder, exposing their burns to the mirror. Hers was a full foot lower than his.

"Wait here." She brought a padded stool that sat beside the door. "Here, kneel on this."

He watched her. She did everything with an incredible grace. The way she picked up the stool; the way she carried it over as if it were made of feathers; the way she bent her legs to set it down; the way she said "kneel on this." No woman could move or speak so gracefully.

He knelt on the padded stool. Now they were at roughly the same height.

"It's hard to believe, isn't it?" she said. "Your mother did this to us so we could find each other."

Stephen focused on her scar. Here they were, kneeling in front of a mirror, Esther and David, the two children from the camps, shoulders bared, branded for each other. The sight was so perfect. Terrifying. He jerked his shirt back up to cover his chest.

"Please, Esther, we have to leave."

She covered her shoulder and turned away. Was something wrong?

"Esther?"

She walked to the window, peered out, and then turned back. "You have to understand something, Stephen." The fire flashed in her eyes again. "I can't leave here yet. Not as long as Braun is alive."

"What? We don't have time for that! We should be somewhere else. As far away from here as possible. Why can't we just leave? He has nothing to gain by coming after us."

"No. He won't permit me to leave." Her jaw was set.

"What can he possibly do?"

"More than you can know."

"What do you mean? We *have* to leave. Now!"

She closed her eyes and took a deep breath. "I'm a prisoner of Braun." Her eyes snapped open. "Believe me, he'll find us both, and when he does he'll kill us. I can't leave as long as he's alive."

"You have to. We have each other; we can run."

"Where can we go that he will not follow? No. I will not run."

Urgency swelled in Stephen's chest. "He'll kill you if you stay."

"That is why I have to kill him before he gets to me. Leave if you have to, but I can't. There are other reasons."

"I can't leave you!" He placed both palms against his forehead and paced. "That's crazy. If you only knew what I've been through."

"I'm sure it's no more than what I've been through. Or my mother. Or your mother. This doesn't end as long as Braun is alive. The man is obsessed."

Her use of the term stopped Stephen. "And so am I."

"Then go find your obsession."

"I already have."

Her eyebrow arched.

"You," he said. "You're the obsession I've searched for my entire life."

"Really? We met only an hour ago. In an alley, if you recall." She looked deep into his eyes. "To what ends will you go to protect this obsession of yours? Will you kill the beast who threatens her, or will you hide so that he can live to stalk her another day? Believe me, Stephen, there's more here than you can know. I can't leave this place as long as Braun is alive."

He frowned, struck as much by her suggestion that he would do anything less than protect her as by the sudden realization that he had to do exactly that.

He had to kill Braun.

He swallowed. What was he thinking? He had to kill Braun? He had to *run*! With Esther.

"But . . . if we kill him, aren't we becoming like him?"

"No. We're doing what Ruth and Martha would have done if they had the chance."

"Okay. Okay, then maybe we should kill him." Hearing his own words, Stephen felt dizzy. Would he actually kill a man? Should he?

"Just like that?" Esther asked.

"I won't let anybody hurt you. Never again."

She walked up to him, eyes searching. "Are you a dream, Stephen?"

"No."

She was putting on a brave face, but he could see the fear in her eyes. She didn't know if she could trust him. Yet he was giving her no choice. *Dear Esther, what have they done to you?*

She suddenly turned and hurried for the sanctuary.

"Follow me."

43

THE BELL TOWER ROSE HIGH ABOVE THE CHURCH, AND BY THE looks of the aged bricks that lined the bell housing, it had been built long before the war. Stephen stood against one wall, staring at Esther, who scanned the street over an old hidden rifle she'd extracted from the back of the tower's only closet.

"No sign of him," she said.

Her voice rose just above a contralto, impossibly sweet. He knew what was happening. Now that the truth of her identity had settled fully in his mind, the fixation he'd had with the Stones of David had been transferred, heart and soul, to Esther. He felt like a puppy in her presence. He'd followed her up the stairs, lightheaded as much from the scent of her perfume as from the climb, and listened as she explained how she knew the rifle was there. Something about having smuggled it there years ago during a lapse in her captors' attentiveness, but he was more interested in her.

"Stephen?" Esther turned her head.

She'd caught him staring? He jerked his eyes from her, aware of his flushed skin. Could she read his thoughts? No, how could she know his mind by looking at him? He was overreacting, which explained the hot and cold waves that spread over his skull and down his neck.

"Are you okay?" she asked.

"Yes. Yes, of course I'm okay. What are you doing?"

"I'm waiting for Braun—what do you mean, what am I doing?"

"Of course. What I meant was, why? Or . . . what are you thinking?" Stupid. Stupid question!

Esther turned back to her study of the street without betraying any problem with his question. "I'm thinking that the moment this pig shows himself, his life is going to end."

"Sure. Of course. Makes perfect sense."

Did it? He hadn't been able to think clearly enough to imagine actually killing a man. The whole plan—coming up here to pick Braun off—seemed surreal.

Was he thinking straight?

Another thought occurred to him. How could a preoccupation that impaired his reasoning be a good thing? If God had created man to obsess, had he also created him to trade reason for intuition? Or worse, sacrifice reason for emotion? The rabbi would never agree. Not even Gerik would agree.

Stephen watched her as she peered over the rifle. Her lips were parted slightly, but she was breathing through her nose. A wisp of dark hair rested on her cheek. Her right hand, tender and white, gripped the trigger. This was the image of God before him. He was staring at a piece of God, and he could hardly stand the wonder.

Chaim had often preached passion for God. In this moment, Stephen thought he understood what the rabbi meant. If man could be as obsessed with God as Stephen was with Esther—what a thought.

And if Chaim was right, if man's emotions were only a dim reflection of the Creator's emotions, wouldn't God also have feelings like Stephen had? Was God obsessed? Was he preoccupied with an extravagant love for man?

How reasonable was dancing naked in the streets, as King David had done? How collected was Noah in building his huge boat in the desert? Or the prophets, being fed by birds or crawling around like an animal for years? Whatever had motivated those great shapers of history had been sparked by a moment of the deepest conviction and passion— maybe not so different from his own.

The entire line of reasoning took no more than ten seconds, and Stephen felt his confidence surge as a result of it.

"Are you really going to shoot him?" he asked.

"Do you have a better idea?"

"It just seems so . . . illegal."

"How can you stand there and talk to me about laws? This man kills. His father killed your mother. He will kill you too. And me. What he's done to me is illegal. Foul!"

She straightened and walked three steps to the still bell, then back to the window, tucking a strand of hair behind her ear.

Foul?

Rage blackened Stephen's vision. "What . . ." *No, not now.* He took a deep breath. "You're right; I'm sorry," he said.

"What am I supposed to do? You can run; I can't. He'll hound me!" For a moment, Stephen thought she might cry.

"No, I was wrong," he cried. "Kill him! We'll kill him for sure!" He took two steps toward her, sick that he'd hurt her again. What was his problem?

Chaim's words were burning a hole in his soul, that was his problem. *This obsession business is dangerous, Stephen. You can't break laws in the name of love.*

Esther's eyes darted about the room and briefly settled on his face. She looked like a child caught between terror and hopelessness.

"Esther . . ."

She spun to the window and froze.

"What?"

She leaped forward and crouched at the sill. "He's here!" she whispered.

Stephen sprang forward, saw the black car roll to a halt across the street. How Esther knew it was Braun, he didn't know, but neither did he doubt. One glance at her face, and he knew this man was a living demon to her. Her lips quivered with fury.

Esther brought the rifle to her shoulder and angled the barrel toward the car. She was breathing hard, and the gun wavered with each breath.

The car's rear door swung open. Braun stepped out.

Stephen bent behind Esther, beating back panic. How could he stand here like a mouse while she fought off the beast?

Esther began muttering under her breath. Bitterly.

Stephen stared at the unfolding scene, aghast. *Foul,* she had said. Roth had abused her.

He lunged for the gun; grabbed the barrel. "Wait! I'll do it!"

The gun boomed in the enclosed tower. Stephen jumped back, rifle in hand. Below them, Braun ducked and ran across the street toward the church's entrance.

"What are you doing?" cried Esther, jumping up.

"I should do the shooting," Stephen said.

"You made me miss!" She gaped at him, and he wanted to explain, but words seemed inadequate.

Esther clamped her mouth shut and ran past him. "Hurry, we're sitting ducks up here!" She disappeared through the tower door.

"Esther!"

From the corner of his eye, Stephen saw the driver's door fly open. Lars dived out.

"Hurry, Stephen!" She was calling him.

His lover was calling his name.

"Esther!"

He worked the bolt, pivoted the rifle out the window, lined the sights in the man's direction, and jerked the trigger.

Boom!

Lars staggered.

Stephen ejected the spent cartridge and shot at the large target again. This time, the man turned and hopped back toward the car. He'd hit him! He'd shot at a man through his leg! Or maybe his hip.

Stephen whirled and raced for the stairs. "Esther!"

She was running straight for Braun! Stephen took the stairs three at a time, rifle flailing overhead. His foot missed one of the steps and bounced over the edges of three more before finding purchase on the fourth. The rifle sailed free as he grabbed at the air. It clanged down a flight and came to rest on the floor directly below him.

"Es—" He cut the yell short. Braun would hear him screaming! The thought sent him flying down the stairs for the gun. He had to get into the sanctuary and cut Braun down before the man found Esther, assuming she didn't find him first.

Stephen reached the rifle, grabbed metal, and came up in a run.

The blow came out of nowhere, a sledgehammer that crashed into his head and sent him reeling back to the floor.

Braun, he thought vaguely. *That was Braun.* But his vision had clouded over, and he couldn't make sense of his surroundings. The gun lay on the floor to his right. He was sitting down. Maybe he'd run into the wall.

No, he'd seen movement. He tried to stand, but his muscles weren't cooperating.

Hands grabbed his collar and jerked him to his feet. "Where is she?"

The stench of the man's breath buffeted his face. Stephen's world cleared. He was standing just inside the sanctuary, supported by Braun. The man's white knuckles gripped a fistful of shirt and pressed against Stephen's nose. He nearly opened his mouth and bit the man's fingers but quickly decided that angering Braun more would only make matters worse.

"Where is she?" Braun said.

She'd eluded him! Esther had eluded this monster and, fortunately, Stephen had no clue where she could be. Hopefully halfway up the hill headed for Hamburg.

A hand slapped his face. "Where?" Braun dragged him into the sanctuary.

"She's gone," Stephen said. "She ran away when I told her about Martha. I told her Alaska would—"

"Jews don't run. They wait obediently; don't you know your history?"

"You'll never find her."

Braun dropped him to the floor by the altar and stepped back. He held a pistol in his right hand, angled casually at the ground. But there was nothing casual about the man's grin. Sweat wet his flushed skin, and his nostrils pulled at the air.

He pulled out the red scarf Stephen had found in the safe and wiped his face as he glanced around the sanctuary, searching the dark corners by the confessional and the doorways.

"She's gone," Stephen said. If he could keep the man occupied long enough, Esther could make her escape. Surely she would know to run. Without a gun, she would never confront Braun, no matter how much she despised him.

"I know what happened to the Stones of David," Stephen said. "Esther doesn't, but I do."

The man cast a sideways glance at him. He wasn't buying it.

Stephen cleared his throat and tried again. "She doesn't know because they belonged to my mother, not hers. You think I would tell her? I've been searching for them my whole life—I'm not about to confide in someone I hardly know."

Braun turned to Stephen and watched him for a moment. Slowly his face settled with a cold determination. "You'll tell me where she is," he said.

"Aren't you listening to me?" Stephen demanded. "She's out of this! Me, I alone, have what you want."

"The city inspector has what I want?"

"You think I would lie with a gun to my head? I didn't even know she existed until you told me. I'm after the same thing you are."

Braun's left eye twitched. "I doubt it."

Stephen was pushing—maybe too much.

"I'm just saying that we need each other," Stephen said. "I have what you want, and you have what I want."

"What do I have that you want?"

"My life! Obviously. You're standing over me with a gun. You let me live, and I'll split it with you."

"The Stones of David. Split them. You are more stupid than I thought, inspector. You think I would share the Stones with a Jew?"

"If you kill me, you'll never find the other four Stones."

A grin nudged the big man's lips. "I do not live for the Stones." Braun glanced around the room again. He dropped one end of the scarf so that it hung from his fingers. "I love games. Shall we play a game?"

He walked forward and held the red silk out so that it hung above Stephen. "You've become useless to me. The only reason you're still alive is because there's a slight possibility that the girl is as stupid as her mother. We'll find out soon enough."

Braun dropped the scarf. It spilled over Stephen's shoulder and hung down his chest. "My father selected your mother, Martha, to die. It seems fitting that I should select you. Unless your guardian angel sweeps in to take your place, I will put a bullet in your forehead. Ten seconds." His voice rang throughout the auditorium.

"Let me live, and you can have it all," Stephen said. "I'll show you exactly where the treasure is, and then you can kill me if you want."

"Seven!"

"She's gone! Kill me, and it's over. I have the information."

"Five."

Stephen knew that his prodding had probably sealed his death, but he couldn't just sit here and die. *Dear Esther, what have I done?*

"Three!" Braun raised his revolver.

"Okay, you win," Stephen said. Panic swarmed him. He was going to die. A bullet was about to punch a hole through his head. He sat up, furious. "I said you win! I'll tell you everything!"

"Stop!" Esther's shrill cry echoed through the chamber. Stephen turned toward the sound of her voice. She stood at the entrance to the stairwell, arms limp at her sides, feet together.

44

STEPHEN FELT HIS HEART SINK TO THE FLOOR OF HIS STOMACH. "Leave," he demanded. "Get out! Run!"

Esther regarded him with a casual glance and then stared at Braun. "There's an exit behind me," she said. "If you kill him, I will run, and you should know that I have a way out of this village that no one knows about. You'll never know what I know; I can promise you that."

"I don't need anything you know," Roth said. "And I don't think hiding will be so easy."

"Then let him go, and I'll cooperate." Her voice held a tremor.

"Esther, please," Stephen pleaded.

Esther ignored him. "Let him go."

Braun could hardly hide his excitement. "Like mother, like daughter. Take the scarf, and I won't kill—"

"I know how your disgusting game is played. How do I know you'll keep your word?"

"Did my father kill Martha when Ruth took the scarf?"

Esther shifted her gaze back to Stephen.

"Please, Esther, don't do this," he said. "He'll kill me either way."

"Maybe. Maybe not. But either way, I'm finished." She looked at Braun. "You hear that, you pig? I know that my life is worth something to you. If you kill him, I'll run, and you'll have to shoot me. I don't know what you have planned, but if I had no value to you, you'd have killed me long ago."

Braun tilted his gun up to the ceiling. "You have my word. He'll go free."

"I don't trust your word," Esther said. "Throw me the scarf."

"Come and take it."

"Do I strike you as a fool? You need me alive, so throw me the scarf."

Braun eyed her, clearly caught off guard by her audacity. But she was right. Braun wanted her alive.

Why?

Braun snatched up the scarf and flung it at Esther. She caught the material, looked at it for a moment, and then casually draped it around her neck.

"Stand up, Stephen," she said calmly.

He scrambled to his feet.

"You'll find another exit through those doors behind you," Esther told him. "Walk out."

"No."

"Then my own life will be in vain," she said.

"He'll kill you," Stephen cried. "I couldn't live with myself."

"He'll kill me anyway," Esther said.

"If you run now, you can still make it. He probably won't kill me. I'm an American citizen, and the district attorney in Los Angeles knows I'm here with Roth Braun."

It hadn't occurred to him until he said it, but this did present a potential problem for Braun. Assuming the man cared.

Braun chuckled. Evidently not.

"Why are you arguing with me?" Esther asked, eyes now moist with tears.

"I'm not arguing—I'm trying to help you!"

"Why would you risk your life for me?"

"You're . . . you're Esther," he said.

"I am. I'm Esther, and no one has ever loved me."

Stephen took a step in her direction before remembering that Braun was in the room. "That's not true. *I* love you. I love you more than anything I can imagine."

"You don't even *know* me." Tears began to slip down her cheeks.

"I was *made* for you," Stephen said.

"Enough," Braun said.

Stephen ignored the man. Esther was offering to give her life for him, not because she loved him so dearly, but because she saw her own life as worthless. The few minutes of tenderness he'd shown her were more valuable in her mind than her life.

Dear Esther. My dear Esther! You are willing to throw your life away for a moment's love.

"Don't you see, Esther? Our hearts have been beating together for thirty years. The truth is, I don't think Martha hid the other four Stones of David. *We're* the Stones of David. I . . . I don't think I can live without you. Please, just run."

"I can't just—"

Boom! Stephen jumped. Braun had fired into the air.

Braun waved the gun at Esther. "Come here, please."

"Not until Stephen leaves," she said.

"You think you can outwit me at my own game?"

"Shoot me," she challenged.

The quiver in his fingers told the truth. Their ploy had stalled him. He couldn't kill Esther, not yet.

Braun twisted his head toward the door. "Lars!"

Lars?

It occurred to Stephen that Braun could easily stop Esther. A simple shot to her leg, and she would be powerless. He was either lost to this fact, or he was playing another game altogether.

If Stephen didn't move now, they could both be dead in a matter of seconds.

"Wait." He could hardly stomach the thought of leaving her here with Braun, but he had no choice. "She's right."

Stephen took a step back. "Okay, I'll leave. I'll leave."

THE GAME had been played out like chess match: for every move a counter-move, for every victory a defeat, for every hope a helping of despair. Roth could not have hoped for more.

He was quite sure that he could be completely satisfied standing here for hours listening to their desperate ploys. But little did they know. It was just getting good. Really good.

He could toy with them both as if they were made of clay. And compared to him, they were. Next to him, most humans were merely dirt that had been fashioned into walking objects.

Stephen backed toward the door. "I'm leaving. And since I'm an American citizen and people know I'm here, shooting me would be a mistake. I'll go."

Braun swung his gun in line with Stephen and waved at Esther. "I want you here, beside me, before he leaves."

She walked toward him slowly. "I'm coming. Now let him go."

Stephen took another step back, hands up. "Easy. I'm going. I'll be going." His back hit the door, and he felt for the knob.

Braun turned the pistol back on Esther. Stephen pulled the door open, stepped quickly through, and slammed it shut.

45

STEPHEN HEARD A SLAP THAT SOUNDED LIKE ONE OF THOSE TINY firecrackers, followed immediately by Esther's muted cry. The world tipped crazily. He had to go back in. He gripped the doorknob but stopped short. Braun was yelling at her in German.

Time was running out. Stephen turned, bounded for the outer door, and threw it open. A back alley; empty. He had to find his way back to the bell tower.

Hold on, Esther!

Stephen gritted his teeth and tore down the alley toward the door below the bell tower. Tugged on it.

Locked! Dear God, it was locked!

He sprinted around the corner, but he was running farther from her, not to her rescue. What if he couldn't find another way in? Inside, Braun was brutalizing Esther, and her only hope for survival was running in the wrong direction.

The species of panic that swallowed him in that moment was a rare kind, debilitating in dreams and deadly in waking life. His legs felt numb, and he wasn't running nearly as quickly as his heart suggested he was.

He ran straight for the street, barely aware of three women who gawked at him from across the lane. Rough brick tore at his fingers when he grabbed the building's corner for the turn.

The steps leading to the front entrance loomed, gray and empty. No other doors. The steps, the foyer, and then the sanctuary. And in the sanctuary, Esther.

From the corner of his eye, he saw Lars, limping, pulling something from the back of the car.

Stephen took the steps at a full run. A faint cry of pain drifted from the church. He was out of time.

He slammed through the heavy church doors. He crossed the foyer in three long strides and headed up the center aisle at a full sprint.

Braun knelt on the floor, directly ahead, bent over Esther.

A terrifying, throaty scream echoed off the arching walls, and Stephen realized it was his own. He rushed forward, blindly, pushed by the power of his own rage. Braun stared at him, frozen by the sudden intrusion.

Still Stephen ran. Still he screamed.

He was halfway up the line of pews before a thought redirected him, an image of that rifle he'd dropped at the base of the tower stairs.

He veered to his right, vaulted a pew, landed his foot on the seat of a second, and hurdled the pew tops toward the bell tower.

A gunshot boomed, but he didn't duck or stop. His momentum permitted neither.

Another gunshot. Stained glass shattered high above and rained down.

Stephen skipped over the entire bank of pews before his left foot finally betrayed him and came up short on the last bench. He threw himself forward in a dive, banged his shin hard, toppled over the pew, and landed on his side with a tremendous grunt.

Wood splintered above his head—Braun's shots tore at pews that momentarily shielded Stephen. He couldn't breathe. The bell-tower door was open, two yards away.

He clambered for it on his hands and knees.

Click! Click!

The gun-hammer fell on an empty chamber. Braun was out of bullets?

Stephen was still out of breath. He shoved himself to his feet and lunged through the door. The old rifle lay where it had fallen.

He snatched it up.

Chambered a round, desperate for breath.

Whirled back.

Lurched for the doorway, feeling faint.

His reason was making a comeback, and for once it sang in harmony with his passion. Kill Braun. He had to kill Braun.

Still no breath.

Stephen staggered into the doorway, gun extended, trigger halfway through its pull, sights lined for Braun.

But Braun didn't fill the sights. Esther did.

Stephen blinked. Braun had pulled Esther to her feet and stood behind her. A large, shiny blade pressed against her throat.

"Drop it," the German said. "Drop it, or I cut her and drink her blood here before it's time."

Stephen's lungs finally inhaled a pocket of usable air.

"Lower the weapon."

Stephen held the gun as steadily as he could, which amounted to wavering in favor of jerking. He had no chance of picking off Braun's head like they did in the movies. Esther's shoulder was exposed, baring the scar. Her eyes stared at him, glazed with indifference. She'd resigned herself to die.

"Let her go," Stephen said, still gasping.

"Drop the gun, and I'll release her."

Stephen groped for a way out, but came up empty-handed.

"I can't put the gun down, and you know it," Stephen said. "But I can promise you that if you draw blood, I'll take my chances and shoot."

"Then you'll kill her," Braun said.

"You'll kill her anyway."

The front doors crashed open. A woman's muffled cry.

Stephen froze.

A sick grin distorted Braun's mouth.

Lars staggered into the back of the sanctuary. Shoved a woman down the aisle. Her hands were bound. Lars held a gun to her back.

It took Stephen a few seconds to realize who he was looking at, not because she looked any differently than he might have guessed, not because the gray tape over her mouth hid her facial features, but because he simply couldn't understand what he was seeing.

Esther. Only older.

Ruth.

But this couldn't be Ruth.

Ruth was dead.

"Hello, Ruth," Braun said.

46

Toruń
May 8, 1945

MARTHA STEPPED INTO THE YARD BEHIND THE COMMANDANT'S red house and let her eyes adjust to the darkness. Ordinarily, the lights would be blazing from tall posts throughout the camp, but not since the Russians had begun their air raids. Not even the front gate was lighted. It was so dark tonight that Martha had to choose her way carefully. If the perimeter fence wasn't flowing with high-voltage electricity, she might have been able to find a way out with the children under the cover of this darkness.

She made it as far as the tool shed at the edge of the yard before a sound stopped her dead in her tracks.

A cough.

From the shed? Did Braun keep prisoners in the shed? She wouldn't put anything past Braun, but why? Most of the barracks below were empty.

There it was again. The cough.

It didn't matter; she had to keep her mind focused. She had to hurry, or she could endanger the children's lives. The fate of one or two prisoners locked in a concrete cell was no longer her concern. Maybe on the way back she would—

"God forgive me. God forgive me." The voice came now, a soft, mumbling voice that stopped Martha in her tracks. Didn't she know that voice?

She heard it again, coming from a small, barred window to her left. "God forgive me."

Martha held her breath and stepped up to the bars. "Hello?"

Nothing.

"Is anyone in there?" she whispered.

"Martha?"

"Ruth?" A knot tried to choke her off. "Is that you, Ruth?"

Hands grasped the bars. A face pushed up between them. Ruth's face.

"Ruth! Is it you? How . . . ? I thought he—"

"Martha! Thank God, Martha. You're alive!" Ruth frantically searched her face. "The children! Are the children—"

"Yes! Yes—oh, yes. I can't believe it's you! I was so certain that . . . I saw your body!"

"It wasn't me. I don't know who."

"But you're alive!" Martha kissed her fingers, then her forehead. "Oh, I have so much to tell you. So much! Esther is the most beautiful child. He won't let me see David."

"They're here? Can I see them?"

Martha glanced back toward the house. "They're here, but the commandant . . . I can't bring her out. She'll wake up. We are being liberated tomorrow, Ruth!"

"You're sure?"

"Yes! Yes, I'm sure of it." She had to leave; she knew she did. If Gerhard found them . . .

"Listen to me, Ruth. There is so much I will tell you. Tomorrow. If we get separated, then you should know that I've marked Esther, and I am going to mark David. Each with half a circle with a star of David in it. The Stone of David. You know it?"

"Yes."

She stepped back and lifted up the boxes. "I have them. And I am going to hide them. If for some reason we get separated from each other, or from the children, remember this."

Martha told her how she planned to hide the treasure.

"What good will that do? His gold is filthy!"

"Do I care? It's for the children, Ruth."

"They will have each other."

"He's . . ." Should she tell Ruth? She had to. "He's taking the children with him, Ruth."

"No!"

"Yes. I'm so sorry. Don't worry, God will protect them. You said so yourself. As long as he thinks I have stolen his treasure, he won't hurt them. Do you see? He'll keep them alive until he finds it. It's the only solution I have. We must have leverage. I have to go." She kissed Ruth on the forehead and nose.

"Thank you, Ruth. You saved my life. I love you more than I would my own sister. Tomorrow we will talk, okay?"

"Pray that God will draw the children with his hope. Like desperate children seeking the pearl of great price."

"I will, Ruth. I will pray it every day."

"God be with you."

"God be with you."

She hated leaving, but she walked with a new urgency. Ruth had survived! Think of it. A great weight was gone from her shoulders.

It took her half an hour to pick her way through the camp toward the barracks she thought would be David's. The door was unlocked. She slipped in and shut the door quietly. "Rachel?"

Silence.

Louder now. "Rachel?"

"Yes?"

Martha ran past empty bunks toward the sound. "Rachel. It's Martha."

"Martha?"

The woman lay on a lower bunk, one of only a few people in the beds as far as Martha could see. She set her bundle on the bed and threw her arms around the woman, noting Rachel's frailty through the cloth immediately. She was nothing but bones!

"Thank God you're alive."

"Martha?"

"Yes, it's Martha, dear. You have my baby? David. Where is David?"

Rachel shifted to reveal a small lump in the blankets behind her.

"This is David," she said very quietly, almost as if it were a question. The woman's mind was slipping.

Martha stared at the form, afraid to ask anything more. She leaned in and eased back the blanket. There lay a small boy, white chest rising and falling slowly. Dark hair covered his head. Her David.

She lifted her fingers to her mouth to hold back an urge to cry. But this scene was too much for her. She sank to her knees, folded her hands in gratitude to God, and began to shake with soft sobs.

Her son was more beautiful than she had ever imagined in thousands of hours of imagining. He lay with all of his arms and legs and a nose and such tender lips and eyes with long lashes. And he was breathing.

Martha knew she had to hurry, but she hadn't counted on such brutal emotion. The thought that she was about to lose her precious child again, this very night, consumed her.

She couldn't wake him.

Did she dare hold him? If he awoke, she would never have the strength to mark him. If she didn't mark him, she might never see him again. She might never see him again anyway. Shouldn't she just hold him now—her baby in her arms, his soft cheek against hers, his breathing in her ear?

She reached a trembling hand for his body. Touched him lightly on his head, pushed his hair back. He took a deep breath and turned his head toward her, still deep in sleep.

"This is David," Rachel said quietly.

Martha nodded but couldn't speak. There was no possible way for her to take him away from the commandant. Marking her beautiful baby boy might be the only way to find him again.

Martha closed her eyes and gripped her hands to fists. *Strong, Martha. You have to be strong.*

With Rachel and two other gaunt women in nearby bunks now staring on, Martha heated the brand until it glowed. She'd reversed it on the ladle to make it a companion to Esther's mark.

She could barely see to press the hot brand into David's flesh for all her tears. To make matters worse, Rachel began to hit her feebly as soon as the metal made contact. As with Esther, it took a moment for David to wake, but when he did, a scream was already in his throat.

For the first time in nine months, Martha pulled her baby boy to her neck and held him tight. His cries tore at her heart like knives, and she did her best to comfort him. He didn't know who she was, didn't recognize the scent of skin or the tone of her voice. Slowly, he calmed.

"It's my mark, Rachel," she said as she put the salve on David's burn. "Do you understand? My mark. So that later I will be able to find him."

Rachel stared at her with hollow eyes, but Martha thought she might understand, might remember what she had done once for her own son. One of the women looked out the dark window to their left. Martha followed her gaze and froze. A light! A guard was coming!

Now, so late? It couldn't be possible!

She spun to Rachel. "Where's his shirt?"

Rachel blinked.

"His shirt—we must cover this! Hurry!"

The woman picked up a small cotton shirt from the end of the bed, and Martha snatched it from her hands. If the guards caught her in here, all would be lost.

The light approached steadily, swinging at the end of the guard's arm. Had Braun discovered her missing? She began to panic. There was no time. No time!

She handed her child to Rachel. "Lie down! Pretend you're sleeping. Don't let them see!"

She scooped up the ammo boxes, ran to the back around the last bunk, and climbed through a window just as the front door opened. If they would have turned on a light, they might have caught her with one leg still hooked in the window, but with the raids, they couldn't chance the brilliance.

Then Martha fled as fast as she dared in the darkness, pulse hammering in her skull, certain that all was lost.

47

Germany
July 27, 1973
Friday

OTHER?" ESTHER'S EYES WIDENED.

"Esther?"

Esther stepped forward, but Braun grabbed her collar and yanked her back.

"Drop the gun," Lars said, shoving his pistol into Ruth's back.

Ruth's face wrinkled in empathy. She looked at Stephen. Then at Esther. Her eyes flooded with tears. Ruth began to cry.

"I thought . . ." Stephen didn't know what to say.

"Yes, you thought she was dead," Braun said. "She is. She's been dead for thirty years."

"Mama?" Esther gazed at her mother. There was something between them, Stephen thought. Something they knew that he did not.

The rifle wavered in his hands. "She . . . she's been alive all these years?"

"Naturally," Braun said. "My father's foolishness in allowing any of you to live has created several problems, but it would take too long to explain how the powers of the air work."

He ran a fat tongue over his upper lip. "When he found the journal and the Stones missing, Gerhard was . . . let us say, disturbed. Martha had outwitted him, and Gerhard was forced to keep Ruth alive. In the event we found Martha, she would reveal the location of the Stones if we hung Ruth's life over her head. So we kept Ruth alive, in my father's house."

He paused as if to let comprehension of Ruth's plight sink in.

"And, of course, what better way to keep Ruth in humble service than to let her know that her daughter was also alive, and would remain so only if Ruth stayed faithful? We told Esther the same about her mother. They've never met, as you can see, but they've lived in respect of each other's life."

Braun's smile faded. "You see what happens when you don't follow the rules? My father should have killed Martha when he selected her with the scarf. Instead she stole his power and handed him thirty years of misery. Today I intend to take that power back." He shivered.

"I'm sorry, Mother," Esther said. "I'm so sorry."

"Don't be. God has answered our prayers."

An awkward moment of silence passed.

"Please lower the gun," Braun said.

Stephen's head buzzed. Slowly his rifle came down, as if it had a will of its own.

"Rifle on the floor," Braun said.

"Forgive me, Mama," Esther said.

"Rifle on the floor!"

Stephen set down the rifle and stepped back.

"Don't be sorry," Ruth said. "Never. Every minute of my life has been worth this one."

Braun clasped his hands behind his back and spoke in a low voice. "Go on. Go to your mother." A chill descended over Stephen. Braun's eyes held wickedness.

Esther walked down the aisle, then hurried the last few paces and embraced Ruth. She kissed her graying hair and her cheeks, then turned to Braun.

"Untie her! What kind of animal leads a weak woman around by a rope?"

Braun's eyebrow arched. "The master of that woman. Back!"

Esther hesitated then walked back.

"David. You are such a lovely boy." Ruth looked between them.

It occurred to Stephen that Braun was reloading his pistol. He exchanged a short glance with Esther.

"And Martha?" Ruth asked. "How is my Martha?"

"She . . . she's dead," Stephen said. "She died in America two weeks ago. She died happy, and she led us to you."

"Did she?" Braun snapped the clip home in his pistol. "Let's give Martha credit, but not too much, shall we?"

Meaning what?

"This moment is . . . invigorating, it really is," Braun said. "But I'm afraid we have to shift our attention back to the Stones." He looked at Ruth. "I trust you don't need any more convincing."

Ruth didn't seem to have heard the man. She was captivated by Esther and Stephen.

Braun pressed his gun into Esther's hip. "Or do you?"

Ruth's face settled, and her jaw firmed. Her eyes met Braun's.

"You had us fooled all these years. Bravo. You convinced us that you couldn't possibly have known what Martha did with the Stones. Martha wasn't even aware that you'd survived your little hanging." He pulled the hammer back on his revolver. "But now I know the truth. You know where Martha hid the Stones. Don't you, dear Ruth? Martha's letter has spoken from beyond the grave."

No one moved. Stephen's mind tripped back to the letter. He could see the last sentence in his mind's eye now: *As for the Stones, their hiding place will go to the grave with Ruth and me.*

"As you can see, your daughter is as healthy as an ox. You have five seconds to begin speaking."

One glance at Ruth, and Stephen knew she had the information Braun wanted.

"If you kill her, I won't tell you," Ruth said.

"I will do much worse than kill her."

Braun lifted his pistol to Esther's head. The gun jumped in his hand. Esther jerked and cried out. Blood oozed from a crease in her skin where the bullet had grazed her neck.

Roth wiped the blood from her cheek and then sucked it off his finger. "That was a warning. I imagine she can take ten carefully placed bullets without dying."

Ruth stared at the man for a few seconds. There may have been a day when she would have called his bluff. But today she looked like a woman who'd been beaten down one too many times.

"They are buried at Toruń," Ruth said without batting an eye.

———

THE SOUND of the words sent a tremor through Roth. The Stones were buried in Toruń. His focused intellect had assumed as much for years. Gerhard had even swept the camp with electronic gear once without success.

Still, Roth knew. He had always known. His whole plan practically depended on Toruń. Which is why hearing that name brought such relief.

Toruń.

Toruń, Roth's spiritual birthing place. Where his father had shown him how to harvest souls.

Toruń, where his father had lost all of his power through one asinine decision.

Toruń, where Roth would finally become a god.

He could barely speak for all of his pleasure. "Where?"

Ruth hesitated. "Under the gates. But I will only show you when you have let her go as agreed."

It was too much! Under the gates! The confession was nothing less than an announcement from Lucifer himself. *Lead them like lambs to the slaughter, and I will deliver myself unto you.*

Roth wanted to shout out his joy, but he held it back in a final act of control. He would have to spread some joy throughout Hamburg to celebrate, but only when he'd finished what his cowardly father had failed to complete himself.

———

A FIRE had entered Roth Braun's eyes, Stephen thought. His eyes danced; an obscene grin tugged at his lips. Sweat dampened his face.

He walked to Stephen. "I want you to listen carefully, Jew, if you want to live. I'm sure the police in Los Angeles will have a problem with your disappearance, so go set their minds at ease. If you ever look for us,

I'll kill them both. One word to the wrong people, and Esther will pay with her life. Carry that with you to your grave."

The man's arm flashed out. His pistol crashed against Stephen's skull, like bricks hurled from a catapult. He felt himself fall.

Hit the pew. Heard a sob.

Esther's.

Then nothing.

48

ESTHER DRIFTED BETWEEN REALITIES, VAGUELY AWARE THAT something was wrong. Something had happened—something furious and explosive—followed by the smell of a strong medicine, but that was surely a dream.

They were in a dark car, she and Ruth in the back, men's voices in the front. She thought they might have driven through a city some time ago, collected an old man with tubes in his nose, but he was surely a dream. The kind of nightmare the mind fabricated in deep, deep sleep.

In reality, she was driving with Stephen. Stephen and her mother, Ruth. They were going to Poland to deal with Braun, or they were running from him. She wasn't sure which. Mostly, they were just going. Together. In his car. She and Stephen in the front seat, Ruth in the back. Stephen obsessing after her from behind the wheel, she pondering him from the passenger's seat, her mother smiling with approval.

They were passing through the border into Poland, going after the Stones of David.

Stephen smiled and she smiled back, dreamy and hazy.

When the border guard waved them through, Stephen revved up the van and took off with enough acceleration to produce a tiny squeal.

"Slow down." Esther objected. "You're driving as if we've just robbed a bank."

Stephen slowed and glanced in the rearview mirror. "Sorry. We're okay." He grinned. "Peachy."

"Peachy?" It was the American colloquialism he'd used during their long discussion in the church while waiting for Braun.

"Peachy."

"Peachy?" Ruth said. "I love peaches."

Esther chuckled. Her mother was here, safe and together with her for the first time in her memory. She couldn't stop looking at her, this woman who'd given birth to her and then given her life.

Then there was Stephen. Everything about Stephen struck her as a bit funny. Not funny as in comical, but funny as in nice. This man—who'd jumped out of the alley at her, who'd ruined her first good shot at Braun, and then who'd come screaming back into the church for her—made her feel funny. A nice kind of funny.

Esther turned and felt something that smelled like leather press against her face. Was she sitting up front with Stephen, or had she climbed in the back with Ruth?

Up front with Stephen, of course.

She'd never felt this way about a man before. Here was a man who claimed to be obsessed with her, a savior who'd come blazing out of the past to rescue her from her eternal prison. David, who had been born because of her mother's sacrifice and who now seemed willing to give his life for hers in repayment. No, not in repayment. In love.

With each passing minute, the realization that Stephen really did love her grew, until she began to wonder whether she herself was smitten with this obsession of his. For him. How ridiculous! Was his disease contagious?

How could any sane woman find herself so hopelessly attracted to any man in such a short time? This couldn't be love. It must be her irrational response to the first sign of real kindness shown her by any man in years. She'd been smothered by Braun's thick hand since birth, a bird caught in a cage, a tiger whipped into submission, a butterfly snagged in a web. And now she was suddenly free because of these two people. Her mother and her . . .

Her what? That was the question, wasn't it? Here was the kind of man she had longed for all these years. Here was her knight in shining armor.

Here was the one who really did think she was beautiful. How could she possibly resist such a love? She couldn't. And Ruth, her mother, didn't want her to resist either. It was meant to be, and they all knew it. A fairy tale come true. She felt like laughing.

She sat with her hands folded in her lap, smiling, bouncing quietly along, wanting to see if he might be looking at her. She couldn't very well just turn and stare at him, now, could she? When they talked, she would have ample opportunity to look directly at him.

"I can't believe I actually found you," he would say.

Esther would face him. He would make a show of looking at the cattle in the field they were passing. But she could tell that his mind was lost on her. Why else would he swallow like that, or lick his dry lips and then bite them? His hair curled around his ear, dark strands moved by a hidden breeze. He was such a gentle man, beautiful to look at and fascinating to think about. She could still see him running over the pew tops, screaming. What kind of man would do that for her?

"Right?" he asked, glancing at her.

He'd caught her staring? But she had the right to look at him because he said something and wanted a response. Still, she'd looked at him too long. Her face flushed. She'd betrayed herself. But she didn't look away.

He'd asked a question. What was the question?

"What?" she asked.

For an eternal moment, they stared deep into each other's eyes. "I was just thinking of how incredible it was that I actually found you," he said.

"Yes." She cleared her throat and looked at the cows he'd pretended to be interested in. "Incredible. Like finding a mouse in a haystack."

"A needle," he said.

Another of his colloquialisms.

"How silly. Whoever heard of losing a needle in a haystack? We say mouse. Have you ever tried to catch a mouse in a haystack?"

"No." He chuckled.

Another good opportunity to look at him. She did so, laughing with him. "What's so funny?"

"You."

"I'm funny?"

"No. You're . . . cute."

She blushed again. "Mice are cute; needles are not."

Why was she disagreeing with him? She should be throwing herself at him and thanking him from the bottom of her heart.

"Touché," he said.

"Yes, touché," Ruth said. They both looked at her and smiled.

"Talk, talk," Ruth said, waving her arms in encouragement. "I've waited my whole life for this moment; please don't spoil it for me. Talk about love."

Tears blurred Esther's vision. She reached a hand back and squeezed her mother's. "I'm so happy. Thank you." She looked at Stephen and touched his arm with her other hand. "Thank you both. Thank you for finding me. I feel . . ." She paused, suddenly unsure of what to tell them. She couldn't say she was falling madly in love with Stephen. That would sound stupid. She couldn't say she was so glad Mother was free. That sounded too plain.

David's right brow went up, urging her to continue.

". . . found," she finally said.

Esther rubbed Ruth's hand and smiled through tears.

David frowned and nodded. "Hmm. Found. Like the treasure in the field. Wow, that's perfect."

It was? *Wow.* The American expression was new, and she liked it.

"If I'm right, he's already on his way," an uncomfortably familiar voice said.

Esther moaned and rolled. Funny how it felt as if she was lying down somewhere. And where was Stephen?

Maybe she was dreaming.

―⁓―

A FIERCE odor stung his nostrils. The sound of running feet. Stephen pulled himself from darkness. Slowly, he remembered what had happened. What was happening.

Braun had knocked him out and dumped him in the alley. He'd then taken Esther and Ruth and was on his way to Toruń.

This simple thought was filled with complex details. Details like Braun, the beast, and Esther, the beauty, and Ruth, his savior, and Toruń, the place where the beast played his game with the red scarf and killed the beauties.

Details like the fact that someone had waked him.

He pushed himself off the cobblestones in an attempt to stand. But his muscles weren't ready to execute the maneuver, and he fell flat on his face.

Roth Braun had let him go. Why?

Stephen moaned, rolled, and desperately willed his body's cooperation. Slowly, his arms and legs responded. Then he was tripping down the alley, one hand dragging on the wall, the other flailing for balance.

The panic hadn't abated. Nor could it. Surges of hot and cold swept over his body like storm-driven waves. They had taken Esther. They were taking Esther to Toruń. They were going to kill Esther at Toruń.

Stephen staggered down the alley and began to cry uncontrollably. His sobs echoed off the walls. When he broke into the street, people were staring at him.

"You should be ashamed of yourselves!" he cried.

The statement sounded absurd. Stephen began to run. There was no way to even begin telling them what they had just done. A princess had lived among them, and they had just killed her. Every last one of them should pay for their sin!

His vision was blurry. He overran himself and slammed into the Volkswagen van. He quickly recovered, tore the door open, and slid in.

How much time had passed? What if they weren't going to Toruń?

Pain hollowed his chest, a pain worse than long swords running him through. Nothing could be worse than this. Nothing!

Never had he wanted anything as terribly as he wanted to save Esther. His desire for the safe in Los Angeles paled by comparison.

And he knew that this was precisely what Roth expected. Stephen's reaction was the object of this mad game Roth was playing. He was lifting and dashing hopes as his father had with the women of Toruń.

He knew it, and he was powerless to stop it.

Stephen yelled at the windshield and slammed both hands against the steering wheel, once, twice. He fired the van up and screeched through a U-turn. A man on a bicycle dived for cover.

"Get out of my way!" He was briefly tempted to drive straight over the spinning wheels.

He roared from the village, redlining the VW's small motor before remembering to shift. When he did, he went right through the gears, blasting down the road.

The incline out of the village slowed the van, and he cursed his decision to rent the van over a Porsche.

Somewhere ahead on this very road, another car carried Esther, his dear, precious Esther, bound and taped and being led to her slaughter.

And what if he was wrong? What if Braun was still back in the village, beating the truth out of her?

Stephen shoved the brake pedal to the floor, sending the van into a precarious skid. A few hours had passed, judging by the light. Braun *had* to be on his way to Toruń. Either way, Stephen didn't have time to run through the village searching, while in all likelihood Esther was on the way to Poland.

He gritted his teeth and slammed the accelerator home.

The first fifty kilometers flew by. He didn't encounter any more than three vehicles. But then he pulled onto the autobahn headed east, and cars abounded. He felt lost in a sea of thugs, even though he knew these weren't the thugs. A hundred cars faded in his rearview mirror before it occurred to him that getting pulled over at this speed might actually put him in jail. Then again, he was on an autobahn, wasn't he? The square blue signs said 130 for cars and motorcycles and 80 for trucks.

He pushed the van to 140 km/h.

A hundred scenarios played through his mind. Images of Ruth. Of Esther speaking her mind and putting Braun in his place. Or being gagged and drugged. Or dead.

God, please. I beg you. Whoever you are, whatever your purpose, I beg you, bring Esther back to me.

He still had to cross the border into Poland. Thank God he had a

Russian passport and the twenty thousand dollars he'd brought with him. He only prayed it was enough to buy his way across without the right visa. He still had to reach Toruń; he still had to avoid the police while shredding whatever speed limit lay in his way.

Esther still had to be alive.

Ruth still had to be alive.

And even if they were, what then?

49

ESTHER AND STEPHEN AND RUTH HAD A DOZEN EXCHANGES, ALL dreamy, all vivid, all beautiful. And all while they were driving straight for this snake pit once known as Toruń.

What they would find there, she really had no clue, and she really didn't want to discuss the matter. There seemed to be an unspoken agreement between the three of them not to discuss the place, which was strange, considering they were headed straight for it. Stephen's preoccupation with her provided enough of a distraction.

Why were they going after the Stones of David? After all, she and David were the true Stones.

The car slowed, and Esther suddenly realized she was leaning against the door. And to her right, Ruth was also slumped over, sleeping. They apparently had fallen asleep while talking to Stephen.

She sat up and looked outside. Night. It was quiet, dark except for the bright moon. They were driving past a large, abandoned camp that looked like it had been turned into a museum. The sign over the gate . . .

STUTTHOF

Her heart bolted. Tall trees with sparse foliage surrounded the huge complex like shamed sentinels, bared for the whole world to see. Barbed fencing still surrounded the compound, and inside, dozens of identical barracks had fallen into various stages of disrepair.

A motorcycle headed the opposite way rushed past with a whine.

351

How could anyone live near this place? But then, she'd lived in a place like this since her birth, hadn't she?

". . . after all these years. How can we Germans stand by and let them pretend this is a monument to the Jews?" The man spit in disgust. "It's a monument to the greatest time in history. The Third Reich."

For the first time in many hours, Esther began to realize that not all was as she'd imagined. She wasn't in the front seat. Stephen wasn't sitting next to her. She wasn't even in his car!

"She's awake," someone said. The old man she'd imagined in her dreams.

Adrenaline began to clear Esther's mind. She jerked her arms and found that they were bound behind her back. She cried out, only to discover that her mouth had been taped. And next to her, Ruth lay bound and gagged as well. She was still sedated.

The full reality of her predicament settled on her mind like a massive boulder, crushing any attempt to rise above it. Braun had struck Stephen in the church, maybe leaving him dead, and then left the village with her and Ruth drugged and bound. They'd stopped somewhere and collected the old man, who sat in the passenger seat now, breathing through an oxygen tube. The father. The one who'd hanged the women. With the son behind the wheel and the father in the passenger seat, they'd rolled through Poland, and had just passed Stutthof.

They were going to Toruń.

Esther leaned back, swung her feet up, and kicked at the heads on the other side of the seat. Her right foot struck the old man. She kicked at Roth, but the car swerved and she missed him. She struck out again, screaming through the tape, shutting out their curses.

The son reached up and wrenched her foot. Pain shot up her leg, and she arched her back.

"The next time I will break it," he said, and she had no doubt that he would. The father was silent.

She yelled at Roth through the tape, "What are you doing? Let me out!" But he couldn't understand her, and even if he could, the demand wouldn't generate a response. She knew the answer anyway.

They were taking her to Toruń because that's where the treasure was. Because that's where the hangings were.

The old man slowly twisted around and stared at her, and for a moment she thought he was part animal. Deep lines like canyons ran across his white face. His eyes looked black in the dim light, abysmal holes. She returned his gaze, terrified.

Gerhard turned back without speaking.

Silence settled around her once again. She was in a black car with leather seats, wet with her own sweat, sitting next to Ruth, who was still mercifully separated from consciousness. The drug had affected her older, frail body more severely. Her mother was a fighter to the end, though. Ruth had bought them some time, knowing that the moment she revealed the location of the treasure, their usefulness would end.

Esther forced her mind to dig deep, as deep as it could through the lingering effects of the drug. But she couldn't fathom a way out.

The car crested a small hill, and both men looked to the right. Two hundred yards off the road stood two old wooden posts with a crossbar, and beyond that the ruins of buildings jutting from tall grass. A second hill rose to the right of the dilapidated compound, and on that hill was a very old building that was shedding its red paint and looked to be hardly standing.

A pale moon hovered in the graying dusk sky.

Toruń.

Esther's heart hammered. The gates still stood! She had heard that most camps had been leveled.

They turned onto a gravel drive and drove across the field toward the looming gate.

Roth stopped twenty meters from the gate and turned off the engine.

Silence smothered them.

The engine ticked softly.

Esther stared past the entrance. She could see them now, as ghosts, a thousand starving women, dressed in gray clothing, standing in formation, waiting orders from a ruthless commandant.

"Parts still stand," Gerhard said. He slipped out of his nasal cannula and looked at the gate in wonder. "This is better than I could have hoped for." He faced Roth. "You knew?"

Roth didn't respond. He opened his door and stepped out.

A new sound filled Esther's ears. A field of crickets sawing at their own legs, like an orchestra greeting the new prisoners.

Roth's feet crunched on the gravel as he stepped forward, then stopped by the hood. For a moment he just gazed at the camp, then he lifted his chin, put both hands on his hips and breathed deep.

Gerhard stepped out and walked up to the gate. He touched the wood and brushed his hands together.

The crickets seemed to scream now. All of them.

Finally Roth retreated to the back of the car and pulled something from the trunk. He met Gerhard in front of the gate and they approached the entrance to Toruń together, father limping along slowly on thin legs, son holding a shovel and a large coil of rope.

The shovel was to dig. The rope . . .

Esther leaned back and shifted her gaze. She would not think about the rope. Ruth slept on, nostrils pulling audibly at the air.

When Esther looked back up, they were looking up at the crossbar. Even from here she could see the white mark worn on the wood. A rope mark from hundreds of hangings. Roth threw one end of the rope over the wood, lined it up with the groove, and then stood back.

This was their plumb line, Esther thought with sudden hope. The falling rope marked a spot directly beneath the worn mark. They were going to dig under the spot where they'd hanged their women so many years ago.

But couldn't they as easily estimate the center without a rope?

ROTH BRAUN could feel the power. What he now felt was new. How many souls had he stolen since the war? Too many to count.

These would be different.

These were the ones who'd stolen part of his soul first, a feat far more damaging to him in spiritual terms then any occurrence since.

As he saw it, the only way to undo his father's grievous sin was to return Gerhard's full power to him by beating these Jews in their own game, using as much cunning as Martha had.

Now he would outwit them, not by retrieving the Stones of David—although that was no small accomplishment—but by returning these Jews to the very fate they should have suffered in the first place.

By hanging them and then bleeding their souls.

Roth was in a very good mood.

He glanced at the road that led to the camp. Still no sign of pursuit.

"I know why you insist on the ritual," Gerhard said, "but please remember that the Stones are as important."

Roth's mood dimmed. But he was a patient man who could handle the weakness of others when required.

He couldn't bring himself to speak to the old man. Dealing with him would be the least of his pleasures, certainly not something to dwell on. Tragic how this man who'd introduced him to the great war of life—the struggle between God and Lucifer over the passions of man—now served the lesser master of greed and self-preservation.

But this would not stop Roth.

He turned away from his father and went to get the younger one.

—∿—

THE SON walked back toward the car. Opened the door. "Get out."

Esther pushed herself away from the door and cocked her legs to protect herself.

"Is that necessary?" he said impatiently. His eyes were dark, emotionless.

He grabbed her foot and pulled roughly. She tried to kick—tried to strike him, even though she knew she would only provoke him—but she could not stop her slide. She landed on her back with a dull *thump*.

"Get up, or I'll drag you. And if you kick at me again, I'll put a bullet in your leg."

Esther rolled over, drew her knees under her belly, and struggled to her feet, her arms still tied behind her back. He prodded her and she walked for the gallows, numb.

Gerhard watched her. "Are you frightened now, little flower?"

Esther felt a lump fill her throat. Mama? She wanted to cry out, but her mouth was still strapped with tape.

Roth Braun took Esther's arm and shoved her to the ground. He quickly wound tape around her legs. Silent. Breathing steadily.

The old man stared at her, fascinated. His hands trembled by his sides, and his eyes glimmered with delight.

Roth fashioned a loop with a heavy knot on one end of the rope.

Esther began to panic again. But before she could even whimper, Roth had pulled her to her feet, spun her so she was facing the road, and shoved the noose over her head. He cinched it tight and tied the rope to the fence so that some pressure, but not too much, pulled on Esther's neck.

Braun walked to the car and shook Ruth awake. It took a minute before he finally helped her out of the backseat. Her mother stood unsteadily, gazing dumbly at the camp. Slowly, her eyes focused.

Braun had more rope in hands, from where, Esther hadn't seen.

Roth pulled the tape from her mouth. "No screaming," he said. "You'll have your chance to speak, but not now. Walk."

He directed Ruth to one side, threw the rope over the crossbar and set a twin loop over Ruth's head.

He threw a third length over the bar on Esther's right.

Ruth looked at Esther. A tear on Ruth's cheek glistened in the moonlight, but she showed no other sign of weakness or sorrow. Her mother's strength gave Esther some courage.

"Are we ready?" Gerhard asked his son.

Roth glanced past the car toward the road and hesitated. He was waiting?

He finally put one hand on the rope and faced Ruth. "If you don't tell us where it is, or if you direct us to the wrong location, your daughter will suffer painfully. If you cooperate, you will both live. Do you believe me?"

No answer.

Roth nodded at his father, who approached Ruth.

"Where did Martha hide the Stones?" Gerhard asked.

Ruth stared at him, emotionless. The moment she told them where the treasure was, they would both die, Esther thought, peering down.

"You're thinking that we will kill you anyway," Roth said. "Then what leverage would I have against Stephen? He would tell the world what he knows and I would have a problem. Your choice is a simple one: Either you tell us where the Stones are and live, or Esther dies first, then you."

He pulled on the rope, lifting Esther to her tiptoes.

"One pace south of the center," Ruth said softly. The words horrified Esther. So quickly! Ruth was too weak to resist.

Roth stared at Ruth for a long time as if caught off guard by her response. He had the look of a disappointed man.

He released the rope so that if Esther continued to stand on her toes, the noose wouldn't cut into her skin.

Roth removed his coat, placed it carefully on the fence, took up the shovel, and buried its blade deep into the earth roughly one pace to Esther's left.

She looked at her mother. Ruth gazed at her, eyes tearful. If Esther could speak past the tape, she would tell her mother that she was okay. That her sacrifice hadn't been in vain. That she loved Ruth more than she loved life itself.

Roth swung his shovel. *Chunk, scrape, chunk.* Metal on dirt. But it wasn't as loud as the sound of her own breathing. Or her heart.

It was louder than the crickets, but barely.

Don't panic, Esther. They won't kill you. He's right, they need you alive to keep Stephen from speaking. They've kept you alive all these years. What's a few more?

But she didn't believe it. She'd never felt such lingering horror.

Maybe someone would come over the hill and discover them. The car and the men were visible from the road. Seeing a man digging a hole at the base of this gate would surely draw the attention of anyone driving by. It had to! But whoever would come out to this dreadful place at night?

The old man stood stooped, dressed in wool pants that rose halfway up his belly and a gray sweater that looked as old as the war. Behind him on the hill stood the house from where he'd kept watch over his women.

Esther glanced at Roth steadily digging. There was only one outcome to this madness. Not three or two, but one.

Gerhard was walking around the hole now, like a vulture, waiting. If she could jump and kick him . . .

The shovel struck something solid. Gerhard stepped forward and stared into the hole. He dropped to his knees, thrust his arms below the dirt, and yanked on something that came loose reluctantly.

A container. Small, like a shoe box, maybe an ammunition holder, though she could barely see it.

They'd found Martha's treasure.

She closed her eyes. She heard a small whimper. From her own throat. Panic edged into her mind.

"Shh, shh, shh," Ruth whispered. "I will hold you in my arms forever, my dear Esther."

"Mama . . ."

"Be strong, Esther."

But Ruth was crying as well.

50

I N ROTH'S MIND, FINDING THE STONES WAS MERELY A BONUS. NOT a small one, but still only a bonus.

Roth's skin buzzed with anticipation now. They'd set the table up ten meters from the gate, directly in front of Esther. It was a small folding table, not the lavish spread Gerhard had used in the war. But they had a white tablecloth and three crystal goblets. One tall bar stool.

And a silver knife.

The ammunition box sat on the ground behind them. Esther teetered on her toes, struggling to keep the rope from choking her. Ruth stood next to her. Gerhard stood by Roth's side before the table.

They were all here except Stephen.

The only thing that dampened Roth's spirits was Gerhard's obvious eagerness to hurry the ritual. The Stones were his prize.

Or were they? He hadn't actually opened the box yet.

Gerhard fidgeted and looked at him. "He may not come."

Roth watched the road. Still no sign.

"What are you waiting for?" Ruth demanded. "You have what you came for, and you're too cowardly to keep your word, so finish it. We've defeated you already."

He would have to be careful with Ruth. She was still capable of lowering the heights to which he anticipated ascending today.

"I have no intention of killing you, Ruth," he said. "Your daughter, perhaps, but not you."

359

"I don't believe you."

Esther's body was shaking with fatigue.

The road was still empty. Roth's eagerness to move forward forced him into a decision. Although patience was a strength, it had to be balanced against ambition and passion.

On balance it was time to move forward.

Roth picked up the bar stool. He stepped around the table.

"Think about it, Ruth," he said, but he was looking at Esther's frantic eyes now. He'd tried to do this once when she was a sleeping baby. It was immeasurably more satisfying now that she was fully aware.

"As stated, I need Esther alive to keep Stephen under control. And I need you to keep her in line. We really are one big happy family, just as we've always been."

"If you'd wanted to bleed us for your sickening ritual, you could have done that years ago," she said.

"Yes, but not with the same results. Bleeding is pointless unless the subject is in a particular state. I don't expect you to understand."

Esther stared at him with wide eyes.

He set the stool against her legs, ripped the tape off of her mouth, and walked toward the fence where the rope was tied off.

"I'm going to pull . . ." He untied the rope and applied some pressure, forcing her to stretch higher. "I advise you to climb the stool as I pull so that I don't break your neck."

Roth pulled. She stabbed at the stool with her legs and drew it under her. Clambered on the first rungs.

Roth snugged the rope. Watching her filled him with pride. His power was superior to hers. It always had been, but until now he'd never had the true opportunity to express it.

He pulled harder. "That's it. Up. Up, up."

She winced when the rope tightened on her neck, but she managed to get her knees on the round wood seat.

"Up, up."

He helped her by pulling her up, like drawing a caught fish out of the water. One leg under. The stool tipped, nearly spilled. That would have been disappointing. But she was a capable woman. She stood on the stool, trembling like a leaf, coughing and gasping. But standing.

Roth fed out a couple feet of slack and tied the rope off.

He walked to the table, picked up the knife and one of the glasses, then faced Esther, whose wrists were still taped together behind her back. Ruth had said nothing. He would have to watch her.

"I'm just going to cut you, Esther. If you look at your mother's palms, you'll see a scar. She's been cut before. Now it's your turn. The only reason I put you on the stool was to control you. If you try to kick me while I'm bleeding you, the stool will probably tip over and you'll drop."

She was trying so hard to be brave. But her face was white and stretched paper thin. She was balanced on that razor edge that divided hope and fear.

He stepped up to her hanging arms and held the glass under her fingertips. He set the blade against her white wrist, just below the gray tape, and pushed lightly.

She whimpered.

"You're in good company. Another Jew was bled by his enemy. Few think of Jesus Christ as a Jew, but he was. It's why we hate him."

Sweat ran down Roth's lip. His own hand began to shake.

Then Roth couldn't hold himself back any longer. He pressed the sharp silver blade down and slid it toward him.

Esther groaned. Her knees began to buckle, then found strength again.

A thin trail of blood seeped out of the cut, over her palm, down her forefinger, into the glass.

"You are a devil," Ruth said.

"I am," he said.

Roth was temporarily frozen by the moment. Lost in his own glory.

A tear slipped down his cheek.

He held the cup out to his father, who took it, mesmerized. Subservient.

"Drink it, Father."

"Not you?"

"She undermined you, not me."

"All of it?"

"All of it."

Gerhart tilted the glass back and swallowed the small pool of blood.

Roth trembled with anticipation. He turned to Ruth.

"It's your turn, my dear. Just a little blood."

"You are very sick," Ruth said.

"The power of life is in the blood," he said.

51

S TUTTHOF.

Stephen roared by the old camp as the sun slipped closer to the horizon, choking on his own heart. The steering wheel was slippery from his sweat, but that didn't matter—there were no turns in this road. Stutthof was on this road, and Toruń was on this road. Sickness and death, that's all. Sickness and death and lots of buried Jews.

He would do anything to prevent Ruth's and Esther's names from being added to the long list.

Maybe he'd passed them on the autobahn. After an hour at 140, he'd pushed the van to its limit and held it there all the way to Poland. The border crossing had slowed him half an hour, but his money had bought a crossing. He could only hope that the border had slowed them as well.

Assuming they had even come this way.

He was driving blind, praying incessantly, hoping that he hadn't misjudged Braun's intent.

If he reached Toruń before them, he would dig a hole and pretend he'd found the treasure only to hide it again. If . . .

The camp suddenly rose into view like a monster from the sea. A black car was parked in front of the gate. Two people standing.

A body hung from the crossbeam. A second next to it, lower.

Stephen's heart seized. He barely glanced at the shoulder before yanking the van off the road, directing it through a shallow ditch and straight for the camp, two hundred meters off.

The van pounded over clumps of grass, threatening to wrest the wheel from his grasp, but Stephen hardly noticed. His eyes were locked on those bodies, and his mind was screaming bloody murder.

Esther's legs were partially obscured by the black car from this angle. He could no longer see Braun. He was bouncing over the field and whimpering and seeing nothing but red. Red and the black forms, hands tied, neck crooked, dangling on the end of the rope.

A sliver of reason sliced into his consciousness. Other than the knife in his right sock, he had no weapon. But the van was a weapon. They would begin shooting at the onrushing van at any moment—he had to bob and weave and he had to actually hit Braun.

One hundred yards. No shots.

Stephen swung the wheel to the right, sent the van into a fishtail. He began to weave through the grass.

—⁓—

AT FIRST, Esther thought the blur on the horizon was a bird, diving into the field for prey. Gerhard Braun was drinking their blood, and there was a bird diving from the road.

A car sliding into the field.

Stephen!

Esther couldn't hear the van streaking for them; her ears were filled with rushing blood and her heart was knocking. The old man might be half-deaf, and Roth too distracted, but sooner or later, they would hear. She had to distract them!

But she was still in shock. Her mind was hardly working, much less her mouth.

The van fishtailed crazily, only a hundred yards off now. She could already hear the racing engine as it bounced.

Behind her, Roth began to chuckle.

"The boy does not disappoint," he said.

—⁓—

STEPHEN SAW that the rope around Esther's neck was loose when he was still fifty meters out.

She was alive.

The sudden relief vanished immediately. She was on a stool. If she fell, she would die.

Three choices. He could try to angle directly for Roth Braun. He could ram the car and hope that it ran Braun over. Or he could crash into the gate, hoping to bring the whole thing down, including Esther.

Angling for Braun was a problem because he still couldn't see the man at thirty yards out. Ramming the car could be a problem because the black vehicle looked pretty solid—he might accomplish nothing except his own dismemberment. And rather than saving her, crashing into the gate might turn out to be a deathblow to Esther.

He slammed the brakes and brought the van to a skidding halt three feet from the large Mercedes. Esther stared, white-faced.

Stephen began to scream.

At the top of his lungs, as he threw the door open, as he vaulted the Mercedes' hood. He was nothing more than an enraged savage pushed to his limits by this brutal attack on Esther. His woman. His life.

The rage became awareness in the space of two steps. He pulled up abruptly.

Roth stood beside Esther, gripping one of the stool's legs, ready to yank it out. A gun in the other hand, hanging loosely by his side. Face amused.

"Nice of you to join us," Roth said.

"Stephen?" Esther's voice was breathy. High-pitched.

Ruth stood strung to Esther's left. Only then did he see the third rope, hanging on Esther's right. This was for him?

An old man stood by a small table behind Esther. This was Gerhard, Ruth and Martha's tormentor. There were three glasses on the table. One was stained dark; one held a small puddle of black wine; one was empty.

Then he saw the blood dripping from Esther's bound hands. And Ruth's hands. Their wrists had been cut and still bled.

Their predicament settled into his mind. He heaved and vomited on the hood of Braun's car.

Roth smiled softly. "That's right, the situation is quite hopeless, isn't it? For you, that is. For me . . . I'm pleased to have played you so well."

Stephen's head was reeling. It struck him that Roth would now kill all three of them.

"Played me?"

"Surely you don't think you're here without my approval? I'm after more than the Stones of David. The fact is, I've played you like a fiddle from the moment you showed up at Martha's apartment in Los Angeles, as I knew you would. Assuming you were still alive."

"You were there for the Stones," Stephen said.

"I was there for you. I knew the minute I read the news story in the *Los Angeles Times* that Martha suspected you were alive and was calling out to you. She was, and now here you are. Consider yourself called."

Stephen laughed bitterly.

"I'm here because Martha was one step ahead of your father," Stephen said. "I'm here because I've stayed one step ahead of you." His voice held no conviction.

"Have you? I drew you, Jew boy. I let you find the scarf. Build your hope to the point of a mad obsession."

Roth Braun spoke the words as if tasting each with immense satisfaction. Stephen had underestimated the power of this man.

"How do you think you escaped unharmed from the basement? Why did I let you walk out of the church in Greifsman and have my men wake you in the alley? I had to make you believe it was all your own doing—this fuels courage—but you've done nothing without my allowing it."

Roth glared at him smugly.

"And why am I now telling you this, knowing that the game isn't yet finished? Because I know how it will crush you. I intend to return all of you to the death you should have met thirty years ago. I intend to bleed and hang all three of you."

He swayed slightly on his feet.

"Desperation, do you feel it working on your mind?"

The words bounced around Stephen's skull like a Ping-Pong ball.

"Turn around."

52

EVERYTHING WOULD PROCEED EXACTLY AS ROTH HAD planned now.

All three faced him, Esther on the stool, Ruth and Stephen on either side, necks tight in their nooses, hands bound and bleeding behind them.

Gerhard tipped back the chalice containing Stephen's blood and drained it. The evening air was cool, silent except for the cricket's song, screeching through the fields. Tears stained the faces of all three Jews.

Roth trembled.

His father set the glass on the table, eyes closed, face tilted to the dim sky. *Can you feel it, Father? I have restored your power to you.*

Gerhard said nothing. His frail frame looked white in the moonlight. For a moment Roth couldn't help thinking that he was one of the starving Jews that had filled the camps, a ghost of his former self.

But inside, where it mattered, Gerhard had now recaptured the full power once lost to him by his own stupidity.

Roth walked toward the car slowly, a master committed to the grandest of all ceremonies.

He withdrew a rope from the car and brought it back. Without looking at his father, he slung the noose over the cross bar. It slapped the wood noisily, then swung into place, eight feet from the ground.

Gerhard's eyes grew wide. With wonder though, not fear. He still did not understand.

"How do you feel, Father?"

Gerhard glanced at the rope. "A fourth rope?"

"For Martha," Roth said. "All four have to hang, even if Martha's hanging is only symbolic. How do you feel?"

Red stained the man's lips. He looked dazed. Drunk on the blood.

"You were right," he said. "Forgive me for ever doubting you. I feel alive."

Roth stepped to his side, withdrew the pistol from his belt, and slammed it into Gerhard's temple.

His father slumped, unconscious.

The Jews seemed too shocked to express their surprise. Good.

Roth hefted his father up under the arms, dragged him to the rope, and dropped him on the ground. Working calmly, he strapped Gerhard's wrists with tape as he had the Jews. Then he pulled the noose down, slipped it over his father's head, and drew it tight.

———

STEPHEN COULD not comprehend the events playing out before his eyes. The ache in his wrist where Roth had cut him faded when Gerhard collapsed in a heap.

The rope was cutting off the circulation in his neck, but he found that if he stood on his tiptoes, the blood flowed freely. This, too, was now only a distraction.

To his right, Esther's knees were shaking on the stool.

To his left, Gerhard Braun lay bound and noosed.

Roth was going to hang them all, including his own father.

"I have decided to let each of you witness a hanging before I hang you," Roth said. "I want you to see the horror on a man's face when he realizes that he has not found freedom and glory. He has to die so that I can take his power."

Roth's face shone with sweat, not from exertion. His eyes fixed on his father.

"I would have to say that it's worked out better this way. You've all spent your lives searching. Whether you knew it or not, seeking, seeking. And tonight you've found your treasure. But it isn't the treasure you were hoping for, is it? Not what Martha had in mind at all. Your hope for love and all that nonsense is now smothered by horror. Emptiness. Death. Hope, on the other hand, will belong to me."

An image of Chaim and Sylvia flashed through Stephen's mind. A week ago he'd been busy trying to convince Dan what a good investment the property in Santa Monica would make. He'd forsaken all that was once dear for the woman who now teetered on a stool beside him.

What had happened to him? He'd lost his mind.

Or had he? No, he'd found his heart.

Esther, I am so sorry.

"If you can see his eyes, watch them carefully," Roth said. "You can see the horror in the eyes."

He looked at Stephen for a moment, and then frowned as if disappointed that, in his current state, Stephen wouldn't be watching Gerhard's eyes, at least not carefully.

Roth suddenly stepped forward, grabbed the end of Gerhard's rope that hung free, and began to haul his father off the ground, headfirst.

The father came to his knees.

Gerhard coughed once, sputtered, and threw his hands around his neck. He clawed at the rope, disoriented. Finally he got his feet under himself and staggered to his feet.

"What . . ." he screeched. He began to cough before he could finish the sentence.

Roth tied his end of the rope around the post, walked to Gerhard, who was now hacking and wheezing in agony, and spread gray tape over the old man's lips. The father's eyes bulged wide and he strained to breathe through flaring nostrils.

Roth uttered a short cry of delight and jumped back to the post. He grabbed the rope with both hands and yanked Gerhard off the ground.

His father began to kick.

"You should have let me kill her, Father," Roth said. "Now look what you've gone and done."

Roth tied the rope off again. Gerhard's struggles eased. His wheezing was choked off. Only the crickets screeched.

Roth bounded behind his father, slipped a silver knife from his belt, and lined it up along the man's wrists.

Another kick from Gerhard.

"Be still!"

Roth cut him. Then jumped back, delighted. He ran to the table, scooped up one of the glass chalices and hurried back to his father. He worked frantically now, driven to drain his father's power and satisfy his obsession.

Gerhard went limp.

Roth lifted the glass and drank.

And then the air went silent again. Even the crickets had momentarily stalled their wails.

All the while Ruth had kept her eyes fixed dead ahead. Esther had followed her mother's cue and stood tall, despite the trembling in her legs.

And Roth . . . Roth stood panting behind them.

Stephen wasn't sure why, but the entire scene suddenly struck him as nothing more than child's play, which was odd because his quest for power certainly wasn't child's play. Still, in context, it now seemed hardly more than silly.

Foolish ambition in the face of far greater power.

What could possibly drive a man to such insane depths? What made one man crave another man's blood?

Obsession. A craving to have what he could not have. Power. Like Lucifer himself defying God in hopes of elevating himself. This moment was nothing less than the collision of two obsessions, theirs and Roth's. God's obsession with man. Lucifer's obsession with himself. Humankind's obsession with God on one hand, or themselves on the other hand.

Stephen turned his head to Esther and Ruth. He smiled. "I love you, Esther. God has given you to me as my obsession, and I love you."

"And I love you, David," Esther said bravely.

"Take courage," Ruth whispered. "God is our deliverer."

------⚡------

THE JEWS were talking, but Roth couldn't make out what they were saying. His head throbbed with an expansive pride that elevated him to a state of heavenly perfection.

It was finished. He had restored his father's power and now taken his soul. Even the Stones of David were now his. The Jews were cowering. He would hang them next. Then he would cut down the bodies and bury them behind the forest.

"Roth!"

The sound of his name cut through his heavy head.

"Roth. Oh, Roth, you do have a problem."

It was the Jew. Stephen. What was he saying?

Roth turned around and stared at them blankly.

"You're drunk on your father's blood, so you may not realize it yet, but you have a very significant problem," Stephen said boldly. Too boldly. "Your plan to harvest souls in anguish has failed."

Roth's mind started to clear. The Jew was trying to sabotage this glorious evening?

"You have not killed our hope. You can't."

———

THE MOMENT he saw Roth's bewildered expression, Stephen knew he'd struck a chord of fear in the man. This simple yet genuine display of courage undermined him in a way that no physical power could.

Stephen laughed, loudly, deliberately. "Ha! You've lost the upper hand, man. Our simple love overpowers you with a single word. Hang us! Hang us and see that it gains you nothing!"

He felt giddy. Perhaps it was the result of the emotional strain he'd suffered for a week now. Perhaps there was some truth in his claim—surely some of that. But mostly Stephen yelled the words because they really did fill him with a sense of power.

He laughed again, louder this time. "You've taken nothing from us!"

———

ROTH STARED at him. This was a farce.

Stephen was smiling because he'd gone mad with fear.

Then the Jew looked up at Esther, but continued to address Roth. "You thought you brought me for a death, but instead I have found love." Stephen faced him and set his jaw. "I love Esther!" he cried, eyes bright with passion. "I love her. I love her deeply, and I can die easily, happily knowing that I have found my love."

He kept laughing. A genuine laugh.

Roth was too shaken to move.

"And I have found love," Esther said. "God has given me love instead of fear."

Roth slammed his fist on the table. "Stop it!"

Ruth was smiling.

This couldn't be! He couldn't hang them while they were in this frame of mind. It would undermine his whole plan. Anguish! He had to return them to a state of anguish!

"I am about to hang you fools by the neck until you are dead!" He thrust a finger toward Gerhard. "Look at my father. Look at his white, dead face!"

They did not look.

The mother, Ruth, stared at him between the eyes. "You have another problem," she said. "The box that you believe holds the Stones of David is empty."

What was she saying?

"Don't be a fool," he said.

"Check it."

"You're lying."

"Check it," Stephen said. "Then hang us if you want. You've lost whatever you came here to gain anyway. We have no regrets, no fear. Only love at finding each other."

Roth didn't want to check the box. He knew that even considering their lies was a sign of weakness. But the thought of owning the Stones had set its claws deeper into his mind than he had guessed.

He walked to the box as slowly as possible.

———∞———

THE MOMENT Roth turned, Stephen lifted his right heel and grabbed at his ankle with his bound hands.

He managed to grab his slacks and support his leg with one hand while he groped for the knife in his sock with his other hand. His fingers closed around the handle. Pulled it free.

He lowered his leg. If he dropped the knife now, there would be no retrieving it. He had to saw through the tape that bound his wrists before Roth returned his attention to them.

And if he did, then what?

Yes, then what?

He pointed the knife up and dug at the tape. Missed. Stuck his wrist instead. He ignored the pain and sliced upwards again.

Roth dropped to his knees by the box. He clawed at the lid.

Come on, Stephen.

The lid flew open. Roth stared into the box.

Thrust his hand inside. Pulled out bundled cloth. Stephen recognized it as one of the old shirts issued to prisoners in the camp. Martha had wrapped the Stones in a shirt.

Stephen felt something cutting, but he couldn't tell how much progress he was making. *Come on, Stephen, cut!*

Roth stood slowly to his feet, kneading the cloth, feeling for the Stones.

He turned to Ruth, eyes frenzied. Or delighted?

He let one end of the shirt fall. The cloth unraveled.

Empty.

Ruth was right; the box was empty.

Their tormentor began to moan. He faced them all, eyes darting, arms spread like a gunslinger. A white ghost in the moonlight, living on rage now.

"Where are they?"

Ruth said nothing.

Stephen prayed the German wouldn't see his shaking as he sawed at the tape. But he had no choice. He had to cut himself free now.

"Where are they?" Roth screamed. "Tell me, you filthy Jew!"

Ruth stared at him defiantly. "Now it is you who are in anguish. You've lost all of your power."

Roth rushed forward with surprising speed. He rounded the table, headed straight for Ruth. But he didn't go to Ruth.

He veered toward Esther at the last moment, grabbed the stool with both hands, and yanked it out, just as Stephen felt the tape give way behind his back.

Esther fell a foot before reaching the end of the rope. She bounced and swung three feet off the ground.

He'd hung her!

——∿∿——

WHEN ESTHER saw Roth veer toward her, she knew the worst was about to happen. She instinctively took a huge gulp of air, tensed her muscles, and clenched her eyes.

Then she was airborne. She hit the bottom and bounced. Pain flashed down her spine. She swung like a piñata.

It took a moment for her to realize that she was alive. Not only was she alive, but her neck, though stretched, wasn't broken. And she could breathe. Barely.

She opened her eyes. She was dangling from the rope above the ground, but fully conscious and fully alive. Was this what it felt like to be hanged? Others' necks were broken by the snap, but hers wasn't. How long would she swing here before dying?

Stephen was swinging too! Had he been hanged as well?

She moved her legs but immediately felt pain stab at her neck. At any minute her neck could break. She wondered if it might be easier to just relax and let the noose take her life quickly. A buzzing began in her ears.

Her vision began to cloud.

——∿∿——

ROTH LIFTED the stool and smashed it on the ground. It splintered into a heap of sticks.

Stephen wrenched his wrists free from the tape and grabbed the rope above his head for support. He threw his weight forward, lifted both legs as high as he could, and struck out with as much force as he could gather.

Roth spun, stunned by the sudden movement.

Stephen's heel caught him square in the temple. Any smaller of a man and he might have broken his skull. The impact sent a sharp shaft of pain clear up to his hip.

Roth staggered back several steps, fell heavily to his seat, then fell on his side, unconscious.

———~~~———

STEPHEN WAS only halfway out of his noose when Roth moved.

Already?

Stephen ripped the noose from his head and dropped to his feet, facing the German, who was now pushing himself up.

Behind Stephen, Esther hung on the end of the rope.

Roth stood, blinking. His eyes darted to the left, and Stephen followed them to a black lump on the earth, behind the table.

His pistol.

Esther began to rasp.

You have time to save her. Not much, but enough.

Stephen spun and grabbed Esther before realizing his mistake. He couldn't turn his back! The snake could easily have a second gun and put a bullet into both of their heads.

He whirled back, Esther in his arms.

Roth was withdrawing a small, snub-nosed revolver from his pocket. The man was still dazed, which slowed him down.

Stephen let Esther go, tore for Roth, and swung his hand, open palmed, for the man's face. The night crackled with a loud snap, like a firecracker.

Stephen's hand flashed with pain.

He formed a fist and drove it into Roth's nose. *Crack!*

Roth grunted and fell back to his seat.

"Stephen!" Ruth was crying out for him. "Esther . . . you have to get Esther."

Esther's rasping had intensified. He grabbed the fallen gun, smashed its butt into Roth's head, and hurled the weapon into the grass as Roth slumped to the ground.

He should have kept the gun, he thought. No time now. He had to get to Esther.

"Stephen!" Ruth cried.

He leaped for Esther and grabbed her legs and shoved her up to ease the pressure on her neck.

"Are you okay?"

She coughed and gasped.

"Are you okay?" he demanded.

"Down!"

Stephen glanced around, suddenly struck with the slight problem of getting her down. Ruth stared at them helplessly. He wasn't quite sure what to do. So he asked her again, "Are you okay?"

"I'm hung!" she barely croaked.

"Are . . . are you hurt somewhere?"

"Everywhere!"

"But not bad?" Surely not a broken neck!

"Bad!" she said.

"Is your neck broken?" he cried in alarm.

She looked down at him and held his gaze. She let out a breath and her face wrinkled, but it was relief, not pain in her eyes.

Stephen's vision blurred with gratitude. "Thank God."

"Stephen?"

"Yes?"

"Free my hands."

"How?"

"Stephen!"

He twisted at Ruth's cry and saw that Braun was struggling to lift his head. Ten yards from him lay the pistol that had fallen free during the confusion.

This was not good. He couldn't let go of Esther. Couldn't get to Braun. Couldn't reach to untie the tape around Esther's wrists. He saw it all, and he knew in a single, dreadful moment what he must do.

Roth slowly pushed himself to his knees.

"Esther, please—"

"Yes!"

"Hold on!" He eased her down, felt the rope take up her weight, felt nauseated. He took two long steps, snatched his fallen knife from the ground, and hurried back. If he thought she could withstand the pressure, he would have gone after Roth before returning to support her.

But the risk of her neck breaking was too high.

He grabbed her legs and shoved her back up. She gasped.

Braun got one leg under himself. Started to rise. Settled back down and tried again.

"Hurry!"

"I'm hurrying!" He held her up with one arm and searched for the tape with a shaking hand. He pressed the blade against it, afraid he might cut her skin.

Braun faltered, then staggered toward the gun.

Esther wheezed a cry.

Stephen sawed, wincing. The tape came apart.

She struggled above him, gripped the noose under her chin, and wrestled with the rope. "Go!"

He ran for Braun like a place-kicker running for a kickoff. His foot landed in the man's rear.

Braun grunted and sprawled to his face.

Stephen flew over him and scooped up the handgun. "Ha!" He spun around, knelt by the killer, and hit him on the head with the butt of the gun.

"Ha!"

This was the third major blow to the man's head. Surely it would keep him out.

In his peripheral vision he saw that Esther was falling.

She'd freed her neck and dropped cleanly to the ground, where she tried to hold her balance and then sank to her seat. She tried to stand, but fell back.

Stephen scrambled to his feet. "Are you okay?"

Esther touched her neck. The bleeding from her wrist had stopped.

Stephen jumped over Braun's prone body and rushed to them. He grabbed the knife and attacked Ruth's bonds. Freed her from the noose.

Dropped the knife.

Faced Esther. They were free.

Stephen sat and took Esther in his arms. She clung to him and began to cry softly.

"It's okay. It's okay, you're safe now."

He wanted to wash away her tears and squeeze her forever. Instead, he took her face in both hands and kissed her.

"I love you."

She couldn't respond for her tears. She didn't need to.

Stephen held her tight, her face planted in his neck as she wept. His eyes swept the camp behind her.

Roth Braun lay still.

This is where we were born. This is where our mothers' lives were once stolen.

He'd never felt so full of life as he did at this moment.

Epilogue

THE AMMUNITION BOX WAS EMPTY FOR GOOD REASON, RUTH told them. Martha had buried two boxes in the event that the treasure's location was forced from them. She would confess taking one Stone and burying an empty canister. When they dug it up and confirmed her story, they would assume someone else had stolen the other four Stones at the end of the war.

But Ruth knew the location of both boxes. Now the second ammunition box sat on the ground—green, dirty, and latched shut. Martha had buried it five paces from the other, directly under the same beam.

They knelt before it in silence.

They'd wrapped their wrists in cloth and then strapped them tight with gray tape. Stephen had gagged and bound Roth like a hog, lowered Gerhard to the ground, and dragged them both around the fence, where the authorities would find them once the call was made. He'd then dug in the spot Ruth had indicated as her best guess.

She'd been right. What thirty years of mystery had covered, five minutes of digging had uncovered.

Ruth unceremoniously reached out, flipped the latch, and pulled open the lid.

On one hand, Stephen wasn't sure he wanted to see what was inside. Considering all the impossible directions the road had taken them these last two weeks, nothing would surprise him. The box might contain the Stones of David. It might just as easily contain a letter. He wasn't sure which he preferred any longer. He had Esther. Didn't he? They had Ruth.

Martha's plan had succeeded. In the end they had beaten the diabolical plan to steal their hope, their love, their very lives.

On the other hand, he was desperate to see what was inside this box.

"It's . . . it's full," Ruth said.

"Full?" Stephen leaned forward.

Gold coins.

His heart pounded.

"Coins?" Esther reached her hand in and pulled out one of the coins.

"It's . . . it's Roman," Stephen said. He was staring at a single coin worth at least a hundred thousand dollars.

He pulled the canister closer and tipped it to one side. Gold clattered from the tin box, the unmistakable sound of priceless metals. The treasure rushed out all at once, gold coins, emeralds, rubies, diamonds, others he couldn't immediately name. There had to be a hundred!

Stephen dropped the box and gawked in silence. There on top of the pile rested a round lump of gold. Imprinted with a five-pointed star. And another . . . three more similar . . .

The Stones of David.

Esther touched one, then lifted it up. "The Stones of David?"

"Yes," he whispered. He cleared his throat and said it again. "Yes."

Her eyes were round and bright, like the diamonds.

"Is this worth very much?"

They both looked back at Ruth. She gazed at them, smiling. She didn't know. She didn't care. Her eyes were on her treasure.

"A . . ." Stephen cleared his throat. "A hundred . . ." He didn't know how much. "Yes."

She set the Stone back on the top of the mound. "Wow," she said. "Ha."

They looked at each other. A mischievous smile slowly lifted her cheeks. Stephen felt like hollering, like yelling, like screaming for joy. Not simply for the treasure on the ground, but for the treasure before him. For all of it. For the reward that had been bought and paid for by his mother. By Ruth. By Esther. And now by him.

This was their inheritance.

"You are my Stone of David," Esther said.

"You are my Stone of David."

"I was born for you," she said.

"I was born for you."

She leaned forward slowly, then kissed him on the lips.

Beside them, Ruth began to cry.

THE KINGDOM OF HEAVEN IS LIKE A TREASURE HIDDEN IN a field. A certain man learned that the treasure existed and he developed a terrible obsession to possess it. He wasted all of his wealth and secretely sold everything he had to purchase the field so that he could own the treasure.

Again, the kingdom of heaven is like a pearl of great price. When a man found it, he sold all that he had and purchased the pearl.

Unless you, too, obsess after God's kingdom, like this man did over his treasure, you will not find it.

Knock and keep on knocking. Seek and keep on seeking. When they send you away again and again, come back and seek still again. Then you will find the treasure you seek.

Parables of Jesus
Paraphrased and expanded
Found in the book of Saint Matthew

IN STORES
SEPTEMBER 2005

What happens when we begin to see ourselves as the utopian-like
Christian that God intends instead of like the imperfect
human the world insists upon?

Discover other great novels!
Join the WestBow Press Reader's Club
at WestBowPress.com

WestBow
PRESS

A Division of Thomas Nelson Publishers
Since 1798

visit us at www.westbowpress.com

DON'T JUST
READ THE TRILOGY . . .
ENTER THE
CIRCLE

VISIT TEDDEKKER.COM AND . . .

- view the exciting promotional video trailers for the trilogy
- read missing chapters—available nowhere else
- experience illustrations from the Other Earth
- listen to excerpts from the Circle Trilogy soundtrack by Jagged Doctrine.

WANT EVEN MORE?

- Join "The Circle" for exclusive updates and contests
- Read Dekker's personal essays
- Discover Dekker's other best-selling novels
- Connect with other readers in "The Circle"

IT'S FREE AND ONLY AT
TEDDEKKER.COM

The Circle Trilogy

Book One
ISBN 0-8499-1790-5

Book Two
ISBN 0-8499-1791-3

Book Three
ISBN 0-8499-1792-1

Fleeing assailants through an alleyway in Denver late one night, Thomas Hunter narrowly escapes to the roof of an industrial building. Then a silent bullet from the night clips his head and his world goes black. When he awakes, he finds himself in an entirely different reality—a green forest that seems more real than where he was. Every time he tries to sleep, he wakes up in the other world, and soon he truly no longer knows which reality is real.

Never before has a trilogy of this magnitude—all in hardcover format—been released in an eight-month window of time. On the heels of *The Matrix* and *The Lord of the Rings* comes a new trilogy in which dreams and reality collide. In which the fate of two worlds depends on one man: Thomas Hunter.

Each book in the trilogy is also available in abridged (CD)
and unabridged (CD and cassette) editions.

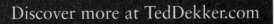

Discover more at TedDekker.com

A NOVEL OF GOOD, EVIL, AND ALL THAT LIES BETWEEN

ISBN 0-8499-4512-7

Imagine answering your cell phone one day to a mysterious voice that gives you three minutes to confess your sin. If you don't, he'll blow the car you're driving to bits and pieces. So begins a nightmare that grows with progressively higher stakes. There's another phone call, another riddle, another three minutes to confess your sin. The cycle will not stop until the world discovers the secret of your sin.

THR3E is a psychological thriller that starts full tilt and keeps you off balance until the very last suspense-filled page.

This novel is also available as an abridged CD audio edition.

Discover more at TedDekker.com

THE FUTURE CHANGES IN THE BLINK OF AN EYE . . . OR DOES IT?

ISBN 0-8499-4511-9

Seth Borders isn't your average graduate student. For starters, he has one of the world's highest IQs. Now he's suddenly struck by an incredible power—the ability to see multiple potential futures.

Still reeling from this inexplicable gift, Seth stumbles upon a beautiful woman named Miriam. Unknown to Seth, Miriam is a Saudi Arabian princess who has fled her veiled existence to escape a forced marriage of unimaginable consequences. Cultures collide as they're thrown together and forced to run from an unstoppable force determined to kidnap or kill Miriam.

An intoxicating tale set amid the shifting sands of the Middle East and the back roads of America, *Blink* engages issues as ancient as the earth itself . . . and as current as today's headlines.

Discover more at TedDekker.com

The Blessed Child Series

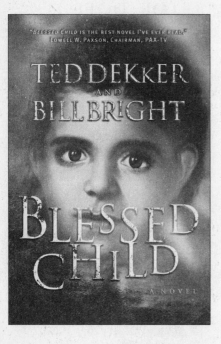

BLESSED CHILD
by Ted Dekker and Bill Bright
ISBN 0-8499-4312-4

The young orphan boy was abandoned and raised in an Ethiopian monastery. When relief expert Jason Marker agrees to take Caleb from the monastery, they begin an incredible journey filled with intrigue and peril. Together with Leiah, a nurse who escapes to America with them, Jason discovers Caleb's stunning power. Jason and Leiah fight for Caleb's survival while the world erupts into debate over the source of his power. In the end nothing can prepare any of them for what they will find.

A MAN CALLED BLESSED
by Ted Dekker and Bill Bright
ISBN 0-8499-4380-9

In this explosive sequel to *Blessed Child*, Rebecca Solomon leads a team deep into the Ethiopian desert to hunt the one man who may know the final resting place of the Ark of the Covenant.

But the man in their sights is no ordinary man. His name is Caleb, and he, too, is on a quest—to find again the love he once embraced as a child.

The fate of millions rests in the hands of these three.

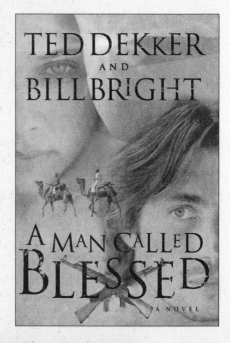

Discover more at TedDekker.com

The Martyr's Song Series

HEAVEN'S WAGER
ISBN 0-8499-4241-1

He lost everything he ever wanted—and risked his soul to get what he deserved. Take a glimpse into a world more real and vital than most people ever discover here on earth, the unseen world where the real dramas of the universe—and of our daily lives—continually unfold.

WHEN HEAVEN WEEPS
ISBN 0-8499-4291-8

A cruel game of ultimate stakes at the end of World War II leaves Jan Jovic stunned and perplexed. He's prepared for neither the incredible demonstration of love nor the terrible events that follow. Now, many years later, Jan falls madly in love with the "wrong" woman and learns the true cost of love.

THUNDER OF HEAVEN
ISBN 0-8499-4292-6

When armed forces destroy their idyllic existence within the jungles of the Amazon, Tanya embraces God, while Shannon boldly rejects God, choosing the life of an assassin. Despite their vast differences, they find themselves in the crucible of a hideous plot to strike sheer terror into the heart of America.

Discover more at TedDekker.com